Praise for *Hidden Agenda* . . .

"Colorful . . . fiendish . . . good entertainment . . . could be a heck of a movie."
—*Publishers Weekly*

"A timely story . . . filled with recognizable people."
—*Library Journal*

"*Hidden Agenda* is a wild romp through my news terrain. . . . I had a great time with it!"
—Kelly Lange, NBC news anchor, Los Angeles, and author of *Trophy Wife*

"*Hidden Agenda* is a thrilling and savvy ride through the worlds of broadcasting, politics, and religion. Real names make it feel chillingly nonfictional, and the ending is a triumph of integrity over hypocrisy. It's unique, and I was spellbound."
—Sally Sussman, head writer, *Days of Our Lives*, NBC-TV

(*continued on next page* . . .)

"The power of television news taken to its logical extreme. Thom Racina's ingenious story gives the reader a peek into the media's well-hidden backstage."

—Bill O'Reilly, anchorman, Fox News, author of *Those Who Trespass*

"Four stars! . . . A thrilling tale. . . . Highly recommended."

—Harriet Klausner

"One of the great 'What if?' stories of the last five years. Racina has done it again, kept me awake for twenty-four hours straight! Clever, and controversial enough to drop-kick any drifting table reviewers."

—Bill Hersey, writer/producer, PBS, NBC

"Great read, wonderful characters and plot, boffo finish. . . . I loved this book."

—Bob Healy, The Music Network

Praise for *Snow Angel*

"Fast-moving. . . . Racina spins a highly cinematic tale set against dramatic backdrops . . . a memorable villain who generates considerable suspense."

—*Publishers Weekly*

"A chilling cliff-hanger chase." —*Booklist*

"A tale of obsessive love run nastily amok."

—*Kirkus Reviews*

"Powerful, compelling. . . . A highly charged thriller with a surprise ending." —*Tulsa World*

"A breathtaking read, a devilish treat that will leave you crying for more. One of the most exciting tales of the year."

—*Romantic Times*

ALSO BY THOM RACINA

Hidden Agenda

Snow Angel

Thom Racina

SECRET WEEKEND

AN ONYX BOOK

ONYX
Published by New American Library, a division of
Penguin Putnam Inc., 375 Hudson Street,
New York, New York 10014, U.S.A.
Penguin Books Ltd, 27 Wrights Lane,
London W8 5TZ, England
Penguin Books Australia Ltd,
Ringwood, Victoria, Australia
Penguin Books Canada Ltd, 10 Alcorn Avenue,
Toronto, Ontario, Canada M4V 3B2
Penguin Books (N.Z.) Ltd, 182–190 Wairau Road,
Auckland 10, New Zealand

Penguin Books Ltd, Registered Offices:
Harmondsworth, Middlesex, England

First published by Onyx, an imprint of New American Library,
a division of Penguin Putnam Inc.

First Printing, November 1999
10 9 8 7 6 5 4 3 2 1

Printed in the United States of America

PUBLISHER'S NOTE
This is a work of fiction. Names, characters, places, and incidents either are the product of the author's imagination or are used fictitiously, and any resemblance to actual persons, living or dead, business establishments, events, or locales is entirely coincidental.

For Susan Feiles,
with a wink and a smile only she will understand

Thanks to all my friends in Hawaii for the pleasure of their company and the inspiration they provided—what fun! My gratitude to Jane Dystel for selling it, Joseph Pittman for buying it (and giving it an edge), and Idell Larson, for her early and welcome enthusiasm. Thanks also to Ricka Kanter Fisher and Joe del Hierro for their suggestions and support.

And to Mark, who keeps the spirit moving, my deepest gratitude.

Prologue

Maui, Ten Years Ago

From merely the passing glance of silky black hair cascading behind the girl on the bicycle, he knew it was her. She was battling the salty ocean breeze, riding along the sun-swept road in Kihei in only her bikini. He immediately got an erection. Which, being seventeen, was no surprise. In fact, it was pretty much an hourly occurrence.

The second reaction was, however, far from natural: a surge of hatred. The sight of her reminded him of the man he had hated for five long years. Like the sexual arousal, it was out of his control.

He spun a U-turn and followed her. The road was clogged with tourist-driven rented cars belching exhaust fumes that shouldn't have been allowed on Maui. He was sure that's why the brush on either side of the road was so brown. Even the palm trees looked sickly. Development was the worst thing that had happened to this tropical paradise. Kihei especially was becoming a real toilet. He was surprised to see her down here, for she was too classy for this area of cheap condos and time-shares. This was trailer-trash country. Well, maybe she was going to Wailea, where the money was.

His wheezing, rusted Suzuki Samurai had seen better days, but it still coughed up pep and vigor when the pedal was put to the floor. Where was she going? He'd not seen her on Maui since they finished the hotel in Wailea, just before his life went down the crapper. He'd heard that she had gone off to college on the mainland after living a year in Hong Kong with her father, getting to know the family business. In other words, learning how to swindle people. He wondered if she had graduated. He was finishing high school this year. That was, if he could manage it and still support his mother.

He was right behind her now, could pass her easily, but he slowed down, not wanting her to see him. He watched her lithe, golden body pedal for all it was worth, that black silky hair streaming in the wind. He could imagine it flicking against his face, his chest, his prick. The teenage fantasy died as revulsion overtook him. How could he be thinking sexy thoughts about someone he wished was dead?

She sailed past Wailea and its high-end hotels, manicured lawns, and gorgeous gardens. She was going to Makena! He couldn't believe it. That's where he'd just come from, from four hours of hanging out, sunning, doing nothing on his precious Saturday before he had to go home and deal with *her* again.

His mother had been soused by noon, and he couldn't take it, had to get the hell away. The routine sapped the life out of him. She'd sleep it off by five or six, he'd make her some food, she'd start drinking again as they watched a little television, then she'd start in with the moaning, the complaining, the what-ifs and the why us? Questions that couldn't be answered.

Sure enough, the girl on the bike turned onto the dirt road that led down to the beach. He stopped, giving her time to position the bike against a fence post, lock it, grab a towel bungee-corded on the back rack. When she pulled off her sandals and started walking over the cliffs to the sand, he got out of the truck, readjusted his rod in the liner in his trunks, and followed her. He was curious, excited and, conversely, filled with loathing.

As she walked along the shore, he matched her stride step for step on the cliff above. He brought the binoculars hanging from his neck up to his eyes to bring her image closer to him. When she turned and suddenly sprinted toward a secluded cove, he ducked right above it, afraid he'd be spotted. When he popped his head up again, she was nowhere to be seen. A quick scan of the beach through the binoculars produced nothing. Where could he have lost her? For a second, even though he knew it was impossible, he wished she'd run into the water and been swept out to sea and drowned. He'd go to her funeral and face them all, the Dragon Lady and her servants, the dog pack of brothers, and Hiram himself, good old Dad, and he'd walk up and spit into his face. In front of everyone. Maybe he'd even whip it out and piss on the coffin. And then he'd laugh. *You took one of mine,* he'd shout, *God took one of yours in return.* No, that wouldn't work exactly. *He'd* have to have drowned her for it to balance the equation. *I took one of yours!* God could have nothing to do with it.

She was right under him. He glanced down and saw her feet lying over the edge of her beach towel. He moved closer to the edge of the cliff and saw her knees, then crept closer as her thighs came into view. Then he realized she had taken her bikini top off and was lying bare-breasted in the late-afternoon sun. He thought he was going to have an orgasm just looking. He sat back and took a deep breath. And thought, maybe he'd marry her instead. It wasn't impossible, she was only about five years older. That would be a different kind of revenge, to take her, have her as his own, let them think he forgave them for what they did to his father. Then they'd invite *her* father to dinner one night and he'd shoot him in the head. He knew he could do it, too. He had done exactly that to his dog the month before.

He lifted the binoculars to his eyes again for a

close-up view. The girl on the sand below ran her fingers lightly from her neck to her thigh, pausing for a slight moment on her left breast, then over her belly button. As she brought her arm back down to the towel, she grazed the shining yellow material of the bikini bottom. He closed his eyes and imagined her sliding those fingers over his cheek and into his mouth. And that's when someone almost kicked him over the edge.

He was knocked forward by the force of the blow, stunned. The binoculars cracked off against a rock. As he rolled in the dirt, he saw the shadow of a figure towering over him. A voice taunted, "Peeping Tom!" He knew at once it was Lawrence Zarian, the school bully, who lived to terrorize him. "Binocular Boy gettin' his rocks off?"

"Eat shit and die." He got to his knees and rubbed his stung buttocks. The boot blow had been hard.

Lawrence poked his head over the cliff. "Corky's gettin' an eyeful."

"Don't call me that." Corky had been his nickname as a kid, but once he got to high school he'd tried to stop everyone from using it. He hadn't succeeded. So he added, "Larry," which he knew Lawrence felt the same way about.

"Fuck you, man, that's not my name."

"You can't even spell your name."

"Don't like Corky? How 'bout 'Orphan'?" Lawrence let out a laugh. "Like that better?"

"You sick Armenian moron."

Lawrence's face flushed red. "You ain't callin' me—" He launched his fist before Corky could respond.

He felt a dull ache shoot through his head and reverberate. He pulled himself to his feet and regained his equilibrium, spit out blood, and struck back. After a moment of grappling, he had the bigger boy pinned to the ground.

"Orphan!" Lawrence laughed up into his face.

"You're so dumb, you don't even know what an orphan is."

"Your old man's gone—"

Corky pulled his hair and rapped his head against the rock.

"And now your lush old lady!"

This statement seared him like wildfire. He knew Lawrence would say anything to upset him, but he also somehow knew it was true. He froze.

Lawrence took advantage of that and pulled himself out from under him. "Just dragged her outta the house in front of everybody," he said. "Still on fire, her skin was still fucking burning!"

"Wh—what?" He could feel his heart starting to sink.

"Didja know skin can burn, Corky?"

He felt the same hollowness inside his stomach he had when they told him about his dad. He thought he was going to vomit. "What are you talking about?"

"I'm saying you're an orphan, asshole. Drunken old hag burned down your house a little while ago. Greg said he thought you were at the beach, so he went along the water. I said I'd check up here—"

Lawrence was suddenly talking to the wind, for Corky was running toward his beat-up truck in horror and disbelief. Lawrence let out a nasty laugh. Then sat down and peered at the half-naked girl, who was unaware of the fight that had just taken place above her. "Oh, baby," he said softly.

The fire had started in the bedroom. She had been smoking when she drifted off, and this time Corky wasn't there to pull the cigarette from her lips and place it in the seashell she used as an ashtray. Her smoking had always been the next topic of concern after her drinking. The ceiling liner on her car was burned in a hundred places where she'd attempted to flick ashes out the window as she was driving. The wind had once forced a whole cigarette she'd discarded back inside, into the rear seat, and she'd had to stop the car to douse the subsequent fire with the Coca-Cola she'd just gotten from McDonald's. The drapes in her bedroom were so heavy with nicotine that they appeared fashionably tea-stained. But it was the smoking in bed that worried her son the most.

The firemen had done their best, they said, but the house was very old and very dry, and the flames feasted on it, devouring everything the termites had not yet eaten. The first thing the boy thought when he saw the charred frame of what had been the only home he'd ever known was that his mother had probably been so drunk, she didn't feel a thing.

Until neighbors told him how her screams had alerted them, and how they continued until the firemen went in, when most of the structure was in flames. They told him that she had called her son's name again and again and again, in terror and helplessness. And he wasn't there. He was up on a rock getting *his* rocks off looking at a sexy girl.

But not just any sexy girl. No, this was the daughter of the man who killed his father and set into motion the destruction of everything dear to him. They had ruined his life, left him an orphan—that idiot Lawrence had been right. They—her family—had done this. They'd murdered his mom.

He got on the last Hawaiian Air flight to Honolulu that night with only the clothes he was wearing, his binoculars, and the money he'd saved in the coconut shell in the shed. He didn't know where he was going, or what he would do, but he knew he had to leave Hawaii and the nightmare behind forever. He would work—his father had taught him a little about every facet of construction, from plastering to electrical to plumbing. He could get a job anywhere—and he'd finish school and build a life for himself.

Sitting wide-awake somewhere over the Pacific in the middle of the night, he suddenly became aware of the girl in seat 23C. She was Chinese, had long silky dark hair like the girl on the beach, was even almost as pretty. She was with an older man who he assumed was her father, a man about Hiram's age. And that's when he knew he would return to Hawaii someday. He had to get his revenge. There'd be no more adolescent fantasies of murder, dreaming about spitting in faces at funerals. Tonight he was, for the first time, an adult. He would get them. Hiram Goh needed to suffer the way *he* was now suffering.

Yes, he would infiltrate the Goh family and have his revenge in the sweetest way possible. He would take from them as they'd taken from him.

He would take Hiram's beloved only daughter.

Honolulu, Ten Years Later

The building came into focus through the eyepiece of the binoculars. The dark eyes of the observer peering through it scanned the height of the structure, taking in the massive beams and girders, the buzz of activity of burly workers on nearly every level, pausing for a second on the bright orange construction elevator chugging its way up to the only finished floor. The observer quickly switched from the binoculars to a powerful, sophisticated telescope, jerking it up to that floor, focusing on the huge expanse of windows blocking what had been a great view of the ocean. And there she was.

A rush went through him. His lens was mesmerized by her image. She'd shown up in his line of vision unexpectedly that first time. As he was studying only the building itself, she walked out onto a steel plank that would one day serve as the basis for the lavish model apartment's balcony. He sucked his breath in at the sight, and his stomach tightened. But a daring balancing act some twenty stories in the sky was just her style. He loved that she took the risk, accepting a dare to do a high-wire performance high above the humid streets of Honolulu. She had danced there that day, danced in the sky on a piece of steel no wider than a magazine, stopping traffic, drawing television helicopters (who arrived too late), sending the moronic construction workers into rapture and lengthy applause. Was she a little crazy? Adventurous? A show-off? Or did she actually like—and this thrilled him—danger?

That performance made him more curious about her, and had led to various "sightings," as he categorized them in his mind. He'd glimpsed her showing the model apartment to prospective rich—you had to be *filthy* rich even to get a look at this place—clients, noticed her and her assistant picnicking on the open, windblown twenty-fourth floor, and once when she, in a private moment he felt both compelled and embarrassed to watch, adjusted her bra straps right in the bedroom window, he couldn't take his eyes off her. She thought no one could see her. Of course, she didn't count on the power of a state-of-the-art telescope.

He found her now, talking with someone—looked like her assistant, but he wasn't sure, he couldn't quite see her face and if it was her, she'd had her hair cut—as the construction elevator made contact with the twenty-third floor. A man got off. He looked Chinese. Probably one of the brothers. They embraced. Yeah—he saw the face now—her brother. Half brother, actually, he recalled. Her father had married again; the old bastard had made some sons. This was the one who went to school in Honolulu, Jeff, he thought he'd read. He assumed they were going to fly to Hong Kong together for the funeral.

A moment later, she broke the embrace. He saw her pick up a garment bag, turn to her right, and disappear. Her assistant—yes, it was that dizzy sidekick she had been talking to—took the brother to the kitchen, where the telescope could actually read the words on the coffee mug she handed him: VICTORIA TOWERS. He pulled his head away from the eyepiece for a moment. For four million bucks they throw in a free coffee mug. He laughed out loud.

When he went back to the telescope, he found her in the bedroom, naked. He shivered. He knew he should not watch this, this private moment, but he was compelled to keep his eye pressed on the spot. He felt a stirring in his loins, or was it just in his head? Cerebral hard-on? That's what this peeping was, wasn't it? All of the mind?

He watched her slowly don new undergarments, fitting every crease and curve of her voluptuous body, then what looked like a soft nylon workout outfit, baggy and comfortable. Airplane clothes. It was a long ride to Hong Kong, and nobody dressed up anymore, even in first class.

He studied her every move, how her slender and soft fingers delicately buttoned the buttons, how she bent forward to slide her feet into her shoes, how she checked her dark, silky hair in the mirror with both hands seeming to mess it. Then she turned and faced the window, walked right up to it, looking out, looking right at him—

He jumped. Of course she couldn't see him, he was in a building across the street, and one that had reflective windows to boot, but it startled him nonetheless. When he looked through the telescope again, she'd rejoined her brother and assistant in the living room, and when the coffee was gone, she and the brother disappeared for a moment, then reappeared on the construction elevator as it started down. The observer felt for them both. They'd suffered a big loss, and his heart went out to them.

At the street level, a limousine waited. She'd probably left her car at home this morning, knowing she would be going to the airport directly from the building. The building. Hiram Goh's crown jewel. And hers. What would happen to her now?

Just before getting into the limo, she stopped and turned, and embraced someone else. The observer immediately pulled his face from the scope with a grimace of disapproval. She was hugging one of the construction workers, one of her friends. Saying her good-byes, accepting condolences. He felt jealous. He wanted to be that man right now.

He glanced at the newspaper open on the desk to his left. There was Hiram Goh's obituary, along with a smiling, benevolent photograph. The man looked almost angelic, which only proved the power of photography, wrecking the old adage that cameras don't lie. When he looked back, the car—with Audrey—was gone.

But he'd see her again as soon as she returned.

Watching her was something over which he simply had no control.

Chapter One

Hong Kong

Audrey Goh was dressed in black, standing inside the ferry building on the Kowloon side, looking out at Hong Kong harbor—Fragrant Harbour—drenched in rain. The Star Ferry was pulling in, and in a few minutes she would make the harbor crossing. As a girl, she found this the most exciting ride on earth. She had charmed her parents into taking her back and forth, back and forth, until they could stand the monotony no longer. These old, proud workhorse boats hadn't changed one bit in her lifetime; they represented a consistency in her world that told her she could count on certain things never to disappoint her. But the man who'd first introduced her to this experience, the one man she'd shared this ride with more than any other, was now gone. Her beloved father lay in a funeral home just a short distance away by ferry, in Central, and she was about to join all the other grieving relatives to put him to rest.

Mark Carson, the man she hoped to marry, gently draped his arm around her. "I know what you're thinking." She moved closer to him. "I know how much you miss him."

Oh, no, she thought to herself, you don't really have a clue. No one did. "The rain seems somehow fitting."

"I hate rain," he muttered.

"I love it. Without rain, Father would say, nothing grows, including people. *Rain washes away that which is not essential.* He read that somewhere and loved it. He always felt it nourished him."

"Let's go," Mark said, as the gate opened. They walked onto the aged white-and-green ferryboat and took seats.

Audrey saw an enormous colorful junk floating by, appearing almost as an apparition in the rain. The gold trim on the intricately carved bow sparkled even through the mist. It bobbed and heaved, and Audrey wondered what legends it evoked, what generations it had transported, what adventures it had seen. Rather like her father, she thought.

A small, hunched woman hesitantly approached her. She made sure it was Audrey, then bowed deeply. *"Neh ho mah?"* she asked. Mark knew that meant how are you? He was studying Cantonese because it was more widely used in Hong Kong than Mandarin. It would help in the banking business, for most of his clients were Asian.

"Ho, yow sem," Audrey said softly to the

woman. He knew she was thanking her for her concern, saying she was well, which was a lie. She wasn't well at all. She had a broken heart. She turned and introduced Mark.

He extended his hand, and said, *"Hun woo."* Pleased to meet you.

"Mm-goy," the woman said, thank you.

Mark added you're welcome, *"Mm'sai mm-goy."*

Audrey nodded to him, as if to say he was doing very well. Then she turned back to the woman and accepted her condolences about her father's passing—some of which Mark was unable to understand because they spoke too fast—and something about how her brothers would make her father proud in the afterlife (a thought that Mark and Audrey had to keep from laughing at), how Hiram had left a great legacy, so on and so forth.

When the ferry started to move, the woman finally decided to stop. *"Hoh goh hing gin doe nee,"* Mark said, nice to have met you.

"Wah-boo-dong," the woman said, good-bye, good-bye. It was primitive, but he had not made any mistakes and felt rather proud.

They crossed the windswept harbor, the rain spraying in from the open sides of the boat. Mark put an arm protectively around Audrey. "Are the jerks upset we decided to stay in Kowloon and not with the family?" By "jerks" he meant her four younger half brothers.

"I don't think they care one way or the other."

She was looking at a little girl who seemed oblivious to the rain, enchanted with her ride in the big boat. "Darren and John are too preoccupied over who gets the house in Paris; Bruce got plastered on the plane from Vancouver, and is probably still too drunk to know what's even happening; and the wives are no doubt busy counting the cash."

"How about Jeffrey? He's the most decent of the four."

She smiled. "He's only twenty-two. Give him time."

The boat rocked sharply, not because of the storm but from the waves of the wake of a large motor yacht steaming through the harbor, one of the busiest ports on earth. A bell clanged. They had to hold on. "You will find the funeral interesting," Audrey told Mark, as they swayed from side to side.

"You mean for all the infighting, the subtext?"

"Well, that too. No, I meant that it is going to be a traditional Chinese funeral, old style. They don't do it like this much anymore."

"Is it what your father wanted?"

"It's what Aunt Melba wants." That said it all. Then Audrey, whose expression usually turned to ice when she mentioned her father's sister, softened. "Father was her only brother, older and wiser. There was a soft spot."

"He helped her build the empire," Mark offered.

"That too," Audrey said with a grin.

They reached Central, bumping hard against the dock. They waited until they heard a clank of chains and the engines slowing down. The overwhelming scent of diesel fuel attacked their nostrils. Energetic young Chinese sailors secured the boat to the moorings with ropes the thickness of a wrist, and the gangplank flipped down.

Audrey and Mark put up their umbrellas and made their way into the rain. They didn't have to go far, for a black Rolls-Royce, which her father had always joked were so common in the colony as to be called the HK Chevrolet, was parked in the rain, chauffeur standing with raised umbrella, waiting to take them the rest of the way.

The dark and musty funeral home on Ving Lok Street smelled of ancient wood, fresh flowers, and pungent incense. The old floors creaked under the weight of hundreds of mourners who had come to view the body of Hiram Goh. His real birth name was Li Yuang, the only member of his family up to that time to be born outside China. His parents managed to flee before the Cultural Revolution destroyed their dreams, stopping long enough in Hong Kong on their way to America to give birth to a fat baby boy. They put down roots in the Hawaiian Islands, and had a daughter two years later. The elder Gohs named their daughter Melba, and started calling Li "Hiram," after Hiram Fong, an island politician who became his father's friend. Years later, after the death of Audrey's mother, Hiram moved to Hong Kong full-time—his British colonial citizenship allowed him to do that—and became wildly successful. Now all of Hong Kong was paying its respect.

When Audrey and Mark walked into the funeral home, the eldest of the brothers, Darren, was burning money in a pot up front near the casket. An old woman sitting on a hard wooden bench was wailing. Audrey and Mark were given black armbands, and Audrey was led to the group of relatives seated up front, who were soon covered with a white sheet, which signified hiding their grief from the rest of the crowd. A cousin went up and burned more money.

Mark thought there couldn't be a flower left in all Asia. The floral tributes were astonishing, and not only the large formal arrangements. As in London following the death of Princess Diana, hundreds upon hundreds of people had brought small bouquets, some from their gardens, or from pots on their high-rise balconies of buildings Hiram had built, to pay tribute.

A Buddhist priest led the short service, and then they all walked several blocks to the cemetery. Umbrellas provided only minimal protection because the rain was coming down in torrents, not especially surprising during typhoon season. And somehow fitting, Audrey thought, for her father had been a dynamo, the harnessed energy of a great storm in a human soul. He was probably looking down and smiling.

* * *

As the funeral procession made its way up Aberdeen Street, Audrey walked slowly inside an enclosure, another sheet carried by four men which surrounded the grieving relatives, to mask their sorrow and tears. Her father had been everything to her. His only daughter, she'd been the apple of his eye. The desire for a son had forced him to remarry when her mother died early in their young and happy life together, and while living in Hong Kong, he'd fathered four more children, all of them boys, which pleased the gods and traditionalist relatives, especially his old-fashioned sister, Melba. But none of the boys could measure up to Audrey in their father's favor. She had wit and grace, beauty and brains, and gave every indication that she would turn out to be a bigger success—the ultimate judge of worth in the Goh family—than the four of them combined.

Aunt Melba walked to her right. The tall woman took rigid short steps, her head covered with traditional Chinese mourning garb, an ever-present fan, so damp that the colors were running, grasped in her left fingers fluttering before her face. In front of the women were the brothers, showing their rightful place in succession, men before women, despite the fact that all of them were gamblers, boozers, and overprivileged snots—or, in the case of Jeff, a boy so afraid of the real world he'd decided to remain a student forever. Audrey thought it must have been the second wife's genes.

In the enclosures behind walked the cousins, Old Uncle from Canton, assorted nieces and nephews, and Mark, not only because he was Audrey's boyfriend, but because Hiram had liked him, to the extent that he had made him his financial liaison in Honolulu. Mark was going to miss him personally, but his bank would miss him even more.

Despite the rain, spectators lined the streets of the procession, for Hiram Goh was one of Hong Kong's most colorful characters, and one of the richest men in the colony. From his multimillion-dollar penthouse high on Victoria Peak, he used to call the city "my little nest." He had flourished both before and after the British left, restructuring his politics to the regime currently in power. His motto for survival was simple: grease the palms of those in charge.

He built several of the buildings the power brokers worked in and most of their homes. He was one of the most successful real-estate barons in Southeast Asia. He was also a smoker, drinker, bon vivant, and raconteur. He lived an affluent lifestyle in five residences on three continents—Hong Kong, Honolulu, New York City, London, and Paris. He dined in five-star establishments, rubbed shoulders with the rich and famous, and took great enjoyment in the opera and symphony, for he loved music as much as making money. He had outlived two wives, but his death still came as a shock, for his passing was untimely; though he had lived what seemed to be three lifetimes, he was only seventy-two years old. He would be missed.

Hiram was buried high atop a hill overlooking his beloved harbor city, facing the ocean, as is Chinese custom. Mark and Audrey lingered till the last mourners had left for the lunch, standing silently under their umbrellas. Because of the rain, no one could tell how hard Audrey was crying. But her father knew, she was sure. Her father knew there would be an emptiness in her heart that no one would ever fill. "*Wah-boo-dong,* Daddy," she whispered, and tossed a lei she had brought made from his favorite flowers, the same kind she had greeted him with whenever he came to Hawaii, onto the soaked ground. "I'll always love you."

Luncheon was served at Guangzhou Garden, on the mezzanine level of one of Hong Kong's glitziest glass, marble, and chrome harborside office towers, which, of course, Hiram Goh had built. Normally filled with upscale clientele, financiers and other businesspeople, today the restaurant was closed to the public. The Cantonese cuisine was distinguished by its subtle flavors and artful presentation—Mark marveled at the garnishes of fresh sliced fruits—hallmarks of the Ta Leung style. The main dish for the mourners was pan-fried milk with crab meat and olive seeds. Audrey told Mark that when they departed, everyone would take their rice bowl and chopsticks and a slice of orange with them, as tradition dictated.

The most interesting facet of the funeral day for Mark was the laise, a butterscotch candy and either a nickel or dime or quarter wrapped in red paper. "My mother used to tell me to buy sweets with the laise, for good luck," Audrey explained. "In my youthful ignorance I almost wanted people to die because then I'd get chocolates and jelly beans and—"

She stopped in mid-sentence as a hush settled over the place. Everyone's attention turned to the rotund man dressed all in white who had just entered the doors, flanked by six burly men. Everyone knew who the man was, and little by little, conversations were resumed. Soon the room was cacophonous once again.

But Mark had no clue as to who the man was. "What was that all about?"

"Pearl River Tung," Audrey said.

"Pardon me?"

"The gangster."

It registered now. "Of course. Your father's friend." Mark saw the man was heading toward Audrey. "Come to pay his respects?"

"We'll know in a moment," Audrey said. She was aware that almost everyone in the room was watching. A hundred pair of chopsticks were pointed her way as people whispered over their rice. Tung had controlled organized crime in nearby Macao for years and was now, according to her father, in trouble. Hiram hadn't told her much more than that, but Audrey had read that he'd been feuding with other tong leaders and was under investigation by the Chinese government. Audrey rose, and Mark did the same.

"I offer my deepest respect," the man boomed, bowing lower to Audrey than she thought possible given the size of his belly. "Hiram was my dear colleague and friend," he continued, "and I shall miss him greatly."

Audrey said, "We all shall miss him greatly."

One of the bodyguards produced a chair, which he handed over some seated mourners to another bodyguard, who planted it directly under Tung's rear end. "Sit," Tung offered Audrey and Mark, though it sounded more like an order. He dropped into the chair beneath him and folded his hands on his lap, pulling slightly on his colorful tie. "So, we mourn."

"Yes," Audrey agreed, with an uncomfortable glance at Mark.

"I hear you are working in Victoria Towers," Tung said to Audrey.

"I'm the sales agent."

"Your father has an apartment there?"

"It serves as the model."

"The safe?"

She blinked. "What about it?"

"You have access?"

"No."

He blinked. "No? Who does?"

"No one that I know. Perhaps Aunt Melba." Audrey turned to glance at Melba at a nearby table.

"That old hen won't even speak to me," Tung growled. "I tried to call her last night. Her servants refuse to put me through."

"I'm sorry, but it's not my business," Audrey said as nicely as she could.

"Listen, dolly," the man suddenly said, bending closer to Audrey's ear, "I need to get into that safe."

She was curious. "Why?"

"I have things in there."

She remembered a shipment that had arrived last week. Hiram had told her the boxes were "immensely important, but not mine." She'd noticed that they were made of metal, and were locked. They probably were Tung's. "I know nothing about it."

"Who does?" he snorted. His pinkish face was turning red.

She shrugged. "Perhaps you'd best speak to my father's lawyers."

Mark butted in. "I'm Mark Carson, Mr. Tung. I was Hiram's person at the Bank of Hawaii. Perhaps I could help—"

Tung stood. The chair fell backward to the floor. "You have a key to the safe?"

"No."

"Then you can't help." He looked back at Audrey. "I would have expected Hiram's daughter to accommodate me."

She could only tell him the truth. "I don't know how to help you. I don't know how to get into the safe. I'm in the same position you are in."

"Not quite," he said with a snide laugh to the bodyguards, who nodded in unison. Then he pointed a finger at Melba, who was ignoring him, talking to relatives. "She will not stop me," he promised ominously, "and neither will you."

Audrey shrugged. "I'm not trying to stop you from anything, Mr. Tung," she said. "It's just that I'm powerless to—"

"I know what you meant to your father," he said as if to insinuate that she was lying. "I know his sons he shared nothing with. You are the savvy one, you are the one the old bastard trusted—"

"This is my father's *funeral,*" Audrey reminded him.

"I mean no disrespect," the man growled. "But I will have my way." And with that, he walked out.

When the sun shone through the black clouds the next morning, Hong Kong seemed to steam in the incredible humidity. Aunt Melba flew back to Honolulu, but Audrey and Mark chose to stay a few more days and pamper themselves at the Regent. They went to Repulse Bay the next afternoon, shopped the Stanley Market there till they could carry no more bundles, ate pizza and drank salty, strong Chinese beer, then found a beach where they soaked themselves in the South China Sea.

"He thought Stanley was fun," Audrey said to Mark, as they lounged on the sand. "Used to buy jeans there."

Mark shook his head. "One of the richest men in the colony and he looked to save twenty bucks on Gap chinos."

"He could spend it as fast as he earned it," Audrey said, "but he did muster up a dose of frugality now and then."

"Did the letters stop?" Mark asked, changing the subject. It's something he had wanted to inquire about earlier, but knew it was a difficult subject.

"I don't know," Audrey responded. He was referring to the cryptic letters her father had started getting a few months before, first in Hawaii and then in Hong Kong as well. They were the kind of notes kidnappers sent, words clipped from newspapers, pasted with glue onto a piece of paper. Audrey had found the first one tossed on Hiram's Honolulu office desk. IT IS TIME NOW read the pasted words. "What's this?" she had asked.

"Nonsense," he had said, and tossed it into the trash.

But recently he had admitted to her that he'd received more such notes. He told her they all said something about "it being time" and "it will happen soon." He had no idea what that meant, and even less who might be sending them. "A prank," he had said, and dismissed it.

But when he had returned to Hawaii a few weeks back, he seemed very troubled when another one arrived at Aunt Melba's compound addressed to him. TIME TO PAY was the message that time. They'd talked about it, Hiram, Melba, and Audrey, but without coming to a conclusion. Melba felt the police should know about the notes, but Hiram laughed at that notion. "They don't threaten me in any way," he reminded her. Audrey felt it was some business deal gone sour and told her father that it was just some "nut," and that it would stop.

It had not. The last one, which had come just before Hiram so suddenly died, read TIME TO LOSE SOMETHING PRECIOUS. Audrey had never even been able to show it to him. It was still in her purse. She found it and showed it to Mark.

Mark studied it. "Mailed from Honolulu. Like all the others?"

She nodded. "One was from Maui, Father said."

"Strange."

She mused on the content of the letter. "Something precious. Wonder what it means?"

"Jesus," Mark exclaimed. "His life? Audrey, you don't think—?"

"No! He died of natural causes, the autopsy proved that. No one killed him."

Mark shook his head. "They do things with poison these days that can't be detected."

"Give me a break, no one poisoned Father." She stared at the cryptic note. "I wonder if they'll stop now?"

"Should. No one left to send them to."

"I suppose." She ripped up the note, got up, and deposited it in a receptacle on the sand. But as she walked back into the South China Sea and swam out a few yards, she had the creepiest sensation that the letters would not stop, and that they, in some way, had something to do with her.

Chapter Two

On a woven ABC Store beach mat on the sands of Waikiki in Honolulu, a pair of scissors rested atop a folded newspaper. Next to the newspaper was a worn backpack. Inside it were plain white envelopes, white notepaper, and postage stamps bound by a rubber band, a tube of glue stick, and an address book which held all the addresses where mail could be sent to Hiram Goh. A muscular man wearing black surfer trunks walked out of the ocean, shook the salt water from his body like a dog, and flopped on the mat in the sun. His shoulder rested against the backpack.

He looked like just another aging surfer, skin bronzed the shade of leather, hair and eyebrows bleached from salt and sun. He unpopped a tube of zinc, greased his upper lip first, then the lower, and put it back into his backpack. Then he stretched out on his side and opened the newspaper he had bought a few days before. It was the seventh or eighth time he had read it. HIRAM GOH DIES IN HONG KONG the headline blared. And more.

TRIBUTES POUR IN. GOH BUILDINGS GRACE HONOLULU SKYLINE. CONTROVERSIAL FIGURE. Ain't that the fucking truth?

He turned to page three and stared at her picture. It identified her as: *Audrey Goh, Hiram's only daughter, Head of Sales for the Goh Corporation's Victoria Towers.* There was a photo of Hiram's sister, Melba, and assorted others of the man himself, one with Audrey and Melba and his sons at his sixtieth birthday party some years back. How young she looked, like she could have been fourteen! Just as he remembered her, just as he'd seen her through the binoculars the other day.

There was one of Saint Hiram, standing with a group of poor people on the day they moved into one of his public-funds-assisted complexes. He could read the loathing on the man's face. This was no Mother Teresa. He hated the poor the way people hate cockroaches. Saint Hiram was Saint Sham.

His rage started to fill him as it had for the past fifteen years. He reached for the scissors. A babe was walking by in a bikini that should have been against the law, but he hardly noticed her. He was staring at Audrey again. And cutting around her picture. Once he'd clipped it, he found the words he needed, some in headlines, some in the text, and once he completed the cutting, he began to glue them to a piece of white paper. A woman from a nearby blanket, a busybody who'd been watching him, got up and walked over. "Excuse me," she said in a grating voice, "but I couldn't help but wonder. Whatever are you doing?"

Jesus. Just what he needed. He hid Audrey's photo. "Therapy," he said to her.

"What?"

"Calms the nerves."

She laughed slightly. She dropped to her knees in the sand, and said, "I write things down myself. You know, just make notes. It helps."

He had to get rid of her. "Well, only works for me for a while," he said. "See, the addressee will become the victim when the nerves get jangled."

She blinked. "What?"

With dead seriousness he said, "I'm a serial killer. These are the warning letters."

First she smiled, then she must have put together that he was being facetious and attempting to get rid of her, so she gave him a nasty frown, got up, and marched off.

Which was just what he wanted. He addressed the envelope with the usual childish printing he knew no one could ever trace. He lifted a self-adhesive stamp from its paper backing and put it on upside down. Then he licked the flap and it was done.

He looked out over the water he loved so much. He was glad he'd returned to Hawaii. This was where he was meant to be. Above him was Diamond Head. He'd climbed it yesterday. He'd had a day off from work and felt energetic. People thought it was a forbidding mountain, kind of like an icon. He knew it to be intimately accessible.

He watched two boys walking along one of the paths above him. They were laughing as they played and chased and seemed to be having the time of their lives. As he'd had with his buddy, Gregory, until the death of his father changed everything and made his world one without joy. A sand crab tickled his big toe. He kicked it away.

He slathered his body with baby oil, the cheapest stuff he could find. Why spend a fortune for the Coppertone name when this did the trick? Sunscreen? Forget it. He'd grown up on Maui's beaches, and the sun was his friend. It made him strong, healthy, helped him think clearly.

And he always seemed to be thinking about Audrey. And what he was going to do when she returned. He felt a devilish thrill just imagining it. Oh, it would be different from what he'd been planning for ten years now, very different. The old man's death had changed everything. He had been engulfed with anger when he learned the old fart had up and died on him. The fucking nerve! But after thinking it through, he realized that just because Hiram had croaked was no reason to discontinue his plan. In a way, it might be better.

He closed his eyes and flipped to his stomach, stretched his legs out wide. Can't have dark skin only in front. Then he realized he was erect. Just like the horny teenager that day in Makena, the day he saw her naked, the day his mother died.

He pushed his pelvis into the sand. It always happened when he thought about Audrey. Even in funereal black, she was the sexiest woman on earth.

Then he realized it was getting late, and the last mail pickup was at five. He sat up, gathered his towel, and slung his backpack over his shoulder. But he stopped. He had an idea. To hell with mailing this one. It was time to take a step further, to begin his new plan. This one he would deliver in person.

He found the Kahala complex nearly empty. Whenever he'd come here before—always from the beach, never the road up to those imposing gates—there was a swarm of activity, with maids and servants rushing about. Today, deserted. The old woman probably packed them all off to the funeral. Hell, they might have chartered a plane to Hong Kong, they could afford it. He guessed no one was back yet.

He made his way through the sand to the property, put his butt on the short wall that served more as a symbol of demarcation—the privileged cut off from the masses—than any kind of barrier, and lifted his feet over. He tiptoed through the lush foliage, which changed from beach vines and ivy to manicured gardens overflowing with tuberose and ginger as he neared the houses. He was standing on the lanai of the main residence. It was quiet here, almost too quiet. Like a churchyard or a cemetery. It gave him the willies.

He peered into the windows, into what he'd only been able to imagine from the beach. Churchlike as well, dark and forbidding, all cinnabar and gold, fucking Chinatown-depressing. All the times he'd done this, come close, even watching her through the lens from the beach, he'd never seen inside, much less been able to enter. But today a door was unlocked.

He used it.

It was like stepping back into time, into an ancient dynasty that he'd only read about. The air was cool, humid, dank. It was dark and mysterious. Audrey grew up in this house, he realized, and he thought he could almost smell her there, a fresh scent of plumeria blossoms amidst the depressing aura of the old taste. He knew she lived now in the cottage to the other side of the compound, had peeked in the windows several times, once just to watch her sleep. But the big house fascinated him.

So this is where some of the money went, he thought. This is where all the riches the old man had bilked from poor people was spent, on silk robes from Shanghai, jade dragons from Beijing. He held an exquisitely carved one in his hand. Worth a fortune. Fucking fat old bastard. Money that rightfully should have been his father's, and now his.

He heard the sound of a car. He froze with the dragon in his hand. A big black vehicle was pulling into the drive, he could see it clearly through the front courtyard. Dragon Lady herself, probably. *Adios.*

But before he left, he set the envelope on the carved antique Chinese sideboard just inside the main door of the house, between the two beautiful blue-and-white fishbowls.

Down the beach, he broke into a trot along the water, and then a full run. The thrill exhilarated him. It was the next step. Then the time would come—the opportunity would present itself, as it had in his dreams—when he would carry out the plan he'd sworn when flying over that very ocean so many years ago.

He stopped dead in his tracks. A collie was ahead of him, leaping into the air to clamp its teeth into a yellow Frisbee its master had tossed, rushing in and out of the water, playing a game of I-won't-give-it-back. He looked and acted so much like Kam, his loving shaggy dog, whom he'd shot through the head when his mother, in a drunken rage, ordered it. He sank to his knees, tears welling up in his eyes. Kam, dear old beautiful Kamehameha.

He turned back to face the compound. The hatred made him rigid, causing the veins in his neck and forehead to protrude. He brushed the tears from his cheeks and steeled himself to the business at hand, the goal that would make the pain go away: getting her.

Chapter Three

Bobbi Kicherer was waiting in the humid sunshine just outside U.S. Customs at Honolulu International Airport. Audrey smiled at the sight of her perky, ever-devoted assistant, for the plane ride had made her a bundle of nerves. She needed a girlfriend to talk to, and Bobbi was the closest thing she'd ever had to a sister. "Welcome home," Bobbi said, giving her a hug and placing a lei made from fresh, sweet pikaki blossoms around her neck.

"Hi." Audrey drank in the scent, one of her favorite in the world. She managed a smile for a moment, but she was preoccupied.

"Was it just awful?" Bobbi asked.

Audrey nodded. "But we knew it was going to be."

"Where's Mr. Wonderful?"

"Mark discovered someone he knew as we were getting off the plane. They were exchanging business cards last I saw."

"Was he being an asshole?"

Audrey looked taken aback. "Why would you think that?"

"You sound annoyed with him."

"I'm just a mess for its own sake. Something happened that really worries me."

"What?"

Audrey took a deep breath. She fingered the lei flowers nervously. "The last morning in the hotel, I—" She stopped as Mark emerged from the doors and headed up the customs ramp toward them. "To be continued."

"Damn right," Bobbi muttered, hating to be cut off just before the good part. "It's like missing the Friday episode of *Days of Our Lives*. Hi, Mark."

"Bobbi," he said with a nod.

She had come prepared. She placed a lei of woven maile, the traditional flowering vine worn by males, over his head.

Audrey said, "How lovely of you," knowing that Bobbi had never liked Mark much and this was a very generous gesture.

"Smells great," Mark said, smiling, happy to be home.

"Anything I should know about?" Audrey asked Bobbi in her business tone of voice.

"Closed the Choi deal yesterday."

Audrey was surprised. "They went through with it? What kind of hoops did you have to jump through?"

"Ate fire, and had to sleep with the husband, but it worked."

Audrey played along. "He's got to be eighty."

"Like I said, no problem. It was over very quickly." Bobbi sounded so honest that Mark gave a look that said, are you kidding me? "Yes," Bobbi added, "I'm kidding." But she rolled her eyes as she turned back to Audrey.

Audrey ignored her.

"Where's Dragon Lady?" Bobbi asked, expecting to see Audrey's aunt coming down the ramp behind Mark, thinking they were waiting for her.

"She flew home right after the funeral," Audrey explained.

Mark added, "We wanted to spend a little time together. Even though I worked with Hiram, I'd never seen Hong Kong."

"So what am I doing here?" Bobbi asked.

"I've got a meeting," Mark explained.

"Going directly to the bank," Audrey added.

"And I'm late," Mark said, checking his watch.

Audrey looked at Bobbi. "So, it was either you or a ride in Aunt's big old Town Car."

"My Bug or a comfy Lincoln? No contest." Bobbi grabbed Audrey's bag. "Come on, I'm illegal. The car may be cute, but it's no limo, so they ticket."

Mark kissed Audrey on the cheek, pulled out his Jaguar keys. "See you later, honey, and stop worrying."

"Worrying about what?" Bobbi asked.

He didn't answer her. He looked at Audrey. "Promise?"

Audrey nodded. "We'll wait and see if they stop coming. But if they don't, we'll go to the police."

Mark looked exasperated. "Honey, you don't send threatening cryptic notes to a dead person."

Bobbi couldn't stand it. "What the hell are you two talking about?"

Neither answered her. Mark kissed Audrey again and headed off to the cab stand, calling, "Thanks for the lei," as he hurried away. Bobbi and Audrey skirted a Roberts Hawaiian Holidays tour guide passing out cheap leis to a hundred overweight Midwestern tourists, and walked to the curb. "What was that all about?" Bobbi asked.

"I'll tell you later."

"All right, I can wait. So, did you have *any* fun?"

"It was a funeral, Bobbi."

"You can still have a good time."

"I loved my father."

"Hiram would have wanted you to enjoy yourself. Celebrate his life, you know?"

"The Chinese aren't like the Irish, no dancing a jig."

"What do you do? Weep and wail?"

"Burn money."

"Huh?"

"I'll explain *that* later as well. Where's your car?"

* * *

Nestled inside Bobbi's sparkling new, bright yellow VW Beetle, on the H1 toward Waikiki, Audrey filled Bobbi in on the somber details of her father's rainy send-off to another life. She explained the significance—the next life would be rich and prosperous—of the burning of the money, how the brothers had treated her with kind indifference, how she felt out of place and ill at ease, as usual.

She touched the delicate orchid Bobbi had stuck into the dashboard bud vase and told of her and Mark's excursion to Stanley Market, how for only one moment she didn't feel irritable and lost. "We were dragging heavy bags filled with all the cheap clothes we bought but didn't need, waiting for the bus back to town, when I spied a sign that said BEACH. We trudged through a residential district and finally found the sandy expanse of beach about a mile away. It was serendipitous. Sun going down over the water, a junk bobbing in the distance. We didn't have swimming suits, but there were few people left on the sand, so I peeled down to my bra and panties, and Mark swam in his boxer shorts."

"Amazed he had the nerve."

"He's got a great body. You always remark on that."

"And that's all one can say, isn't it?"

Andrey didn't pursue it. Bobbi had never liked Mark, and Audrey was through trying to convince her otherwise. She went back to her story. "It was amazing, Bobbi, I was buoyant and went into a trance. I thought to myself, I'm floating on the surface of the South China Sea, on the other side of the globe, and I don't have a care in the world."

"Fab fantasy, honey. Wish you could have stayed there?"

"I never wanted it to end."

Bobbi exited the freeway. "What did Joe Boxer do?"

"Mark—that's his name, remember?—was very understanding."

"Understanding how?"

Audrey shrugged. How to put it? "He felt my grief."

"Who wouldn't? You lost your father suddenly, after all."

"I felt . . ." Her voice drifted off, not sure.

"How?" Bobbi probed.

"Vulnerable. Emotionally."

"Did you tell him?"

"Sure."

"And?"

"I asked about his feelings, about the future, since we were both left unsure by Father's death."

Bobbi gripped the wheel and yelled. "Unsure? You want to marry him, you want a life with him, you want his kids, you want out from Melba's domination—what do you mean you're unsure?"

"I'm not positive about what Mark wants. He's a complex person."

Bobbi blinked. "This is a guy who gulps Creatine, clips coupons 'cause his mother did, watches television wrestling, and cooks a good pot roast. I'll say he's complex."

Audrey threw it right back at her. "He takes care of his body, he's frugal, he was captain of his college wrestling team, and thank God he cooks because I sure don't." Bobbi passed a flatbed truck filled with palm trees. "Let me remind you also that he's successful, smart, and sexy."

"You don't have to convince me," Bobbi said. "I'm not the one marrying him."

Her response only made Audrey angrier, so she changed the subject. "What's happened at the office?"

"You know some asshole named Tung?"

Audrey sobered. "Pearl River Tung?"

Bobbi blinked. "Pearl? No, this was a guy."

"Never mind. He called?"

"Several times. Left you this basic message: cooperate."

"He showed up at the funeral luncheon. It wasn't pretty."

"Who is he?"

"A very powerful sleazeball my father knew from the old days."

"What's he want?"

"I'm not sure I even know."

Bobbi waited for more. When none came, she offered, "I saved all the messages he left."

"That's a waste of time."

Bobbi felt Audrey wasn't giving her a chance. "Hey, how was I to know they weren't important?"

"Sorry." Audrey bit a nail. "I'm just a little edgy."

"I'd be edgy, too. I mean, I heard you and Mark talking about the police. That about this Tung guy?"

"No, something a little more frightening." Audrey told her about the cryptic notes cut from magazines, and how she and Mark had discussed it that day on the beach. "We calmed down, believed it would stop. But then we had dinner with Father's attorney that night at the Chinese restaurant in the Regent, and he showed us one that arrived that very day."

"Mailed before Hiram died?"

"Yes, actually the day of his death. What was so troubling is—" Audrey stopped.

Bobbi changed lanes. "Continue."

"I'll show you." She dug into her briefcase and found the envelope.

"I can't look till I get off the highway," Bobbi said, "or I'll roll this thing like a hot baked potato." She changed lanes to the right again. "We should have let Melba's driver do this. So, home or to the office, Miss Goh?"

"Any appointments?" Audrey asked in response.

"Cleared the afternoon for you. I know how nasty you can get with jet lag."

"Thanks. Let's go to Aunt's, then."

"That's worse than jet lag." Bobbi took the exit for Kahala, and didn't say another word. She'd look at the envelope when they got there.

Melba Goh's oceanfront compound in Honolulu's exclusive Kahala area was a blend of cutting-edge contemporary mansion and back-alley Chinatown. Gates worthy of a Sung Dynasty palace opened to reveal a winding driveway lined with pakalana flowers, which meandered around towering coco palms. A six-car garage to the right of the entrance door had roll-up doors as common as in the cheapest apartment complex, yet were adorned with dragons in gold leaf and cinnabar. The intricately carved wood entrance door, which led to a soothing, welcoming courtyard with fountain and pond, had been shipped from Shanghai, where it had withstood the onslaught of centuries, welcoming people to a grand villa that was finally razed by the Cultural Revolution.

The interior of the courtyard was an oasis of falling water, lily pads, singing birds, old teak benches, and a view of the Pacific that stretched as far as the eye could see. Red, yellow, and white ginger grew all around the buildings, and vines and ti plants with their enormous leaves abounded.

Audrey had grown up in this house, which had gotten larger and grander every year. Her mother had suffered from toxemia during her pregnancy, and had had a difficult childbirth, and it was a wonder that the little girl survived. Though it should have been, by tradition, a source of shame to Hiram Goh that he fathered not a son and heir, but a useless daughter, the man doted on the girl, in whom he saw the beautiful eyes, dark eyes, deep jade green eyes, of his beloved wife. The fact that the little girl's birth was a near miracle endeared her to him all the more. When his wife, who never recovered her health after the delivery, died only four short years later, his relationship with little Audrey was set in stone. Even when he remarried a nice, if dull, Chinese girl and produced four sons, Audrey remained the favorite.

Hiram was a resident of Hong Kong, however, not mainland China, and he felt the relatives and their old-style thinking had to change, for things were different there. The old traditions were dying, and girls could be as smart, cunning, and successful as any man. Hiram measured success in gold. So did Aunt Melba, who treated Audrey as if she were her own daughter.

Melba and her older brother were determined that little Audrey would grow up to make a fortune. She would be taught that goal early in life, and never allowed to question it.

Until now. For that was part of the unrest, the churning in Audrey's stomach, the empty place in her soul. Was this all there was? Was this what she wanted? Didn't anything else matter? She had talked to her father about it before he died, just a few weeks ago, on Hiram's last visit to Hawaii. And yes, he admitted, he'd known love as well, and it was a reward better than the next million, the new contract, the latest acquisition. That was why his second marriage was about the business of fathering sons and nothing more. He never loved his second wife, who had also died before him. He did love his sons, but was gravely disappointed in their lack of ambition. Audrey thought he seemed almost more fond of Mark, who was already his liaison at the bank in Honolulu, and he urged Audrey to marry Mark and be happy, and to give him grandchildren. But he did not live to see that happen.

To the right of the entry courtyard was the living area, an expansive parlor with two walls of sliding glass and plantation shutter panels which could open or close the room to the elements. Outside, a marble patio guided the eye to the sparkling swimming pool anchored on one end by huge stone Foo dogs, and the blue ocean just beyond the other.

There was an intimate dining room, crowded with Chinese antiques, which Audrey felt was a mistake because it was dark to begin with and the pieces overwhelmed it and made it feel dingy. It reminded Audrey of an old-style funeral parlor, as musty as the one they had just buried Hiram from. Disguising the entrance to the kitchen, two large and exquisite Ming Dynasty pots were displayed on pedestals. They were so big that once, as a child, she hid inside one for nearly three hours to keep from having to go to school.

The kitchen looked like a small hotel's, with its chunky restaurant range, commercial dishwashers and refrigerators. Audrey never used it. She chose instead to cook for herself—when she had the time and inclination—in the privacy of her own place, one of the compound's guesthouses. Her idea of dinner was to send out, let Mark do it, or simply go to a restaurant. She could do simple things like roast a turkey, but she didn't find it at all compelling.

Her cottage was on the beach to the far left of the main house, around the corner from the bedroom and office wing, past Aunt's private quarters, almost to the edge of the property. Audrey had grown up in the main house, where she had a frilly, little-girl pink bedroom, which transformed to a less feminine abode during her teen years, with rock-star posters on the walls. The same room was re-created in her father's apartment high on Victoria Peak in Hong Kong, but when she turned eighteen, she wanted something to call her own. That wasn't possible in Hong Kong, for the apartment could not be expanded (Hiram already owned the entire floor), and Hiram wasn't about to lose precious time with her by putting her in her own unit. But it was possible in Kahala, and the cottage was built just for Audrey.

It consisted of a comfortable living room, decorated almost exactly like one of the rooms in her favorite hotel in Waikiki, the Halekulani, with soft light filtering in through the plantation shutters and rattan furniture with cushions in tasteful off-whites, natural tans and creams, and just a touch of robin's-egg blue. She'd gotten the inspiration from meeting with friends from China at that very hotel. A year later, when Aunt had thrown a large and lavish dinner party to celebrate Chinese New Year, one of the honored guests, a gracious, quite stunning businesswoman with an eye for elegant taste asked to see Audrey's cottage. "Well," the woman remarked with a smile, looking around after Audrey had opened the doors, "in case anything ever wears out, just call us and we'll replace it."

Audrey, not knowing who the woman was, blinked and asked what she meant.

"I'm Patricia Tam," she said softly, adding, "general manager at Halekulani."

Audrey felt deeply embarrassed.

But Patricia Tam said, "And you have fine taste."

Which was true in the bedroom as well. It was simple and sparse, and the focal point was a red antique Chinese chest which had belonged to Audrey's mother. The bath was filled with light, the shower stall built completely of glass blocks, and the little kitchen featured a bistro table for two, where, when it rained, Audrey took her morning coffee and read the paper. Mainly, though, the ocean was her parlor; she lived outside on the lanai, facing the Pacific. She loved the little house, but it had one major drawback: it was on Aunt's land. Part of her compound. And Audrey wanted out.

She handed Bobbi a glass of iced mango tea, and they sat on the lanai overlooking the water. Trade winds were blowing, keeping them cool despite the fact that the temperature was near ninety. The afternoon sun filtered through the lush island foliage, and they could hear the sound of a Hawaiian guitar somewhere in the distance. The scent of the ginger blossoms filled their nostrils. While Audrey looked over the final papers on the Choi deal, which Bobbi had produced from her briefcase, Bobbi opened the envelope Audrey had shown her in the car. She was confused as to what the words WILL YOU MISS HER? meant. Audrey made a few notes on the contract, capped her pen, and answered Bobbi. "I think it refers to me."

"You?" Bobbi gave her an inquisitive look. "How so, you?"

"The cut-out notes all said Dad was going to have to 'pay,' that he was going to suffer somehow—"

"For what?" Bobbi interjected.

"We don't know. This is the one that was sent the day he passed away. I think *her* means me."

Bobbi was aghast. "Someone was going to hurt you to make him pay?"

"Could be," Audrey said matter-of-factly.

"That's crazy."

"So is the guy who cuts out words to paste into frightening messages."

Bobbi set the scary letter down. "What did Mark say?"

"He's sure that there won't be any more now that the intended victim of his wrath is dead."

"*You* are the intended victim," Bobbi reminded her, "if what you think is true." Then she realized she was upsetting Audrey. She changed her tone. "Mark's right, it'll stop. Someone must have had a bad business experience with Hiram and took it a little far."

Audrey brought up another possibility. "Or just a sick prank."

"Yeah." Bobbi didn't believe it, but she wanted to. Then she looked at Audrey's face, studied her eyes. "So, what else is wrong?"

Audrey bit her pen. "I'm okay."

"Come on. It's not just your Dad passing, not just the nutty letters. There's something more. When you got off the plane, you started to say something about that last day in the hotel."

"It's nothing, honest." Audrey gathered up the papers and began to stuff them into her briefcase.

"I know you like a sister would. I've worked for you for four years now. You can't fool me."

"Bobbi, I—"

"You got off the plane looking like hell, and

you said you needed to talk to me, and I know when you're in denial mode."

Audrey shrugged. She wanted to talk about it, thought of nothing else in the last hours of the plane ride, but it was hard to bring out in the open. Bobbi was right, denial was almost a family trait, but she knew she couldn't get away with it anymore. "Okay, you're right. When I saw you waiting at customs—"

Audrey was interrupted by the voice of a third person booming through the bird-of-paradise leaves: *"You do not wish to say hello to Aunt?"*

"I thought you were resting," Audrey lied. The imposing figure of Aunt Melba, dressed in a flowing Chinese gown, moved through the foliage toward them.

Bobbi stood, greeting the anachronism. "Melba," she said, a little too loudly and too warmly, "you got new face powder in Hong Kong!"

Aunt stepped onto the lanai. And pointedly ignored Bobbi's dig of an observation. "Audrey, I trust you had a comfortable flight."

"It was fine."

Aunt wrenched her nose. "Pikaki?" she asked, focusing on Audrey's lei. "It overpowers the ginger and the ocean."

Audrey said, "It's wonderful, isn't it?"

"I will ask that you remove it," Aunt ordered.

"Why?"

"The scent is too strong for me."

Audrey glanced at Bobbi.

"Tourists like pikaki," Aunt chided, "but I could never acquire the taste."

Bobbi said, "I gave it to her. I happen to love it."

"Yes," Melba said pointedly, "of course you would."

Audrey, just as pointedly, did not remove the lei.

Melba sighed. "Brother has left me with a great burden. To run the empire alone."

Bobbi quipped, "Some burden."

Aunt nodded to her. Bobbi nodded back.

Melba Goh was seventy, severe, and humorless. Towering over most people at six feet, she was intimidating and powerful. Her demeanor was royal, her disposition difficult. She had the dark eyes of the family ancestry, but unlike Audrey's green jewels, they were muddy and deep-set, resting atop high cheekbones that she first powdered white and then dabbed with the reddest rouge. Her skin, with few wrinkles, defied her age, but the alabaster color made her look like a ghost. Bobbi swore she applied it with a paint roller. Once, when she and Audrey had finished touching up the paint in Hiram's apartment, Bobbi sealed the can of Ralph Lauren Polo Mallet White and handed it to Audrey, saying, "Don't let it go to waste; take it home for Melba's face."

She dressed only in traditional Chinese costume, wore too much jewelry, and moved in a little-bitty-step stride rather than a true walk. People often inquired whether she had had her feet bound as a child.

She was imperious and incapable of lasting human relationships outside the family; she had never, to Audrey's knowledge, had a friend. She was surrounded by sycophants, secretaries, butlers, drivers, servants of every kind whom she treated with indifference and sometimes outright cruelty, but whom she paid very well. She was a real-estate and investment dynamo, and commanded the respect of Honolulu's business community, as well as investors across the ocean in both Hong Kong and China. Audrey respected her, loved her because she was family, but she simply didn't like the woman, and never had. She could not warm up to her, because Melba simply had no warmth herself. And the one thing that Audrey really wanted in life—freedom—was the only thing Aunt would never give her.

Aunt softened and asked Audrey, "How are you holding up?"

"Strong as steel. Isn't that what I was taught?"

Aunt gave a sly grin. "We must be strong in our mourning. And we must attend to business at hand."

"Sold the twenty-seventh floor to Mr. Choi," Bobbi said brightly.

Aunt perked up. "What did they pay?"

Bobbi knew the figure to the dime. "Seven million, eight hundred seventy-five thousand, three hundred and fifty dollars and ninety-seven cents."

Aunt was shocked. "Why?"

Bobbi said, "They needed extra parking for their security detail. Four vans, can you imagine?"

"I see," Melba said, nodding.

"And the ninety-seven cents is for moving a light switch."

Aunt looked aghast. "You charged them for such a thing?"

"It was a joke," Bobbi offered. "You and Mark need humor lessons. Lighten up."

"Money is seldom a laughing matter." But Melba smiled. She was obviously pleased. Then, from somewhere under the folds of the red and gold and black embroidered fabric draped over her tall frame, a cell phone rang. She slid her hand inside and pulled it out, turning to the ocean for privacy.

Behind her back, Bobbi said, "I wonder what people think when she goes to the supermarket in that drag."

Audrey giggled. "She's never been to a market in her life," she whispered, "except maybe to cut the ribbon on one she built."

"Why does she insist on wearing the Chinese Museum's drapes? Isn't she hot under there?"

Audrey thought about it and suddenly realized she had never seen her aunt perspire. But, then again, she'd never seen more than her face, neck, and hands. All the rest had been covered from the day little Audrey's eyes began to focus.

Aunt turned back, finished with her conversation, replacing the phone wherever inside the garment it had come from. "I have something for you," she said, reaching this time into a pocket.

Audrey and Bobbi watched her hand over a white envelope addressed to Audrey in the same childish print that adorned all of the threatening notes. It had a stamp on it, but it had not been canceled. "Where did this come from?" Audrey asked in alarm.

"It was on the table inside when I arrived."

"Christ," Bobbi gasped.

Audrey picked up the envelope. She saw it had been opened. "You read it?"

"Yes," Aunt said simply.

Audrey would normally have objected to such an invasion of privacy, but this was a special case. Melba knew about the earlier letters to Hiram. She could be forgiven for being curious. Audrey opened the envelope and withdrew the folded white piece of paper.

"Here," Bobbi said to Melba, handing her the one Audrey had brought from Hong Kong, "one good psychotic note deserves another."

Melba read the words WILL YOU MISS HER?

Audrey found her eyes focusing on THE PAIN OF YOUR LOSS WILL BE GREAT. It sounded like a grim Chinese fortune cookie. But what upset Audrey was what had been pasted underneath the words:

her photograph. And not just any photograph, a picture of her that the newspaper ran *after* Hiram's death. Meaning Mark was wrong. The notes hadn't stopped because Hiram died, and they weren't going to. "You know," Audrey said softly, with real fear, and showed Bobbi, who bit her lip in concern, "I'm afraid this is serious."

Aunt announced that she was taking care of it. "I have seen Detective Wong. He is a good man whom I know quite well. He is looking into it."

Bobbi wasn't sure how good he sounded. "He didn't want to take this? Analyze it or something?"

"He took all the others," Aunt answered. "I asked him to leave this one so Audrey could see it."

"Great homecoming," Audrey quipped, and sat down again. It weighed heavily on her fright. "What did the detective say about it?"

"Could be a prank, could be more. He took it seriously enough. He will investigate."

Audrey shrugged. How? She felt it was a dead end. And she really felt frightened for the first time.

Aunt slapped the letter from Hong Kong against the back of her other hand. "This person is deranged. Perhaps worked for us, holds a grudge. The police will find him before he can act."

"He got into the house!" Audrey exclaimed. "That's acting already, as far as I can see."

Bobbie piped in. "Someone must know how the letter got there."

"The exterminator, Don Hirsch, might be helpful. He said he saw someone walking through the gardens shortly before my return from Hong Kong."

"What did he look like?" Audrey asked, hopeful.

"Mark."

Audrey bristled. "What?"

"Mr. Hirsch said he thought it was Mark."

"Wonderful," Bobbi groaned. She turned and rested her hand on Audrey's arm. "Come sleep at my place."

Aunt said, "I have ordered security to send extra men to watch the house at night. I can get you a bodyguard if you—"

Audrey shook her head. "It's just some nut," she said, trying to lessen the danger in her own mind. Denial again. "We are getting paranoid and jumping to conclusions."

Aunt nodded. "I hope you are correct, Niece. Now, I have something else for you." She clapped her hands to summon a servant, who seemed to appear magically from the antheriums.

"Christ," Bobbi muttered, when she saw the old man tottering down the path, "that wasn't enough?"

The servant handed Melba what looked like a small green-velvet pillow embroidered in gold and disappeared again. Aunt handed the pillow to Audrey.

But when Audrey took it in her hands, she realized it was not a pillow at all, but an envelope made from rich velvet, which was closed by a gold braid. She looked at Aunt. "What is it?"

"You will see," Aunt said. "I leave you now to rest," she added with a bow, and with a look to Bobbi that said get lost.

As the woman moved away—it looked like someone was pulling her on a sled because of her little steps—Bobbi said defiantly, "I'm staying a while."

"And I'm glad," Audrey said warmly. Then she reached into the velvet bag and withdrew a thick envelope with her name on it. On the back was her father's seal, imprinted with his chop that she knew so well. "It's from Father," she said softly, breaking the seal to open it.

Bobbi smiled. "He left you the whole shebang instead of Dragon Woman?"

"The brothers got it all, you know that."

"Your dad didn't leave you anything? I was hoping he'd buck Chinese tradition and slap your goofy half brothers in the face by giving you the empire, lock, stock, and buildings. It would have been so gutsy, so great."

Audrey read silently for a moment, then looked up. "I guess I did get something." She held up a key.

Bobbi joked, "To Victoria Towers? That would be a nice consolation prize."

"I'm not sure what it's for."

"Doesn't he say?"

Audrey read the note again. "He's given me this key and a combination." She looked at the numbers. "At least I think they're a combination."

"To the big vault?" Bobbi joked.

"I don't know."

"Or a bank?"

Audrey studied the key. "It doesn't look like it fits a bank's safe-deposit box. Too small, too funny-looking. Father didn't believe in them anyway. He had his own vault in the Hong Kong apartment."

"And you've got the only key?" Bobbi said hopefully.

"No. Bruce and Darren were already carting files out the day we buried him."

"Well," Bobbi reminded her, "he transferred lots of stuff to the vault in the apartment here."

Residence Twenty-three, which was being used as the model, was Hiram's own, and he had planned on living there when the building was completed. Audrey nodded. "He did."

Bobbi bubbled. "There could be a fortune in there, cash and gold and jewels."

Audrey shrugged. "I doubt it. He said he sent over records for safekeeping. And Tung's stuff."

Bobbi dreamed of a cache of buried treasure. "Jewels, diamonds, emeralds, cash, lots of cash."

"I can't imagine," Audrey said with caution.

"Tomorrow, when we open the place, first thing we do is try that door, I'll help you dig through the rubies."

Audrey corrected her. "Tomorrow when we open, we've got Mr. and Mrs. Yee to pitch."

"Tough?"

"If you thought the Chois were no picnic, just wait. Father always said Curtis Yee was the best businessman he knew. Meaning brittle."

"I like a challenge," Bobbi said perkily. "We going for the top floor?"

"They can afford it." There was a long silence as Audrey looked out at the sun melting into the water to the west. Then she took the lei off her shoulders and held it in her hands before her face, drinking in the sweet, captivating scent. When she placed it on the table between them, she looked again at the beautiful velvet bag which quite possibly encased her entire future. Her eyes went oddly sad, and then she seemed lost, almost irritable.

"What is it?" Bobbi asked, without any hint of joking now, a friend reaching out to someone loved who was in trouble. "Scared because of the notes?"

"It's what I started to tell you in the car." Audrey took a deep breath, summoning courage. "I think," she finally said, measuring her words carefully, words that explained so much, "that I'm pregnant."

* * *

The observer trained the telescope on the kitchen of the apartment and found the spice rack. He focused on the labels, but found they were too small to read. He turned his attention to the catalog of lenses open on his lap. Perhaps he could find one better, one that might open the very pores of her skin to him. He knew he was becoming obsessed with her, but was that so bad? There were worse things, and more dangerous and harmful things he could find that might take up his every conscious moment. It was like being drawn to a great painting, a beautiful statue, a stained-glass window or constantly being on the search for the perfect orchid. A new lens. She would come closer, almost into his arms.

Then it occurred to him. My God, he thought, is she back?

Chapter Four

When Audrey woke at dawn, the sky was heavy over the Pacific. Wrapped in a white robe, she ground Kona beans, poured the water through the machine, and sifted through a stack of mail while she waited for the coffee to brew. When it was ready, she parked herself on the lanai and sat staring out at the water. The two security men who had spent the night waved to her from the oceanfront wall and went home. Jet lag made her mouth feel like cotton, and she knew she should be drinking water, not coffee. But she needed to wake up. Coffee. Would she have to give up coffee if she was pregnant?

This was the first day of her new life. If she could think in those terms, she could begin to face the future. Her father was dead. There was no more trying to please him, lead her life the way he wanted.

She sipped the rich deep black coffee heartily and leaned back in the wicker chair, letting her long black hair fall over her shoulders. She made herself a promise: today, not tomorrow, not next week, she'd talk to Mark, pin him down, have that discussion about their future, their life together. Plan a wedding, then a lifetime. Yes, today. After the gynecologist. For if the doctor told her what she anticipated, a long talk with Mark was imperative.

She reached for her cell phone and dialed. The machine answered. He wasn't there. Odd, she thought, for it wasn't likely he was already at the bank. Maybe he was in the shower. She took another sip of coffee, then remembered that Bobbi had said she'd saved Tung's messages. She dialed her voice mail and pressed a button to hear the first of twelve messages in her mailbox.

As Audrey sat listening to the collected voices on the telephone, a man stepped carefully through the open side window into her bedroom. He had come up the beach at dawn, watched through his binoculars until the security men left, and made his way through the ground cover and foliage to the right of Audrey's cottage. He had pressed himself flat to hide against the wall while she ground the coffee beans, then peeked through the slits of the shutters as she tightened the luxurious white robe around her freshly showered body. He'd been waiting hours for her to awaken. Now he was in her bedroom, invading her most private place, listening with one ear to be sure she was still on the lanai. This was risky—this was insane!—but it was also impossible for him to stop himself.

The browning, dying lei hung limply on the back of the vanity chair. He lifted it and brought it to his nose. Pikaki, the sweetest blossom in Hawaii, less fragrant today but still intoxicating. He placed it over his head. It felt cold against the flesh of his chest. He thought how it had rested atop her bosom, and a ripple of excitement bolted through him.

He ran his fingers over the silver picture frame set on the lacquered Chinese chest to the right of the bed. He felt the grooves of the etched, precision craftsmanship. He lifted it—heavy, best quality sterling—and looked at the back. Beautiful dark blue velvet, looking like new even though he was sure it was very old. The word *Tiffany* stamped in small letters at the bottom. This was class.

He replaced it exactly where it had been and picked up a Limoges ashtray. She didn't smoke—he was sure of that, for he would have seen her do it at least once—but he knew right away why she had this piece here: its beauty. A thousand tiny stars painted on the blue of coral and sunlight streaming through ocean waters.

Near it was another treasure, and he admired the exquisite charm of the oval painted box. On the top were Chinese letters and Audrey's name painted in red and black over a luminous orange.

Wrapped around the sides was a depiction of the Forbidden City.

When his thumb unclasped the lock, and he pushed the lid up, he saw delicate flowers and water reeds on the inside lid, with the green of a mountain spring beneath. What surprised him, however, was what was in the box: a velvet bag, the kind he'd seen jewelry kept in, and a ring. He picked the ring up first and slipped it onto his little finger, but it only went halfway. It was a small emerald, exquisitely cut and mounted on gold. He kissed it, and just the feeling of the cold stone on his lips made him tremble.

He heard her move, dropped the ring back into the box, and closed it. He sat there, frozen, trying to determine what she was doing. She was moving, pacing, looking nervous and agitated, but still out on the lanai. He still had time. He opened the box again, curiosity getting the better of him. He opened the green bag and shook the contents out into his hand. He was surprised to find a key. And then he pulled out a piece of paper, crinkly Chinese rice paper, on which was written a combination. He promptly copied it down on the back of a business card Audrey had on the bureau.

He inserted the paper back into the bag, and then assessed the key. Should he or shouldn't he? He was sure what it fit, sure what safe the combination was for, especially when Hiram Goh's chop was on the bag. He didn't have trouble making the decision; he slid it into the pocket in his shorts.

Then he replaced the lid to the box and set it where he'd found it.

He eyed the bed, and his hands caressed the tousled sheets. Rich Egyptian cotton, slinky and sexy and expensive. A sexual excitement that was uncontrollable came over him. He could smell her naked, soft body wrapped in the sheets. He was rock-hard.

He removed the lei and slipped his tank top off his head. His heart was racing in his chest. He dropped the shirt on the floor and hooked his thumb in the waistband of his baggy volleyball trunks. On the sand he'd looked like just another surfer, with well-developed arms from all those years riding the waves. Here, he was putty, a boy feeling the first thrill of forbidden sex. He yanked his shorts down to his ankles and stepped out of them. He stood there, erect and trembling, bare naked in her bedroom. Then he crawled into her bed and closed his eyes. He felt the same surge that he had that afternoon ten years ago on Makena Beach.

The sound of the ringing cell phone jolted him. She'd hung up, and he hadn't realized it! Thank God a call had come in. He looked out the window. Sure enough, she seemed to be on her way inside, but the call had stopped her. Ah, she was chatting now. No problem.

"Miss Audrey Goh, please?" The man's voice was deep, strong, and warm.

After listening to Tung's messages for the last five minutes, Audrey was glad for the pleasant tone. "This is Audrey Goh."

"Aloha. I'm calling on behalf of Curtis Yee."

"Oh, yes."

"The Yees wanted to confirm this morning's tour of Victoria Towers."

"Absolutely, ten o'clock. I'm looking forward to showing them our wonderful building myself."

"Fine, fine." The man seemed distracted for a moment, and Audrey heard other voices behind him. "Miss Goh, excuse me a moment, but—"

Audrey waited. Then she heard the sweet voice of an old woman. "Audrey, Patricia Yee here."

"Hello, welcome to Honolulu."

"So very sorry about Hiram, we are still in shock."

"Everyone is. So, I'll be seeing you soon."

"Curtis and I are looking forward to it. We came to the islands just for this."

"We won't disappoint," Audrey promised.

"Wonderful, see you in a little while, then?"

"My pleasure, Mrs. Yee." And she meant it. The commission on the one apartment alone would give her the money to make that break with Aunt—leaving her job behind as well—and get things off to a good start with Mark. Money didn't hurt any new marriage.

The man lying in her bed heard her voice no longer. Silence from the lanai meant it was time to go.

He flipped the covers off and swung his feet to the floor. His thigh was sticky, still wet. He wiped it with part of the sheet, and then quickly slid on his shorts and tucked the tank top into the waistband. He bent over and straightened the satin linen, fluffing the down pillows. He looked at the emerald ring in the little box again, tempted for a moment to swipe it, but thought twice about that. He would be getting more than that from her very soon.

Then he left something on the pillow that he hoped would have the desired effect. And he put the lei back on.

At the door, he peeked into the hall, looking down the long corridor of limestone squares to see her standing on the lanai, her back to him, looking out at the ocean. She raised her arms and stretched, jumped up and down slightly, and he knew why. The prick she was talking to said the right things, making her momentarily happy. Well, let her think she was happy. She would learn the truth very soon. He would make her understand.

He slipped out the way he'd entered, through the window, into the jungle growth of plants to the side of the guesthouse, and in moments he was just another person walking along the beach, kicking sand, jogging for health. She looked right at him from her position on the lanai and didn't even recognize him. He had faded into the landscape, just as he'd wanted.

* * *

Audrey rinsed her coffee cup, thinking about toast and papaya, but she knew she could get that at work. Her refrigerator was bare because she'd been gone, and she didn't want to trouble one of the maids, they always fussed. She dialed Mark's cell phone. "Where are you?" she asked when he answered.

"At work already. Didn't sleep well. Jet lag."

"Just talked to the Yees; they're here."

"That's good."

"We have to talk."

"We are talking." He laughed.

"Really talk. With no one else around. We can't put it off."

Mark complained, "I've got four meetings, the woman who runs the escrow department is out sick, we're way behind. Besides, I spent too much time in Hong Kong. Eckhart is on the rampage. There's a closing on land on Kauai, there's a—"

"Mark, today." Her voice was firm.

"I can't get away." He was silent for a moment. Then he came up with an idea. "How about the weekend?"

"Sure."

"We'll run away."

"We just got back."

"Honey," he reminded her, "you're the one who wants to talk. *With no one else around,* you said. What better than a secret weekend?"

"Secret?"

"Yeah. We'll go somewhere secret, tomorrow night, not tell anyone, just you and I."

"Tonight!"

"I don't know if—"

She liked this. "We'll leave tonight. Where?"

"Your call."

She thought about the trip home from Hong Kong. "I couldn't bear another plane ride over an hour. How about the Lodge?"

"Koele?"

"It's private, romantic, can be secret."

She smiled. "Perfect. If I don't tell Aunt about it. When can you get away?"

"How about you?"

She said, "I could be out of the building by three." Then she remembered her doctor's appointment. "No, five. I couldn't leave till at least five."

"I'll be done . . ." His voice trailed off. She knew he was checking his appointment book. ". . . after six."

"Mark!"

"Honest, honey, don't worry."

"I do."

"I'll book a flight at seven," he promised. "Want me to pick you up?"

"No," she said, "I don't want to leave my car at the building. I'll come to the bank or meet you at the airport."

"Fine."

"Aloha or Hawaiian?" she remembered, wondering which airline.

"I get frequent flyer miles on Hawaiian," he joked.

"See you then."

"I'd better get back to work." There was a pause. "Audrey, you okay? You worried about the note you told me Melba showed you?"

"Yes. No. I mean, she had guards here through the night, I'm going to be all right."

"No, you're not. I can hear it in your voice."

"I'm fine."

He didn't believe it. "You've sounded this way since we left for Hong Kong."

"That's why we need to spend some quality time alone," she responded.

"I love you," he said.

Those words made all the difference in the world.

In the bedroom, she threw things into a duffel bound for Lanai: shorts, T-shirts, a linen dress for dinner, bikinis. God, how much longer could she get by wearing them before she started showing? No, she wasn't sure yet, it wasn't official. She zipped up the bag, put it near the door, then chose a white suit, white shoes with gold accents, a gold belt and white purse to match, to wear to work. Then she thought twice. It was a little flashy for Patricia Yee, she thought, remembering how her father described her as a down-to-earth, no-nonsense woman. In fact, the skinny on the Yees was that they were very private people, deeply conservative and humorless. So she decided against the gold, replacing it with more white. She laughed aloud. She looked like a snowball, but a demure one, and that's what counted. Mrs. Yee would approve.

After putting the finishing touches on her makeup in the bathroom mirror, she walked back into the bedroom, tossed her keys, sunglasses, notes, and things into the white bag and slipped into her shoes. It was only then that she realized that the bed had been made, and it startled her. She walked to it, saw the fluffed pillows, the comforter folded expertly. How in the world . . . ?

She hurried outside, where one of the maids was sweeping the walkway with a primitive palm frond broom. "Gloria?"

The maid turned, gave her a little curtsey. "Very good morning, Miss Goh."

"Gloria, did you do my bed?"

"Excuse, Miss Goh?" The old woman who had worked for Aunt for what seemed like a hundred years said.

"My bed, it's been made. I was on the lanai. Did you do it?"

"No make bed," Gloria responded. "Am doing now." She bowed again and hurried toward her cart, sweeping a path as she did.

Audrey stood dumbfounded. She hadn't made the bed. She hadn't made her bed in years. Why bother when her aunt's maids changed the sheets every day? But if she hadn't done it herself, and Gloria hadn't either, who had? The thought made her shiver. She started back toward the guest-house, but then stopped in her tracks. She was positive she knew the answer: Gloria, in her old age, had simply forgotten a moment after she did it. She was dotty, had to be in her eighties. Her memory was going, that was all.

Satisfied, Audrey returned to her cottage, grabbed the duffel and her white bag, and realized something else: her lei was missing. Gloria had probably trashed it, she thought. She couldn't wait to get out of here, live without so much help and interference. She hurried to the garage and pressed the button for door number six, where her little BMW sat awaiting her. She tossed the duffel into the trunk. As she slid into the driver's seat, however, something nagged at her. If Gloria *had* done it, how did she get herself and her cart into the guesthouse without Audrey seeing her?

She ran back to her cottage to find Gloria vacuuming the bedroom. The little woman jumped in fright when Audrey tapped her shoulder, and it took her several tries to turn off the Hoover with her toe. "Miss Goh, no making bed, bed no making right." To prove her point, she got down on her knees and showed Audrey the distinctive non-hospital corners. "No do this way," Gloria snapped, showing Audrey the correct way. "Do like this. Right way. This way mess." With that, the woman turned the vacuum back on.

Audrey shook her head. Was it him? Her blood went cold for a second at the thought that the person writing the notes could have actually been in her bedroom. No, she told herself, it couldn't be. There had to be some other plausible explanation. Then she asked, "Did you take my lei?" Gloria didn't hear her over the noise of the vacuum. She tried again, louder. "Gloria, did you—?"

She froze when she saw Gloria put the nozzle of the vacuum to the little scrap of paper resting on the pillow. "What was that?" she asked.

The woman was deaf, went back to the floor.

Audrey turned the machine off. "What was that?"

"Sand," Gloria snapped. "Sand on carpet, no picking up good."

Audrey hadn't been in sand. Her shoes had not gotten sandy. But someone had dragged sand into the room. And her lei was gone. "Gloria, did you take the lei that was hanging here?"

Gloria held the vacuum nozzle high. "No sucking lei, Miss Goh."

Audrey got down on her knees and practically ripped open the canister on the Red Devil. To the maid's horror, she dumped the dirty contents right on the Tibetan rug and dug through the debris for the scrap of paper she saw the woman vacuum up. When she found it, her heart went cold. It was a piece of paper cut from a newspaper, just a word: *revenge*.

She hurried to the garage and backed the car out, shivering with fear, wanting to get out of there as fast as she could. It hadn't been taped to white paper this time, but it was as clear to her as all the others: the madman had violated her most private space and left a calling card. She dialed Mark on her cell phone and told him what had just happened, swearing she would never return to Aunt Melba's, ever. "We're going to Lanai together, and I'm never leaving you," she said.

"That sounds perfect to me," Mark replied.

That made Audrey feel safe. With Mark, she would be protected. And the man writing the notes would give up.

Or would he?

Chapter Five

Victoria Towers, slowly taking its majestic place in Honolulu's skyline, was set on land that had originally been owned by the Dole Corporation and at one time had held warehouses for the pineapple cannery just a short distance away. By the 1980s, the buildings had gone to seed, and Hiram and Melba Goh were smart enough to foresee this area being Honolulu's next big boomtown long before anyone else did. They'd bought up most of it. Hiram built three modest buildings on the land, ensuring the viability of growth in the area. *If you build it, they will come.* And they had. The buildings, both commercial and residential, were eighty-eight percent occupied. Not bad for the city. Not bad for the economy. Not bad, either, for the Goh Corporation.

Now that the rusting historical waterfront buildings were being developed and renovated into a shopping/media complex, the area was hot, and Victoria Towers, Hiram Goh's much-touted, multimillion-dollar high-security building, was going to be the crown jewel. It was named after the peak in Hong Kong that Hiram loved, and would have been the crown jewel in any development. The apartments *began* at three million dollars.

Audrey tapped the horn at the construction gate, and Gary, the affable gate man, waved her in with a smile. All the guys loved her, for she was, even decked out with Manolo Blahnik heels and Prada bags and Versace dresses, one of the boys. Feminine and possessing an elegant sophistication, she still could joke, smoke, and hang with the roughest of them. She drove the car up the ramp to the fifth floor of the parking lot, the only other finished floor in the towering mass of steel. One day this parking garage would be protected by steel-and-concrete doors and infrared coding to be sure no one who didn't belong got in.

The ground floor was reserved for high-end retail shops, with Gucci, Vera Wang, Armani, and Jil Sander already signed, and a sleek Starbucks coming. Pottery Barn had been lured to the islands by the expansive space on the second floor. Offices would be let on the third and fourth levels, while five through seven were reserved for parking. The construction guys called level eight, just above parking, the moat, because it would have nothing but open marble flooring, wall to wall, glass to glass, with a security desk in the center. That was where the elevator went from the parking garage. Someone sneaking through there would be shot.

It was designed to be the most secure apartment building ever constructed. Level nine was reserved for a state-of-the-art health club, indoor pool, and a banquet room.

The apartments, lavish, luxuriously overdone "residences," one to a floor, started on level ten and went all the way up to the penthouse on thirty, for which the occupants would pay somewhere in the vicinity of an astonishing fourteen million dollars. It was not yet sold. But Audrey had hopes that the Yee family would take it. They were famous for being intensely private—she could never recall seeing even a picture of them in a newspaper—and shunning publicity, so the building was made for them. Her father had told her they desired the security, wanted a "view," and loved Hawaii. It was also the smallest apartment in the building (because the walls tapered up toward the top, like the John Hancock Building in Chicago), perfect for a family which was "downsizing." If she could get them to purchase, the memory of her father would be well served. In designing the building, Hiram had said, "Old Curtis Yee, we're going to get him out of the colony. He's not gonna like the Communist regime. He's gonna take the top floor." It would be the perfect legacy for Hiram Goh.

Audrey headed down the ramp from the garage, grabbed a hard hat from a basket filled with them, and waved to Ben, the head electrician and her good buddy, who was eating his breakfast from a dented green lunch pail. "Morning," he said, when she got into hearing distance.

"Morning," she replied, and immediately snatched what was left of the cinnamon roll from his hands just as it was about to enter his mouth. "God, that's good!"

"Audrey, goddammit, bring your own breakfast."

"I don't know where to find these gooey things."

"Cinnabon, they're all over."

"No time. Besides, why bother when you supply them?"

"Cute." He laughed and reached up and wiped the sticky-sweet frosting off her chin with his fingertip.

He was about to put it in his mouth when she grabbed his hand and brought his finger to her lips, lapping up the thick white sugar. It wasn't sensual as much as it was silly, like a kid eating cotton candy at a carnival. "I don't suppose you have any extra coffee?"

Ben shrugged. "Don't they pay you well here? You could stop on the way to work, even bring me some better brew than this crap I get out of the machine."

"I promise, promise," she said with a grin.

"Yeah, sure. I won't hold my breath." He stood up, tucking his plaid shirt into his khaki work shorts, grabbing his coveralls. "So, how did it go?"

"It was tough. Funerals always are."

"You okay?"

She nodded, feeling it would be less a lie than saying something. "I've got a lot of thinking to do. About the future without Father."

"And Dragon Lady."

She smiled. Everyone on the island called Aunt Melba Dragon Lady. She had a reputation that reached far beyond Audrey and the family. Everyone found her austere, eccentric, or downright scary. "Dragon Lady I still have to deal with."

"How's the fiancé?" Ben asked.

"He's not quite that yet. But I'm working on it."

"I thought maybe he'd spring the big question on you in Hong Kong."

She shrugged. "Me too."

"He working today? Or did he take the day off? I wouldn't go back to work the day after I'd made that trip."

"Working. Mark's always working. I wonder if I'll ever see him after we're married. I don't now."

"Come on."

She grinned. "Actually, I really do wish we'd married before Father died. He liked Mark a lot. It would have made him happy."

He grinned. "With Auntie as flower girl?"

"Could you imagine?"

"Over Auntie's dead body?"

"An added bonus," she giggled, but then felt terrible, for she certainly didn't wish Aunt any harm. "That just sorta slipped out. Strike it."

"Deleted," Ben said. "Hey, speaking of the delete key, HAL is on the fritz again."

"Oh, God," she said, paling. "How bad this time?" HAL was the name they'd given to the building's state-of-the-art computer system, named for the talking computer in *2001: A Space Odyssey*. As head electrician, it was Ben's duty to tend to it when it went haywire, which it seemed to do on a daily basis. She was panicked. "I've got clients any minute now."

"It unlocked the gates at eight-fifteen this morning instead of six. It sent the freight elevator on a run just for fun, up and down, for about half an hour till I literally pulled the plug."

"It's like I used to do with the Star Ferry."

"Huh?" It was lost on him.

"Never mind."

He said, "It may not work at all today."

"Curtis Yee has got to be seventy," she reacted. "He can't walk up twenty-three floors!"

"Calm down," Ben said, in a reassuring voice. "Right now we're running it manually. Let's just hope it holds."

"I need that elevator, Benjamin!"

He used her tone of voice. "I need that elevator, too, Audrey. We're pouring the top-floor cement this afternoon."

"Wish it was done already. I'd like the Yees to see it."

"They can walk on the plywood."

She nodded. "You sure about the elevator?"

He assured her, "Everything's fine for now."

"That's what worries me, that 'for now.' "

"I think you'd better get Carlucci over, the trouble's in the software. It isn't electrical."

Dean Carlucci was the man paid by Hiram Goh to create the building's computer system. Paid handsomely. "I'll tell him we need him again," Audrey said. "Maybe he should just move in here."

"His fault," Ben muttered.

"No love lost between you guys, huh?"

He changed the subject. "You dolled up for this Yee guy?"

"I'm being a bit demure, don't you think? He has a wife." She twirled. "How do I look?"

"Sexy as always, though I prefer your shorts and wet T-shirt routine."

"Sexist pig," she teased.

"Give a guy a break."

"Only when I don't have clients. The clothes, not the break."

"You actually look rather subdued. In a pretty way, of course."

"You don't look so bad yourself." She looked him over from head to toe, her dark eyes smoldering. "I can't resist a man in work shorts," she fake-panted. "And with such hairy legs as well."

"Tease," he jeered.

And with a sexy grin, she sauntered off, giving him and the other men sitting around her best Marilyn Monroe walk as they catcalled and whistled. Then, just as she approached the construction elevator, Ben yelled back to her. "Audrey, hey!"

"What?" she called back.

"I think your clients are here." He pointed to a huge car lumbering into the drive. The Mercedes S600-based limousine was spit-polished black, and the bulletproof windows glinted in the sun.

Audrey muttered, "Shit. They're an hour early." She hurried back toward Ben, pulling out her compact, frantic that she look presentable.

"They're buying an apartment, not you," Ben assured her.

She laughed. "Wish they would, my worries would be over."

"What worries?"

She just shrugged.

"Wipe your chin one more time," he suggested, "a little frosting left there—"

She gasped and wiped her mouth with her hand. Then she turned toward the anthracite steel bunker with wheels and put on her sales face.

At the car, Curtis Yee, looking a lot more spry than his seventy years would suggest, shook her hand. "You must be Audrey. Oh, yes, you so resemble your father."

"I'm not sure that's a compliment," Audrey joked. "Daddy looked like a walrus."

Mrs. Yee spoke up. "Never mind him," she warmly said to Audrey. "We knew your mother, too, and I think you look just like *her*."

"I didn't know you knew her," Audrey said,

surprised. "They spent such little time in Hong Kong." She thought her father had not met Curtis Yee till he became a backer on a project in Hawaii Kai.

"We wanted so to attend the funeral," the woman said, "but we were in Paris."

Audrey remembered they had a son living there, a diplomat. "I love Paris. Father did, too."

"We dined with him there several times," Curtis told her. "You have our deepest sympathy."

Audrey bowed slightly. "Thank you. Dad was very fond of both of you, and he predicted you'd one day live in the building he was so proud of. Ready to take a look?"

Mrs. Yee reached into the car and grabbed her handbag, which Audrey thought was large enough to contain the gold bricks necessary to purchase the apartment. The bodyguard handed Mr. Yee his cane. "Ready," the sprightly old man then pronounced.

"Just follow me," Audrey said as she led the way to the construction elevator.

The images sharpened as the observer's fingers turned the focus knob. He watched with interest as she led the elderly couple toward the construction elevator. Their burly bodyguard followed. He looked like a stock Secret Service sharpshooter, beady-eyed and all muscle from the neck down, and perhaps the neck up as well. But then, you didn't need brains for the kind of job he did. Just brawn and a sense of timing.

The observer laughed as he saw her put hard hats on the old man and woman and prod them into the caged, open-air elevator. Their bodyguard did the same, constantly looking over his shoulder as if he were waiting for someone to start shooting. Chinese Mafia, the observer thought, come to seek protection in the sky.

The telescope followed them up to the twenty-third floor, and then fixed its Cyclops eye to the living-room windows and waited for their images to appear once again.

"Welcome to the formal entry hall," Audrey gushed in her much-practiced sales pitch, "from which you can access all the major areas of Residence Twenty-three, or arenas: the living arena, entertaining arena, relaxation arena, and service arena. Just look at that view, even from here."

"Yes," old Curtis Yee said, "oh, look at that." All of Oahu was visible from the windows, the peaks of the mountains with the storm clouds hugging them, the spires rising from downtown, the blue of the endless ocean, Pearl Harbor, planes on their approach to Honolulu International Airport. It was simply breathtaking.

"Lovely," his wife pronounced, seemingly less enchanted.

Audrey indicated the large hall table with its magnificent bouquet of pastel mums and birds-of-paradise. "If you'd like to put your bag down, Mrs. Yee, feel safe."

"That's quite all right," the woman said politely, reaching up to touch the blossoms lightly with her fingertips. "I'm an old-fashioned gal, feel naked without it."

Curtis smiled. "Thinks she's the queen of England."

Mrs. Yee eyed the mirror behind the bouquet. "I'm more curious about the feng shui."

Audrey waxed poetic. "The building was designed for the most harmonious feng shui, from the lobby all the way to the top residence. A feng shui master is on retainer to work with each buyer to create a perfectly balanced environment as you decorate. He worked with my father and the architect, planning every door and window, discussing where every mirror would be hung, so that the residents would live in perfect harmony."

Curtis Yee smiled.

His wife nodded. "Excellent."

"And now," Audrey said with a grin, "leaping from ancient custom to the new millennium, let me tell you about HAL, our computer—that's the staff's nickname for the system. It was designed by the former Olympic skier Dean Carlucci."

Curtis Yee brightened. "Really?" This obviously meant more to him than good feng shui.

"Yes. He's a brilliant man."

"Still in a wheelchair?"

"Yes," Audrey said, "and he's a testimony to rebuilding a life after enormous tragedy."

Mrs. Yee said, "Who are you talking about?"

Mr. Yee explained. "The great skier from Hawaii—Maui, wasn't it?"

"I think so," Audrey confirmed.

"He lost his wife and child in a terrible car accident, got paralyzed, confined to a wheelchair for the rest of his life." Curtis turned back to Audrey. "He worked on this building?"

"He designed computer programs when he was a skier, and had worked on construction when he was going to college. Dad felt he was well suited to the job."

"His story is an inspiring one," Mr. Yee remarked. "I'm a big sports fan."

His wife laughed. "Some big fan, sound asleep ten minutes into a game."

Audrey smiled. "Dean did a marvelous job here, as you'll see as we continue through the apartment."

"I'd like to meet him one day," Yee said.

Audrey gave him a dazzling look. "You live here, and you'll see a lot of him." Then she pointed out the rare marble floor, a green of such depth you thought you were walking on a pristine lake, the hand-rubbed cherrywood paneling, the lead crystal chandelier which was just a bit too much for her taste, but the decor wasn't completely her doing. She'd been consulted, but her father had definite opinions that had made their way to the finished product. And, of course, this apartment was going to be his one day, so why shouldn't he have a few tacky chandeliers if that's what he desired?

Audrey asked them to notice the wide corridors, the expansive feeling, showing them a floor plan of the planned penthouse, so they could see what the difference would be so many floors higher. She indicated that the halls up there would not be quite as long or wide. "But your view will more than compensate for it." She led them from the corridor to the living room, gesturing with a sweeping hand to the flank of windows. "Here you see other buildings, but from the top floor you'll be above the clouds, a watchtower over the Pacific." She let them ooh and aah a moment as a British Airways 767 looked to be on the same level that they were. "And remember that up there, if you truly value your privacy, as I know you do, no one can possibly see in."

Audrey watched the Yees study the living room, peeking up the fireplace flue, checking the placement of outlets, sitting on the furniture to get a feel for the joint. Whenever Curtis Yee asked a question, he pointed with his cane. Like he did with the windows, inquiring whether they were bulletproof. Audrey wanted to say, "Up here?" But the answer was yes.

It could have been real overkill, however, if her father had gone through with his plan for the steel window covers. He'd envisioned rolling steel doors that would cover all the windows in moments—in case of air attack. She'd howled at that one, reminding him Pearl Harbor was history. Who was going to "attack" an apartment by air? Hiram had given up the idea when he saw how truly ugly metal shutters would make the building look. "Like one of Suharto's tenements in Jakarta," he'd growled.

"Could we have travertine?" Mrs. Yee inquired.

"Pardon me?" Audrey answered the woman.

"On the mantel?"

"You can have one encrusted in diamonds if you like," Audrey said with a smile. "Come, let me show you the sumptuous bedroom . . ."

It was that and more. Another fireplace at the foot of the bed, flanked by two tall windows looking out at the ocean, with bookshelves and entertainment center on one wall and two closets larger than some apartments. In the master bathroom, Audrey pointed out the gold-plated fixtures rising from the Lucio Marron—coffee brown—granite, the top-of-the-line Jacuzzi tub, the "drying stall" where a whoosh of hot air did in seconds what it took a towel three minutes to accomplish, and even though Audrey thought it as silly as walking naked through a car wash, she kept a straight face as she demonstrated it.

But when she showed them the steam room, pointing out the intricate Portuguese tile, and she touched the computer pad to input temperature, time and aromatherapy—just press "eucalyptus"—HAL acted up, blasting Mrs. Yee's butt with a shot of steam. Audrey apologized, the woman took it good-naturedly, but Audrey worried what was next.

When they exited the master suite, Bobbi was just arriving, and Audrey promptly introduced them. Bobbi chatted them up a moment, telling them what a joy it was to come to work here each day, she could well imagine what it will be like to live here. Audrey rolled her eyes, knowing Bobbi felt the place was like Aunt Melba: cold, austere, and overwhelming. She also hated heights, and stayed well clear of the windows. "HAL is challenging us again this morning," Audrey sang.

"Oh, dear," Bobbi said with a phony smile. She knew it might mean the sale. "What's that prankster up to this time?"

Mrs. Yee put her hand on her backside.

Mr. Yee said, "A little steam cleaning my wife's dress," in a joking manner, poking her devilishly with the tip of his cane.

Bobbi shared a look with Audrey. They'd have to work harder. Bobbi complimented Mrs. Yee on her snazzy outfit—the woman was the epitome of quiet taste—and inquired where she'd gotten such a beautifully woven bag. Bobbi said she'd love one for the beach. "India," was the answer, and Patricia Yee graciously offered to send her the name and address of the vendor. "You couldn't put a plane ticket in the envelope, too, could you?" Bobbi joked.

Mrs. Yee smiled politely.

"Listen," Bobbi said, "I'll put on some tea, how does that sound?"

Audrey said, "Swell. So, shall we continue?"

"Forge on!" Curtis Yee said loudly, stabbing the air with his cane as if leading a landing party to the beach. His wife giggled.

Audrey continued the tour. She pointed out that there were working fireplaces in the living room, master bedroom, dining room, and library; more could be added at the client's wish. She showed them the climate-control system, where a temperature just needed to be spoken—a gentle "Seventy-two degrees, please!" would do it—and the A/C would kick in. "Fire!" turned on the sprinklers, also notifying the security lobby and fire department. "Mood" produced indirect, muted lighting. "Lock" instantly secured any door in the apartment ". . . should you have houseguests you really don't want to see for breakfast." Audrey usually got a laugh with that one. Not today. The Yees took it dead seriously. Audrey wondered if they did often have houseguests they wanted to lock up. "Our children have threatened to visit," Patricia Yee said with a grin.

"Carlucci did all this?"

"Everything connects to the computer, Mr. Yee, so yes, he did actually," Audrey answered.

"Very impressive," Yee said.

Audrey explained there were steel panels that cut off corridors in case you wanted to leave a section of the residence uninhabited, or in case of thwarting intruders. As she was telling them this, a huge bucket of wet, slopping concrete compound sailed past the living area windows, on its way up. "Look," Bobbi called out, "that's yours."

The Yees didn't understand.

"Your flooring," Audrey explained. "The cement is going to thirty."

"We have not made a decision as yet," Curtis Yee reminded her.

She smiled and said, "Let me help convince you. Follow me . . ."

In the cavernous, dark-wooded and stainless-steel kitchen, a Gaggeneau commercial cooktop and ovens the size of some apartment kitchens were the focus, complemented by two built-in refrigerators, two freezers, two commercial dishwashers, another induction cooktop (in case you didn't want to use gas) and a built-in wok. "I'm sure you'll love that feature," Bobbi offered.

"No," the man said firmly, "I'm afraid we send out for Chinese."

Bobbi looked a little embarrassed. "Ah, like Audrey does."

Patricia Yee laughed. "I'm just a terrible cook. Probably because I hate it."

Audrey couldn't believe what she was hearing. "My father talked of wonderful meals at your home."

Mrs. Yee looked flustered. "Oh?"

"Honestly," Audrey said, "I swear Father told me you had a way with a wok."

The woman looked a little lost. She turned to her husband. "Well, maybe a long time ago."

He coughed up a nervous laugh. "We are just too Westernized now."

"Truth is," Patricia admitted, "I'm too lazy. And Curtis loves a good steak more than anything." She examined the Gaggeneau cooktop, suddenly interested in cooking. "Does this have a grill?"

"Absolutely," Audrey offered. "The center two burners become a griddle or grill. Finest forty-eight-inch unit on the market."

While Bobbi puttered around—wearing an apron, a nice touch, Audrey thought, for a girl who could just barely boil water—Audrey demonstrated how the computer would actually cook for you, or for your chef. "Recipe" would bring up just about every cookbook in the world, which were already logged into the database. "Roast Beef," for instance, would bring up on-screen questions for the chef to answer, from when do you want it done, and just how rare? But for shoving the meat in one of the ovens, the rest was automatic. The kitchen could hold a staff of ten working at one time, for those "important dinner parties."

"Or," Bobbi interjected from her vigil over the

teakettle, "when you invite the poor relation from Taiwan to brunch." They all laughed.

Mr. and Mrs. Yee felt the kitchen was entirely too large. Audrey again reminded them that the apartments got smaller as the floors got higher, and they were glad, for, as they kept reminding *her,* they were downsizing from their palatial villa on the slopes of Victoria Peak. "If you decorate that way," Audrey said instead, "it will be like a private little retreat. Of course, with your taste, Mrs. Yee, I have no doubt it'll be charming."

"How do you know my taste?" the woman inquired.

"I was at your house once."

They looked positively shocked.

"What's wrong?"

Curtis said, "I'm just surprised. I don't recall." He shot his wife a glance. "Do you, dear?"

"No," Patricia said.

"I was nine. It was my first time to the colony. I know it was about twenty-six years ago, but I remember."

"Oh, yes," Patricia said, "I think I recall now."

Curtis Yee just nodded.

"It was the most beautiful house I'd ever seen, I thought."

Patricia smiled. "I'm flattered, dear. Thank you."

Audrey was sure they were lying to save face, for she remembered distinctly that they were in Europe when her father took her there. But that was fine, for if they were indeed lying, so was she. She couldn't remember their decorating at all. Just that they had a great pool.

After a discussion of how they could cut the size of the kitchen in half, to create a sunny "sewing" room, she led them down the hall to the library, her favorite room in the apartment. It was paneled in mahogany, with a burnt sienna ceiling, fireplace with stone mantel, and endless bookshelves lined with worn, leather-clad volumes. It made her feel like she was in a dusty villa in Tuscany, which, of course, was the objective. Mrs. Yee sat on the damask sofa and looked very comfortable. "It's heaven, isn't it?" Audrey asked.

"It is nice," the woman only replied.

Audrey pointed out a small six-drawer safe for jewels hidden behind bookshelves, again computer controlled. However, when she pressed the button that was supposed to close it, all the drawers suddenly became projectiles that shot across the room. Bobbi walked in, asking if they preferred green Earl Grey, or Darjeeling, and was hit in the foot with a metal drawer. Audrey slapped a computer button, and Bobbi, seeing the look on Audrey's face, said she'd put in a call downstairs to Ben. "There's a little glitch in the computer," she apologized to the Yees, and then she wondered, had she blown it? Were they in or out? She'd guess it was fifty-fifty at this point. She had a little more work to do.

She led them to the command center, the security staff room, showing them the bank of computers which ran the apartment, where their security detail could monitor every move. The bodyguard, who had not uttered a word till then, said, "Cool."

"I'll say," Audrey added. "This is Dean Carlucci's pride and joy." She demonstrated the features of the room, the computer, then showed them a fire door which could be used in emergency. It opened onto the small corridor where they'd gotten off the construction elevator, an area adjacent to the center stairwell, an easy exit in emergencies.

Then she took them to the spacious room that was suggested as an office, and showed them the walk-in vault that looked like it could hold all the gold in Fort Knox. The safe to which she had the combination at home. It could not be opened for showing; this was Hiram Goh's own apartment, his personal safe. Audrey stared at the vault a little longer than she might have, wondering what was in it for her.

Then Curtis Yee started asking questions that made her think they were serious: Could they eliminate the fireplace in the master bedroom. (Sure.) What were the condo fees? (Four thousand, monthly.) What was the estimated date of occupancy? (Eight months from now.) How about guest parking? (Lots.)

Mrs. Yee wandered toward the expansive windows in the living area once again just as a crane was moving past it with a huge air-conditioning unit, destined for the roof, swinging from it. "The view of the ocean is astonishing," she commented, looking as far as the eye could see, with the Aloha Tower and Diamond Head focal points in the distance.

Audrey said, "I like the bird's-eye view of Pearl Harbor from the dining room. And this building is just as defensible."

Old Mr. Yee rubbed his chin. "Pearl Harbor certainly was vulnerable to an air attack." He pointed his cane in that direction.

Audrey couldn't help but start laughing.

"What is it?" Mr. Yee asked.

"My father might have been right after all!" And she went on to explain the steel panels that had been nixed.

"But they might have been helpful in case of hurricane," Mrs. Yee suggested.

"No worry," Bobbi chimed in, entering sans apron, with a tray of tea in her hands, "the windows are all hurricane proof. Audrey, darling, will you clear that table?"

The observer saw them taking chairs at the game table right against the window. The bodyguard remained in the kitchen. Audrey's assistant was pouring tea. Darjeeling, if he could read the label correctly. Wait, there were two pots. Only Audrey was having the Darjeeling; the old Chinese couple were being poured green tea. Ah, details. His life through the scope was a simple matter of details.

He suddenly wondered what she would think if she found out about him. Would she be flattered, or horrified? Upset or curious? This kind of thing was frowned upon, of course, invading privacy and the like. On the Net it was accepted behavior, justified by the thousands of photographs that "amateurs" had posted of scenes he'd found in so many windows. Everyone was a voyeur, it seemed, and if that were true, everyone else was an exhibitionist. He even wondered, suddenly, if someone, somewhere, secretly was watching *him*.

Audrey and Bobbi sat drinking tea and eating cookies with the Yees. More cement sailed upward. The Yees explained that they had tried to lead an insular life and didn't want to stop now. That's why this building appealed to them. They did not like what was happening to Hong Kong since the Chinese takeover, so they were looking to retire in the Hawaiian Islands, where they had long-standing friends and life was simpler. They wanted Audrey's assurance that the building would not be "flashy" or given to "great publicity." In other words, they wanted to remain as private as they always had.

"All the other residents who have bought so far have said the same thing," Audrey assured them.

Bobbi added, "No movie stars, no rock stars, no jet-set trash, nobody looking to make headlines."

Curtis Yee smiled.

But his wife, who had been looking out at the terrace, asked why the floor of the balcony had not been finished when the rest of the apartment was. "I would love to see what it feels like out there." Indeed, the terrace was still just open girders.

Audrey explained, "We're waiting for the bulletproof glass panels which will form the sides of the balconies to be bolted in place; then the flooring can be laid." She got up and demonstrated how the balcony's doors opened just by speaking to HAL. "Open balcony," she said softly, and the beautiful French doors opened wide. But the wind was howling, and she instructed the panel to close them. "Close balcony doors." Nothing happened. "Close! Close!" she shouted, trying to keep her composure but joke about it as well. "I'd love to give this computer a kick, but I'm afraid how it might retaliate."

The doors didn't close. So Audrey did it by hand, putting a foot out on one of the girders to give her the leverage she needed, for the door was eight feet high, and Mrs. Yee gasped, "My dear!"

"Careful—" Mr. Yee called out.

"No problem," Bobbi said, trying to lighten the drama and danger. "She's done this before. Cookies?"

Mr. and Mrs. Yee chose their sweets, with nervous eyes on Audrey, who was having real problems getting the door to move.

"Bobbi?" Audrey called inside. "Give me a hand. Hit the close button on the computer panel, I think it's sticking because its memory is locked on open. This voice-command stuff isn't working—"

Bobbi pressed the button. And it worked. Too well. For the computer popped the door closed with such immediate force, that Audrey was knocked backward.

Into the bright blue sky.

Chapter Six

Audrey grabbed for one of the balcony girders as she fell, clasping to it for dear life, a leg dangling. Then her shoe fell off.

Her heart in her throat, she swung her right leg up on the girder. She tried to bring her left foot up, but when she did, she lost her balance and knew she was going to spin around on the girder and tumble. She let her left leg dangle.

But how long could she hang on? She was suspended twenty-three stories above the ground. Her head was pressed against the hot steel—the sun had heated it like a charcoal grate—and she could just barely make out the horrified faces in the window. She dared to glance down. The ground was far away. Roofs of cars and trucks and vans parked around the building looked like flat rectangles, playing cards made of steel. The swaying palm trees made her sick. She felt she was on some kind of island carnival ride. She closed her eyes, hoping the dizziness would pass. She couldn't risk losing her equilibrium, for it would mean losing her life.

Inside the apartment, the horrified onlookers didn't know what to do. Even the burly bodyguard was unsure about how to help her. Curtis Yee suggested she grab his cane, but they couldn't get out there, and even if she could grab the cane, how would they help get her back inside? As they stood helpless at the window, the doorbell rang, and Bobbi remembered she'd called Ben. She rushed to open it. "Audrey's stranded out there!" she shouted at the man, whose shorts and T-shirt were covered with work coveralls.

"Out where?" Ben said.

"The girders, the balcony," she said, pointing toward the three people standing with their faces pressed against the window glass. "She's out there, and HAL's locked the doors!"

Ben hurried to the doors, saw Audrey clinging to the girder and sucked in a breath. He said, "Don't worry," and got the doors open with a few inputs on the keypad. "Audrey," he called out to her, trying to make light of the danger, "I told you no more dancing out there."

"I promise," Audrey said weakly, trying to mask her fear, "I'll never wear heels to work again."

"Not like doing stunts this time, is it?"

She shivered. He was talking about the time she had walked out on the girders. "That was choreographed. This is HAL trying to kill me."

Ben studied how far away her hand was. He assessed that to try to grab it and securely hold her while pulling her in was to risk her life with very bad odds. "I can't reach you to help you," he said.

"Could you maybe send a helicopter?" she moaned.

He put a foot out on the girder to see if he could hold fast with one hand to the doorframe while pulling her up with the other. "Audrey, think you could stand up with my help?"

"Oh, God," was the answer.

"That a yes?"

"I'm feeling dizzy."

That being the case, it was too risky. "Audrey, can you hold fast for—?"

Suddenly, a bucket of cement moved within feet of her, on its way up to thirty. She reached out a hand to grab it.

"No!" Ben shouted, but she missed it by several inches. "Just hold tight, right there. You grab a line, and you could swing back into the girder and crack your head open!"

"Okay," was the terrified reply.

"Hold tight," he ordered. "If you loosen your grip a little, you'll relax your muscles and you still won't fall."

She muttered, "Easy for you to say."

"Hang on, just hang there, rest there, and don't look down."

"Did that already."

Ben pulled out a walkie-talkie from one of the pockets in his coveralls, and immediately communicated with the crane operator. "Chuck, we've got a rescue mission here . . ."

"Crane ride?" Audrey moaned.

"Know another way down?"

He had a point.

The observer was flabbergasted when he saw the crane descending toward the balcony girders. On the end of the arm of the crane was a basket, and in that basket was a hard-hatted man, and after several attempts to line him up with the girder Audrey was clinging to, the man reached Audrey and scooped her into his arms and pulled her into the basket with him. He could see the word ELECTRICAL on the back of the man's coveralls and knew, though he couldn't see his face, that it was Ben, the worker she horseplayed around with all the time. He could see now that she and the construction worker were laughing as the crane descended the twenty-three floors to the ground. He wondered if they had something going more than friendship and being coworkers. No, she was engaged, or close to it. She was sexy and seemed carefree and loose, but he was sure she, being Hiram Goh's daughter, had the morals of a woman of her stature.

He glanced at the apartment once again, to see four astonished faces looking down from the windows. They were smiling.

He was not. The construction worker's arms around her bothered him.

Bothered him a great deal.

* * *

Dean Carlucci, a wheelchair-confined but rugged-looking man in his forties, was trying to figure out what was up HAL's high-tech butt. Audrey—shoeless now, for she didn't have a spare pair in the car—and Bobbi and Ben sat at the tea table, finishing the cookies, talking about the close call Audrey had just had. And the loss of the sale it had caused. The Yees had fled.

"They were horrified, absolutely panic-stricken," Bobbi said. "I thought the woman was going to pee in her pants. She went into the bathroom and stayed for like twenty minutes."

"I might have done the same," Ben said. "It's not every day you see a beautiful woman hanging from a piece of steel high over Honolulu Harbor."

"Damn computer," Audrey muttered.

"You're okay," Bobbi said reassuringly. "What's important is you're fine."

"I'm fine, but the loss of the sale may kill me." She shook her head. "Boy, that was strange."

"Their exit?" Bobbi asked.

"That stuff about cooking. If there's anything my father talked about, it was the wonderful dinners Patricia Yee prepared. He used to call her the best Chinese chef he knew."

"You sure?"

"In a restaurant once, he muttered something to the effect that they should hire Pat Yee in this dump. Maybe that way they'd get the dim sum right."

Bobbi looked as curious as Audrey did. "Odd."

"Very odd."

"You think it's hopeless?" Ben called out, working on the panel.

Bobbi said, "Let me put it this way. When a prospective client says fuck the feng shui, you know you're cooked."

"They said that?" Dean called over his shoulder.

Bobbi answered, "The woman muttered something in Chinese that sounded like it could have been worse. I wasn't going to rattle them more by asking for a translation."

"It's hopeless," Audrey added. "In any language."

But Bobbi was a cockeyed optimist. "They could still come around. Don't rule them out completely."

"He was impressed with you, Dean," Audrey called out to him. "I thought they were going to buy it just for that reason."

"The last of the diehard fans?" Dean joked.

"*He* certainly was."

"Hey, Dino," Ben said, looking at Dean, who now had what seemed like a hundred wires pulled out of the nearby control panel, "can we charge the loss to the computer man?"

Dean hated being called Dino. "Yeah, right," Dean said without looking at him. Then he added, "It's Dean."

"You owe the building about twelve million," Audrey laughed.

"But we'll take it in installments," Bobbi joked. "Just make the checks out to Audrey and me."

"Fucking electrical, that's the real problem," Dean snapped. This was a man who was seldom in a good humor, but today he seemed especially nasty. "Who installed these?" he barked, knowing damn well that Ben himself had.

"What's wrong?" Ben asked, getting up, moving over to him.

"The glitch isn't in my software, or even the goddamn program. It's in the wiring."

Ben shrugged. "That's what you always say, Dino."

"Screw you. Your fuck-up is shorting out the system."

"Listen, Carlucci, I'm sick of being your whipping boy, you know?" Ben glared at him.

But Dean had an answer. "If you and your gang of electric morons had installed the wiring according to specs, we wouldn't be going through this shit. You realize this is the fourth time in a week you've gotten me over here to undo some mess the installers made?"

"Fifth," Bobbi corrected him, "but who's counting?"

"Redo these wires," Dean ordered Ben.

"Do it yourself, man," Ben said. "You're the expert, *you* do it according to 'the specs.' Just have yourself a ball." He turned and stormed out.

"Tea?" Bobbi deadpanned.

* * *

As Dean worked with the computer's apartment control center, Audrey and Bobbi went over the rest of their day. There were two problems: she needed shoes, and there was another tour and inspection by prospective buyers that Bobbi had scheduled that overlapped Audrey's doctor's appointment. "I'll handle it," Bobbi assured her. Audrey wasn't worried. Bobbi, with her dizzy energy and perkiness, was not at all a bad sales agent in her own right; she'd already sold two of the apartments herself. And the Choi deal was half hers; she'd completed it while Audrey was in Hong Kong.

"Who are they?"

"The Johnsons."

"Johnsons?"

"From Texas."

"Any relation to—?" Audrey was starting to look impressed.

"No, the Johnsons who called a few months back."

"Oh, God, *those* Johnsons. The woman who went on and on that her oil-well land was too dusty for her sinuses."

"So move to the islands." Bobbi laughed.

"She's all yours."

Bobbi smiled, then hit her with the big one. "So, did you tell Mark?"

Audrey shook her head. "Not yet. I was so jet-lagged I just went into a coma last night. And this morning was too upsetting."

Bobbi looked concerned. "Why?"

Audrey decided not to tell her about the piece of newspaper on the bed. She did mention the letter sender but Audrey assured her she was going away for the weekend with Mark, and that they'd never be apart after that, she would be very safe.

"They've got to catch this guy!"

"Yeah, and in the meantime I can't hide," Audrey reminded her.

"What did Mark say?"

"I called him from the cell phone on the way to work. He agreed getting away was the best thing to do. We were going away just so I could talk to him about the baby and our future, but now there's a whole other reason."

"Honey, don't tell anyone where you're going. And get the cops working on finding who has been sending that crap. This is serious."

"The baby is serious, too. If there is a baby."

"Why didn't you tell Mark on the plane?"

"I want him to marry me because he loves me, not because he's forced into it."

"These days a pregnancy doesn't force anyone into marriage."

Audrey laughed. "It's still a pretty strong incentive, I'd say. No, I'm going to wait. If the doc says I am, then I'll tell him this weekend on Lanai."

"Why Lanai?" Bobbi inquired.

"Because I know what'll happen if we stay in Honolulu. We won't find a chance to talk, no matter how much we try. His cell phone will ring, they'll want him at the bank, Aunt will pretend one of her seizures just to keep me waiting on her—"

"Mr. Yee will return asking for a second look—"

"From your lips to God's ears. No, they're probably on their way back to Hong Kong, fleeing for their lives. We've seen the last of them."

Dean wheeled in, clutching a fistful of wires. "Where's that asshole?"

"Which asshole?" Bobbi responded. "The place is full of them."

"Your head electrician."

"I assume Ben went downstairs," Audrey responded.

"To turn in his resignation?"

"Come on."

"Problem's on the floor above," Dean muttered, "in the—"

"In the wiring," she said, beating him to it, "I know." Audrey picked up the phone, dialed the construction trailer, which was the building's computer nerve center until the ninth floor was completed. She asked that Ben be found and instructed to meet them on the twenty-fourth floor in fifteen minutes.

When she hung up, Dean said, "I hope we can get this rectified fast. It's Friday, the time lock sets at six, and I'd hate to leave this unfinished till Monday morning."

"We've got most of the day," Audrey reminded him, checking her watch to see that it was only ten in the morning.

"This could take most of the day," Dean said.

"Thing is," Audrey said, "this has to be fixed for good. We can't lose buyers because this system hits them with flying file drawers."

"I'll recheck the software again this weekend," Dean promised, "but I'll bet you anything it's the installation that got things screwed up. It's all in the hardware."

"Hard, soft," Bobbi interjected with a pixieish twinkle "it doesn't matter, it's the performance that counts."

Audrey grinned. Dean did not. He seemed almost embarrassed. "I don't think that's an appropriate analogy," he said, and wheeled himself to the apartment doors, adding, "I'll see you upstairs."

When he was gone, Bobbi said, "You know, I've really had enough of that chip on his big shoulder."

"He's had a rough time, Bobbi."

"Yeah, well so have I, so have you. Life ain't a picnic."

"Think what he went through," Audrey defended.

"Big-shot Olympic gold-medal winner loses the use of his legs. Awful, but get over it already. He's still alive."

"And bitter."

"It's not our fault," Bobbi muttered.

"He's bitter because he feels guilty for living through the accident."

"Oh, come on, that was four years ago."

"Bobbi, he was driving. Wouldn't you feel responsible for the death of your wife and child?"

"He just shouldn't take it out on us." Bobbi picked up the tea tray and carried it back into the kitchen.

Audrey followed her, stopping to stare at the stove. "It's just so strange about what she said," she remarked. "I just can't get it out of my mind."

The bulletproof limousine made its way down the Nimitz Highway toward the airport. In the back, the elderly Chinese couple were each heartily sipping a gin and tonic, talking about the fortunate circumstance of Audrey having nearly fallen off a girder. "I thought yes, God is on our side," Patricia said. "It gave me the perfect opportunity."

Old Curtis nodded. "And she certainly made it easy for us to decline to purchase."

"Serendipity," Patricia said, smiling from ear to ear. "But lousy feng shui."

"Horrible feng shui," the man agreed.

They clicked glasses when she held hers up. "To Hiram!"

"To Hiram, who I doubt is going to rest in peace," her husband agreed.

"Not after tonight."

The driver turned to the elderly couple, and

said, "Gimme a smoke." It was the first words the bodyguard had spoken since they got into the construction elevator. They had been wondering when he would say something.

Patricia Yee, who had lit up the minute they left Victoria Towers, handed him a pack of Parliament Lights from her big woven bag.

"Garbage," the driver said when he saw what brand she'd given him, but lit one nonetheless. Then he braked for a traffic light. He slid down in the seat somewhat, looking relaxed. "Gotta hand it to both of you. Nice work. The cane was a great touch, by the way."

"Thank you," Curtis Yee said.

"What did you expect?" snapped Patricia.

"Perfection," the man said. The light changed. Next to them was an open Jeep filled with teenage boys and surfboards. He gave a wave.

"Well, you got it," the old woman cackled, enjoying her gin. She let out a nervous laugh. "I must say, there were a few moments I wasn't so sure."

Curtis nodded, agreeing heartily. "When she said you 'had a way with a wok'!"

The woman nodded. "I thought I'd have heart failure. Me, a great cook, can you imagine?"

"You never fried anything more than a burger." The old man laughed.

"And that she'd been to our house," she said in the enthusiastic voice of someone who was trying to calm herself after an intense ordeal. "I thought, shit! We're in trouble here."

"You covered fine," the driver again assured them, seeing the signs for the airport now. "But Jesus, I really thought we'd lost her when she toppled off that girder."

"It was the chance we needed," the woman replied. "It was just as good as if she'd fallen."

"I'll drink to that," the old man said, laughing heartily.

The limo driver chuckled as well.

"Watch this," Dean instructed, wheeling his chair back toward Audrey, Bobbi, and Ben. They were standing on the poured concrete expanse that made up the twenty-fourth floor. Only a few of the future apartment's wall frames had been constructed yet, and they could see out in all four directions.

They stared at the control box, a panel of wiring on one of the central supporting columns, near where the elevator would one day be. In a moment, it started to smoke. "See!" Dean shouted. "The fiber optics are melting because some clown didn't tape correctly, leaving the wire exposed." He snorted, and then said, "Help me."

Ben, silent, burning, followed him to the box. Dean reached up to it to deal with the wiring, but he couldn't quite get his hands up far enough from the wheelchair. Ben reached over him, stepping on his tiptoes in his construction boots, and pulled out the offending wiring and loose electrical tape. Together they worked on the fix, and when they turned on the juice, in the apartment below, the ovens beeped, water rushed into tubs, stereos suddenly blasted, windows opened and closed, doors slammed, steam shot from wall jets, lights flashed and dimmed as the computer reset itself and things went back to normal.

The men faced off. Ben seemed slightly humbled—you couldn't argue with melting wires—and felt he'd give a little. "I try to tell my men not to be sloppy, not to be in a hurry." But his voice was filled with masked rage. It was an error common to any new building, one of the kinks to be worked out. But Dean was right, it *was* his fault, and he had to eat crow. "I'm sorry."

Instead of accepting his apology, Dean drilled him. "Sorry doesn't do it, man. Sorry is for losers, and this is a building for winners. It's being advertised as the most technologically advanced residential structure in the world. And your crew acts like morons building tract houses."

"Jesus," Ben muttered, trying to keep his mouth shut.

"*You* know what I mean," Dean said pointedly, needling him.

Ben grabbed Dean by the shirt collar and lifted him a foot up from his wheelchair. "You talk about that, and I'll toss you off this level. And there won't be a crane nearby to pluck you outta the air."

"Ben!" Audrey shouted.

"Come on, fellas, let's keep our cool," Bobbi added.

Ben dropped Dean back into the chair, turned on his heels, and walked away.

"Prick," Dean cursed, straightening his collar.

"You didn't have to go that far," Bobbi told him, unafraid this time. "You take out your frustration on everyone else. Gimme a break." She walked away as well.

Dean looked up at Audrey. "I guess I was a little out of line."

"A little."

"I just never liked that guy."

"Feeling's mutual, I would surmise."

He nodded. Then he started wheeling his chair toward the construction elevator. Audrey noticed how developed his arms and chest were, the result of having to compensate for the loss of his legs. Then his voice changed, growing warmer and slightly sad. "I was sorry to hear about your father."

"Yes. It was a shock. He had the zest that made you think he'd live forever."

"Bigger than life."

"Like this building."

Dean looked her in the eye. "Will anything . . . change?"

"How do you mean?"

"With the building, with you?"

She shrugged. "It may change things for me."

"You going to leave?"

She shook her head. "Oh, I don't know. Sometimes I think I want to leave Hawaii forever."

"I understand. But I hope you don't. You're one of the nicest people I've met here."

"Thanks," she said, and meant it. "Dean, what made you come back here?"

Dean closed his eyes, hiding the pain she might have seen in them. "I guess," he said softly, "it was just what I had to do. Just part of my mission. Part of my journey."

She didn't ask any more.

The Mercedes limousine approached the airport. "We're early," the bodyguard said.

"We can kill time here," Curtis said. "I'm hungry."

"I can do some shopping," the woman said.

But the bodyguard turned onto one of the airport access roads which led toward huge warehouses and hangars that most people never saw. Curtis Yee put his drink into the mahogany holder. He looked out and saw a sign for air cargo. He looked puzzled.

"Where are you going?" Patricia voiced, realizing now that they were headed somewhere other than the check-in area for United.

"Picking up some cargo," the driver said.

"Cargo?" Curtis said.

"Some papers the boss wants you to take with you."

"To Chicago?"

"That's right," the driver sang.

"I see."

The car stopped in the bright humid sunlight between two huge white buildings. The area was deserted but for a big Singapore Airlines catering truck parked about fifteen feet away. The driver pulled the car in behind it. "Gotta go inside the building and get the courier envelope."

"Want us to come?"

"No," the man said, bending down to reach under the front seat of the car, "not necessary." He seemed to be fumbling with something. "The key's under here somewhere."

Old Mr. Yee looked at the woman and gave her a mystified glance. He wrapped his hand tightly around the cane, which was lying to his side, against the passenger door.

His wife gave a nod that said she understood, and yes, it bothered her as well.

But the bodyguard put his head up before they could say a word, and he suddenly seemed to be glowing. "Gotta say again, you did a swell job."

"We take pride in what we do," Curtis said, with a slight edge.

The woman added, "I just wish we could stick around to see it happen."

"Yeah, too bad you can't." The bodyguard pivoted so that he was kneeling, facing them through the open partition between the seats. He held a gun in his hand.

"What—?" Curtis started to say, but the blast hit him square between the eyes. His hand tightened around the crook of the cane, then went limp.

The woman sat paralyzed as his body oozed blood in her lap. But she never took her eyes off the gun. "No," she said softly, her whole demeanor changing from sarcastic pride to putty, as if begging the gun itself not to go off. "No, no, don't. We would never—"

"Shut the fuck up," the bodyguard said as he pulled the trigger again.

"No—" The bullet pierced her throat and came out the back of her neck, imbedding itself into the leather seat. Her hands came up to grasp her windpipe as blood spurted as if from a fountain. There was a gurgling sound. The look in her eyes was one of disbelief, and then, as the second bullet shot through her brain, the eyes locked in position, and she toppled onto the old man.

"Shit," the bodyguard muttered, unfastening the silencer, putting the gun back under the seat. He unfastened his tie, opened the button on his collar. Then he looked into the backseat, and groaned, "Man, I hate blood."

The Texas Johnsons were due to arrive at one-thirty, and Audrey considered staying to greet them, then going to her doctor's appointment, but decided against it, fearing if she did that she'd never get away. Still, she was intrigued. The man was the Larry King of Houston oil barons, already on wife number seven, and he'd been said to have bumped off number three. In fact, he'd stood trial back in the seventies in a salacious mix of money, sex, and scandal as only the Texans can do. Audrey was curious about number seven, a former Miss America, an "entertainer" of dubious talent, enormous bust, and lots of bleached blond hair. Still, Audrey figured, if they bought into the building, she'd see more than enough of her in the future.

Besides, she needed shoes desperately.

She decided to go home and get them, grab the safe combination and key, then see her gynecologist on the way back to the building. Bobbi took Audrey's hand and squeezed it tight before she departed. "About Mark," Bobbi said.

"What about Mark?"

"Listen, I know I'm a terrible judge of character, and you shouldn't even listen to me—"

"You're right," Audrey hit back. "Your parents have a great marriage and you'd probably say *they* aren't suited for each other."

"Probably. But part of me wants you to really know if Mark is the right guy to father your children."

"Bobbi—"

"Honey, I know you think I just hate him. That's not so. And whether or not I like him means nothing. The only thing I worry about is that you don't really know him."

"Stop harping on it, Bobbi. I've dated him for almost three years!"

"I know; I've been here the whole time," Bobbi said. "It's been a wild, fun ride. I just wonder about his depth."

"He's smart, hardworking, kind, thoughtful, and caring. What's not to know?"

Bobbie pressed the point. "You know him, yeah, but I mean *know* him. What kind of life is he looking to have with you, how many kids does he want, how will he—?"

"Bobbi," Audrey said, "not now."

"Audrey, answer that. How many kids does he want?"

Audrey stammered.

"Come on, tell me."

"I don't know." She was ashamed this was her only honest answer.

"He's never said?"

"No."

"You strike me as smarter than letting some guy you don't really know knock you up."

Audrey hit the ceiling. "Damn it, Bobbi, he didn't 'knock me up.' It was an accident. We've had safe sex, but that one time—"

"Settle down."

"How can I settle down when you make me rattled?"

"It's just 'cause I care!"

"You just think I could do better than Mark, always have."

"Audrey, I believe some of your attraction to Mark has been the fact that it's a rebellion against old Aunt's domination. You've had a fun time with him, which is great, the opposite of the way you grew up. Now things are more serious."

"It's not like we just partied this whole time," Audrey said in defense.

Bobbi said, "I know that, but I think, despite how smart and caring he is, that he's not grown-up yet. I don't sense the responsibility in him, and you need that if you're going to have a kid."

"Bobbi, I gotta go."

"Wait." Audrey turned. Bobbi continued. "I just never felt Mark is deeper than that beautifully tanned skin of his. Before you leap—before you tell him about the baby, if it's not just gas and there really is one—find out, talk to him, get him to open up. I don't want to see you unhappy, honey, that's all."

"That's why we're going to Lanai."

"Make sure nothing stops you."

"Nothing will." But the sense of danger made Audrey shiver. "Right now I'm more worried about whoever has been sending the notes than the depth of Mark's feelings."

"Something else happen?"

Audrey told her about her bed being made.

"He was in your *bedroom*!" she gasped.

Then she told her about finding her lei missing, and about the piece of newspaper he left on the pillow.

"Honey, go to the police."

"Aunt told me last night that a Detective Wong put the letters through forensics and came up with nothing they could trace."

Bobbi rolled her eyes. "Honolulu's finest."

"It'll be okay."

"But you're not safe."

Audrey looked around. "I feel safe here—"

"Pol Pot would have felt safe here. This is a goddamned fortress."

"I'm going to move in with Mark when we get back on Sunday night."

Bobbi paled. "Does Dragon Lady know this, by any chance?"

Audrey answered with a wicked wink. "We'll surprise her."

"Thanks."

Bobbi stopped her halfway out the door. "Audrey, you coming back here after the doctor?"

"Yes. I'll go to the airport from here. My bag's in the car; I'm all set to meet Mark."

"See you then."

Audrey started out the door.

Bobbi called out, "He'll cancel. Mark my words, something'll come up, and he'll cancel."

Audrey gave her a knowing grin.

"Don't let him this time," Bobbi ordered, and Audrey was gone.

The bodyguard retraced the route he'd taken to the airport, and now turned into a driveway leading to a long-shuttered Asian import store off the Nimitz Highway. He drove around back, pressed a button on a remote on the visor, and the huge shipping-dock door rolled up. The sleek black limousine rolled in. When he turned the ignition off, he lifted the cell phone from the leather seat next to him and dialed an international number. It took a while, then the phone was finally answered. The voice spoke Chinese, but when he heard the driver identify himself, he switched to English. "Is it in place?" the voice asked.

"Not exactly where you wanted it," he admitted, "but close enough."

He sounded worried. "It went well?"

"Precision. She was good. They both were."

"Are they gone?"

"Boy, are they gone."

"No one saw you?"

"Nah."

"Leave the car and go about your business. But call me after it happens. I could watch CNN, but I want to hear firsthand."

"I'm gonna be on the beach like the Fourth of July," the bodyguard said.

"Good-bye," the voice said, repeating the sentiment in Chinese.

"Over," the bodyguard muttered, and turned off the phone. Then he took off his jacket, reached into the back of the car, and grabbed the woman's purse and the man's cane and tossed them into a trash can. Then he rolled up his sleeves and pulled a bottle of 409 and a towel from the cavernous trunk. He had a lot of blood to clean up.

Ben brought her car around, anticipating that's what Audrey was coming down for. "Where's the barefoot contessa off to?" he asked.

"Shopping," she lied.

"Didn't do enough of that in Hong Kong?"

"Never do enough of that."

"Shoes?"

"Yes." But she didn't get into the car.

He sensed she wanted to talk. "What's up?"

"Ben, you have a girlfriend?"

"Yes."

"Do you really know her, I mean know what makes her tick, what she's all about, her desires and dreams and all that?"

He looked like he was hit in the face with a girder. "Huh?"

"I know that's a lot to swallow. I just wonder how well anyone really knows anyone."

"We've only been dating a few months, so I think the answer is no, I don't know all that Takes time."

She nodded. "But Mark and I have been together almost three years."

"Then it's no secrets."

"Bobbi's really confused me."

He laughed out loud. "Bobbi's *confused* herself."

"I'm serious. She sees Mark through different eyes. Maybe she's more objective."

"Maybe. Different perspective, I guess," the construction worker offered, trying to help her.

"What do you think?"

That caught him off guard. "Me?"

"You. You know me pretty well. You've seen me with Mark often enough, I've certainly talked about him a lot. What's your gut feeling?"

"He's a nice guy."

She put her hand on Ben's shoulder. "Don't tell me what I want to hear."

He thought about it. "Okay, well, the way I see it is this. You've called him your 'fiancé' for a year, but he's never given you a ring that I can see."

She held up her naked fingers. "Listen, if Mark had given me any ring, from cubic zirconium to the Hope Diamond, I'd be flashing it everywhere."

"Okay, so what's he afraid of?"

She didn't understand. "Huh?"

"Well, he knows you love him, everyone knows that. So what's keeping him from popping the big question? I know a dude who doesn't ever plan to marry, but he sure gives the current girlfriend the impression he's gonna spend the rest of his life with her."

Audrey started to sink. "Till she presses?"

"And he moves on." He shrugged. "Hey, I didn't mean to depress you."

"It isn't like that with Mark; I know so."

He said, "I hope so, for your sake. I really want

to see you happy. Hey, maybe you better ask *him* to marry you."

She said, "No, I think I'll just lead the horse to water."

She opened the car door. "And what if he doesn't drink?" Ben asked.

She giggled. "I'll marry you instead." And she gave him a big hug.

The telescope framed this show of emotion. The construction worker wrapping his arms around her, holding her for what seemed a little too long for such a casual gesture between friends. It bothered the observer, bothered him greatly. How deep was their relationship? Did she see him away from the building? Was there more to this than he had previously thought? Questions like those kept him looking.

He saw her pull away, laugh about something. They both turned as a Cadillac pulled into the curved building entrance, announcing its arrival with a series of cacophonous horns. It was a flashy candy apple red, with one of those fake cloth tops to make it look like a convertible, but this one was unique, in a ghastly black-and-white cowhide. From the chrome on the grill protruded a huge set of steer horns. The Texans had arrived.

Even more comical than the car was the couple who emerged from the backseat. The man had to be pushing ninety, wearing blue jeans and boots, while his wife looked like an old showgirl who looked like a hooker trying to look like a schoolgirl. She balanced a head of teased hair, wore a dress as tight as a condom, and sported the biggest knockers the telescope had ever seen. But the observer wasn't focused on the arrival. He was still watching Audrey, who was now in her car, waving to the construction worker, driving out alone, and away.

Just blocks from the building, at a red light, a bright blue convertible made its way through the intersection at which she was stopped. Had her mind been on what she was looking at, she would have seen it was the Yee's bodyguard, rippled muscles now visible in a yellow tank top and reflective sunglasses.

But her mind was on Mark. And the growing suspicion that there was more about him that she needed to know.

Chapter Seven

Audrey waited impatiently as the Goh palace gates parted, then quickly parked her car in the center of the courtyard. Her hurried walk toward her cottage was cut short by Aunt suddenly standing in her way. "Audrey, I must speak with you."

"I'm in a terrible hurry, Aunt."

The woman did a double take. "Where are your shoes?"

"Some bird's probably wearing them. I've come home to restock."

Melba would not let her brush past so easily. "There is something troubling."

"I'll say." Audrey glanced at her watch. One-thirty. Her appointment was at two. "Sorry, Aunt," she said, dismissing her, "but I don't have time." And she hurried to her little cottage.

She sat on the edge of the bed—creepy feeling—and yanked off her torn panty hose, put on a new pair, and slipped into flats. She looked in the mirror and saw that they didn't fit the outfit, so she kicked them off and stepped into short heels. She checked the clock. She was right on time, twenty minutes to get to the doctor's office.

She opened the porcelain box and withdrew the little velvet bag with the combination and the key, and slid it into her purse. She noticed the emerald ring. She'd not worn it in a long time. Impulsively, she slipped it onto her finger and smiled. Then she grabbed a bottle of water from the fridge and walked out the door.

Aunt stood with folded arms where Audrey had left her, her face twisted in a snit. "Why are you being disrespectful?"

"I have a doctor's appointment," Audrey explained.

Instead of asking if she was feeling ill, Melba said, "This cannot wait, Niece."

Audrey gave up and shrugged. "What?"

"We must discuss things."

Audrey repeated the sentiment, louder. "What?"

"You will dine with me tonight."

"I can't."

"I demand it. Eight o'clock."

"I'm going somewhere with Mark."

The ghostly woman stared at her, as if assessing her priorities. "Aud-reeeeey," she said as if chiding a little girl.

"I'm an adult, Aunt. I'm going away with the man I love."

"You were just away."

"I don't have time for this." She started toward her car.

"Wait." The woman hurried in her baby steps toward her, suddenly flourishing a thick folder from the folds of her sleeves. "I need you to sign this." One of the servants appeared to her right, holding a pen and inkwell.

"Ah, the truth rears its ugly head," Audrey said snidely. "You weren't inviting me for shark fin soup. You need me."

"Just your signature."

Audrey was filled with distrust. "Another transaction in my name that I'm not supposed to know anything about?"

"Pardon, dear Niece," Melba said, "but it is a courtesy to you not to involve you in the boring details."

"On the contrary, Auntie dear," Audrey quipped, "bore away."

"Audrey, please just sign." She nodded to the craggy servant, who held out the pen and inkwell in a shaky hand.

"Want my chop, too?"

"Your signature will do nicely."

Audrey pulled the file from her aunt's long fingers. The title jumped out at her. "The Kaneohe Project?"

"A simple real-estate transaction on land we have owned there for some time."

Audrey flipped through the pages. In the past she would have signed without a thought. Her name had been used several times so Father and Aunt could save on taxes or somehow manipulate a deal to their gain. She never argued, feeling it was her duty to obey. But Hiram was gone, and she felt more responsibility to herself now, and that included documents with her name attached. She would read the contract, and sign only after she understood what she was putting her signature to. "I'll take them with me."

Aunt was genuinely alarmed. "I cannot allow that."

"Why not?"

"You . . . you won't understand it." She was obviously trying to remain unflustered, but it was clear she was shocked that Audrey would suddenly take an interest.

"I'm in real estate, Auntie dearest, so give me a little more credit." She closed the file and thrust it into her bag.

"Audrey, this is most disrespectful. I need these signed now, time is of the essence—"

"Then you should have given them to me last night. Dear Aunt, I must go now."

"Audrey!"

Ignoring her plea, Audrey got into her car and started the engine. Then she put her head out the window. "One question. Was Patricia Yee a good cook?"

The old woman looked startled. "What?"

"Just what I said. Did Mrs. Yee have a way with a wok?"

"Yes. She was a Chinese Julia Child."

Audrey shook her head. "God, how strange." The window went up, and she was gone.

And a perplexed Melba Goh hiked her skirt and disappeared into the house, slamming the ancient carved doors.

Dr. Thomas Rickerts, a good-looking man with ocean blue eyes, said, "You're pregnant."

Audrey, though expecting those words, nevertheless gasped. "My God."

"God had little to do with it, I'm afraid," the doctor joked.

Audrey smiled. Rickerts was a good man, smart and caring, and she'd been going to him since she'd had her first period. Aunt Melba objected, wishing Audrey would see her Chinese practitioner, but Audrey would have none of that deer-antler and ancient-curses stuff. She wanted a modern doctor who'd deliver her a healthy, bouncing baby.

"Audrey," he cautioned, "I want you to know your options. It's still early enough to terminate, if you have any doubts."

"No. I want this baby. Mark and I both want this baby."

He nodded. "I'm happy for you, then."

And she knew he was.

But would Mark be?

Thrilled, scared, dying to share her joy with Mark, but knowing she had to wait till he declared—better yet, when he declared by *slipping a ring onto her finger* in the moonlight—she imagined her wedding and a beautiful child in eight months, moving away, breaking forever that choking bond with Aunt for a life of her own.

She was glad that because her father had been a rich man, she would never have to worry about money. But that didn't mean she needed to dedicate herself to the relentless pursuit of making more. Perhaps she would become the only Goh in history just to want to be happy and contribute more than she took.

At her car in the parking garage, Audrey leaned against it for a moment, just to steady herself from collapsing into the fantasy that seemed so lush and ecstatic.

The man sitting behind the wheel just a few cars down and around the pillar from Audrey wanted to jump out and rush to her. He could tell she had learned something important upstairs, something that had affected her deeply. It wasn't a terminal illness; you didn't see your gynecologist for that. It looked more like happiness. Could she be pregnant?

Yes, he'd followed her here before. He knew exactly where she'd gone upstairs. That first time he actually walked twenty paces down the hall behind her. Taking risks like that thrilled him, and made him feel closer to her. Maybe one day he'd walk down the hall right next to her, with her proudly on his arm.

Once she knew the truth about Mark.

Audrey called Mark from her cell phone as she drove back to Victoria Towers. She had never felt so excited in her life. She tried to mask it, but it was difficult. "How's it going?"

"Terrible day," he said. "But you sound good."

"It is. I mean, I am. Mine's great."

"Don't rub it in."

"I have a surprise for you," she said, wanting to tease him slightly.

"I have one for you, too, actually."

She smiled. *Not as good as mine.* "Really?"

"I went shopping at lunchtime."

Her heart raced. "Hmmm." She tried to sound demure. She wondered how big the box was. Ring size? Tiffany? Cartier? "Do I get the surprise this weekend?"

"That's why I bought it today," he replied. "Do I get mine then, too?"

"That depends."

"On what?" he asked.

"On how things go. Actually, it probably depends on *your* surprise."

"Then I go first."

She was delighted. "Of course."

Then she heard a voice in the background, his secretary telling him something, and he said,

"Gotta run. See you at the airport. Flight 334 at 7:14."

"Tell Irene I said hi. I love you—" But he was gone.

Ben greeted Audrey outside the building. "Shit-kickers left."

"Nice car, huh?" Audrey deadpanned.

Ben said, "Told me they ship it wherever they travel."

"Couldn't rent one of those if you tried."

"Stop making fun of our tenant's automobile." It was Bobbi's voice. She was behind them with the opened bottle of champagne they kept in the apartment's refrigerator for just such an occasion. "Proud new owners of Residence Twenty-four."

Audrey was thrilled. "You pulled it off?"

Bobbi spit on her nails and rubbed them against the sleeve of her dress. "Just promised parking places for their horses."

Audrey gave her a big hug.

"Champagne?" Bobbi asked.

"No."

Bobbi froze. She'd never heard Audrey refuse champagne in her life . . . unless she was . . .

"Yes," Audrey confirmed, reading her mind.

Bobbi jumped for joy. "Congratulations, honey!"

They hugged and danced like two schoolgirls on the last day of classes. Ben said, "What the hell am I missing?"

Bobbi looked at Audrey, willing to keep it a

secret if she wanted. But Audrey was so delirious with happiness she blurted it out. "I'm going to have a baby."

Ben gasped. "A baby? Honest?"

"No, she's making it up," Bobbi deadpanned.

"Oh, man, that's pretty cool," Ben voiced.

The cell phone in Audrey's purse rang. To her surprise, it was Mark. Her blood turned to ice. She knew what was coming. Why had she really expected him to go through with their plans this time? This is what always happened, and she could predict his next sentence: *Something came up here at the bank . . .*

"Audrey, something's come up here at the bank, and I just can't get away."

"No!"

"Honey, this problem might be solved by tomorrow night. We could go then."

"No!" She didn't realize it, but she was actually shouting. Ben and Bobbi stared at her.

"I don't like it any more than you do. But work is work. There's an escrow that's got to be accelerated—"

She turned away from her friends for more privacy. "Care more about us and less about accelerated escrows, Mark. You cancel every single time we plan anything."

"I went to Hong Kong!"

"You had to."

"Honey, it's not like I want to do this, or even like it."

"I wonder."

"I hate it. I want nothing more than to be with you tonight on Lanai—"

"Then do it!" She was shouting, sounding desperate. She didn't care now who heard her.

There was a moment of silence. Then he disappointed her: "I just can't get away."

She thought for a moment. And then, without another word, she clicked the phone off and the line went dead.

Ben clearly felt uncomfortable being privy to her disappointment, and didn't know what to say. "I'm sorry," he whispered softly, again clasping her hand. "But it will work out," he added encouragingly.

Bobbi had a different take. "That shit."

Audrey just shook her head.

"I mean it!" Bobbi was spitting fire. "He's got some damned nerve. Too busy making a loan?"

"Accelerating an escrow."

"What the hell does *that* mean? Honest, Audrey, why do you want to marry a guy who treats you like this?"

Audrey's eyes held back tears. She couldn't say anything because of the flood of emotion hitting her all at once, but she answered with a gesture; she placed her hand on her stomach.

Bobbi looked disgusted. "You know," she said, "Mark just doesn't deserve it. Run off and have the kid yourself. Ben and I will come and help you raise it, won't we, Ben?"

"Sure thing," he said, a little confused.

"Bobbi and I disagree on Mark," Audrey explained.

"You told me."

"Give up on the jerk," Bobbi said.

"That's not fair to him; nor to me."

"Then do something to uncork what might be inside of him."

"How?"

Bobbi shrugged. "Go into escrow. You'd get a lot of attention."

Ben's beeper sounded. "Gotta run." He winked at Audrey. "It'll work out." And he was off.

But Audrey didn't even realize he'd left. A plan was taking shape in her mind, a crazy and outrageous plan, a plan that just might work—if she had the time. She looked up at the enormous building. "What time is it, Bobbi?"

"Almost four," Bobbi answered.

Audrey looked at her watch, wanting to be sure. "Exactly."

"Three forty-nine. Why?"

"Because . . ." And that was all she said as she stared up again at the building, then looked around the construction area, through the fence, down the street, at the parking structure. Her mind was reeling.

"Honey, care to clue me in?"

"I have an . . ." Audrey suddenly started walking toward the parking ramp.

Bobbi followed. "What? You have a what?"

Audrey hurried up the ramp, toward her car. "Idea," she answered. She stopped dead. "Bobbi, what kind of food is up in the apartment?"

Bobbi blinked. "Um, the champagne's gone. There's tea and crackers and cookies. Maybe half my sandwich from yesterday. Some chocolates, I think. Why?"

"This could work!" Audrey exclaimed.

"What could work?"

Audrey ran to her car. Bobbi watched her open the trunk and lift out a duffel bag. "Will you take this back up to the apartment for me?"

"Huh?"

"Just do it!"

"Sure," Bobbi said, surprised at Audrey's sudden enthusiasm.

When Audrey slammed the trunk, she suddenly looked unsure. "The tux. Gotta get his tux."

"Huh?"

Audrey threw her purse into the front seat and opened the door. "I think I can make it."

"Make what? What's going on?"

"I've got a plan."

"Want me to close up for the weekend?"

"I'll be back."

"Back? This afternoon? You've got less than two hours."

Audrey started the car. "That's why I've got to hurry!" And before Bobbi could ask anything more, Audrey had zoomed down the ramp, leaving Bobbi standing in a small cloud of dust.

Chapter Eight

Audrey got to Mark's apartment sooner than she thought, thanks to Feng Shui Traffic Master for providing harmonious clear lanes and directing all the idiots onto roads other than the one she was on.

She parked in his carport, used her key, only to step into the living room to find the phone ringing. She answered it. And she wished she hadn't.

"Audrey," Melba Goh shrieked, "when you disrespect me, you disrespect your father."

"Father is dead, Aunt. And why are you calling me here?"

"To talk sense into you before you go off with that boy."

"He's thirty-nine years old."

"But he isn't family. Audrey, I am your family! Your only family."

"Mark will be one day."

"Heresy."

"I have brothers."

"Worthless playboys."

"They're still family." Audrey knew there was no point in this. Time was not on her side. "I have to go."

Aunt wasn't about to drop this. "Mark is not part of your future."

"Visiting the fortune-teller again?" Audrey asked sarcastically.

"Yes. That is what she said. It validates my own intuition: this is not the man for you."

Audrey remembered something that had happened that last day in Hong Kong. She and Mark had visited one of the fortune-tellers up on Wan Chai Road, in the old Chinese part of town. The shriveled elderly woman had two blue beetles walking around in a cardboard box. Into it, she set a matchbox and had Audrey and Mark hold hands over the box. It took a while, but the two beetles finally crawled into the matchbox together and stayed there. "Ah, you have long and happy life together," the fortune-teller pronounced, revealing a toothless smile.

When they emerged, Mark had said, "She didn't tell us there was food in that matchbox."

Audrey had just chuckled. Now she felt strong and brave as she said to Aunt, flatly, "It's time I make my own future."

"Audrey—"

"Good-bye, Aunt."

Through the high-tech receiver she heard Aunt's booming alto. "Dinner at eight o'clock. I *demand* you to be there, do you understand me?"

Audrey hung up.

* * *

She virtually ransacked the place. The kitchen was first, where she grabbed Mark's bottle of Polish vodka from the freezer, and a jar of mail-order chocolate sauce she loved. She rustled through cabinets, choosing some spices and herbs, and then a bag of Italian arborio rice, thanking God that Mark loved to cook and had just what she needed. He loved risotto. She needed to plan the menus, for it wasn't like she'd be able to dash out to the store to get something she had forgotten.

She opened the storage closet to the left of the refrigerator and grabbed a folded shopping bag, tossing the food into it. Carrying it into the bedroom, she went into the drawer where Mark kept a few things—shorts, tees, tanks, socks, swimming trunks. She emptied it into his classy leather weekender, zipped the bag shut, grabbed the hanger with his tuxedo still under dry cleaner's plastic, and hoped he was wearing black shoes. But if he wasn't—she laughed aloud at this thought—who would see?

In the living room, she flipped open the Honolulu phone book and called the number on the full-page ad for Lotus Taxi. Then, with the tux and leather bag in one arm and the food in the other, she went outside to wait.

Standing there in the shade of a huge old banyan tree, which romantically filtered the afternoon sun, she felt truly free for the first time. She would never return to Aunt's compound, she knew that now. A stranger had made her bedroom unappealing to her, as was the whole complex and what it represented.

Fifteen long minutes later, a cab's horn tooted as it rounded the corner. Audrey saw a beater of a car wheezing, the meter already running. All the windows were open, and just looking at it she knew that it was the only car on the island without air-conditioning. She couldn't be choosy at that point.

She indicated for the man to open the trunk, and when he popped it up from inside the car, she dumped the suitcase and shopping bag into the trunk, and jumped in.

"Where we go, missy?" the sweaty, jovial Polynesian driver asked.

"Any supermarket on the way to the Bank of Hawaii on Bishop Street."

The man tried to joke: "Hungry?"

"We'll be making a second stop."

"Yes, my little fortune cookie." His eyes seemed to sparkle at the thought of a longer fare.

"I'm not your little anything," Audrey reminded him with a scowl, fastening a seat belt that she was reasonably sure had never been buckled before. "God, it's hot in here."

The jolly driver giggled and clicked on a little round fan that had been attached to the dashboard with silvery duct tape. "There, no more hot."

Audrey rolled her eyes. "Okay, let's go."

"Holding your horses!" he howled, gunning it

so hard the engine vibrated and squealed. They did two blocks in two seconds.

"Hey, take it easy," she cautioned.

"You say go!"

"Go, fast, yes, but not suicidal. I don't want to join Father quite so soon."

Soon the driver careened into a Safeway lot. "Pull up right in front," Audrey ordered. "Right there, by those carts."

The man parked next to three haphazardly abandoned shopping carts as she unbuckled and unlatched the door. "I'll be right out."

"Take your time, please, missy," he said with a grin. "Meter happy."

"I'll bet." Audrey rushed into the store. Meats first. What would Mark want to cook? Beef? Veal? She grabbed a leg of lamb, knowing Mark loved it. And a chicken. Mint jelly, she needed mint jelly. In rushing for it she smashed into a cart being pushed by a woman who asked her if she was crazy. A little, Audrey thought. Tossing the jelly jar into the cart, she headed for liquor, knowing champagne would be necessary besides Mark's vodka. Dom Pérignon would do, one bottle. No, two. No, she was pregnant, Mark would be drinking alone.

Then she went to the frozen foods, where she almost had to fight a man for the last quart of Starbucks low-fat latte ice cream, perfect when drenched with the chocolate sauce in her bag. Chocolate eclairs grabbed her fancy at the bakery counter, plus some healthy nine-grain bagels, rolls, and a dreamy feta foccacia. And chicken broth for the risotto. Just in case, for she'd heard this all her life, she got some pickles to go with that ice cream, if the baby dictated.

When the girl started ringing her up, Audrey opened her purse and pulled out her billfold. Inside were about twenty coupons Mark had given her the last time they'd gone shopping together. She just laughed. If she told anyone her boyfriend, a banker, gave these to her, they'd laugh in her face.

Outside, the driver seemed to be napping. "Help me!" she called to him. He didn't move. Because both hands were holding plastic grocery bags, she kicked the side of the cab to get his attention.

"Hold on, cookie, I'm coming," he said, opening the door with a creak. He unlocked the trunk, helped her set the bags inside. "Looking good. You chef?"

"Are you nuts?" she snapped.

He spied the buns. "Lousy buns, Safeway. Old King's Bakery, now those were buns."

"I'm sure, let's go."

As he got in, he suggested another stop. "Missy, I take you to Leonard's Bakery, getting the best malasadas on the island. Yes?"

"No. Bank of Hawaii building on Bishop Street, best mortgages on the island. Take King Street."

"I do better than that."

"Faster?" she asked, stepping back inside.

"You leave route to me, missy." He gunned the engine. They took off, back onto the street for half a block, and then into an alley that led to another alley, down a side street, into another alleyway, through what appeared to be someone's backyard, and then onto Bishop Street, to the bank building where a young escrow officer was about to be very, very surprised.

"Keep it running. The minute I get him into the car, take off, no matter what he says!"

"Who he?"

"You'll see."

He looked at his fake Rolex. "No problem, missy."

She rushed inside the bank. The interior was cool, woody, and hushed, like a church. Audrey thought that might be right on target, for if you worshiped money, this was the place to pay reverence. She calmed herself and slowly ascended the stairs to the real-estate department's welcome desk, where she knew the receptionist sitting there. "Audrey!" Irene Lim said, looking up, thrilled. "Hi, it's been a long time."

"Hello, Irene."

Irene stood up, warmly clasping Audrey's hand. "I'm sorry about your father; it was a great loss."

Audrey nodded, and couldn't help but add, "Especially to this bank."

Irene slightly nodded, an irreverent smile creasing her pretty face. "You can't see Mark, if that's why you're here."

"I know."

"Want to leave a message? Or are you here for business?"

Audrey grinned. "Business like you wouldn't believe. Where is he?"

Irene rolled her eyes. "In the conference room, for hours already. I open the cage door once an hour and toss peanuts in."

"That bad, huh?"

Irene nodded. "I had planned to get out of here at five, but I'm gonna have to stick around till they're done, which could be after midnight."

"Which conference room?"

"Number three. Why?"

"Irene, would you really like to go home at five?"

Irene didn't quite understand. "Sure, but—"

"But nothing. Now, I'm going to jazz up this stuffy place just a little, and I want you to say, 'I'm sorry, Miss Goh, but you can't go in there!' Can you do that?"

"Oh God," Irene said, fearing what was cooking.

"Right," Audrey said with a wink, and then hurried past her.

"Audrey," Irene called in a slight voice.

Audrey ignored her, walking toward the third conference room, where a Do Not Disturb sign hung on the door.

"I'm sorry, Miss Goh," Irene said, louder now so others could hear, as Audrey put her hand on the doorknob.

"Come on, Irene," Audrey whispered, "like Pavarotti. Let them hear you downstairs. Give it to me!"

Irene virtually shouted, *"I'm sorry, but you can't go in there!"*

But she did.

Five startled faces looked up at her from a slab of black granite covered with real-estate documents. Mark's was the only mouth that dropped open. "Audrey?" he whispered in shock.

"Darling!" she cried, rushing to him, putting on a performance. "Hi, everyone! Excuse me for the interruption, he'll only be gone a minute—" She kissed him on the cheek and began pulling him out of his swivel chair.

"I can't leave," the bewildered man said, "even for a minute—"

"Honey, I have a surprise for you. No one will mind if you step out for a second!" She was pulling his arm so hard now that the chair began to move. She just pulled him along the length of the table, past a well-dressed woman, past a sophisticated-looking man, past Mark's boss, and one other person she didn't even look at. Mark shouted, "Audrey!" and pulled back near the door and the chair stopped moving. He stood up on his own accord. "Um, everyone, this is my . . .

girlfriend, and she . . . we . . . I mean . . ." He didn't know what to say.

She noticed his closed briefcase sitting on the side table, next to the coffee and fruit bowl, so she grabbed the handle and took it. "We'll be right back, I promise, so just carry on, carry on . . ." She smiled a big grin and moved to Mark's side at the door.

"What *is* this?" he whispered. "How can you embarrass me like—?"

"Mark just won a yacht!" she said to the group watching them. "Egg Harbor, forty-foot, charity raffle, drawing, you know, and he's got to choose a color scheme or he'll forfeit it." She had no idea where this babble was coming from, but she couldn't stop now. "So we'll just run out, I've got the brochure in the cab—what goes well with teak, darling?—and be back in a jiff." She grabbed Mark's hand and yanked him out of the room.

Irene was still standing there, looking both worried and amused. Everyone in the building who'd heard this was now watching. Audrey said, "Sorry, Irene. You did a valiant job, but this is just too important." Irene looked on as Audrey dragged a protesting Mark down the stairs and out the front doors.

"This is crazy," he said out on the street. "What do you mean, I won a yacht?"

"Maybe it was a car."

"What the hell is going on?"

"Trust me, Mark."

"Trust you? I could lose my job over this."

"You won't. They need you too much."

"This is a very big transaction."

"But not as important as this."

"As what?"

"Us."

He shook his head in desperation. "What are you talking about?"

The cab's engine was running, the driver alert. She pulled the door open. "Get in."

Mark was dumbfounded.

"Where are we going?"

"Never mind."

"How long? I've got to get back to that meeting!"

She growled, "Get into the cab, Mark."

"Best taxicab in islands," the Polynesian driver sang.

Mark still protested. "What are you doing, kidnapping me?"

Audrey said, "Sort of."

"Audrey, get serious."

"Damn it, Mark, I am serious. I need you to come with me now more than ever. Give me that. It's the only demand I've ever made of you."

Mark was silent. He shrugged his shoulders, looked at his fellow employees staring at them from the windows. The cabbie gunned the engine. "We're coming," Audrey said.

"Take time, missy, fight all you want. Best fare I ever get."

"Mark, please?" She looked into his eyes. Love and desperation mixed to send a signal which he could not refuse. He was risking his job—or, certainly, the huge corporate real-estate transaction he'd just walked out on—and perhaps his future, but this was the woman he loved, damn it, and she was either hysterical, a little crazy, or very serious. He had to do it.

The telescope found its focus. Friday. Five in the afternoon. Cement all poured up on thirty, construction workers streaming out. The prison gates had just been sprung. The observer laughed at that. Idiots, most of them. Had trouble tying their bootlaces, much less erecting a building of such height, sophistication, and intricacy. He saw the coveralls again. The ones with ELECTRICAL printed on the back. Ben, her buddy, cinnamon-roll addict, lolling around. What they must pay that asshole, he thought, and he works maybe a third of the day. What in the world did she see in him?

She wasn't around, or at least wasn't visible. Maybe she wasn't coming back. The assistant was up there, pacing, it looked like, in the living room. He wondered why Audrey had left early. It wasn't like her, not on a Friday. For some unknown reason the building's sales office was closed on weekends, which, in his mind, would be the perfect time to sell apartments. Hell, he'd bought his place on a Sunday. Isn't that when everyone went looking, when they were off work? Maybe it had to do with her father's arrogance, creating the impression that this was the most exclusive building in the world. Why should he cater to the masses by opening on weekends?

In any case, it gave Audrey weekends off. Which she must have already started.

He turned the scope to the Pacific and found one of the booze cruise boats already floating a contingent of drunks. Ah, Honolulu.

Audrey, despite what the man looking through the telescope thought, had not left for the weekend. She was on her way back to the building in the backseat of a taxicab. Mark had gotten into the taxi to appease her, hoping whatever this was about would be over soon and he could return to the conference table with little harm done, except for the embarrassing explanation that his girlfriend was a little wacky. But now he realized they weren't going back to the bank, not soon at least. He demanded to know what the hell was going on. "I'll tell you when we get there," was Audrey's response.

"Get where?"

"Where we're going."

"Where *are* we going?"

"Somewhere to talk."

"We can talk later."

"No. Not after your 'conference.' You'll be too

tired at midnight, and then we'll table it and never get around to it."

"Sure we will." His voice was softer. He was trying to appease her.

She would have none of it. "No, we won't. We never do."

Mark slumped down and rested his head against the cracked plastic of the seat. "I don't believe this." Then he looked out and realized they were on the Nimitz Highway. "We're going to the airport. You still intent on taking this trip? 'Cause, Audrey, I'll take another cab back. I can fly and meet you tomorrow—"

"Does it *look* like we're going to the airport?"

He realized it did not. "Oh." The man had turned onto Pacific Street.

"You rather going airport, cookie, I going airport," the cabbie said.

"No!"

"Aye-aye, Kapitan."

Mark looked at her. "Seriously, honey, where *are* we going?"

Audrey saw a sign and it gave her an answer. "To Hilo Hattie's to buy Aunt a new muumuu."

"Audrey, are you losing your mind?"

"Quite the contrary. I'm saving it."

The observer tired of the monotony of the waves, so the telescope changed windows and focused toward Waikiki. He could see Aloha Tower, but nothing ever happened there, and his lens wasn't good enough for intimate details at that distance. So he zeroed in on nearby buildings, his usual sightings. The woman on the sixteenth floor of a building just past Victoria Towers, who liked to wash her windows in the nude, was nowhere to be seen. She provided interesting diversion now and then, especially when she stood on the inside window ledge and reached high to do the tops—her breasts then rubbed against the glass, and she'd have to clean there all over again. He always wondered what he'd do if he passed her on the street or down in the convenience store on the corner. Probably turn red. Maybe he'd meet her in the checkout lane, and say, "Stocking up on Windex?"

There was a guy—maybe a kid, he couldn't tell, a teenager probably, because, as he recalled from experience, they were always horny—who liked to jerk off in a window in the same building. Maybe they only rented to oversexed individuals.

Now and then he'd see an older woman in the apartment—the teenager's mother? But mainly he just happened upon the kid sitting on a desk chair facing the window, probably very aware that someone might be watching him, giving him an extra kick, stroking it while he looked at what the observer assumed were dirty pictures on the Net. Internet porn was addicting. He knew; he went there a lot too. The anticipation . . . *what's the next picture going to be like?*

Looking into apartment windows was much

like looking into the windows filled with porn on the computer. He moved the telescope now to more familiar windows, those of Victoria Towers. Where no one fascinated him as much as Audrey. Her delightful smile, the way she teased the workers, her dedication to clients, that pretty upturned nose, fine delicate hair, the most smooth, silky skin he'd ever seen on a woman, incredibly happy disposition. It was because he liked her so much, was so powerfully attracted to her on more than a physical level, that he always felt guilty for spying on her. Even now, he turned the scope back on the lavish apartment on the twenty-third floor, hoping against hope that she had returned and he could have one more look at her. But it was not to be. The place was empty.

He looked down to see Ben shedding his coveralls outside the construction office trailer, tossing them into a big receptacle along with hundreds of others. He looked as if he were wishing other workers a good weekend. Then he went into the trailer, emerged in a moment with his lunch box in hand and walked off into the parking garage. So much for him till Monday.

The observer turned away from the telescope and booted up his computer. One addiction replaced another, and he told himself he was going to stay away from the scope for the rest of the night; at least the computer offered more rewards, could be more creative. But he was going to stay away from the Net. He had a job to do this weekend.

And it had to do with Audrey.

Most of the construction crew at Victoria Towers had already left for the weekend when the beat-up taxi rolled up to the chain-link construction fence. Audrey got out as the cabbie went around to the trunk. Mark was shocked to see his leather weekender bag and his freshly cleaned tux lying there. And all the grocery bags. The driver started putting them at Audrey's feet. "What's this stuff for?" Mark demanded of Audrey.

"Bobbi."

"Bobbi?"

"We have to take them up to her." It was a silly excuse, but it stopped more questions. Audrey handed Mark the groceries, let him grab his bag, while she put his tux over her arm. "Why my tux?"

"For Lanai."

"Then we are going to the airport?"

The Polynesian gave Audrey an inquisitive look, and Audrey answered it: "No, we're not going to the airport." She paid the driver the outrageous fare, adding a modest tip.

"Been fun, cookie."

"A delight," she said.

"Anytime you kidnapping someone, you calling me," he urged, giving her his card. Then he got into the cab and drove away, leaving them standing there facing the building.

Audrey read Mark's mind. "Mark, don't say it, just go with it, okay?"

"Jeesh." It was an expression of utter frustration.

"Come on," Audrey urged, looking at her watch. It was after five. Time to start walking.

"Your car here?" Mark asked.

She thought lying would be the best possible choice. "Yes."

"Then we *are* going to the airport."

"Stop saying that!"

"If you would tell me what the hell is going on, then maybe I wouldn't have to keep guessing."

"I can't. Not yet."

Two workers got off the elevator, waved goodbye to Audrey as she continued walking toward it. Mark grabbed her hand, stopping her. "I'm gonna lose my job because of this."

"Mark, if you don't do this, you're going to lose *me*."

He looked at her, realizing she was dead serious. "Okay, let's get the car."

"We're going upstairs first." She nodded toward the groceries. "I've got to give these to Bobbi."

"You go upstairs, I'll put our things in the car."

"No. Come with me. Say hi to Bobbi."

"I don't even like Bobbi."

"Get to know her better, then."

"Audrey, I'm not going to sneak out on you and drive back to the bank."

"Craig!" she suddenly shouted to one of the few workers left on the job.

"Audrey!" he called back.

"We need to get upstairs, fast."

"Sure thing!" He disappeared into the operations trailer and as soon as he did, she saw the construction elevator lumbering its way down to fetch them.

Craig put his head back outside the trailer. "Better hurry. Lock time."

"Don't worry," she said, smiling.

"This is nuts," Mark muttered.

"Yes," she agreed wholeheartedly, "it is."

Bobbi was in the doorway. "Craig said you were on your way up. It's almost—"

"I know," Audrey said, "and here's everything you wanted for that dinner party."

"Dinner party?"

"The Texans, remember?" Audrey coached.

Mark said, "Texans? Yees are Texans?"

"They were. Are. I mean, they were on my mind. No, Bobbi's clients are the Texans."

"Lunch for the Johnsons, dinner for the Yees." Bobbi was fast, she played along.

"You two opening a restaurant?" Mark looked dumbfounded. "Or you been smoking something illegal?"

Bobbi did her best to cover, but she wasn't even

sure what she was hiding. "I'll just put them vittles away, then." She left them.

Audrey looked at her watch again. They had about thirty minutes. "Let me talk to Bobbi for a second, then we'll go."

Mark slumped into a comfy chair. "Oh," he deadpanned sarcastically, "take all the time you need."

Audrey found Bobbi shoving the leg of lamb into the freezer. "No, just refrigerate it."

Bobbi whispered, "What are you up to?"

"I wish I could tell you, but it's better no one knows."

"Huh?"

"You just go on, I'll put the rest away. See you Monday morning."

"Audrey, something's fishy."

"Honey?" Audrey called into the other room just to make sure he was still there.

Mark's muffled "Yeah?" bounced off the granite countertops.

"Be right there!" Then, softly to Bobbi, she said, "Make a big deal out there about the wonderful time we're going to have. Come on, do your stuff."

Bobbi followed Audrey into the living room. "You guys, I really envy you. Something so romantic, so private, it gives me chills."

Mark perked up. "We *are* going somewhere. Lanai? Shit, I've got to at least call work and say something." He reached for the closest extension.

"Somewhere wonderful, I'll bet," Bobbi giggled, thinking she'd figured it out. "Like some hotel where you'd be almost home, but still removed from the world?"

Audrey got what she was thinking. Bobbi believed they were going to the Halekulani. "A house befitting heaven," Audrey added, leading Bobbi on with the translation of that Hawaiian word.

"Have fun, you two!" Bobbi sang as Audrey rushed her to the door. Then, in a lower voice said, "And be strong. Get to know him or get rid of him."

"Bye, honey," and Audrey closed the big door behind her.

"Give me Irene Lim, please," Mark muttered into the phone behind her. While he waited, he said, "Wonder if Eckhart's still in the meeting?" And that made him look at his watch. "Christ, Audrey, it's twenty to six!"

Audrey looked at her watch. She lied. "It's only five-thirty, you're fast."

"Mine's never fast, it's a—" But Irene Lim answered and he started talking to her, and as the conversation went on, he forgot all about the time. Audrey moved to the big gilded clock on the wall of the entry hall and opened the back. Mark listened to Irene inform him how outraged the couple were that their escrow officer left in such a bizarre way—with the papers they were discussing, no less—and how they walked out in a huff. Then Audrey turned back the minute hand and closed it. And smiled.

". . . I'll call Eckhart tomorrow, see what we can do to put this back together. Gotta run now. I think I'll be at the Lodge, but"—his eyes found Audrey with a God-only-knows look—"but who the hell knows for sure. Aloha." He hung up. "Ready to go?"

"In a minute." Audrey went back to the kitchen and reset the clock on the microwave. She continued putting things away until she heard the ten-minute warning beep through the computers in the apartment. Last call for the trip down. She wondered if Mark would realize what that meant. No problem, not a sound from him. She put the ice cream in one of the freezers, then found a can of cat food in the bottom of the bag. Where had that come from?

Mark walked in. "Shouldn't we be getting out of here?"

"We still have time. I'm an expert at this." The five-minute beep sounded.

"What's that?"

"HAL has been acting up, making all kinds of noises."

"Come on, let's go."

Audrey pretended to wash her hands. "I'm a master at exiting right on the stroke of six," she told Mark. Of course, he didn't know that everything shut down precisely at six, and the warning signals were meant for the last elevator at five minutes to the hour. It was now impossible to catch the last ride down. Audrey dried her hands, took her time walking to the entry hall to get her purse, then took the tux from the closet.

"Just leave that, we won't need it."

"I want stylish romance!" she sang.

He didn't bother to argue, just put out his hand for it, and she hung it there as he reached for his bag with his other hand. He grabbed his briefcase as well and faced the door.

Just as it locked.

Chapter Nine

"It locked!" Mark gasped as his hands touched the massive brass door handle. He dropped the tux to the floor, put his briefcase and the weekender down, and gave a harder push downward on the lever. Then both hands. It didn't budge. "The lock's set!"

Audrey nonchalantly placed her bag on the big stone entrance-hall table. "It does that automatically at six."

"But you said it's only—"

She nodded, "Ten till." She glanced up, indicating the gilded Rococo clock on the wall just over his head. Then she looked at her wrist. "But I guess both are slow."

Mark saw that the clock on the wall was ten minutes behind his Cartier tank watch. "Mine was right!"

"Pity," she said, almost dreamily. "We don't have any choice but to spend the weekend right here."

"What?" He was incredulous.

"It might not be a bad idea."

He digested that for a moment. And then it hit him. "You planned this all along. This is what the scene at the bank was all about, that crap about winning a boat, all the urgency. Shit, Audrey, how could you do this?"

"How could I not?" She was feeling feisty. "One plan after another goes into the toilet, and this time we promise each other that come hell or high water—"

"I don't need the guilt about me canceling again—"

"—and you call and cancel just like all the other times. I had to do *something.*"

"You could have suggested this. We could have talked about it."

"Right," she replied with a sarcastic edge. She turned and began walking toward the kitchen.

Mark followed. "I think this was a really lousy thing to do, Audrey."

She turned on her heel. "You do, huh? I think it's pretty lousy that the next big mortgage takes precedence over the rest of your life with the woman you claim to love." She continued on.

"That's not fair."

In the kitchen she dumped the potatoes into the sink and began scrubbing them with a vengeance. Mark looked incredulous. "What are you doing?"

"Cooking."

"You must be kidding." He leaned against the island, where he set his briefcase. "All that stuff about Bobbi cooking, that was bullshit. You got all that food for us."

"Risotto and all your favorites," she said with some sting. "I thought you'd be thrilled."

He started to feel like a jerk. "Hey, I'll do the cooking. I love you, Audrey, there's no question about that."

"If you did, you'd stop whining about missing ten minutes of a meeting and be glad we're somewhere private and inaccessible and have more than two whole days alone without interruption."

He took a deep breath. "I'm not whining. I'm being responsible."

She peeled a potato with such force that she almost peeled her thumb. "Scared."

"You're your own boss," he reminded her. "You don't have to live with the fear that one little screwup can get you canned."

"Oh, come on, Mark, no one's going to fire you. You're too important to them."

"You don't realize the responsibility of a nine-to-five position."

"Listen," she said, waving the potato peeler to make her point, "my father adored me, but even though I was his daughter, he would have canned me in a Chinese minute had I screwed up. So don't tell me about responsibility." She dropped a naked potato into a bowl of cold water and started on another. "Besides, if you lose your job over this, you didn't belong there in the first place."

"I've got to call—" He didn't finish his sentence, reaching for the wall phone instead.

Audrey stopped him. "Won't work. Everything shuts down till Monday morning. Power stays on up here—have to keep the heavens gleaming so the masses staring up can dream—but no communication with the outside world."

He grumbled, set the slippery receiver back into its computer cradle, unsnapped his prized Kenneth Cole briefcase and withdrew his cell phone. It beeped when he hit the on button, so he muttered, "This won't last all weekend. And I don't have the recharger with me."

"Pity," she said, delighted.

"You got yours?"

She walked to her bag, lifted her cell phone from it, opened a window, and tossed it out. "No."

While Mark tried to explain his hurried exit to his boss, Audrey finished the potatoes, then left the kitchen and dimmed a few strategic lights. During the day she kept most lamps burning brightly so the apartment was displayed in its finest glow, but she wanted to make it a little more intimate. She pushed a button, engaging the computer to fire up the gas control on the fireplace, and flames instantly roared. She adjusted it to a fine burn, just enough to provide romance, not heat. But would it work? She was not pleased at his response to what she'd done, but could she blame him? He was very responsible when it came to work, and she admired that about him; she'd just have to give him a little time, anyone would be upset. She felt badly that she questioned his love for her, but wasn't that what this was ultimately all about? Whether they spent the weekend here, on Lanai, or on the moon, she was here to learn what Mark's heart felt, not what she told herself, not what Bobbi cautioned, not what anyone else said or thought.

She heard Mark from the kitchen, apologizing, promising, cowering, and finally, she was glad, being bold: "I said I'll pull it all together on Monday, and I think you know me well enough by now, Mr. Eckhart, to trust that." Audrey smiled. Then she heard him hang up.

She was sitting on the floor near the fire when he walked in, cell phone still in hand. "Nice place you got here," he said, grinning.

She smiled back. "Loosen your tie and stay a while."

He put the phone down on the massive stone coffee table, kicked off his loafers, and joined her on the floor. "I think I got things handled."

"I heard," she said, reaching for his tie knot.

"He's gonna call back, I'm sure of it."

She pulled at the knot and undid it. "How much phone time you got left?"

"Dunno. Didn't call out much, probably an hour or so."

"You could just shut it off."

"Audrey—"

"Okay, okay," she laughed, pulling his tie apart, starting to unfasten his crisp collar, "I'll let up."

He took hold of the tie by the large end and pulled it from his shirt collar as she unbuttoned him down to his stomach. "That's better," he said as he felt her hand move over his chest.

"Why do you wear undershirts? In this weather."

"Soaks up the sweat."

"You know, *you're* to blame, guys like you!"

He blinked. "Blame for what?"

"All these buildings in the world keeping their air-conditioning at frigid levels. It's because you wear suits."

He laughed. "I didn't design the male dress code. If I had my way, I'd go to the bank in skivvies." He rubbed his chest through the white shirt. "Anyway, this is faster once you get to the gym."

"We've got a great workout room here."

"On one of the floors we're locked out of," he commented.

"No, here in the apartment. Oh, you've never seen all of it, have you?"

"I will this weekend."

"You sure will." She pinched his left nipple through the soft cotton.

"We're going to make love in every room," he whispered, stretching out on the luxurious soft wool carpet.

"That's just what I had planned," she giggled, moving her lips close to his chin.

They kissed.

And then his phone rang.

The eyes peering through the telescope watched the last of the workers leave the building site. The foreman locked the gates, turned to the security guard, and handed him the key, according to the protocol that had existed from the day the hole had been dug and the protective fence went up. The security guard then went to his truck, got in, and followed the foreman's car down the street. The observer knew the routine well: every hour or so, the security truck would make a sweep of the site, driving around the streets surrounding the building. The security trailer parked inside between the structure itself and the parking garage was locked tight, but if necessary, the security guard could access it. The computers were in a lock position, having shut everything down—the elevator, phones, everything but the airplane lights on the top floors, inner stairwell work lights, and the brilliant lights in Residence Twenty-three—for the weekend; in an emergency, however, they could be up and running in no time.

God, he hated weekends! Audrey would be out of the reach of his lens till Monday morning. Oh, he could follow her if he wanted, bump into her at the Ala Moana mall, find her in a restaurant, and possibly even dine simultaneously, but the real thrill of knowing her—knowing her secrets—would be lost for two whole days. Nothing he observed satisfied him as much as she did.

He panned upward, looking through the building spires to a harbor slip on the other side. A magnificent yacht looked like it was being readied for a dinner party. A woman in a slinky black dress was setting down some kind of appetizers with the help of a uniformed maid. The powerful scope could pick out shrimp on the platter and the small protruding ridges of her nipples. The observer smiled at that. Mighty good lens, he thought, just as the salesman had promised.

The woman was joined by a man in a tuxedo, probably her husband, because as soon as the maid left the boat's salon, the man pressed both hands against those uplifted protrusions on the top of her gown and kissed her full on the lips. The observer looking through the scope pulled his head back and closed his eyes, remembering the last time he'd done that, so very long ago . . .

He wouldn't let himself get caught up in maudlin memories, for it didn't help at all. He forced himself back to the scope, found it aimed right at the model apartment, and just as he was about to direct it to another building where there might be some action—he was feeling a little horny after seeing the blonde in the tight dress, and he knew an apartment a block away where a couple often performed in front of the windows—his eyes caught sight of movement.

No way. Not in the model, not after six o'clock. But he kept the telescope there, just in case. For a whole five minutes. Nothing. It had to have been his imagination.

He moved down the block. Ah, yes, the exhibitionists were in full swing. She was sitting on the dresser, looking out the window, actually, right at him—did she somehow know he was watching?—while the boyfriend was on the floor in front of her, on his knees. The man took a deep breath and focused even closer.

Jeez, he thought, I can taste this myself . . .

Audrey got out a gleaming, never-before-used French copper roasting pan and dumped the potatoes in it. She doused them with Tuscan olive oil as directed by the recipe plus pictures on the screen, grated some sea salt from the oversized grinder, and pushed them to the sides of the pan. Then she set the lamb out, to come to room temperature, readied garlic, fresh rosemary, and opened a bottle of red wine. She wasn't bad at this, she thought. Patricia Yee didn't want to cook anymore, so maybe it was time for Audrey to start.

She poured Mark a goblet of wine and took it to him in the cozy library, where he was lost in papers from his briefcase. "You've got half an hour, tops," she warned him.

"Huh?" He'd heard her speak, but had no idea what she'd said.

"I'm going to get dinner ready to go, maybe work out a little, then take a bath—long and luxurious. You can do the same."

"Shower's good enough for me."

"No Jacuzzi? We have two."

He smiled seductively. "One in the master looks big enough for both of us."

She grinned in the same way. "I'd love that."

He sipped the wine. "Am I drinking alone?"

It wasn't time to tell him she was pregnant. "I'm just in a juice mood." Then she remembered she hadn't bought any. "Or maybe water."

"What's for dinner?" he inquired.

"Leg of lamb. Roasted potatoes. Salad. Fabulous dessert."

"Want me to—?"

"I'm handling it."

"New talents, huh?"

"You ain't seen nothing yet." She kissed him on the forehead. Then something dawned on her. "Mark! I completely forgot, I went home and got the key to the safe."

"Safe?"

"Father left me the combination to the vault. And a key that I assume fits something inside it."

"Really?" He looked curious.

She kissed him again. "I'm going to get dinner ready, then we'll do it. I'm afraid if we go in there now, we'll never eat." She left him to his mortgage papers.

* * *

Back in the kitchen, while chopping garlic, she read the papers Aunt had given her. The first pages of the document were straightforward and common, the kind of stuff she'd grown up on, for real estate was in the Goh family blood. But things began to get complicated on page three, and she had to read a few paragraphs several times to get the gist of what was actually buried in legalese jargon. She was cutting the rosemary leaves with a pair of scissors as she reached the fourth page, and nearly cut through the document. She was troubled because this seemed to be a deal designed only to benefit the Goh Corporation, not the people whose land they were buying. In fact, it made clear to Audrey that the homeowners—poor people along a stretch of road in Kaneohe who'd lived there for generations and finally accepted Aunt's offer to be bought out so the Goh Corporation could develop it—were being railroaded, with promises to provide "low-income housing as an element in the redevelopment" only as a promise, not a stipulation that was legally binding. The grandiose plans for the area, the homeowners thought, included apartments for them, condominiums for their children, town houses that would be affordable, and would appreciate quickly because they would be right smack up against half-million-dollar properties. It was pretty much a lie, and Audrey, though not a lawyer, but a savvy real-estate broker nonetheless, saw through the words immediately.

She pummeled the leg of lamb, then set it in the roasting pan, nestling it into the center of the potatoes. She did what she'd watched Mark do many times, doused it with olive oil, splashed on some wine, rubbed the minced garlic over it, sprinkled the cut rosemary on top, salted profusely, then set it inside the oven. All she had to do was tell the computer to do "Lamb, rare," and that she wanted to serve it at "Ten P.M.," and that was that. She turned her head, hands still covered with oil and garlic, and read the next page of the document. And so on until she was finished.

When she came to the end, and washed her hands with strong kitchen soap from a dispenser built into the granite, she knew she would never sign the document, and that by withholding her signature, Aunt was stymied in completing this deal, for Audrey was the other major stockholder in the Goh Corporation.

She got herself a glass of ice water from the dispenser in the refrigerator door, sat again at the island, and looked at the folder in front of her. She'd seen so many like it, signed so many like it, but always—until now—without reading them. What other schemes had she put her signature to? What other greedy projects at the expense of the poor had she validated? She was no bleeding heart, always believing you had to go out and work hard for your money, and she had no sympathy for those who never even tried to do that, but this was outright robbery. She'd heard the criticism of her father over the years. The *Honolulu Advertiser* called his company the God Corporation instead of Goh Corporation, in a biting editorial over plans to develop the vast hills of the famous Dole sugar plantation, a plan that was killed by public outcry.

In ways, Hiram Goh and his sister were revered in Hong Kong and Hawaii, for they'd erected some of the most magnificent buildings and created countless jobs in the construction of those structures. In other ways, they were despised, because ninety percent of the housing they built could be afforded only by people like Ferdinand and Imelda Marcos (a mansion overlooking Honolulu, a condominium on Victoria Peak in Hong Kong), or the rich Japanese (an entire building on Maui), or people like the sophisticated Yee family or the wealthy, tacky Texans who were buying into Victoria Towers. They were helping drive the middle and lower classes off the islands completely.

But Audrey had always heard her father say, "They're only jealous." And he'd defend himself, his accomplishments, his vision. He had always said he did nothing crooked, nothing illegal, that he was only looking for the best deal for himself and his children, and he needed to do that because his sons were such losers. She had trusted his words. Father taught her not to lie, and he told her to follow his example. He had convinced her the Kanehoe Project was of great benefit to the local Hawaiian people. Yet she'd just read differently. Was it Aunt? Audrey wouldn't put anything past her. Had she been pulling the wool over her brother's eyes? It was a powerful moral dilemma for Audrey, one she had to solve. But how?

"Mark?" she called, surprised to find him watching television in the den rather than deep into his work.

"Yeah?" he said, looking up.

"Brought you another glass of wine."

"Thanks, just put it down." He hit the mute button. "Wanted to catch the news." He gathered up his papers and reading glasses and put them on the coffee table. "What have you been doing?"

"Starting dinner. Don't you smell the garlic?" She waved her fingers in front of his nose.

"Yum. And where did you get that ring?"

She looked down at the emerald and saw there was a little piece of rosemary caught in the setting. She picked it out and ate it. "I bought it long ago."

"Never wear it."

"I know. I don't know why, because I love it."

"It's beautiful," he said, examining it. "Where did you get it?"

"Italy. A wonderful shop in Florence."

He gave her a curious smile. "You like rings?"

"What girl doesn't?"

"You don't often wear one."

"Maybe I'm holding out for the right one." Could she say anything more leading?

"I see," he said, and that was the end of that. "I'm lunching with Millie Reed on Monday."

Audrey figured he changed the subject because it was too close to home. He was saving giving her an engagement ring for later or even tomorrow. "That's nice. Oh, I was on my way to check out Father's safe."

He laughed. "That's an idea." He rose, but something on the TV screen caught his attention. "What's this?" he said, and grabbed the remote to press the mute button again.

He and Audrey watched what looked like a live report from the airport. A female reporter was standing just outside a yellow police line between two nondescript buildings and in front of a fairly large truck. The reporter was saying, ". . . and this particular part of the airport can be desolate. It's in that truck there, a Singapore Airlines catering vehicle, that the bodies were found just a short time ago. We don't have anything concrete yet, Paul, but we are told that the victims were both of Asian descent and were elderly. We are being told that they both were shot in the head, but that's unconfirmed at this time as well. What we are sure of is that two bodies, a man and a woman, were discovered by an employee of Singapore Airlines as he opened a catering truck—that truck you see behind me right now where the coroner is working—which had been parked here for most of the day in the Air Cargo section of Honolulu International Airport. Details are sketchy at this point, and no one here seems to have any clue as to the identity of the two people. We will jump in with our live report as we learn details. This is Connie Suzuki reporting. Back to you, Paul . . ."

Mark hit the off button when the anchor began talking about an accident on the Pali Highway. "Gruesome."

"Sounds like a mob hit."

"Here?"

"There's Mafia here."

"Tongs, you mean?"

"Mark," she said, trying to get him to drop the surprised attitude, "you do business with some of them. Let's be honest."

"Yeah, well."

"Yeah, well what?"

"I only handle real-estate transactions. I don't ask where the money comes from."

She smiled smugly. "You're wearing the blinders I used to wear." Then she shrugged. "With Aunt and Father, you had to."

"Hiram was a good man," Mark said, reassuring her. "He dealt with some unsavory characters—"

"Mr. Tung, for example?"

"—but he was a man of integrity himself."

She smiled. "Thanks," she said. Then she retrieved the green-velvet bag containing the key and the numbers from her purse, and motioned for Mark to join her as she walked to the safe.

She set the bag down on the desk near the safe door, just under the computer screen. With the stroke of a few keys, she called up access. It took time, asking her to input several numbers and dates which she knew well but an outsider would not. This was Hiram's own Fort Knox, not just a residential burglar alarm. She then saw the request for the combination numbers. Mark was standing over her shoulder. She asked him to take the combination from the little bag and read it to her. He opened it, pulled out the rice paper, and set the numbers down next to the keyboard. "You said there's supposed to be a key in here as well?'

She turned, surprised. He shrugged and showed her the empty bag. She said, "Maybe it fell out into my purse." But dumping her purse upside down and shaking it did not produce the key.

"You might have lost it anyplace," Mark offered.

"No. It went from my hands to the bag to the box in my bedroom. Then I lifted it out early this afternoon, put it directly in my purse, where it's stayed. It couldn't have fallen out."

Mark shrugged. "It had to."

Then a look of panic crossed her face. "It was him."

"Him?"

"The guy who was in my bedroom."

Mark remembered her alarming call that morning. "So it was a robbery?"

"Why take a key he can't use when he could

have swiped this ring, or stuff that's worth money there?"

He shrugged. "You said someone saw him that day he left the envelope. Have the police followed up on the description?"

"Mr. Hirsch, the bug man, said he looked like you."

"Me?"

"Apparently you're who he described."

"It wasn't me," he joked, but didn't feel in a joking mood. "Audrey, this is serious."

"You're telling me? That's another reason this was a good idea. We are certainly safe here."

Mark said, "Let's go for it. Type in the combination."

She did. And waited. It took so long that she feared it would not work, but suddenly a window on the screen announced ACCESS GRANTED. They heard a click. The massive door, over a foot thick, popped open.

"Presto," Mark said, reaching out to pull it open farther. "Just like in the movies."

And they entered.

Chapter Ten

The observer watched the couple make love until he could stand it no more. Peeking into people's bedrooms was the eeriest part of his telescope obsession, being there with them—without their knowledge—while they were having sex. It was almost as if he was an unknown participant, completely invading their intimacy. He wanted not to look, ever. He knew how wrong it was, and yet there was something so compelling about it.

Was it him? His condition, the fact that something was wrong with him, that he was different from most everyone else? He knew himself well. This was the only way he was going to get sexual enjoyment. No woman wanted him, no woman would have him—for what would she do once he explained, once it was time to perform? No, this was the only path left for him.

And yet it drove him nuts, this guilt he felt from peeping, the shame he lived that this was what he was reduced to. And yet the telescope—almost as an extension, a replacement, of his penis? he thought—stayed glued to the spot, wouldn't move, didn't budge. It was fixed, permanent, solid. It would stay there till they finished.

The first thing they saw inside the vault was a chair, a comfortable high-backed wing chair which Audrey explained to Mark was her father's favorite, shipped in a container recently from Hong Kong. She ran her hand over it. The worn brocade felt familiar, warm to the touch, as if he'd been sitting there and had just gotten up. Memories flooded her mind.

"Apparently he was planning to spend a lot of time in here," Mark said, noticing the little table, reading lamp, and footstool. "Cozy."

The room was anything but, actually. It reminded Audrey of the sterile safe-deposit room in most banks, with just as much charm. She thought it probably made Mark feel at home. She scanned the floor-to-ceiling filing cabinets. Projects, buildings, dates, banking transactions, tax files, the names of law firms, banks, on and on. Nothing looked as if it needed a separate key to open, except the boxes she knew belonged to Tung, and she doubted her father had offered her a peek in there. Until Mark found the other safe. "Look at this . . ." he murmured.

It was at the rear of the vault, almost overpowered by a pile of loose papers. Audrey thought it looked like the old safes in the movies, a squat little chunk of steel standing on four stubby legs, dark and grimy with age. "This must have been in the family forever," she said.

"Manufacturer is Chinese," Mark said, looking at the gold characters flaking on the side, "and I think the year is 1757."

"My God."

Mark stooped down and studied the antique. "It can't hold much."

She laughed. "Good things come in small packages."

"There's more writing here," he added, "but I don't read Mandarin very well."

She could. And when she did, she gasped. "It was my mother's! This belonged to my mother's family, it says something about the God of Prosperity looking down on the Chin family."

"I hope the God of Prosperity left it full." Mark rubbed where the key needed to be inserted. "And that you find the key fast."

They stood up. Mark said, "Nothing particularly compelling, huh?"

She shrugged. "I don't know. I'm going to poke through some of this stuff."

"I've got another hour's work to do, honey."

"I want to find a project file. You mind if we eat late?"

"Nope. What's time when you're locked in a tower?" He kissed her on the cheek and left.

The God of Finding Things was good to her. She almost immediately located the cabinet labeled GOH CORPORATION HOLDINGS—CURRENT. The master file was two hundred pages long, and read like a computer printout (which it, in fact, was) that cross-referenced every piece of paper in the safe. She wasn't interested in learning everything that was in here, for most of it was not relevant to her. Or even her business. But Aunt had made the Kaneohe Project her business.

Something else struck her as she sat there in Hiram's lovingly oiled teak chair, about to read the secrets which had till now been hidden behind thick walls. Hiram had wanted her to see the contents of his vault first, before Aunt, before the attorneys, before anyone. Hiram could have instructed that Audrey simply be given her mother's safe; anyone could have carried it out of the larger structure. Why had he wanted her to see the whole place, to have these files to access? She almost felt a force compelling her to go on with this, a gale blowing her toward enlightenment.

She found the listing of all the documents relating to the Kaneohe Project. File cabinet 7, drawer B. She got up and located it, pulled it open, and began to withdraw the files.

All afternoon, Melba Goh had paced the living floor of her incense-encrusted mansion. She was worried, worried sick. Audrey was smart, that was the problem, and that had always been to the family's advantage, for she was showing every sign of carrying on after Hiram and Melba. Melba had always written off Hiram's sons, her good-for-nothing nephews who were neither ambitious nor bright—that cursed second marriage!—nor interested in anything other than carnal pleasures, megayachts, horses, and spending. But Audrey was showing signs of independence, and that could do the family irreparable harm.

Hiram and Melba had come from a generation where simple survival was at stake, and thus anything one needed to do to ensure that survival was condoned. Audrey had had everything handed to her: good breeding, fine schooling, all of it. She never had to flee a Communist regime that was about to take away her ancestral home, her land, her independence, her spirit. She never had to start over, sharing space in a cramped room on Tsim Sha Tsui with five other relatives, eating meager bowls of rice cooked on a fire in a bucket hanging outside the window, sustained only by their dreams, their desire to get even—and you got even by getting rich.

Melba shook herself out of her reverie. Communists were not the problem here, Audrey was. Obviously she had not yet read the file on the Kaneohe Project, or she would surely have called by now. Melba never should have let her take the Kaneohe papers. She had to stop her, had to retrieve them.

She looked at the clock. Seven-fifteen. She had told Niece dinner would be at eight. She would wait until eight-fifteen. Perhaps she would still come, happy to dine with her Aunt (if she had not read the papers), or combative (if she had). In any case, once in this room, Aunt could handle her.

Audrey was knee deep in papers when Mark walked back into the vault. "What are you doing?"

"Homework."

He smiled. "And you claim I'm obsessed? Had the television on. They dragged the bodies outta that truck. Old Chinese couple, in their sixties or seventies, can you imagine? Who would do such a thing?"

"I wonder what *they* did," Audrey answered.

"How so?"

"To deserve execution."

He changed the subject. "What did you find?"

She smiled back. "There's something Aunt doesn't want me to know about the Kaneohe Project."

"I'll bet."

"Why do you say that?"

He shrugged. "It's been controversial from the get-go."

"That doesn't mean—"

"That means," he cut her off, "it's good for Aunt, and bad for the people."

She just looked at him. "I'm boning up on the details. She wants me to sign a contract. I don't think I can do that."

"It's almost eight. I thought this was our special romantic weekend."

She said, "Sorry."

"You look so sexy sitting there going over figures."

She laughed. "Tables turn, huh? I'm acting like you at that meeting this afternoon." She reached up to him, pulled him down to her, kissed him lovingly on the lips. He helped her up from where she was kneeling. "I think I should have worked out today," she said as her joints snapped.

Mark nodded. "Why don't you do a little work-out, and I'll put some appetizers out?"

"You sure?"

"Sure. Just don't take all day."

"Maybe fifteen minutes of cardio."

"Work up an appetite. What we got?"

"Smoked salmon in the fridge, crackers, and—"

"I'll find it. That roast is gonna be great; can smell the garlic all the way in here."

She kissed him. "I won't be long."

"Take your time," he said, "I'll bring the feast to you. Just leave the door unlocked."

She winked seductively.

The observer watched the couple finish, watched so closely that he could practically hear them panting. He stayed with them, his blood falling from the boiling point while they stretched out, cooed, relaxed. When the girl reached for a cigarette, the observer looking through the telescope actually laughed out loud—the cliché still exists!—and began to scope out other windows.

But nothing interesting was happening.

He looked at the clock across the room. Eight o'clock. Time for dinner, and he was plenty hungry. He took one last long look over the windows with lights on, just to be sure he'd miss nothing when he left. He even checked out Victoria Towers, for what he wasn't sure, seeing that the place would remain deserted until Monday morning. Maybe just to say good night in his own protective way.

And then he saw her.

Or what he thought was her.

It was just a glimpse, a flash of hair moving through a doorway in the apartment. But he knew he was seeing things. No one was up there, no one could possibly be up there, not at this hour. The place was locked tight, and it would not open until Monday morning.

Yet he stayed glued to the spot. And in another minute someone walked through his sight—but it wasn't her. It wasn't a woman at all. It was a man. Who the hell—? He felt the hair on the back of his neck stand up. He was shocked, outraged, troubled. Who in the world was up there?

He focused the lens and waited. Whoever had rounded the corner would surely come back the way he came. And this time he would be facing toward him.

Chapter Eleven

They were in the exercise room, one of the few in the residence with no windows. Mark had taken the salmon from the refrigerator and left it out on the island while he joined Audrey in the gym. She was moving fast on the treadmill, beginning to sweat. She had slipped into a T-shirt and shorts and tennis shoes. He sat and watched. "You're making me nervous," she said.

"Why?"

"It's like some Peeping Tom watching me perform."

"Only you know I'm here," Mark said.

"Yeah."

"Does it turn you on?" he asked.

"Mmmmmmm," she replied, increasing her speed.

"That a yes, no, or maybe?"

"Why don't you join me?"

"I only like full workouts."

"Come on!" She started running. The pace was 4.9.

"Didn't bring my gym bag."

She shouted, "I got your things. But who needs clothes?"

He nodded, stood up, and pulled his shirt off. He wore a white tank top—what she called an undershirt—under his dress shirt, and she thought he looked incredibly sexy. Then he kicked off his loafers, unbuckled his belt, unzipped his pants, and stepped out of them, neatly folding them and placing them near the shirt. He stood in his socks and boxers, and Audrey gave him a big, sexy smile that told him she liked what she saw. He lay back on a bench and stretched. She increased her speed to 5.2. He picked up forty-five-pound weights and started pressing them, chest muscles rippling. Audrey increased her speed to 5.5 and soon felt the sweat pouring down her brow. Then she remembered the baby and decreased the pace back to 4.7, just in case she was overdoing it.

But this situation, the two of them working out together, mother and father of the child she was carrying, made her feel safe. For this was their common ground. Cardio machines, she fondly remembered, the way they had met.

On the TV screen suspended from the ceiling, Connie Suzuki was reporting the speculation that the dead couple were shot at another location and their bodies dumped at the airport. Tape of the bodies being carried on stretchers from the back of the catering truck ran again and again. A baggage handler was saying he was sure he saw a limousine heading toward the buildings where the bodies were found earlier that day, and he remembered it because he thought it odd. And he was sure it was a Mercedes. He loved Mercedes Benz cars. But Audrey wasn't paying attention. Being with Mark right now, in their routine, made her feel safer and more content than she had for months.

The observer's eyes hurt. It was over fifteen minutes that he'd been staring at the corner of the living room in the model apartment. If someone was in the apartment, it seemed he'd have seen him again. He risked missing him by looking in other windows—the master bedroom, master bath, the dining room, kitchen, the living room again. Nothing. Not a soul, as it was supposed to be. That was enough. This was crazy. This was obsessive.

He was about to remove his eye from the lens when he froze. He'd moved the telescopic sight to the kitchen counter. Something had caught his eye. The oven was on! Why he noticed it, he could not explain, but there it was, the powerful scope had picked up the countdown of the timer clicking off the seconds in blue digital light. He clicked to the next power of the scope and peered into the oven door, where the light showed him a roast cooking there. Somebody—some man—was making dinner!

There he was again. He got a glimpse of the man crossing the hallway—in boxer shorts or swimming trunks, he thought—and disappearing into one of the bedrooms. Which one? The one on his side? The apartment took up the entire floor, and only one guest bedroom allowed him a look. It remained dark.

Then he saw a shadow in the master bedroom. The man was in there, but to the side, out of his sight. He could see his arms moving, as if he were talking animatedly to someone else there. And he guessed—hoped—the someone was *her*.

Audrey stood in her sweaty T-shirt and panties, pointing out the clothing she wanted him to wear. "It's all there, your shirt, the tie, everything you need. New underwear as well."

"Briefs under a tux?" he mused, towel slung over his shoulder. "Yuck."

"Why does that make a difference?"

"You have to be a man to understand. Maybe we should just skip the formal wear."

"Mark!"

"It's silly."

"Why's it silly? If we were at the Lodge, you wouldn't feel silly dressing up for a beautiful evening together."

"We're not at the Lodge. We're here."

"This is even better."

"But it's just us."

"What does that mean?" She tried not to hide her hurt. "You dress up only for others to see?"

"No, that's not what I meant. It's . . . well, I've never done this before."

"You think I have?" She handed him the outfit on the heavy hanger. "We are dressing for dinner, or there'll be no dinner." Then she grabbed his shoulders and started to tickle under his arms.

"No . . ." He pulled away.

But she grabbed him. "Say you'll wear the tux," she ordered, tickling him some more.

He was powerless, bending over, clutching his arms to his sides in an attempt to keep her hands out of his armpits. "Stop it!"

"Say you'll wear it, or I'll tickle you to death!"

"Yes!" he cried, screaming with laughter. "Yes, I'll wear it."

She stopped.

He was giggling and sweating. "My downfall."

"Works every time," she said, getting back to her feet.

He finally got up as well. And took the tux from her and picked up the duffel. "I only have my loafers."

"We'll make an exception for your feet."

He smiled, and said, "Take your bath. I'll bring appetizers in a minute."

After he left, Audrey spoke to the computer panel at the bathroom vanity. "Bath," she said simply, and a menu appeared on the screen. She then read her choices, and moved her finger to the ones she preferred: WARM/HOT, BUBBLES, WHIRLPOOL, CLASSICAL MUSIC, MOOD LIGHTING. And presto, the lights dimmed, soft strains of Haydn filled the air, the water began to run, a perfectly measured burst of bubble-bath gel dropped into the running water, and once the water reached the correct level, the jets would start humming.

Audrey looked into the mirror and smiled. She'd pulled it off. Mark was actually getting into it, in the kitchen preparing the first part of their romantic night. He would tell her how much he loved her, he would *say* it this time, and then she would tell him her secret, and they'd cry and laugh and plan for baby clothes and strollers and saving for college. She admired the beauty of the delicate lavender orchid plant set on the marble. Then she took a whiff from the decanter of Chanel No. 5 they kept there to impress prospective clients like Pat Yee. Yes, she thought, *yes.* Then he would top off the evening by giving her the ring.

Or would he? Curiosity seeped through her as she wondered if that's what his surprise was. She didn't want to see it exactly—she didn't want to spoil the excitement of his sliding it onto her finger—but she wanted some kind of verification that she was right about him. She wanted him to want to marry her as badly as she did him. She had a devilish thought suddenly, and yanked open the bedroom door and took several steps down the corridor to assess where he was. She could hear him in the kitchen. Perfect. She high-tailed it to the guest bedroom.

Where his briefcase sat like a tabernacle on the bed. Her heart in her throat, afraid he'd burst in and catch her snooping, she hurried to it and saw that it was unlocked. Without thinking twice, she popped the beautiful leather case open. And she wished she hadn't.

Staring her in the face were cut-up pieces of newspaper. And a pair of scissors.

Her heart stopped.

As the shock turned her blood cold, she jumped backward, and screamed when she felt Mark standing only inches behind her.

Chapter Twelve

"My God!" he shouted, grabbing her arms so they wouldn't both fall backward. "You scared the shit out of me."

"*I* did?" she said, whirling around to face him. "What were you doing inches behind me? Spying on me?"

He looked startled. "Spying on you?"

"Sneaking behind me."

"I just walked into the room," he explained. "What are *you* doing in here? I thought you were taking a bath."

She accused him right back. "I thought *you* were getting some food."

"I was. I couldn't find a corkscrew for the wine, always carry one in my briefcase—" He saw that his briefcase was open. "What were you doing?"

She wasn't fast enough with an answer. She watched him move toward the bed, to the case and lift the scissors and the folded, raggedly clipped newspaper, to reveal a bright blue Tiffany box under it. Her eyes widened.

"You were peeking!" he admonished playfully, figuring it out. "Like the little girl who can't wait for Christmas morning."

"I didn't look." She tried to cover her fear.

But she wasn't doing a very good job. "What's wrong? That look on your face—" He stopped as he figured it out himself. "Oh, Audrey, you don't think . . ." He looked down at the clippings and scissors. "That's why you look like you had a narrow miss with a shark."

"I didn't . . . it just took me by surprise." But the truth was, she was scared to death. What was he doing with newspaper that had been hacked at with a scissors?

"Honey, it's yesterday's paper, Thursday's food section."

She blinked. And it registered. "Coupons."

He picked up the folded newspaper and opened it. Inside were several grocery coupons held together with a paper clip. "I was killing time cutting them when the meeting started, just tossed them in here."

"I'm sorry." She felt like a heel. "Of all fetishes to have right about now."

He put his hand on her shoulder. "I understand. I'd be jumpy, too."

She tried to shake it off by changing her interest to the Tiffany box. "Gonna show me what's in there?"

He found the corkscrew. "Not till Christmas

morning," he joked, "which should be in about two hours."

She kissed him on the cheek and hurried back to the master bath. Where her bubbles were waiting. And the big bottle of perfume she'd sniffed before she decided to play Sherlock. She dabbed some on her sweaty T-shirt. And laughed. But the laughter didn't erase the fact that she was shaken to the core.

The observer couldn't believe what he was seeing. It was her. Audrey. Standing in a sweaty T-shirt with her nose glued to the top of what looked like a Waterford crystal decanter filled with scotch. No, perfume, of course. As she stood there, hair a mess, dabbing the perfume onto the sweaty cotton material under her arms, under her breasts, he thought she never looked more beautiful.

But what was going on? It didn't take a rocket scientist to figure out that the man in her kitchen was her boyfriend—*fiancé,* he thought—and that they were there together, planned, not happenstance or an accident. Yes, of course, that explained the food, it was all planned, they were spending the weekend there, cut off from the rest of the world. Christ, he thought, with a shiver of sexual feeling, they're there to *fuck.* If that didn't beat all!

He moved his eyes back to the kitchen. The observer watched the man carefully place a corkscrew next to two bottles of wine. Then he set what looked like a side of salmon on a white fish-shaped platter, and lined it with crackers. He seemed not to know where anything was, for every time he went to find something—forks, pumpernickel bread—he rummaged around forever. But that made sense: he'd probably never been there before. They must have brought all the grub with them.

The telescope framed him pulling out a bottle of champagne—Dom Pérignon, the amazing lens told him—and opened it. The cork blew off, right through the plastic panel covering the fluorescent lights in the kitchen, and stayed up there. The man jumped at the explosion, then started laughing as he realized what had happened. He reached up and pushed a cracked piece of plastic back into the ceiling, and then, realizing some champagne had bubbled up over the stem of the bottle, bent down and licked it off the granite countertop. Then he reached and scratched his balls, grabbed two glasses and the bottle, and disappeared again.

The telescope found Audrey before the boyfriend did. Facing the window, she crossed her arms, reached down to grasp the sides of the bottom of her T-shirt, and pulled it up and off her body. His scope fixed on her firm, voluptuous breasts, made to look even larger by the tan line of her bikini. He was a tit man, always had been. These were the most beautiful God created, and he would do anything if he could . . .

He felt a pang of guilt. He had no right to violate her like this. He told himself to turn off the scope, but he kept on watching. She pulled her panties off with hooked thumbs. He gasped for breath. Bare naked in front of him, she was like an apparition, the appearance on earth of an angel, breathtaking and overwhelming. He found the telescope shaking from his excitement.

She stepped into the water and slithered down, almost out of sight (thank God he was two floors higher), into the bubbles, which were rising from the swirling water. He held his breath thinking what it would be like to be there with her, kneeling there, washing her soft shoulders, her smooth armpits where she'd sweated so, gently rubbing the loofah over the flesh, and then moving closer to kiss there, to taste her, to feel the warmth of her skin on his lips . . .

And then the chef appeared, standing at the side of the tub with the bottle raised in one hand, the glasses in the other. Shit. The observer was jealous. Mark—that was his name—had no right walking in on their private moment. He wished she had locked the door. Then she could bathe only for him.

"I just don't have a taste for champagne," Audrey repeated, when Mark questioned her.

"You must be sick," Mark said. "You've never turned down champagne."

She couldn't tell him about the baby, not yet. It

had to come naturally. And she was afraid to drink even a drop of alcohol. She wasn't sure how soon you were supposed to stop drinking and smoking and stuff like that, but she rarely smoked and wasn't about to take chances with booze. "I'm thirsty for water."

He looked dumbfounded. "Water."

"Water."

"You *are* sick."

She grinned. "Champagne doesn't appeal to me right now, that's all."

"I destroyed the kitchen ceiling for this bottle, and you want water."

"Kitchen ceiling?"

"Don't ask." He turned to the marble vanity and set the glasses down. He ran water until it was icy cold and dipped one glass into the stream. Then he poured himself a glass of sparkling amber champagne, handed her the glass of water, and they toasted.

The observer knew what was going to happen next. And he was jealous. He wanted to be the fiancé. He wanted her to reach up and yank down *his* boxer shorts, touch him there, play with him, and then move toward the tub, spilling the champagne down his hairy chest, watch it run down his belly, over the firmness of his gym-manufactured abdomen, down over his swelling penis and into the bubbles floating in a cloud around her breasts, climb into the water with her, his mouth finding hers, kissing, laughing, loving. Which is just what they did.

He couldn't take it anymore. Rage coursed through him. He knew he had no right to feel this way, but it didn't matter. He couldn't stand it. This was the woman he was in love with, and it hurt too much to keep watching. Instead, he had to do something about it. He turned off the telescope, shut the lens cover. He moved away from his desk, clicked off the light, grabbed his backpack, and left the apartment.

He knew the only thing that would rid himself of this guilt. He had a craving that needed to be fulfilled. It was time that he did something about it.

It was now or never.

The security truck moved slowly past the construction gates at 8:40 P.M. The two bozos inside the cab paid little attention to the building they were supposed to be protecting. After all, what was the point in guarding a place that billed itself as "the most secure condominium complex in the world"? Hell, nobody was even living there yet, so why would someone break in?

As soon as the truck rounded the corner, the man who'd been hiding in the shadows crossed directly in front of the locked gates. He stood still for a moment, under the swaying palm trees planted to frame the entrance to the building, assessing the situation both left and right. No one was visible; nothing stirred. Someday this area of Honolulu would be hopping, but tonight it was dead.

The lock on the gate was a cinch to open. And why not? It was the stuff on the inside that would be the problem. The man closed the gate, relocking it. To get in, you had to be an insider. And he was. And he knew she was up there. That was incentive enough to accomplish what he'd thought about for a very long time.

He found the construction trailer, really two motor-home-sized units joined together, fed by computer and electrical cables that looked like tentacles protruding from the sides. There was an intricate control panel on the secure door, accessible only by a specially coded magnetic card. If you didn't have one, there was absolutely no way you could ever enter the trailer without ripping it apart. But that would not be necessary tonight; the man pulled a plastic card from his shirt pocket, ran it in front of the flat black access panel, and presto, red letters appeared atop the panel which said: INPUT DIGITAL CODE ON KEYBOARD. No problem. He punched in seven numbers, followed by the star key and then HG, letters that had to be entered after every input, presumably, he thought, because they were Hiram Goh's initials. It took a few seconds while the information ran through the processor, and then, like magic, the letters said: ENTRY APPROVED. The door lock snapped. He was inside.

* * *

Audrey rose from the tub, looking down to see the bubbles swirling around the fast-sucking drain, and reached for a huge, fluffy white towel—but then stopped herself. There was something she wanted to try, something that had fascinated her from the first moment she set foot in the model apartment: the body dryer. Mrs. Yee had sampled what it could do, but with clothes on it served no purpose other than to remove wrinkles.

Audrey thought the concept was a hoot, kind of like a car wash for the bod. In the corner of the master bath were gold-plated pipes lined on each side of an alcove the size of a person, into which you walked, stood, and pressed a button—or simply spoke to the computer, uttering the word *Dry*. She did just that, dripping wet, and in a moment she felt what seemed like an enormous hair dryer gone berserk blasting hot air over every inch of her body. Sure enough, in moments she was crisp—except for a few private areas where she needed the towel to pat the dampness, and her hair. Thank God it hadn't done her hair, for she knew the kind of frizzy do it would have created. She had always dried her soft, silky hair naturally.

"Champagne now?" Mark said, his still damp body wrapped only in a towel, poking his head in. When he saw she was bare naked he perked up, and added, "Well, hello."

She wrapped the towel around herself, fastening it above her breasts. "Hi. And no, water's fine."

"Took my shower. Is it time to dress for dinner? Don't want to put on the monkey suit before I have to."

"Rather wear the birthday suit, huh?" she joked.

"I think we should get drunk and play." He was still pushing the champagne.

"I can play without getting drunk." She squirted some gel into her hands and ran her fingers through her hair. "And I object to that. I've never been 'drunk' in my life."

"How about Eric Leiberman's wedding?"

"I wasn't drunk."

Mark nodded. "Yes you were. I was. He was."

"The bride was. God, she was smashed."

"She wet her pants."

"Poor thing. I felt so sorry for her. And him. We were all a little giddy."

"How are they doing?"

She smiled. "Got a postcard from Istanbul. Extended the honeymoon."

"Guess it's working for them." He leaned against the marble counter. "Where do you want to go?"

She gulped. "When?"

"When we get married."

"Huh?"

He stared at her in the mirror. "Why do you

look so dumbstruck? We've been talking about getting married for a long time."

She was hopeful. "But we . . . we never pin it down."

And he wasn't about to do it now either. But this was more than they'd ever discussed. "So where do you want to go? Paris? Rome? Rio?"

"Cebu."

"Philippines? Your dad built a resort there, didn't he?"

"No. I'm just intrigued by it."

"How about someplace cold? I mean, we live on an island. Let's expand our world."

She smiled. "Like?"

"Switzerland. Iceland. Alaska, even."

"We'll go around the world, hot to cold to hot." She kissed him again.

But it troubled him. "What's wrong? I know when your heart's in a kiss, and that was missing something."

She shrugged. "I have a lot on my mind."

"We're here for just that reason. Spill."

She took a deep breath. And went for the brass ring. "Mark, when are we going to set a date for the wedding?"

"Soon," he answered, without missing a beat. But it was somehow too expected. He watched her face fall. "I mean it, soon."

"That's what you always say."

He came close and playfully licked her chin, brought his fingertips up to the top of her towel, and unfastened it expertly. The towel sank to her feet. Then he took her jaw in the same hand and held it as he brought his lips to hers. "Tonight," he whispered, with an air of promise and certainty, "we'll talk about it tonight."

She closed her eyes, wanting to believe him with all her heart. But all she could picture was a pair of scissors and words cut from newspaper and she shivered.

The construction elevator was a rackety thing, and the sole passenger riding it worried about that as he passed the seventh floor, the eighth, worried that someone might notice it rising and call the authorities. Yet he was almost there, with her, in her arms. He'd set out to do this at seventeen years of age. It had been ten whole years. He trembled with excitement that he was so close, after all this time.

It stopped at twenty-two. He opened the doors and emerged onto the floor beneath the completed apartment, where he knew something the two occupants above him did not: he could get in this way. Residence Twenty-three was locked tight until Monday, but someone could crawl through the A/C duct from the unfinished twenty-second floor. All it took was a little know-how, strong arms, and an obsessive desire.

He found the grate and reached up, pulling it off. It was only a construction filter, easily pried free. He stood on a ladder that was conveniently nearby, right on the top, and grabbing with his arms, hoisted himself up and into the duct. It was dark, but he'd brought a little flashlight clipped to his jeans. And a backpack filled with essential items he would require. It lit the way. He was on his way upstairs, where, through the ductwork, he could already hear classical music.

Mark's hungry lips pressed into hers as his hands ran up and down her back, from gently brushing her buttocks to holding her shoulders tightly. Making love had erased the image of scissors and pasted threats; she was lost in the magic of the moment. Her breasts felt like steel against the hairs on his chest and below, pressed against the V of her pelvis, his erect penis moved with exquisite sensations as she undulated back and forth with the music. Her glow was made all the more golden by the fact, still secret, that she was carrying life within her, and that their love had produced it.

Mark pulled away. "I'm close," he whispered, "and I'm not going to waste it like this."

She smiled, agreeing. "We have all weekend."

"Mmmmm." He closed his eyes.

She reached down and touched him, wrapping her fingers around him, and then said, "Just stay like this till later."

He laughed. "Being near you, it'll be easy." Then he pulled his towel back around himself, adjusting his cock upward. "I'll go dress . . . slowly."

"Meet you out there for appetizers. I'm starving."

He left.

She wiped the perspiration from her face, and other more private areas of her body. Then she faced the mirror and reached out to draw a glob of creamy lotion from the dispenser built into the marble. And she began to massage the honey-scented cream into every inch of her body.

Directly above her, unseen and unheard over the Vivaldi, a man's eyes peered down through the grate. He watched from that vantage point as she rubbed the cream into her breasts, shoulders, arms. She sat on the stool and massaged it into her feet and legs, up her thighs, then stood up to look back into the mirror to do her butt. He thought it was much like that first time in Makena, when he peered from the top of the bluff down to the sandy cove in which she was lying. He lay flat against the cold metal of the duct, his body pressed to it, his penis in the same state Mark's had been, rubbing in slow rhythm against the cold silvery new metal. She was the most beautiful vision he'd ever seen. And this time there was no bully named Lawrence to interrupt.

When she finished and left the bathroom to dress, turning the lights down to a soft glow, he waited until he was sure she wasn't coming back.

Then he unfastened the grate with his Swiss Army knife. He was careful not to let it fall, to lift it into the duct and set it next to the opening. He was ready to enter.

But he'd made a foolish mistake. He had to turn around. He couldn't very well enter the room headfirst. He would fall and kill himself. His feet were behind him, no way to switch position in the tight space. He had to crawl backward, all the way to the junction where he'd made the turn to the bathroom.

When he had accomplished it and slid backward to the open register grate above the master bathroom, he realized that he wasn't sure if she was back down in the room or not. He waited a moment, listening. There was no sound of perfume bottles being set down or towels being hung up to dry. So he moved back a few inches or so, flipped over onto his back, and let his feet drop from the ceiling.

Audrey looked in the mirror in the dressing room. She held the dress she'd chosen in front of her, thought it looked like a million bucks, but her hair bothered her. Too flat. That was the one real problem being Chinese, that fine, flat hair. Maybe a brush would do the trick, a slight teasing, and a little spray. She hung the dress back up and walked back to the bathroom.

Standing at the mirror, she fished her brush from her overnight kit and gave it a sweep through her hair. Grabbing a bottle of spray, she spritzed lightly. It looked pretty good. She stood back a few feet, checking it from the sides. She didn't see, just two feet above her head, the pair of boots dangling from the ceiling.

When the man realized she was down there again, the feet rose into the ceiling, and just in time, too, for as she reached for the light switch, she would have seen his dangling legs. She looked up, around at all the gleaming marble and brass and white towels and robes, and doused the light so it was all black.

Then she dressed.

Across town, at the Honolulu Police headquarters, Detective Jules Gordon stared at the business card that a cop had just given him. It was ivory in color, silky in texture, embossed and expensive. But then it should be. Victoria Towers was probably the most pricey high-rise in the world. "This was the only thing on them?"

"Woman was completely clean," the cop explained, referring to the two dead bodies found at the airport. "He was, too, except for this card in his right front pocket."

"Sloppy," the detective said.

"Pardon me, sir?"

"That the guy who popped them missed it." The detective tapped the exquisite card on the desk. "Fingerprints?"

"Got clean ones. We're running them now."

"Get back to me the minute you hear something."

The cop nodded and left the room.

The detective leaned back in his chair and reached for the phone. He dialed the home number listed on the card, knowing it would be futile at this hour to call the work number. The phone rang four times, and then an answering machine picked up. He listened to the pleasant female voice and then obeyed the instructions, talking after the beep. "Audrey," he said in a warm, fatherly voice that worked well for him in situations like this, "this is Detective Jules Gordon of the Honolulu Police. We are investigating a double homicide, and you might be able to help us out here. When you get this message, please call me at . . ."

Chapter Thirteen

His heart was beating through his chest. He waited to be sure, completely sure this time. The lights were off so he'd be descending to pitch-blackness, but that was less risky than coming down where he could be seen. He swung his feet down again, then his thighs, then his butt, and then, as he gripped the sides of the opening with his hands, he dropped into the bathroom.

His feet would have thudded on the marble floor, but he landed on a thick white rug that absorbed some of the sound. The gear in his back-pack clattered, too. He froze for a moment just to be sure, and then breathed deeply. She hadn't heard him. Thank God for the music playing.

He moved to the door with careful steps. He could see her down in the sumptuous dressing room, getting into what looked like a slinky evening dress. He'd have to wait till she was gone before he could make his next move. But there were worse places he could be trapped. He sat on the edge of the marble tub, feeling the last of the disappearing bubbles that had caressed her body. He lifted them in his hand, blew them across the room. There was enough light coming from the cracked door to let him see what he was doing. He touched the towel that had dried the private places of her body, pressed it to his face and drank in her scent. He was in rapture again.

But he had work to do. He carefully set the backpack on the marble counter, stood on a makeup stool to put the vent cover back over the hole which he'd come through, then took off his gloves so he could type on the computer keyboard in the next room. He needed to tap into HAL.

He peered around the corner carefully, and was relieved to see that she had left the master suite altogether. He grabbed his backpack, hurried in, sat on the chair by the computer, and started to tell HAL what he wanted him to do.

Melba Goh sat alone at her dining-room table, servants cowering in the corners, not wanting to incur her rage. She snapped her fingers, and a frightened girl quickly fetched her the telephone. She had waited till nine, and now she felt like a fool. Why had she thought Audrey would obey her and come to dinner? She dialed Bobbi's apartment. Her machine answered on the fourth ring. Aunt was about to hang up, but she heard Bobbi's voice suddenly, "Hello, hello?"

"Roberta, Melba Goh here." Her phone manner

was every bit as charming as her everyday demeanor. "Is Audrey with you?"

"Hold on, don't say a word!" Bobbi ordered.

Melba waited what seemed forever. Then she said, "I don't understand why you cannot answer my question."

"Shhh! We have to be silent for it to stop recording. Don't talk."

Melba waited impatiently, tapping chopsticks against the edge of a gold-rimmed soup bowl. Finally she heard a distant beep, and Bobbi said, "Okay, all clear. I just hate it when a whole conversation gets taped."

"Where is my niece?"

"Not with me."

"She was to dine with me. She has not come home. I need to reach her."

Fat chance, Bobbi thought. "Don't have a clue."

"Yes, you do."

That was true. Bobbi did have a clue. But Melba Goh would be the last person she'd tell it to, for if anyone were not welcome to interrupt Audrey and Mark, it was Aunt. She had guessed that they simply went to the Halekulani and checked in under an assumed name and wanted to be left alone. So she told Aunt what the plan had been, which wasn't a lie at all. "She was supposed to go to Lanai with Mark."

"Thank you," Melba said, seething, and promptly hung up.

Melba dialed the Manele Bay Hotel on Lanai. It

was an easy island on which to find someone, for there were only two hotels of any quality. Audrey would be staying at the Bay or at the Lodge. The girl looked up the reservation, and yes, it was made for the Lodge, and she could transfer the call. Melba waited. When she learned from the young man who answered the phone at the Lodge at Koele that Miss Goh had a guaranteed reservation but had not yet checked in or canceled, she left an urgent message for her to call as soon as she arrived. But when Melba hung up, she knew that had been pointless. Audrey would not call her. Especially with *him* there to fuel the fire. But she needed to get those papers back from her.

She picked up the phone again, and as she asked for the number for Hawaiian Airlines, she rapped her chopsticks against the soup bowl so hard it nearly cracked.

Audrey surmised that Mark was still in the guest bedroom when she saw the door still closed. She adjusted the lighting in the living room to the perfect romantic setting, lit some candles, then went to the kitchen, where the appetizers were set out on the slab of granite that made up the island. Mark had done a good job. He was very domestic for a bachelor, probably because, she thought, his mother had produced cooking shows for the Public Broadcasting station in Boston. And he had taste.

She checked the oven, touching the roasting

lamb with her fingers. All she had to do was throw the greens into a salad bowl. Perfect.

She took the salmon and crackers into the living room and set them on the coffee table. "Mark?" she called. No answer. She wondered what he was doing in there for so long. "Mark, you about ready?" Maybe he couldn't get his cuff links in.

Then she heard a rapping. It sounded like a pipe banging, but then she realized it was a knocking on a door. She went to the guest bedroom hall. It was coming from the closed door. "Mark? What's wrong?"

"Door's locked."

"Unlock it, then. It locks from inside."

"I've tried. Nothing works."

"What?" Audrey tried it from outside. No go. And she knew it was useless to attempt pulling it open, or even breaking it down, for the doors were part of the security, filled with metal. "Wait there a minute."

"Where do you think I might go?"

He had a point. She went to the nearest computer panel, in the servant's room in the guest bedroom arena, and called up the security program for that part of the apartment. Sure enough, Guest Bedroom Two had a "door locked" entry. HAL's mistake, she knew, or hers or even Bobbi's. But Mark had gotten in. How could Bobbi have misprogrammed it earlier? It had to be HAL. She overrode it with her personal code, and she heard Mark shout, "It opened!"

She met him in the hall. Dressed in his tuxedo, he looked dashing. She loved a man in formal wear, even if he was a little exasperated about having been locked in a room for twenty minutes. "Yes, twenty minutes, I was dressed and all, kept shouting and pounding—"

"I was dressing, you can't hear in there."

"Shit."

"You're fine. It's the computer. It's a wonder it doesn't just heave us all out the windows."

"Wonderful thought." Then she glanced into the room behind him. The bed was strewn with coat hangers, plastic, the wet towel, the clothes he'd been wearing, even the wretched newspaper and scissors. The Tiffany box sat in the midst of everything now, and she studied it this time. It was a little larger than one that held a ring, but if you wanted to surprise someone by making them think they were about to open a watch or a pin, this would be the perfect size.

He drank her in with his eyes. "You look sensational."

"I forgot cologne!" she cried.

"You smell great."

"That's just body lotion, it'll wear off."

"It's fine."

"I need a splash of the stuff in the master bath over it." She'd always loved Chanel. "Meet you in the living room." And she was off again.

* * *

The man observing the computer screen in the master bedroom saw that she had opened Mark's cage. He was amused. He never counted on having fun with them—well, he'd never counted on being here, actually, especially being here with her and her boyfriend, an added treat. He could drive them both a little crazy if he wanted to, controlling the evening by this panel, but that would take time away from his time with her. But they had till Monday morning, didn't they?

Suddenly, his ears perked. Someone was coming down the hall. It was her, he could hear the heels clicking on the travertine. He touched a key. Snap. The master bedroom door locked.

"Oh, no!" Mark heard Audrey cry. "Damn."

"Now what?"

She appeared. "Now the master bedroom is locked."

"Oh, so what? Come join me." He offered his hands from the sofa.

"I want that cologne."

"I'm just going to lick it off you anyhow, so I don't see the point."

She smiled, gave up on it, and sank into the rich down-filled chenille next to him. His arm came up around her, and his lips pressed against her cheek. "This is our Lanai," she said.

"Yes, it is, and nicer, too, though I miss the sound of the waves."

"I can check with HAL. He probably has that available."

Mark laughed. "We'll skip it."

"So, we have to do what we were going to do on Lanai."

"What's that?" he inquired.

"Talk."

"Ah." He thought about it a moment. "But first we have to do something else we were going to do on Lanai."

"And what's that?"

"Dance."

As Mark took Audrey in his arms and they danced in the living room, the intruder made his way to the guest wing, toward the room where he'd locked Mark in. On the way he spied the unlocked vault. It amazed him, seeing it open like this, the entry to God-only-knew what riches and secrets. He stepped inside it, ran his fingers over the big chair, the fine wooden table, and saw the file Audrey had been studying: *The Kaneohe Project*. He was more interested in another one, and it took only a moment for him to find it, a whole file cabinet filled with documents labeled *Makena Villas*. He quickly scanned the papers until he found the one he was looking for, a letter from Melba Goh to her brother Hiram, strictly confidential, spelling out just what they needed to do to save themselves from prison time. As he started to read it, it took his breath away. He was unsteady, had to sit in the chair for a moment to catch his breath. Tears welled up in his eyes. This was his confirmation.

He took the file with him to the bedroom in which he'd locked Mark. He turned the lock after he entered, just in case. He saw the mess of clothes lying on the bed, and reached for the slacks Mark had been wearing, feeling the wallet in the back pocket. He pulled it out, opened it, and studied everything—from gym card to a photo of Audrey, his Amex Platinum to a Bank of Hawaii business card with Phyllis handwritten on it, along with her home phone number, which he found very interesting—and put it all back the way he found it. Mark was carrying one hundred and twenty dollars in cash, all in new twenties. He must have recently hit a cash machine. His driver's license was about to expire.

Then the intruder spied something even more interesting. The box from Tiffany. He sat on the bed, untied the little string around it, and lifted the top. What he saw surprised him; it wasn't what he expected at all. *What an asshole,* he thought. He lifted it out and studied it. It was beautiful, he'd admit that. But then he had an idea . . .

Chapter Fourteen

Mark pressed his cheek against Audrey's as they danced to Diane Schuur and B. B. King, a slow rhythm and blues number. The reflection of the fireplace flames danced on the ceiling. "I love holding you," he said.

"Mmmm. I love being held. You know, everyone thinks I'm so tough, that I'm like Aunt Melba—"

"No one thinks *that*."

She pulled away slightly and looked at him. "Sure they do. Not as severe, but I'm perceived as being driven, ruthless, career oriented."

"That's what attracted me to you."

"I'm serious. But I want something more than I want all that."

"Which is?"

"A family, a good husband who is also a good dancer—"

"That's necessary."

"—who will be a good father."

He pulled her toward him again. And said nothing.

She gave it another try. "Reading about my father before was difficult for me."

"Because he's gone?"

"Because I'm seeing the truth." She stopped moving in his arms. He stopped as well. "And it's disturbing."

"I'm sorry. If you don't want to know this stuff, why not let it rest with him?"

She sat down in front of the fire. Dancing had lost its appeal suddenly. "I can't. I need to see things clearly, about Aunt, the past, you."

"Me?"

"You. Us."

"I see."

"I think I've blinded myself for a long time because Hiram Goh was my dad, you know? And I overlooked just how cruel and cold Aunt really is. I've got to wake up and face reality."

"You think you're wrong about me, too?"

"No. I mean, I hope not."

"Hope not?" Mark looked hurt. "Are you not sure you love me?"

"Oh, no, I love you, I love you very much. What I'm not sure of is how well I know you."

The intruder tied the ribbon around the Tiffany box just the way he'd found it. He stood up and laughed, tickled at the thought of what was going to happen when she opened it. Then he opened the closet and stepped in. The room was the size of the living room in most apartments, with seemingly miles of rods and baskets and drawers. He knelt in the middle of the far wall, the wall that faced toward the center of the building, toward the elevator shaft and service units, an unseen area where the guts of the building—the wires and pipes and inner workings—came together. He pulled out a measuring tape and measured from the floor up to a height of precisely fifty-three inches. Then he fished a hammer out of his backpack and began to jab the claws into the drywall. He did this again and again, as swiftly as he could so as not to make noise—the place was soundproof, but not completely so—and thereby ruin his plan. After six direct hits in an even line, he did the same running vertically to the floor, three feet apart. He pulled out a small chisel, lightly tapped it to sink it into the Sheetrock, and presto, the whole panel of drywall just fell into his arms, exposing a dark space into which he shined his flashlight and smiled.

There was now a gaping hole in the guest bedroom closet wall. Then the intruder came back through it, but did not set the piece of drywall back over it. He instead went back to the bedroom, unlocked the door, pulled the hammer from his equipment belt once again, and stood behind the door, the weapon ready in his hand, waiting.

"It was the Kaneohe papers that upset you, not the newspaper," Mark said to Audrey.

She nodded. "And more. I read something about this building I didn't know."

"What's that?"

"You know how seven of the apartments were presold by Father in Hong Kong?"

"Yes. I did the mortgages, remember?"

"Yes. So, you knew as well?"

He didn't know what she meant. "Knew what?"

"What was really going on?"

He shrugged, indicating he didn't have a clue. "Tell me."

"People in Hong Kong wanted to get their fortunes out because of the takeover. Some were smart and began doing that ten years ago, but others waited too long, until it was impossible. It's illegal to just walk all your money out of Hong Kong, and now it's even tougher with the Chinese rulers watching."

"So?"

"So, the seven families paid twelve million each for these apartments."

He nodded. "I know."

"But they didn't really," she said. "They only paid six million."

He tried to joke. "Always said they were overpriced."

She didn't laugh. "You know all this, don't you?"

"The mortgages were for various amounts," he admitted, "none over one or two million, if I recall."

"Right. They pay twelve million, the Chinese think okay, they bought an apartment in America for that, nothing they can do about it. It's an allowable investment. But they don't know that the families get six million in cash back when they show up to live here, a secret way to get cash out of China."

"Is that wrong?"

"It goes into your bank—through you as Father's personal banker—and then it comes out of your bank. You never said you laundered dirty money."

He looked uncomfortable. "Why are we going into this?"

"Because the lack of ethics bothers me. And the Kaneohe thing bothers me even more."

Mark said, "Honey, it's business."

She shook her head. "What was my father's take on each transaction?"

"The seven apartments? Two million each."

"My God."

"Which, may I remind you, is probably yours now."

She said, "I don't want it. I was taught to have honor, and this is a sham to launder dirty money."

"And who taught you to have that honor you are being so righteous about? Your father."

She just glared.

"I'm getting more champagne," he said, and walked off to the kitchen.

She got up, too, deciding to make another attempt at getting the perfume. Maybe HAL would let her in this time.

When Mark returned with a fresh glass of champagne, he saw that Audrey was gone. He hoped she'd given up on the line of thought, for it made him very uncomfortable. When she joined him, it seemed she had. But she had an odd, puzzled look on her face. "What's wrong now?" he asked.

She showed him a pair of work gloves.

"I don't understand."

"I don't either. They were in the bathroom."

"So?"

"So they weren't in there when I bathed."

He blinked. "Impossible. You just didn't see them."

"Mark, they were right on the counter!"

He shrugged. "One of the workers must have left them before you locked us in here. Or maybe Bobbi."

She tossed one into his lap. It was huge. He saw her point.

"No," she said emphatically, "I know they weren't there when I finished bathing."

He started to laugh. "This is ridiculous."

"Someone's been following me, Mark. Someone made my bed this morning while I was on the lanai—"

"And you think he's here now?" Mark laughed. "Come on, Audrey, get a grip."

"I'm scared, Mark."

"Honey, you're just unnerved by the scissors thing."

"All of it, the notes, the letters, the missing key, that horrible scene we saw on TV."

He put his arm around her. "We're locked in here, no one else can get in or out, we couldn't be in a safer place."

"I'm not sure this was such a good idea."

"Oh, Jesus, nice time to come to that conclusion."

She was growing more and more upset. "None of this is going the way I'd planned. I thought I was going to find something loving from Father in the safe, something to cherish. Instead I read he's a crook. And I learn that you were in on it."

"Christ."

"Aunt and Father taught me values, but they were hypocrites because they didn't live up to them themselves."

"I don't know a successful businessman who does," Mark stated.

"Are you kidding me?" She meant it.

"Honestly." He did, too.

She was feeling more and more uncomfortable by the moment. She felt more removed from him than she ever had, on a night when she wanted to be feeling closer than ever. She heard a chime from the kitchen that told her that the roast was done, but she didn't care about eating anymore. She was getting a glimpse into a side of Mark she'd never known. "Tell me more."

"More about what?"

"You."

"Audrey, come on."

"No, I mean it. I want to know. I think you admire people like my father, even when you know they cheat and lie. I think you have little concern for the things that count."

"What counts?" He was getting argumentative, probably reacting to her tone. "Morals? Integrity? Honesty? Yes, in personal relationships, but I don't believe those are virtues in business."

"Screwing people is okay?"

"Being successful at the expense of others is okay, and yes, people can be amoral in business, have to be at times."

Mark was silent for a moment as he sipped from his glass of champagne, as if to give him strength. Then he opened up. "I'll tell you what I said the 'important' question I wanted to ask you on Lanai was."

Audrey held her breath. Was he going to ask her to marry him now?

She didn't need to worry. What he said astonished her. "I came up with a way that you and I could profit from the sales here, in this building, to start a venture on the Big Island. We could siphon off some money the way your dad did in hiding the Hong Kong cash, all perfectly legal, just using money that would eventually be paid back to make us a small killing right now."

Audrey could barely believe her ears. Not only had he just told her he approved of the kind of underhanded dealings her father and Aunt made their fortune on, but he wanted to do one himself, with her help. "That's what you wanted to tell me on our romantic weekend?"

"Yes." He acted as if it were the perfect thing to suggest. He wasn't the least bit attuned to the fact that she was so disappointed she was on the verge of tears.

"I thought you were going to ask me to marry you," Audrey blurted out.

It hung in the air for a long moment. Mark slugged down the rest of his champagne. "I was going to tell you I think we should not mess with a good thing."

"What?" Her voice was incredulous.

"I like what we have now."

"That means you don't ever want to get married?"

"Never say never." He grinned.

"Tell me what you feel!" she almost screamed.

"Why do you have to push the issue?"

"Push? We've been dating over two years!"

"So why ruin what we have? Everyone gets married and then it goes to hell. I don't want that to happen. I'm comfortable the way we are."

"I'm not."

"I see that."

"What about kids?"

"What about them?"

The oven beeped again. "I want them."

Mark said, "Aren't we going to eat?"

"Screw eating."

"I'm finally being honest. That's what your integrity wants, right? I'm not ready for marriage, and I hate kids, okay? Even if we married, having children may not be an option, and you'd have to agree to that, and I doubt you would."

But I'm carrying your child! She was aching inside, probably from the tears of the tiny unloved and unwanted baby. Her own tears suddenly flooded her face.

Mark hugged her, "Honey, honey, come on, I didn't want to make you cry. It's just that female stuff kicking in because you're vulnerable after losing your dad; it's understandable." He caressed her shoulders. "Audrey, listen, I love you, you love me, we have a great sex life, I support you breaking from Aunt if that's what you want, I'd love you to live with me, and you'll be safe and together we'll be a marvelous successful team."

Team? She wanted a husband and father to her baby and he wanted a team? What hurt so was that it was clear that he meant every word of it.

And she knew now, in that moment, that she would never marry this man. She was carrying his child, and she was trapped with him twenty-three stories above Honolulu. She would just make the best of it, and read those magazines she'd bought at the Safeway.

But when he got up to get the gift he'd bought her that afternoon, something to make her "feel better," she curled up on the sofa and dissolved into tears. She had never felt so lonely and miserable in her life.

The cell phone sat on the vinyl dinette chair in Room 41 at the Tahitian Princess, a small Honolulu hotel near the beach that had seen better days. The gorilla in the shower, who could not hear the phone ringing, looked like the perfect clientele for the place. This was a dive, where he could certainly keep a low profile. On the bed was the small suitcase, opened, with his chauffeur's uniform and cap lying inside. To the left of the dust-encrusted plastic orchid in a vase on the table was his gun. The television was on, as it had been since the 5 O'Clock News, with that pretty Connie Suzuki updating the airport story every ten minutes. A can of Bud was on top of the television set, almost as warm as it was outside. The air conditioner rattled as it circulated frigid, unfiltered air around the tawdry room.

When the water stopped, the man finally heard the telephone. He'd been expecting this call, fearing it actually. He thought about not answering it, ignoring it for a while, till the anger wore off. But he was supposed to fly back tomorrow, and so perhaps it was best to face the music now. Let him rant a little. He'll get over it when he sees it's going to blow over soon. He wiped his face with the threadbare towel, then flung it over his big shoulder, turned the TV down, and answered. "Yeah."

The voice was measured and slow. "It made the TV here already." And it sounded anything but happy.

"Where are you?"

"Macao. Where do you think I am?"

"News travels fast."

"Bad news travels even faster."

"What they saying?"

"They're saying how could some stupid fuck of a hit man be so motherfucking stupid as to toss the cadavers into a catering truck!"

"The Dumpsters were locked."

The voice was seething. "There are mountains there on Oahu you could have pitched them off, there's an ocean to dump them in—sharks like old Chinese for lunch, some proverb says. There's nice soft earth out in the rain forests to bury them in. You could have dug the fucking grave with your hands. But no, you try to serve them for dinner on Singapore Airlines." He sputtered. "And I *like* Singapore Airlines. I fly them."

"Nobody's gonna get wise."

"I figured I'd read something about it maybe a month from now when some arm washed up on a shore or when some naked hiker found the decomposed bodies in the ravine. No, the day it happens, mere fucking hours later, it's in my face."

"Chill, boss."

"Goddamned moron."

"Boss, it's gonna be big tonight, it's gonna be raining money on Waikiki."

"Yeah, well, after this risk, it had better."

"It'll take their minds off the other stuff."

"You positive no one saw you?"

"Nobody."

The voice, however, sounded no less worried. "You sure she got it in the right position?"

"As good as being inside the vault. It'll take out that entire part of the structure, wham, sideways. It's what should have happened to the World Trade Center had they not fucked it up."

"You should know about fucking things up."

He took a slug of the warm beer and spit it out all over the bed. "Shit."

"What?"

"Nothing."

"All right, now remember, you call me right when it happens; call me from the beach. Things are getting worse here. Stanley Ho wants me outta the casinos. Wan is pushing me out of Macao altogether."

"He's in jail."

"Why would that matter? When you are the biggest gangster in Asia, jail is merely an inconvenience."

"Nobody's got nothing on Pearl River Tung if

they don't get what's in Goh's safe. Tonight, it'll be history." He glanced at the TV screen. Again they were showing the old farts being carted from the catering truck. Didn't they have any other crimes to report in this lousy town?

"What time does it happen?"

"One in the morning on the dot." Then he laughed.

"What's so funny?"

"Think about it. I set it for the middle of the night because I didn't want to hurt anybody. Hah."

Mark entered the bedroom, and out of the corner of his eye he saw something coming down toward his face, but the hammer struck his head so swiftly that he hadn't even time to duck. He collapsed at the feet of the intruder, who immediately dragged him through the bedroom, toward the hole in the closet wall, leaving a thin trail of blood like the drippings of a wet exhaust pipe across the white rug.

Audrey pulled herself into a sitting position. Her world had fallen apart, her dreams, her hopes, her plans. But empty? How could she feel empty when she had life inside her? It was Mark who was empty, and would always be. She felt sorry for him, not for herself. Had she married him, yes, she'd feel sorry for herself, call herself a fool. What she'd done was get the truth in time.

Too many women met guys like Mark, vibrant gym freaks with deep tans and lots of energy, successful young businessmen who were out there to get laid, make money, and never grow up. She was above that.

Something, guts she didn't know she had, some instinct for survival had taken over, and she was suddenly standing tall, knowing that even though she felt terrible, she was better off. She knew the truth now, and you could never argue with that. She would make the best of the rest of the weekend. She would feed him and have fun with him, but she would not make love to him. That attraction was dead, and she would certainly never tell him about the baby. He wouldn't have cared anyhow.

She hurried to the kitchen and looked into the oven. The lamb was crusted with a rich, garlicky crispness, and the potatoes looked to die for. The oven was keeping them at perfect serving temperature. She quickly opened the bag of salad greens she'd bought, dumped some into two bowls, drizzled them with olive oil and balsamic vinegar, and uncorked a bottle of red wine.

As she turned toward the dining room, she realized she had not lit the candles. She would go through with everything as planned. She'd had dinner with a lot of people she loathed. Why not one more? After that, she could lock herself in the vault for the next two days and emerge Monday morning to throw Mark out and start her new life. Hell, maybe if she studied the papers in there closely enough, she could get him sent to prison for embezzlement or something. Someday she would find a man deserving of her, a good man who would also be a loving father and worthy husband.

She found matches, but just as she was about to walk to the dining room to light the tall tapers, she saw that Mark was already doing that. His back was to her as he reached out to put the flame to a wick, and she threw him the finger because she knew he could not see her. He turned the lights in the dining room completely off, so only the candlelight lit the room. She felt terribly ambivalent suddenly, hating him and loving him at the same time, feeling she'd been a fool for not looking deeper all these years, hating admitting that Aunt was right about him, Bobbi had been right about him . . .

She poured two glasses of wine, even though she knew she wouldn't drink hers, then carried them to the dining room. Mark was standing at the windows, looking out at the Pacific. And on her plate was the Tiffany box.

Oh, God! Her heart fluttered. For a moment she wondered if he'd said those cruel things to her only to test her, to see if she'd believe him, to make her feel terrible when she opened the box and found an engagement diamond. She said, "Oh, Mark . . ." Then she put her hands on the box and untied the delicate ribbon. And lifted off the lid.

Her mouth dropped open as she found herself staring at not a ring, not a piece of jewelry of any kind, not anything Tiffany would sell. She was looking at a Cinnabon.

When she looked up at Mark standing there in his tux, and he turned around, she saw that it was not Mark anymore at all.

"Surprise," Ben said with a grin.

Chapter Fifteen

On the twenty-fifth floor of a high-rise building a block away from Victoria Towers, a man opened the double entry doors leading to apartment 2512. He could see the lights of the new structure through the bank of glass that formed the far wall in the sunken living room, and he thought for a moment how breathtaking it would look when it was completed. Then he reached up to the wall and flicked the light switch, bathing the room in white, virtually wiping out the view of Victoria Towers. He set his keys down on the hall table and looked into the mirror above it to see what the humid trade winds had done to his hair. Not much. Too vain, he thought with a laugh. He set his backpack on the floor from where it had hung from the wheelchair handle. Then he looked over his shoulder and talked to Jimmy Stewart. "How vain were *you,* buddy?"

He laughed out loud. Talking to the poster from *Rear Window* was something he often did to pass the time. "Got to keep our faces pretty 'cause our legs sure aren't getting any muscular." Then he felt the grease starting to seep through the bag in which his dinner sat in his lap, and he wheeled down the ramp to his desk.

His desk was his world. On it sat plastic salt and pepper shakers he'd swiped from a restaurant and a stack of napkins for dining in. Which he did a lot, for the kitchen was something he hadn't really learned to conquer in a wheelchair. He wondered if Jimmy had. He laughed at that thought. And at himself. Hey, at least he had humor about his condition. It relieved some of the bitterness, though few might agree with him.

Next to the salt and pepper were a stack of papers, all relating to Victoria Towers, his obsession for the past two years. Then his computer, an IBM wonder he kept upgrading so that the components now bore no relation to what he'd started out with. To the left of that sat his pride and joy, and his problem, his addiction, his guilt machine: his high-powered Meade ETX telescope.

On the wall to the left of the telescope table was a photo that he sometimes found too painful to look at, and other times made him the happiest man in the world. It was of a vibrant woman with blond hair and bright eyes, and a little boy, mop-headed and bursting with life, both of them basking in the joy of his Olympic medal, which, in the photo, he was placing around his son's neck. Four years had passed, and it seemed only yesterday that he finished that slope with a time that shocked even him. Four years had passed since he made that right turn on a snowy night, a decision that had forever altered his life.

He glanced at the other photo on the wall, the picture of Christopher Reeve as *Superman*. It kept him balanced. Whenever he started feeling sorry for himself, all he had to do was look up. Chris had done *Rear Window* as well. He *knew*.

He bit into his teriyaki burger. And spit out the pickle. He always told them no pickles, and he still got them. He thought the guy did it just to annoy him, his best customer. He looked up at a photo of himself in midair, just out of the gate, a still from the CBS video footage of his brilliant winning run. He could feel it right now, feel it in his useless legs, the impact of the snow making contact with his skis, bending his knees just perfectly to absorb the impact, racing downhill . . .

The fries were cold, too. He'd have to stop going to that place, but it was the only fast food around. This part of Honolulu would have Burger Kings on every corner one day, but for now it was no-man's-land.

He wondered if Audrey and her boyfriend were doing it yet. But he wasn't about to look. He knew what would happen, how inflamed he'd become. Christ, he'd thought about it all the way to the burger joint. This was getting more and more obsessive, sicker and sicker. It wasn't like he was a voyeur from birth; before his accident he hadn't even liked porn videos. This was the replacement for what he'd lost. He could no longer get an erection, because he was dead below the waist, and that stirring he'd felt down there his whole life long was missing. But it was still alive in his head. One of his most powerful revelations in the process of learning to live again without his legs—and this from a guy whose life was skiing—was the fact that sex was mostly in the brain. He had the same desire, passion, interest. Which made it all the more frustrating because he could no longer satisfy himself.

He'd moved back home to Hawaii after the accident to be as far from snow as he could possibly get. Park City was where his heart had been, and he hated leaving the beautiful Utah ranch they'd just bought, but he needed to kill all the memories the way the nerves in his legs had been severed. He hadn't wanted to live, much less think about where, but when he arrived home at the ranch—he'd never forget being pushed down that ramp for the first time from the back of a van, like a BarcaLounger arriving from Rooms Express—he knew he could never be comfortable there. He left the next morning, and bought a ticket back to where he was born, to Hawaii. And he'd not been back to the mainland since.

His apartment was a virtual shrine to Victoria Towers, the building for which he'd created the software. It was serendipity, getting that gig. He'd bought into the first Hiram Goh building that had been erected in the old warehouse district, a resale. It was spacious, easy to convert to wheelchair access, had a view of the world, and seemed as unlike their Deer Valley ranch house as would a grass hut. He had already been deeply involved with computers, having devoted college to computer programming to get through with the scholarship that allowed him to ski all the time. It had become his hobby by the time he married Cathy, turning her on to it while she introduced him to her hobby, astronomy. Utah's sky was ripe for plucking stars and comets, and they'd spend hours in the dead of night charting, watching, dreaming. During the day, Dean found himself rewriting computer programs that he found difficult or silly. He sent one back to the company which had issued it, a program about charting moves on a ski slope, and they were so impressed they paid him for the update. One thing led to another, and by the time of the accident, he was creating the software for small office buildings. Victoria Towers was quite a leap.

But a well-placed risk on Hiram Goh's part. They'd met at a party for the opening of the Goh Corporation's second building down there, the one where he now watched the teenager watch Internet porn and masturbate. He'd met Audrey that night, too, although he was sure she'd never remember that. To her he was just another worker, nothing more. His secret was that she was what he lived for.

When he met Hiram in person for the first time,

the man didn't know how to act. Dean found that common. People got so flustered, tried to be so cool, and usually made asses of themselves. They all seemed to want to say they were sorry, but their tongues tied, and usually what they said came out wrong. Either they tried to overcompensate without thinking what they were saying ("So, we'll have to go hiking up Diamond Head sometime!") or they were so condescending ("Are you sure you don't need my help in the bathroom?") that he wanted to just go home and never see another human being again. Hiram had been a fan of his, and quickly found that if Dean could laugh at himself, so could he. He actually called him "Jimmy" because of his *Rear Window* identification, and Hiram always claimed his building, being watched incessantly by Dean, was in "good hands because you don't got good feet." Audrey knew none of this, of course. Or she might have drawn the shades tonight.

He sipped his diet drink—it was tough staying slim when you couldn't exercise like normal people—and finished the greasy fries. He saw the building out there and remembered how he had convinced Hiram to let him have a go at the software, figuring a job like this one would last years and years and be a real challenge besides. The money meant nothing to him. He had what he needed. It was the accomplishment that was important. Almost as good as a downhill win.

He scooped up the hamburger wrappings and

dumped them into the trash can at the side of the big desk. It was full, and he had to push down on things to get them to stay there. He never remembered to empty the trash. He could be a bit of a pig like that. Cathy had complained incessantly, but she had also picked it up. What had Neil Young sung once? *A man needs a maid . . . ?* Would Audrey pick up his junk and dirty underwear and hamburger wrappers? He laughed. Probably toss them in his face.

Audrey. He still felt bad, for he'd become so embarrassed by watching her bathing naked earlier that he had to relieve himself not by going over to the building and asking if he could be her soap (now there was a thought!), but by going out to get dinner. Lousy dinner. He wiped his fingers with one of the napkins, then broke open a Handi Wipe to get the grease off. Probably lard. Maybe that was why the stuff tasted so good.

He dimmed the lights in the apartment till they were almost dark, and turned on the telescope. Victoria Towers came into view, the same room where he'd last invaded her privacy. But she was not there. All it took was a quick sweep of the glass to find her. She looked stunning in a black evening dress. Mark's back was to him, but he could see he was wearing a tuxedo now. *Classy couple, hey, Jimmy?* She seemed to be backing away from him for some reason. Hmmm. She didn't look like she was smiling. He decided to change lenses to see closely. But in doing so, the nose of the telescope moved and focused on the floor below, and when he brought his face back to the eyepiece, he found himself looking at a man standing in his undershorts, a piece of duct tape over his mouth, bound to a steel beam.

He gasped. Sure that he was seeing things, he looked again. Not only was the image more pronounced—he was deep inside the building, but under a work light, which made him clearly visible—this time, but he could see details: the man's eyes were open, blood ran down his face and chest, and he could now see that that face was Mark's.

If that was Mark, who was facing Audrey upstairs in the tuxedo?

The scope went back to the dining room and caught the candles flickering, a blue box on a plate, two glasses of red wine, and Audrey's hand, raised in front of her, as to fend off the man, hold him back, as she stepped backward toward the living room. Dean gasped as she grabbed hold of the handle on one of the French doors, which led to the half-completed terrace which she'd nearly fallen from earlier that day, yanked it open, and stepped out there, hitting something on the computer touchpad before she did, and the door closed after her, and locked. Dean couldn't believe she was going back into the fire, not after what she'd been through earlier. She must have thought the risk was the better choice. He could see her screaming for help from the precarious balcony girders. Only no one could hear her in this deserted part of town.

He shivered, then realized he could do something! He reached to his right and grabbed the phone from where it had been shoved behind the salt and pepper and napkins. He knew the number of the small precinct house near there, for he'd called it several times before, with anonymous tips: 911 worried him because they recorded the calls and he feared he might get into trouble admitting about his telescope. It was the *Rear Window* dilemma that Jimmy had faced. But Hitchcock wasn't directing this tonight, this was real.

"Yeah?" the gruff voice said.

"Who is this?" Dean demanded.

"Officer Holcomb, Alan Holcomb, who's this?"

Dean recognized him as the desk clerk, a slob who no doubt was eating a sandwich and watching moronic television reruns. "There's a woman in jeopardy."

"This Jimmy Stewart?" Obviously the sergeant knew him well.

"This is Dean Carlucci."

"That's what I meant."

"You have to believe me."

"Yeah, yeah, and I just won a Pulitzer prize."

Dean felt the frustration brimming. "Listen to me. A woman is trapped on the twenty-third floor of Victoria Towers—out on the girders—and a man is after her!"

"I hope it's Darlene."

"Who's Darlene?" Dean asked.

"My wife."

"My God."

"And I hope he gets her."

"This is for real!" Dean shouted.

"Jesus," the cop muttered. "What you smoking tonight, Jim?"

"I'm serious."

"That watching could put you in jail, you pervert."

"You've got to help her!"

"Victoria is locked and sealed, and you know that. Go bother somebody else. Hey, I'll give you Darlene's number. She'll talk your head off for hours, might even believe you. Or get some help or something." Click.

Dean had called one too many times, he realized that. At first when he started watching people, he was overzealous. The capper was the time he reported a fire in the next building, which emptied the place but turned out to be an apartment that was being fumigated. The bug bombs looked like smoke to him. No one was going to take him seriously, especially with such an outrageous charge as a woman out on a Victoria Towers girder in the dark of night.

He set the receiver into his lap as he looked through the eyepiece. And he saw what he would have done had he been the man inside the residence wanting to get to her. The guy spoke into HAL's voice-activation microphone. He utilized one of the distress calls which shattered the safety glass of the French door—indeed, the glass just crumbled before Audrey's eyes—and then he reached through and yanked her back into the apartment.

It was at that moment that he realized who the intruder was: Ben Benedict, her favorite electrician. Who knew almost as much as Dean did about the computer system's guts in that building. Fucking nutcase, he knew there was a reason he'd never liked the guy. Fucking psycho!

But now that he knew that, what the hell was he going to do?

"You want to kill yourself?" Ben shouted to Audrey.

"Don't touch me!" Audrey pulled away from him.

"Why are you so upset?" Ben asked gently, giving her a chance to calm down. "We're friends. I thought you'd really enjoy this."

"Enjoy this?" She was incredulous. "Where's Mark? Tell me where Mark is."

"Audrey, calm down."

She had never felt so disoriented. It was as if someone had shattered her and tiny bits of herself were flying in all directions. She tried only to think about Mark. "You're wearing his tux."

"Nice fit, huh?"

"What did you do to him?" she shouted.

"Should have hung him on a meat hook, 'cause that's what he is, a hunk of meat."

"No!"

"Oh, don't worry. He's fine. Let's just say he stepped out for a while."

Her stomach turned over, thinking he had been thrown to his death. "Oh, God."

"Christ, Audrey, I didn't kill anyone! I just put him downstairs so we could have some time together."

"Downstairs?"

"He'll be waiting for you on the twenty-second floor."

Her eyes darted to the gloves sitting on the sofa across the room. "You wore them."

"Nobody's perfect."

She closed her eyes, trying to believe this wasn't happening.

Bobbi Kicherer had just finished painting her nails Positively Peachy when the phone rang. Melba Goh again, she was sure. *"Where's my little Audreeeeeee?"* Bobbi cried in a witch voice right out of *The Wizard of Oz*. She tried picking up the receiver with her palms, but it clunked to the floor. "Sorry, hang on!" she shouted, and got down on all fours to press her ear to the piece of plastic. "Hello!"

"Audrey has not arrived on Lanai," Melba barked without saying hello. "There are no more flights. She did not take the one she was scheduled on. Is she there?"

"Nope." Bobbi rolled her eyes. For this she was contorting herself on the floor?

"I have called Mark's apartment. There is no answer. Is she there?"

"Dunno."

"Where might she be?"

"Shit if I know," Bobbi said, and lifted her head, pressing the button in the cradle with her chin. There. Got rid of her.

She went into the bathroom and turned on the hair dryer to crisp up her paint job. But she worried about Dragon Lady and her zeal to find Audrey. Maybe Bobbi should warn her. No, she and Mark wanted to be left alone. But if Melba found them, it would really ruin their weekend. Knowing Melba, she'd stop at nothing to locate Audrey, and chances were she would figure out Halekulani in due time. Bobbi would risk it. When her nails were dry, she dialed the hotel.

"Good evening, Halekulani."

"Hi. My name is Roberta Kicherer. My colleague Audrey Goh and her fiancé, Mark Carson, are guests there."

"I'll ring them." There was a pause. "Go?"

She spelled it. "G-O-H. Or Carson."

"I'm sorry," the pleasant girl finally said.

Bobbi shrugged. "I didn't think they'd use their real names."

The innocent operator's voice sounded slightly amused. "I see."

"God, how do I find them?" Bobbi thought for a moment. "I know! Mark's cell phone!"

The voice still on the other end of the phone said, "Thank you for calling Halekulani. Good night."

Bobbi was already looking up another number.

Dean frantically typed an urgent message on his computer screen. He told what was happening, asked anyone on the Internet reading it to contact the authorities. He addressed the e-mail to several newsgroups and chatboards, where he knew it would be read instantaneously. But just as he was about to hit SEND, he strained to look into the telescope again, and in doing so pulled the plug out of the wall with the wheelchair's foot rest. "Shit!" he shouted. He tried immediately to reach down to replug the cable, but he couldn't reach it because of the desk. He'd have to get out of the chair, lift himself up with his powerful arms and slide to the floor to replug it. And it would be easier to move to the window, to the side of the desk, so he could grip there—

He stopped himself as he glanced down at the street. Headlights! The security truck was just starting to make its way around the perimeter of the building. That was the quickest way to get help. He probably knew the guys in that very truck. If he hurried, he could get down there and out to the street before the truck was gone. He could roll himself into the middle of the road and flag them down. He glanced up at Chris Reeve. "Give me strength," he said aloud. Then his powerful arms gripped the wheels, and he tore up the ramp with such force that he smacked into the doors of the apartment. Undaunted, he shoved them open, and sped out, not even bothering to close them.

Chapter Sixteen

He slapped the elevator button. It seemed to take forever, but he knew the car arrived in less than forty seconds. The doors opened and he wheeled on. He pressed G and waited. Good, he was moving.

When the doors parted, Dean rolled like a rocket out of the elevator, and he was in luck, for someone was walking through the security doors at that very moment, and he shouted, "Hold the doors, hold the doors!" and blew on through.

Outside, the humid night air hit him, cooler than he'd remembered when he went out to get dinner. He had to maneuver around the usual rock-and-foliage planting area they invariably stuck in front of all of these buildings, but as he did so he could make out that the truck was directly in front of him, passing the building. "Hey!" he shouted, wheeling himself to the street. But as he did so, one wheel hit a palm frond lying on the cement, which acted like a brake. By the time he backed up and turned to his left to avoid it, the truck was passing. "Hey, wait, stop!" But he was too late. The security truck moved on.

He sat there, sweating, exhausted, pissed off. He didn't know what to do. And then he recalled a moment he hadn't thought about in a long time, when a stranger had made a decision the night of his accident, pulling him from a burning car at great risk to himself. You sometimes had to do the impossible, and actually could if you willed it strongly enough. Hadn't he won the gold medal in just that way? Just because he didn't have legs, was that a reason to let a woman be raped or perhaps murdered?

He knew what he had to do.

He summoned courage he long thought dead inside him and wheeled himself back toward his building, but not into the lobby. This time he approached the parking garage gate. He was able to get close enough to the control box to punch in his code. The gate lifted a second later, and he rolled down the ramp to the first level of the subterranean parking structure. If he couldn't get a message out, he would just have to go in himself.

Audrey was trying to figure out just how nuts Ben really was. He was talking like she was the girl of his dreams, but he was obviously some kind of psychopath. She had to get out of this situation, and she knew she would have to outsmart him somehow.

"Come talk to me," Ben said, sitting in the living room playing with his work gloves. "I know dinner's ready; we'll eat soon. I don't want to mess up any of your plans tonight."

She walked over and played along, but keeping a safe distance from him. He had been her friend. It was too crazy to believe he would want to hurt her. "I don't understand this at all. Why did you do this?"

"Do what?" He reached for the salmon. "May I?"

"Sure."

He helped himself. "I didn't really do anything other than surprise you, maybe take advantage of a situation."

"You've been here the whole time? Since before the building locked?"

He shook his head. "Nope. It's not as impenetrable as your brochures make it out to be."

She shivered. "Why?"

"Why not?" He put his hands on the tux lapels and looked around. "Great idea, spending the weekend here."

"You saw me come back?"

He nodded. "With him. And never saw you leave. I just put two and two together, punched my time card, and came back later. What's for dinner?"

She was startled that he was asking. "Leg of lamb. Ben, why did you do this? What do you want?"

"Isn't that what you wanted to know from him?"

She nodded. "Yes."

"Did you find out what a mistake you've been making? I'm on Bobbi's side, Audrey. I hope you realize Mark is just not going to make you happy."

"You think you are?" she blurted.

He just grinned. "You're tough, like your father and Melba. Mark is a putz. Not deserving to be the father of your child."

"I'll be the judge of that."

"I think you already have been. I heard you weeping. I heard his little manifesto about making money and fucking you on the side. I somehow don't think we'll be getting wedding invitations anytime soon."

She closed her eyes. It was all true. "Can I ask you something?"

"Shoot."

She didn't know how to voice it. "Have you wanted me—I mean, have you been in love with me all along?"

"In love with you? I'm not in love with you."

"But you sound jealous of Mark."

"Jealous of Mark? No. Just that I think you deserve better. It never really had anything to do with you, actually."

She was lost. "What didn't?"

"My plan. What I had to do."

"Which is?"

"Revenge."

The word rang inside her head and reverberated like her skull was a bell. *Revenge.* The word in the newspaper clippings. "It was you?" she gasped. "All along, the notes, the warnings, it was you?"

"Put it this way," Ben said, reaching for more salmon and another cracker. "You know how you felt out there on the girder when HAL acted up and locked you out?"

"What?"

"I mean helpless, powerless, your life in someone else's hands?"

She tried to follow him. "Yes. And you saved me."

"I came to your rescue. So you know what it is like to be whisked from utter destruction at the last minute."

"Yes." She waited for more. Nothing. "Ben, I'm still lost."

"My father never knew that feeling. No one saved him, no one rescued him."

"Your father? What are you talking about?"

"My father. The man your father murdered."

The parking-garage gate at Dean's building lifted, and a dark blue, specially equipped van drove up the ramp. Dean's chair was locked into place behind the wheel, controls for acceleration and brakes at his fingertips. He gunned the engine and looked both ways at the street.

All clear. No one around. Well, maybe that might be good, he thought, if someone watched this and called the cops. Maybe then they'd believe him. He drove into the street, went down to the end of the block, and turned around. Then he gunned the engine and peeled rubber, and the van rocketed forward. He braced himself for the imminent crash with the locked construction gates in front of Victoria Towers.

The impact snapped the lock and mangled the chain-link gates. The van sounded like it had been hit by a plane, metal scraping against metal, and Dean's chair rocked back and forth, straining the braces that secured it in place. But he was okay, and best of all, he was inside.

Dean found getting out of the van difficult because it was parked on sand and gravel, and the chair sank where it should have rolled. He had to slide, an inch at a time, till he reached the wooden ramp leading to the trailer. Once there, it was an easy matter of waving his security card and inputting the code to get it open. If anyone knew what numbers to push, it was him.

Trouble was, getting the elevator down would take some doing, for that was not his area of expertise. His knowledge had more to do with the future of the building, when it was up and running, not the construction phase. The construction elevator, that lumbering parasite attached to the shell of the exterior, was going to be a pain in the ass.

He turned on the computer in the trailer and typed in his name and security code. When he was into the system, he called up the construction elevator. What he saw facing him was Greek. And then he had a great idea—why not just slam the fire alarm? It worked once before. Every engine in town came out for that wire-burning party! He almost laughed at how easy it was to hit the panic button for FIRE EMERGENCY. Trouble was, nothing happened.

He stared at the screen and hit a reveal code that showed him the reason. He should have guessed as much. Ben had overridden it. In fact, there was no fire alarm, for, as it showed in the SYSTEM ANALYSIS SCREEN, the wires had been destroyed within the guts of the building itself. Ben had taken every precaution.

He must have wanted her very badly.

And that made Dean shiver.

"My father never murdered anyone," Audrey replied. "That's crazy."

"Is it?"

"Yes."

"This man who robbed people his whole life wasn't capable of harming someone?"

"Not physically. My father was kind and gentle."

"Did I say physically?"

"What? Murdered him emotionally?"

"Destroyed him."

"My father couldn't even have known him."

"Ever hear of Makena Villas?"

She blinked. "Of course. That was Aunt's biggest failure."

"Your father's, too."

"What's that got to do with you?"

"My father was the head contractor."

She gasped. It was like someone had pushed the rewind button in her mind. "Corky?" It all came clear. "They called you Corky."

Ben continued as if he hadn't heard. "Bob Benedict was a good man," he said, talking about his beloved dad, "a decent guy from Virginia. He built houses in developments there."

"That's why you got so upset when Dean mentioned 'tract' houses to you earlier today."

He nodded. "We moved to Hawaii when I was in grade school because it had been his dream. My mom and I had a good life. He wanted me to go to college, but they didn't have the money. He worked first as a foreman for your father, then as a builder in his own right. He built condos and a hotel on Maui. He was successful, but he still wasn't rich, and your father finally offered him that opportunity when he asked him to invest in the Makena Villas project."

"Bob Benedict was your father," Audrey said. It had all come back to her now. "I never connected your last name to the past. Your dad gave you the nickname 'Corky.' "

He smiled at her recognition. "He invested every cent he had into that scheme."

"A retirement complex," she recalled.

"A lie, a sham, just like the Kaneohe Project."

She understood, and replied with a dark "Yes."

"Everything went under. The investors lost all they had put in, and Dad had to walk away from twenty-seven unfinished units the day the government discovered the fraud and slapped on the liens and closed everything down."

"It wasn't my father's fault."

"You think not? You should have read *my* father's suicide note."

She stood up, angry. "My father lost a fortune there, too; he was burned just like yours. He was able to survive because he had money, that's all. I'm sorry about what happened to your family, but it's not my fault."

He, too, got up. "Come here, come with me." He started toward the hall.

"Where are we going?"

"To the guest bedroom where I locked your boyfriend in."

Her eyes flashed with hope.

"No," Ben said, "he's no longer there."

"If you hurt him—"

"Stop worrying about him. Come with me."

"Why?"

"I want to show you something I got out of the vault."

"You were in the—?"

Her words were cut short by the ringing of a phone. They both froze, looking down at Mark's black leather-wrapped cell phone lying on the coffee table. The green light just barely flashed as it pierced the silence with its electronic squeal. It still had some power, but she could tell juice was running out. She reached for it.

"Don't!" Ben warned.

She defied him, grabbing it, clicking it on. Then she raised it to her ear, and shouted, "Help! Help us!"

But Bobbi did not hear her, for the little power that was left was drained just by turning it on. The phone went dead.

Audrey looked at Ben, whose face became enraged. His arm came out in a sweeping movement, and before she could duck, his hand slapped her across the face with such force that she was slammed back into the sofa.

"Don't you ever disobey me again, you understand me?"

She gasped, looked up in shock and fear. *Now* she was afraid.

Chapter Seventeen

Ben forced Audrey into the guest bedroom. When she saw the blood on the carpet, she choked back a terrified gasp. There was a big puddle of it, almost purplish now, just beyond the doorframe, and then a trail leading to the closet. The closet! Mark was in the closet. She ran to it, flung it open—

But Ben grabbed her hand and twisted her around so hard, she didn't really register if Mark was in there or not. He pulled her back and flung her toward the bed, where the file was open. The papers went flying. He quickly found the letter and held it in front of her face. "Read this."

Her eyes focused. She recognized the handwriting. "It's from Aunt," she said.

"To good old Hiram."

She looked at him.

"Read this," he ordered, "and then tell me your father didn't destroy mine!"

* * *

Mark's garden apartment on Makiki Street looked deserted. Melba Goh frowned through the back window of her black Lincoln. She looked at the address, which she'd brought along with her. Yes, this was the place. And there was Audrey's car, under the carport, half-hidden by foliage. So they had been here. She surmised they had driven somewhere in his automobile. "Stop, Mr. Yin," she ordered, just as another car drove up.

It wasn't hard to miss. The minute the Volkswagen announced it was rebuilding the Bug, Bobbi had put money down on one. It was a perky yellow, her pride and joy. Melba watched as Bobbi jumped from the car without even noticing the Lincoln, bounded through the gate, and up the stairs to the front door. She rang the bell, tried to peer in through the living room window, rang again, knocked, and finally lifted a terra-cotta planter to the right of the door and picked up a key. The old woman was quite surprised to see Bobbi Kicherer unlock the door and simply walk on in.

"Hello?" Bobbi called, not expecting an answer. "Audrey? Mark?" No one. She'd called Irene, Mark's secretary, to tell her Mark's cell phone didn't work. Irene mentioned that Mark's car was still at work. He had left in a taxi with Audrey. Yes, Bobbi thought, and that cab had taken them to Victoria Towers, and she'd left just before six and they'd fled the place shortly after she had.

Probably in another taxi for the short ride to Halekulani. She already knew that everything had perhaps been a ruse to give them privacy. But could she have been wrong about the hotel? Audrey had left her car here, so could they actually be at Mark's apartment?

"They are not here," a loud voice boomed.

Bobbi screamed in fright. The woman's shrill tone shook her to the bone. "Christ! Don't do that to me!"

"What are you doing here?"

Bobbi shot right back. "Where did *you* come from?"

"Where is Audrey?"

"Not here," Bobbi muttered.

"She did not go to Lanai."

"I know."

"Where is she, then?"

Bobbi shrugged. "Got me. Her cell phone isn't working."

Melba suddenly looked suspicious. "Why are you looking for her?"

Bobbi blurted out, "We lost the sale of the penthouse to the Yees today." She didn't quite know why she said it. It was all she could think of.

Aunt sucked in her breath. Hearing that almost gave her cardiac arrest. "Unacceptable."

"Yeah," Bobbi said. Now she had to tie that into locating Audrey. "I agree. I'm trying to find Audrey to see if she knows where they are staying so I can give it another shot."

"I need papers I gave her to sign," Aunt explained.

"We're both out of luck."

"Not necessarily," Aunt said. "We can look around and see if there is some clue to where they've gone."

Bobbi pulled open a drawer in the secretary in the corner of the entrance hall. "I'll start here," she said.

Bobbi was sure that her first assumption—the Halekulani—was correct. Now she wanted only to get out of there.

"God damn it." The construction elevator just wouldn't move. Had Ben jammed it? Locked it on the twenty-second floor somehow? Dean had done all he could with the computer, and the hulking box should already have come down. He had one shot left. He exited the construction trailer and wheeled himself to the base of the elevator shaft, where there was a small operator's shed. Inside were the gear controls used to run the elevator manually in case of a computer problem. Nothing happened when he pushed the first one, but the second sent a message to the computer screen that said MANUAL OVERRIDE ENGAGED, and he knew right away that was the problem. Ben had risen on a manual program, not through the computer. Dean disengaged the override on the screen, waited, then heard the sound he wanted to hear. The clackety-clack. The elevator was starting to descend.

Hang on, Audrey. I'll be up there in a minute.

The construction elevator stopped with a thud. Dean's eagerness died when he saw a new problem: the elevator had stopped two feet from the ground, easy enough for a man to simply step up and into, but impossible for a wheelchair to bridge.

He sat still and assessed the situation. In the past few years a lot of progress had been made in helping the handicapped access the world. Curbs were chopped out and replaced with sloping concrete, handles went into every rest-room wall, and ramps to all public buildings. That's what he needed here. A ramp on which to roll up onto the elevator floor. Only where the hell would he get one?

His eyes darted around. All he needed was a long piece of plywood, the kind they used as a form for concrete, or even a chunk of drywall—no, it would break. He needed the cement board they used on the bathroom walls before they tiled. He wheeled over to an unlocked storage shed. Five long pieces of cement board were lined against the wall. He turned around, positioned himself facing the door, then did his best to grab one of the pieces and drag it with him. It was too heavy, though. As he tried to move, he found himself in danger of falling out of the chair.

Giving up on it, he had another thought. He

found himself, as he wheeled out of the shed, looking right at one of the many signs on the property advertising the building's amenities. It was about six feet long by four feet wide, the perfect ramp—if he could only get it down.

He knew the signs were all makeshift, for the workers had to move them every few days or so when they got in the way. Thus, they were easily pulled from their anchors in the earth. He moved to the nearest one, parked directly under it, and found it fairly easy to lift the legs a few feet up, raising it on his shoulders, out of the ground. Then he let it crash to the earth. He coughed as dust caught in his throat, then wheeled back to the shed to grab himself a crowbar. Positioning the chair on top of the facedown sign, he used the crowbar to yank the two four-by-four legs off the sign. He tossed the crowbar aside, wiped the sweat from his brow, wheeled off the sign, and bent sideways to lift it. Gripping his wheel with one hand, and dragging the plywood sign with the other, he managed to get it to the construction elevator. It took four tries to get it into place, but it worked. He had a ramp to wheel up.

Once inside, he leaned over and pushed the plywood off then closed the metal gate. Grabbing the lever, he eased it forward, and the lumbering hunk of steel started to move. The floor wasn't level, and he felt the chair rolling backward. He stopped the roll with his hands, and he started to laugh, because it happened every time he went up the thing, and always forgot to hold on.

He wondered if Mark was still holding on.

And Audrey, too.

Audrey set the letter down and looked up at Ben. "I'm sorry," she said softly. "I . . . I didn't know."

What she had just read disturbed her greatly. Aunt Melba had written in her own hand that Makena Villas was indeed going to be "trouble." She suggested they take a loss on the investment and assured Hiram the Goh Corporation could weather it. As far as the legal impact—for the project was already the subject of a state investigation—she said she had already taken steps to protect them and "thrust the bulk of the blame" onto the man Hiram had suggested become the easy patsy, "the contractor, Bob Benedict." Mr. Benedict, Aunt pointed out, because of his monetary involvement, coupled with the fact that in the past he had several times had trouble with the Internal Revenue Service, was the prime candidate for culpability. She would "whisper" to friends in high places to let them know he was the man to go after, once she had covered the trail leading to herself and Hiram. "Dearest brother," she had concluded, "I trust you will see to this with utmost urgency."

Audrey said, "Your father was ruined financially, wasn't he?"

Ben's eyes became glazed with tenderness, and heavy sadness. "For two years he was a broken man, despised, reviled. We would have people come up to us on the street and spit at him. 'You took my savings!' a man once shouted in church. In church, Audrey! He never worked again. And then he shot himself."

She winced. "Your mother?"

"Drank. When he died, it got worse. She burned to death in a fire she started by smoking in bed."

Audrey's stomach turned. "I didn't know."

He nodded. "That's when I decided I would get revenge. For both of them."

She closed her eyes. She understood his anger. She would have felt the same. This letter was proof, she could not argue, could not suggest he was wrong. It was irrefutable. But the logic of his actions confused her. "Why didn't you confront my father?"

"He was too rich, too powerful. It would have done no good."

"How could you hold something like that in?"

"I found another way to take care of it."

She didn't understand. "How?"

"This. You."

"I still don't understand."

"It's simple, Audrey. Who did I love most in the world? My dad. Your father took him away from me. Who did your father love most in the world? You."

She felt a shiver down her spine. Her feet tingled. A cold spasm gripped her neck. "But . . ." She gasped for the words. "But my father is dead. You can't hurt him now, even by hurting me."

He let out a deep laugh. "Jesus, he up and just croaks! Talk about taking the wind out of your sails, man." Then he twisted around, crying out in wounded pain, shouting at the absurdity of it all. "He fucking dies on me! Isn't that rich? I mean, it takes me almost ten years—ten years of trying to talk myself out of it, ten years of battling with my soul, never resting. I spend all my energy to plot this, for that's the only way I'm going to sleep at night, to watch him suffer in losing you like I did in losing my pop, and what does he do? He buys the farm!"

Audrey stared at him. She knew he was mad, and she knew she was in trouble. She kept thinking if only she could get to that closet to see if Mark was all right. If only she could find a way to run. But she wasn't going anywhere. The only hope she had was to outsmart him. But how?

"But it doesn't matter anymore," he said. He came closer to her, looked her in the eye.

"What doesn't matter anymore?" she asked.

"About making Hiram suffer."

"That's right," she agreed.

"It's my satisfaction now that counts."

"What do you mean?"

"Let me put it this way: I don't need your father here to suffer. The deed can be cleansing enough." He smiled.

She closed her eyes and shivered.

* * *

While Melba Goh searched Mark's apartment for a clue to where he and Audrey might have gone, Bobbi called the Halekulani and spoke to Susan Shackman, the concierge. She explained her plight, who Audrey was—Susan had, of course, heard of her—and what had happened and how it was necessary just to give her a message, but Susan was implacable. The company policy was not to give out any information that a guest didn't want given out. Then she asked Bobbi to hold on for a moment, while she said, "Good evening, Mrs. Yee. In the lounge? Certainly, I'll tell them." Then she was back with Bobbi. "I'm sorry, you were saying?"

"Yee!" Bobbi almost screamed. "Mrs. Yee? Patricia Yee?"

"Yes," Susan admitted. "They frequently stay with us."

Bobbi muttered, "So I was right, they didn't fly back to China right away. I almost sold them an apartment this morning. My God, maybe Audrey doesn't even know." Bobbi laughed. "Isn't that a kicker? Staying down the hall from each other and she probably doesn't even realize."

"I'm afraid I don't understand."

"That's okay," Bobbi said, "but bless you, thank you, oh thank you!"

"Who are you thanking?" Melba bellowed as she strode back into the room with her baby steps.

"Nobody." Bobbi hung up the phone. "I'm leaving."

Melba blinked. "I'm most concerned about Audrey."

"She's fine, just doesn't want to be found." But then it hit Bobbi, suddenly, in her gut. What if she'd been *wrong* on all accounts. What if something *had* happened to Audrey? "Oh, God." Bobbi looked sick.

Aunt said, "I am fearful. The letters, that crazy man."

"But Mark is—"

Aunt cut her off. "With her? You do not think he could harm Mark, too?"

Bobbi agreed. Mark was strong, but that wasn't much assurance. It was possible they never made it to any airport or any hotel. Then another thought occurred to her. And she gasped out loud, "Oh, my God, the baby!"

Aunt's eyebrows lifted. "Baby?"

Bobbi gulped, wishing she could take the words back.

"What baby?"

She knew she couldn't. Oh, well, she had to find out sometime anyway. "Audrey is pregnant."

Melba Goh nearly expired. Her knees gave out, and if Bobbi hadn't helped her into a chair, she might have swooned to the floor. Bobbi thought it was a little over the top, but fanned her nonetheless, asked if she wanted water. All Melba kept saying was, "This is not true, this is not true."

"It is, honey, and you'd just better get used to it."

Melba was clearly worried, perspiring. She pulled her fan from one of the pockets in her silk pants. Then she spoke in a voice that most people reserved for talking about death. "They might have run off to marry. That Howlie. That gold digger. That—"

"We finally agree on something," Bobbi said. "Audrey could do better, if you ask me. But I don't think they eloped. I think something might have prevented them from getting on that plane to Lanai."

Aunt shook her head, not sure what to think.

"I'm going to find out," Bobbi said.

"Where are you—?" But Melba knew she was wasting her breath. Bobbi wasn't going to tell her where she was going. She was out the door before Melba could have gotten the words out.

Melba Goh sat in the chair a few moments longer, thinking. She did not want to overreact, but at the same time Bobbi could be right, and she would never forgive herself if Audrey was in danger.

She picked up the phone and dialed 911. "Young woman, I need police help," she told the operator. "I want Detective Wong, he is familiar with this case."

"What case is that?" the girl asked.

Melba said, "Some madman has been threatening my niece, and now I fear he has harmed her."

* * *

Audrey swallowed hard. "So it was you all along. Sending the notes."

He looked delighted. "Did Hiram squirm?"

"You were in Aunt's house while we were in Hong Kong."

He seemed oddly proud of that fact. "She has good taste, if a little on the dark side. But your place is charming."

"Thank you."

"It was amazing how turned-on I felt when I was in your bed."

She held her breath in. "In my bed?"

"This morning. While you were on the phone."

"*You* made my bed."

"That's not all I did in it."

She blinked. "And you took my lei."

"Pakalana."

"Pikaki," she corrected him.

"Amazing how sweet it still smells. It's under the front seat of my car. Great deodorizer."

"You bastard."

"Did you wear it naked?" he asked with a leering grin. "Did you put the blossoms against your naked skin like I did? I pictured you naked with only the lei around on your shoulders."

"You want revenge on my father, but you want to fuck me first?"

"I didn't have any interest in you that way, at least I didn't think so. Maybe at seventeen, but then I was hot for any girl. It started happening when I got close to you again, when I got this job and all. It's strange. Kinda like a kick I didn't expect."

"I don't understand."

"Don't mean to say you're unattractive, but I'm not sure I really want to have sex with you. I mean, I do and I don't." He rubbed his head. "I think it goes back to the day on the beach."

"What day on what beach?"

He told her about Makena the day his mother died. How he had watched her. "You sunbathed naked."

She recalled. "I used to go down there, a private cove, there was no one around. Ever."

"Bull. You knew the boys hid on the rocks and watched you. You liked it."

She honestly had not. But that wasn't important. "What does that day have to do with me?"

"That's when I knew what I one day had to do."

"What you are doing now?"

He nodded. "Been around you over a year now, working on this building, waiting for the right moment. All your teasing, all your sexy innuendo, it gets to a guy."

"You saying you fell in love with me?" Her voice bordered on incredulous.

"I don't know it's love." He looked in the bureau mirror and adjusted his bow tie. "Passion of some sort, I'd call it." Then he brightened. "So, are we going to eat dinner?"

She couldn't believe he was still suggesting it. "Dinner? I'm so frightened I think I'd throw up."

"Frightened? Think of it as fate, Audrey. The Chinese are taught to accept fate, that it can't be changed. Just enjoy this night."

"But you—"

"No, no, no, don't think about what I'm going to do. Think about the fact that some quality time together might get me to change my mind." He glanced at Mark's clothes on the bed, his dress slacks, undershirt, blue dress shirt, and the striped silk tie he'd been wearing that day. "Spend the evening with a man for a change."

Quality time? She wanted to murder this lunatic and run for her life! She took a chance. She jumped from the bed and ran to the closet, grasping the door lever and pulled it down, trying desperately to see inside.

But Ben was as fast as she was, and he pulled her away, into his arms. Holding her close to him, he started dancing. The music was still coming from the hidden speakers all over the apartment. "Yes," he said, with a hint of passion, "we'll dance the night fantastic, dine together, sleep together . . ."

"No!" she cried out over his shoulder, determined not to cry. She had to be strong, she couldn't let him know how afraid she was, she had to be—what was the word? *Steely.* Like Aunt would be in this situation. She was fighting for her life tonight.

For now she had to play along. "Maybe we should eat after all."

"I'm starving."

"And we can talk."

He smirked. "Sure. And I have a surprise for you."

"Another one?"

He nodded gleefully. "And nothing tacky like Mark was going to give you."

"The box from Tiffany," she said. "What was in it?"

"A bracelet."

"A bracelet?"

He laughed. "In other words, not a ring."

She remembered the things Mark had said about love and children and their future. And she knew now she wouldn't have wanted one from him anyhow.

Suddenly Ben froze. "What's that?"

"What?" She heard nothing.

"That sound, that rumbling—" He flattened himself to the floor, pressing his ear into the deep wool carpeting. "Something's running, some engine or . . . elevator. Shit!" He jumped up. "Construction elevator."

Oh, God, yes, she thought, maybe Mark had gotten out somehow and got help! Yes, go, go look at the elevator, go! He ran from the room. She hurried to the closet, yanked open the door and saw the empty space. It shocked her, for she'd expected to see Mark lying there in a pool of blood. The bloody trail led to the far wall and just stopped. Then she noticed that a square had been crudely cut out and the piece of drywall put back in. Mark had gotten out!

She was about to do the same, but powerful hands grabbed her just inches from the wall. Ben yanked her out of the closet and pulled her down the corridor to the living arena. That's when she figured out that Mark wasn't supposed to be in the closet. Ben must have opened the wall, dragged Mark through it, but to where?

At that moment she realized what he was doing. In an effort to see down the side of the building, he had opened the French door with the shattered glass leading to the terrace. He was on hands and knees, legs inside the apartment, torso out in midair, peering down to see the construction elevator.

It was perfect.

Audrey crept up behind him, positioning herself so that she could send him, with one quick shove, flying into space.

Chapter Eighteen

Bobbi rushed into the hushed, elegant Halekulani reception area. The floral display in the center of the open-air room was bigger than she was. Constructed from orchids, mums, tuberose, ivy and ti leaves, thick white ginger exploding into fragrant bloom, even delicate plumeria, it was a feast for the senses.

In her estimation, this was Hawaii's finest hotel. The din of Waikiki nightlife disappeared the moment you entered the place, and Bobbi always felt a kind of spiritual calm come over her. The gods, she figured, had declared this a true house of tranquility.

She approached the concierge desk and said hello to the pretty, dark-haired woman behind it. "I'm Bobbi Kicherer, we talked a while ago."

"Hello," Susan Shackman said sweetly, as if half-expecting her. "I still can't tell you whether or not your friend is here. I honestly don't know."

"Well, we know the Yees are. See, I work with Audrey at Victoria Towers and—" She stopped herself. She was about to tell the woman that they nearly sold the Yees the penthouse and that she wanted to give it one more shot. But she doubted Susan was going to help her annoy paying hotel guests. "We spent most of the day with the Yees, helped Patricia pick out marble and carpet colors, it was delightful. But they ran off without signing one of the pages of the agreement, and I've been trying to track them down. That's why I wanted to find Audrey, to get their signatures."

Susan hadn't been born yesterday. She looked suspicious at Bobbi's babble.

"I know they'll be very upset if they learn escrow has to be extended because of a technical error like this."

Susan weighed the story. "They *are* leaving in the morning," she said softly.

Bobbi could see she was wavering. "I'm on the level, honestly."

Susan brightened. "All right. They're in Lewer's Lounge. Two friends have just joined them."

Bobbi wanted to scream for joy. "Oh, thank you!" She started out, but then turned back. "Susan, you haven't *seen* Audrey around tonight, have you? Can you tell me that much?"

"No, I'm afraid I honestly haven't."

Ben balanced himself with his weight supported by his hands out on the girder, his knees resting on the edge of the carpeting just before the doorframe, and strained out as far as he could to see down. "I can't tell," he muttered. "I can't tell if it's moved—" He'd left the elevator on the twenty-second floor, just beneath them. "I think it's there. Yeah, I think—"

It was now or never. Audrey set herself to push hard, and then an alarm sounded. As she jumped, he twisted back like a rattlesnake, and she fell right on top of him. The alarm beeped and beeped and then stopped. "The oven," she realized. The overly sophisticated Gaggeneau appliance had ruined her chance. Goddamned apartment. "The oven's telling me it's now or never or the roast will dry out."

He glared at her. "What were you going to do?"

She got to her knees, hurrying to get up. "What do you mean?"

"What were you about to do behind me? Why were you kneeling?"

"To see . . . I was trying to see the elevator, too."

"Bull." He grabbed her arm and twisted it. "Don't you try to hurt me, you hear me?"

It was hurting her. "Yes."

He let go. Then he smiled again. "This could be a wonderful night."

She nodded to that, thinking the gesture was the biggest lie she had told in her life, and walked into the kitchen. He followed close behind her.

She took the roasting pan from the oven and lifted the roast to the serving dish. He tossed the salad with olive oil and balsamic vinegar, chatting on about how many times he had thought about living in this kind of apartment, if only he had the money, which he would if her father had not screwed his. But she wasn't listening; her brain was working overtime. She spooned out the roasted potatoes, still hot with crusty browned garlic chunks from the bottom of the pan, onto the serving platter, then set the roasting pan back on the stove.

And then it came to her. She knew what she'd do. She'd turn on the gas under the two burners on which the roasting pan rested. The fat from the roast would be bubbling in no time. And after dinner she'd get him to help her clear the table, take the things back into the kitchen, get him close to the stove.

He put the salad on the table, and she followed him with the main course. He held her chair for her, and they toasted at his insistence. "To justice."

She felt her stomach turn. This was too sick for words. She set her glass down without tasting the wine. She wanted to stay stone cold sober, and not only to protect the baby. He carved the lamb. It looked a little on the dry side, for it had been sitting in the oven forever. She tried to eat. But she couldn't.

Ben relished his meal. Spearing a chunk of potato, he twirled it on his fork, and said, "You're not hungry?"

"No."

He chortled. "Scared?"

She whispered. "Yes."

"How does it feel?"

"Terrible."

"I bet," he said, chewing the potato heartily. "I'm just so mixed up when it comes to you, Audrey."

"Tell me about it."

He cut a piece of lamb. "Well, it's like I wanted to get you so your dad would suffer."

"You told me."

"Then he fucking croaked, and I wasn't sure."

"You said."

He dipped the lamb chunk in mint jelly. "That really pissed me off, you know? So it almost gave me more reason to hurt you."

She had to say something. But could she reason with him? "I'm your friend. The sins of my father have nothing to do with me. I've always been fond of you. Why would you want to go through with this?"

"Isn't it too late?"

"How?"

He pondered. "If we leave here on Monday, you'll tell people. Call the cops. Or that asshole tied up downstairs, he'll—"

She jumped at that. "Mark is tied up downstairs?"

"Yeah."

"Is he—?"

"I told you he's all right, don't push it!" he

barked. "I barely could bring myself to shoot my dog. You really think I could shoot a person?"

"Your dog?" Her stomach turned. "You shot your dog?"

He closed his eyes. His body seemed to quake with emotion. She could see a flood of feeling flush his face, then he shook with anger again. He opened his eyes and stared blankly at the sparkling buildings of Waikiki out the window. Then he told her the story.

A year before the fire that killed his mother and set him free, on a hot afternoon, his mother had suddenly announced that they couldn't afford to keep Kam anymore. Kam was his beloved Sheltie, his best friend in the world, who as a puppy had been named by his father after Hawaii's King Kamehameha. Now, with Mom drinking up the money Ben brought home from his job helping a builder after school and the mortgage two months behind and old Kam needing an operation for his hip that was going to cost three hundred dollars, she handed him the shotgun and told him to take Kam down the beach and do what "was right." He knew she just didn't want to buy dog food anymore, that she felt it was whiskey money gone to waste.

He begged her to rescind the order, promised he'd get another job on Sundays, he'd sell his surfboard, anything. He assured her Kam wasn't in pain and maybe he could go a little longer before they had to take him in for the surgery. When she remained steadfast, he cried and ached with the longing for this to change, he prayed for the first time since he'd sworn off God after his father died. Dear Lord, please don't make me have to do this. God chose not to intervene, assuring him once and for all that there was no such entity.

"You don't come back with that dog, hear?" his mother had ordered, as they left the yard. He ditched the gun in the back shed and spent a couple of hours in town trying to give Kam away to tourists who might give him a loving home, but no one wanted an old dog or could transport one back home. He thought of his pal Gregory, but Greg's dad said no because they already had two dogs and a cat. He approached strangers, and with tears falling said, "Please take my dog . . ." No one did.

He finally went back to the house, hoping his mother would be so sloshed she'd forget all about it. Kam ran into the yard in front of him and up to his dog dish on the porch, lapping up water after a fun walk through Lahaina. Mom appeared through the screen with a drink in her hand. "I told you, you have that dog, you don't live here anymore." Then she slammed the inside door, which seldom, in this climate, was ever closed. That's when he took the gun from the shed and put it into his Samurai.

He drove north, past Kapalua, walking a path through what seemed like the most private rain forest on earth, covered with vines and dense with exotic plants, to a secluded spot of beach he often ran away to. Kam bounded ahead of him along the water, loving the game despite the limp because of his hip, waiting for him to throw the ragged tennis ball as usual. But there was no tennis ball in the black vinyl gun case.

Ben didn't need to close his eyes when he finally brought himself to do it two hours later. He was so cried out by that time that his pupils were glazed over. He only heard what he did: the blast of the explosion, a slight whimper, then silence, just the sound of the waves. He sat there till dark with Kam's body in his arms, wondering if it had been like that when his dad did it. It was so sudden and irreversible, he was curious if he whimpered or if he just looked forward to the peace. Kam's face didn't look peaceful, however. It looked to him as if the animal were saying, "Why did you do this to me?" It was violent and final. Just like his father. It even was carried out by the same gun.

He buried Kam that night right next to his father. He had a fold-up shovel for sand emergencies in the vehicle, and it was easy to get over the fence surrounding the deserted cemetery. Luckily for him, the earth was sandy, not volcanic there, so he could dig easily, and Kam was laid to rest in less than an hour. But he didn't leave. He sat there, still covered with the dog's blood, between the graves of the only two beings he'd loved more than life itself, Dad and his dog, and went numb. He finally got the gun and put it to his own head.

"But I didn't do it," he told Audrey.

"Why?" she asked, wishing he had.

" 'Cause of my mom. I hated her that morning for what she did, but I still had to go home and make her coffee and put her clothes out. She was helpless wreck, an invalid—"

"You were only a teenager," Audrey said. "You weren't mature enough to be a caretaker."

"But after losing Kam," he explained in a haunted voice, "she was all I had."

She poured him some wine. This was good, getting him to talk. He was trusting her more. Maybe, in sharing his painful story with her, his rage toward her had lessened. "Listen, let's help Mark. Let's get him and bring him back here and we'll all talk about this. We won't tell anyone. This could all work out."

"No, it can't." He continued eating.

"What do you mean?" Icy fear gripped her insides again.

"The only way I can get away from here is not to leave anyone behind who can talk."

She bit her lip.

"That scare you?" he teased.

She nodded. "You're talking about killing both of us so we don't talk? Of course it scares me."

He ate for a few minutes, silent, seemingly thinking. Then he said, "If we did have this little party, the three of us, what would we discuss?"

"Revenge," she said, jumping on the fact that he was considering it, "and rage and anger—I'm feeling some of that for my father right now, too—and how to deal with it constructively. You're letting hate control you, Ben. Maybe some therapy would help you channel it."

"You're saying I'm nuts?" he snapped, tossing his fork down. "You want me to go to a shrink?"

"If you have the flu, you go to a doctor. If you have an emotional problem, you should also go to a doctor. There's no stigma attached."

He laughed at her. "You don't know shit, baby."

"What?"

"My mom went to therapy, for a long time after my old man killed himself. Lot of fucking good it did her."

Audrey wouldn't give up. "Ben, you're confused. You're here partly because you want to harm me, and partly because you feel an attraction to me. One repels the other. You probably want to talk to me more than you want to hurt me or make love to me. Why don't we just discuss our families more?"

He squinted. "Till Mark breaks away and gets the cops?"

"No!"

"Audrey, I've taken this too far, can't you see that?"

"I want to help you!"

"Shut up. Just shut up."

She didn't. "Ben, please, I care about you."

He spooned more of the sweet green jelly onto a new piece of lamb. "You should have made fresh mint sauce."

"I'm not that fancy a cook."

"Mint jelly is pretty pedestrian."

"Mark likes it."

"My point exactly."

She gripped her fork tightly, resisting the impulse to plunge it into his eye. He had hurt Mark, tied him up downstairs somewhere. For all she knew he really had killed Mark, though she wanted not to believe that, and she had to sit here listening to him make cracks about him.

She stopped her train of thought. It was useless to let him upset her by what he was saying; better to concentrate on what she was going to do. She'd seen the hole in the wall in the guest-room closet. That was where she had to go, her goal. All she needed to do was to detain him long enough to reach it.

"If we knew our fate," he continued, "we'd all live in constant fear. We would never want to know what day it was. Never turn a page in the calendar."

"I'm not fatalistic."

"Not very Chinese."

"Aunt would agree with you. I don't believe in hocus-pocus. I believe that you make your destiny, you create it, and you can change it."

"Change what is going to happen here?" He

grinned again. Then he sipped some more wine. "It might be set in stone."

"No! For ten years you've pondered this, you said. You've tried to talk yourself out of it. You're confused, you don't know what you want to do, you aren't sure what to do to me. You're trapped because you went this far and now you're having second thoughts. You may have shot your dog, Ben, but you're right, you're no killer."

"I think maybe you should go join your father." He lifted his glass to her with a grin. "To Audrey and Hiram, reunited. Building mansions in heaven, or condos in hell." He laughed out loud.

She was aghast. "How can you toast to murdering me like you're saying happy anniversary or something?"

"You'll never know," he said, placing a forkful of flavorful lamb in his mouth, "how sweet revenge can be."

"Don't be so sure," she muttered.

"What does that mean?"

She said nothing more.

Dean had a terrible time getting the elevator to stop so it was lined up with the concrete slab of the twenty-second floor. With the computer's help it might have been easy, but manually it took an expert, and he was no elevator operator. Had he been able to walk, he could have easily jumped up to the floor. But the chair wouldn't climb stairs, so it wasn't about to accomplish this either, and he had no makeshift ramp there to help him. Finally, after adjusting the elevator again and again, up and down, down four inches, up seven inches, back down ten inches, he finally wheeled off onto the floor. He was inside the building, just beneath her. First thing to do was to find Mark.

It was almost pitch-dark. He made his way to the interior of the building, to the center core, where the elevator shaft would one day house the high-speed cars filled with the very rich inhabitants. Where was Mark? He remembered that he'd seen Mark bound to a girder almost directly beneath the living-room windows of Residence Twenty-three. "Mark?" he called out in that direction, softly but loud enough to be heard.

There was no answer. Only the warm, humid trade winds blowing steadily from the sea. Everything in sight glittered from up here. Honolulu looked like it did from an airplane. He was momentarily a little dizzy, never having seen this at night before. The lights of his own building gleamed in the distance, the beacons of boats bobbed on the ocean, the airplane lights at the corners of every floor of the structure dazzled like Christmas lights. He moved around the elevator shaft toward the perimeter of the building, until he was standing where the living room would begin in the finished Residence Twenty-two. "Mark! Can you hear me? Answer me, man!"

Dean heard a moan.

Or did he? It could have been the wind. But he

moved in the direction of the girders, where he was sure Mark was secured, and as he did, the moans got louder. "Mark?"

"Yes," the reply was faint, but clear. "Help me . . ."

"I'm here, I'm here, man," Dean said. He was just behind the girder now, where he could make out the hands securely bound with duct tape. He hurried to them, and started pulling the tape apart, ripping it with his teeth. When he had freed Mark's arms, he moved in front of him and let Mark fall into his arms. Mark slumped onto the wheelchair, and Dean eased him down to the concrete floor, saying, "It's okay now, you're gonna be fine."

"My head," Mark moaned.

Dean examined it. The blood was already drying, caking up most of his hair, but the bleeding had stopped—there was none running down his neck that Dean could find. "I think it stopped," he assured Mark. "You might have a concussion, but you'll be fine."

"What happened?" He hadn't a clue. "Where am I?"

"In Victoria Towers," Dean said. Apparently the blow to the head had been worse than he thought. Maybe Mark didn't even know who he was.

"I know that," Mark snapped. "I mean what *happened*? Who did this? Why am I down here? Where's Audrey, what's happened to Audrey?"

"She's still in the apartment—I think—with that psychopath."

"Psychopath?"

"Ben."

"Ben who?"

"Ben Benedict."

Mark blinked. "The electrician?" He shook his head. "No way. He's her good friend."

"Fucking nutcase is just above us dressed in your tux, dancing with her."

Mark felt the wind knocked out of him a second time. "How did—?"

Dean anticipated the questions. "I was looking at the building through my telescope, saw what happened. I tried to get the cops; they wouldn't believe me. I came over here myself, and now it's up to us to help Audrey."

"Cops wouldn't believe you?"

"It's a long story." He knew he couldn't go into the *Rear Window* thing. "You able to walk?"

Mark closed his eyes for a moment. "I'm okay." Then he tried to get to his feet. He was wobbly, but did it. Dean supported his elbow and shoulder just in case. "I'm all right, honest."

"We've got to get up there. How did he get you down here?"

Mark shook his head. "I don't know. I went into the bedroom, I think—yeah, to get the gift. Audrey and I had just had words and I upset her and I thought the bracelet would—"

Dean was impatient. "Yeah, yeah, and what happened?"

"Shit, I didn't have a clue. I'm in the clouds, bleeding, tied to a chunk of steel and—"

"He had to have gotten the door open," Dean surmised.

"What can we do?"

Dean thought about it. "Get in there. Get him."

"We need the police. He's violent. He could kill—"

"Audrey," Dean filled in. "He could kill Audrey."

"Jesus. That's who's been sending the notes."

"Huh?"

"Someone has been mailing threats to her father for months now. This guy has probably been watching her every move."

Dean lowered his eyes. Guilt ran through his blood, that familiar feeling he'd experienced again and again while looking at her. "No," he said softly, "that wasn't him. I don't know anything about notes, but that was me watching her."

Bobbi walked into Lewer's Lounge, the lovely, dark, wood-paneled bar in the old building at the Halekulani, where the entertainer, an earthy, elegant singer named Loretta Ables finished her set with "Can't Help Lovin' That Man of Mine." As everyone applauded, Bobbi scanned the room for the Yees. Her heart fell. She didn't see them.

Susan said they had been joined by two friends,

so she zeroed in on every table of four. No go. Plenty of Asians in the place, but Patricia and Curtis Yee were not there. Damn, she must have just missed them.

She walked over to a waiter. "Excuse me, do you know Mr. and Mrs. Yee?"

"Sure do," he said with a smile.

"Did they just leave?"

He blinked. "Leave?"

"Susan the concierge sent me here to join them. Which way did they go?"

The boy gave her a look as if to say calm down. "They're sitting almost immediately behind you."

"Huh?" Bobbi turned around. The four people sitting behind her were strangers, two men in spiffy casual suits with an elderly Chinese couple. They saw Bobbi staring. The well-dressed woman smiled. Bobbi turned again to the waiter. "Them?" she whispered.

"Them," he said, picking up some empty glasses.

"Oh, God, just my luck. The wrong Yees." But Bobbi was trapped now, because the curious Chinese matron was starting to rise, sure they were talking about her.

"Do we know you?" the woman asked in a pleasant voice.

Bobbi felt mortified. "I'm sorry, I was looking for Mr. and Mrs. Yee."

"I'm Mrs. Yee."

"The other Mrs. Yee," Bobbi said. "Patricia Yee."

"I'm Patricia Yee."

"The Patricia Yee from Hong Kong," Bobbi said, trying to differentiate.

Her husband stood now as well. "We are from Hong Kong."

"No," Bobbi said, "you're still the wrong people. I work at Victoria Towers, a building here in— "

"Hiram's pride and joy," the man said.

Bobbi blinked. She felt a cold sweat starting in her pores.

"Actually," the old man added, "we planned to view one of the apartments this week. We must call Audrey. Audrey Goh. You must know her?"

Bobbi could barely speak. "I'm her . . . her partner."

The woman loved it. "Oh, how delightful," she said warmly.

Curtis Yee continued, "Hiram was one of my oldest friends. I'll always regret not being able to attend the funeral."

His wife said, "Let's not dwell on that, darling. Just remember the good times." She turned back to Bobbi. "I'll never forget, we met Audrey only once, when she was about—"

"Nine," Bobbi said, her stomach turning over. Something was very wrong here.

"Oh, forgive me," the man said, turning to the two young men who now rose, "these are our good friends from San Francisco, Tim Hillard and Jesse Walker. We've been friends since they visited the colony a few years back."

"Hi," Bobbi intoned, but she felt like she was drowning.

"Please, join us," Tim said, pulling a chair up from another table.

Everyone sat down. Bobbi slumped into the fifth chair and stared at the elderly couple with grave suspicion. "You really are the Yees who knew Hiram Goh? Live in a villa on Victoria Peak, promised Hiram you'd buy the penthouse—"

"No promise," Curtis said, "but we'll have a look."

"Do you have a surly bodyguard whose neck looks like a sausage?"

"No," the man said with a laugh. "I don't believe we do."

"Do you use a limo when in Honolulu?"

Patricia shook her head. "None of those trappings for us; they make you a sitting duck. We rented a Toyota. I love to drive." She sipped her drink.

Bobbi asked Mr. Yee, "Do you like steak?"

He seemed amused at the question. "Not particularly, why?"

His wife's curiosity had grown even stronger. "Now, my dear," she said politely but firmly, "may we inquire why you are asking these strange questions?"

Bobbi grabbed one of the drinks sitting on the

small table at their knees. She didn't know whose it was, or even *what* it was, but she downed the full glass in one gulp. Then she said, "Boy, do I have a story to tell you . . ."

Chapter Nineteen

Dean steered Mark away from the edge and led him to the central core of the building. There were steel fire stairs there connecting all the floors. Dean wheeled into the stairwell. "Okay, help me get up there."

"Why don't we just take the elevator?" Mark inquired.

"It's too difficult."

Mark stared at him in the dim work light. He was curious. "You said it was you watching her. What did you mean?"

"I'll explain later."

"No, now."

"I have a telescope. I watch the place. Now come on."

"But we're defenseless. We don't have a weapon."

"Jesus!" Dean worried that Mark wanted to stand there and talk all night. "We'll use our fucking brains."

Mark looked very unsure. "One of us has to get the cops. They'll believe me; they'll listen to me."

"I need you, man!"

"I don't believe she's in any real danger," Mark said unconvincingly. Dean could tell he was scared. "He could easily have killed me, but he didn't. I think he's harmless."

Dean snapped, "You say that after he cracked your skull? You think raping her is kinder than killing her?"

"I'm going down," Mark said again. "I'm going down and getting help."

"Fuck you!" Dean shouted. "You're not going anywhere till you help me get to the next floor. Now lift me out of this chair and put me over your arm. I don't care how scared you are, this is what we've got to do!"

Audrey could barely swallow her food. She pushed it around her plate as she had as a child. Her body was shaking, and her mind was reeling. She had to go through that hole in the wall and find Mark, and they'd get to safety.

Ben seemed to act as though he were having dinner at Alan Wong's, happy and carefree and savoring every morsel. "You're a great cook," he complimented Audrey.

"It's dried out."

"How do you know? Eat something. You're a talented woman."

"Any idiot can shove a roast in the oven."

"No, it takes skill. Like your sales skills. Most

people can't do what you do. Most people aren't as smart as you."

She saw he was finished. "Dessert?"

"Ummmm," he said, cartoonishly rubbing his stomach. "And coffee."

"That sounds good."

"You shouldn't have caffeine with the baby coming. I thought about that after you refused the wine."

"I have decaf."

He nodded. "We'll both have that."

She got up and cleared the plates, took them to the kitchen, where she looked at the fat bubbling in the roasting pan on the stove. The grease was boiling. But how would she do it? She couldn't bring the pan to the dining room. He was sitting with his back to the windows, watching her through the kitchen opening. Had he been turned around, she could sneak up on him from behind. Maybe she could get him to change places. "Ben?"

"Yes?" he called from the dining room.

"Give me a hand, all right?"

"Sure."

"Get a couple of plates down for dessert," Audrey ordered Ben as she set the dinner dishes into one of the sleek stainless-steel dishwashers.

"Sure." He did so. "I don't think I'm going to hurt you, Audrey."

"I hope not." She didn't trust him for a moment.

"What we having?"

"For dessert? It's a surprise."

He smiled. "Good. I've got one for you, too."

"You said. Can you come over here a minute?"

He said, "Let's wait a while on dessert."

"What?" Damn. So close.

"I want to give you your surprise first."

She had to play along. She left the heat on under the grease and followed him into the living room, but he didn't stop there. He made his way down the hall toward the entry arena and walked into the library. "Come on in, I like this room the best."

She joined him on the sofa when he patted it, just as she'd done with Mark earlier in the evening. He reached out and took her hand in his. She tried not to cringe at his touch, and felt how absurd a feeling it was, for this was the same man who had hugged her every morning for the past year. "Let me ask you something," she said.

He said, "Anything."

"Did you make HAL go a little nuts this morning when I went out onto the balcony?"

He grinned. "Maybe," he teased.

"Trying to kill me then? Without me knowing it was you, without knowing your revenge agenda?"

"I knew you wouldn't fall."

"I don't understand."

He said, "I needed you to trust me. I didn't know tonight was going to happen, I mean I never planned on this. I had imagined something different, needed your trust so you'd come away with me somewhere."

"A secret weekend," she muttered ironically, recalling Mark's words.

"It certainly is," he reminded her.

"What's the surprise?"

He stood up and took off the tuxedo jacket, reaching into the inside pocket to withdraw a red-velvet bag, almost cinnabar in color. Audrey recognized it. "Looks like the one my father gave me."

"Yes, apparently he had several colors." Ben laughed. "Probably bought the company that makes them."

"Where did you get it?"

"The safe."

"I didn't see it."

He grinned. "I looked deeper."

"What do you mean?"

"I looked in the safe within the safe."

"What?" She was startled. "How? I wanted to, but I lost the key. It must have—" She stopped herself the moment she realized how stupid she must have sounded. "My God, *you* had the key. You took it from the box in my bedroom this morning."

He slid his hand into his pants pocket and withdrew the key, dangling it in front of her. "This?"

She took it and closed her fingers around it. "You opened my mother's safe. What was inside?"

"This," he said, handing the bag to her now.

Audrey felt it was heavy, very heavy. She ran her fingers over the velvet to see if she could determine what it was, but as she did so, Ben produced another envelope, a paper one this time. Audrey recognized it as her father's stationery. "I think you should read this first," he said.

Audrey saw her name scrawled on the front in her father's hand. Surprisingly, Ben had not opened it, it was still sealed with his chop on the back. She broke the seal, and withdrew a folded piece of paper on which was written a heartfelt letter. She unfolded it and began to read.

Dearest Daughter Audrey . . .

Bobbi was holding the Yees in rapt attention as she described the two people who had shown up that morning claiming to be them. With a chauffeur/bodyguard no less.

"It's absurd," Curtis said, "simply crazy."

"I know," Bobbi agreed. "Let me ask you this. Does the name Dean Carlucci ring a bell?"

Curtis thought about it. "No."

"You a sports fan, Mr. Yee?"

"Good God, no."

Bobbi gritted her teeth. "They may have played you to the hilt, but they were certainly sloppy about it."

"How do you mean?" Patricia asked.

She told them.

* * *

"Listen!"

"What?"

"That, hear that?" Dean said with urgency.

Mark had just lugged the wheelchair to the twenty-third floor and was out of breath. As he opened it and helped Dean into it, he listened in the direction Dean was pointing. "I don't hear shit."

"Listen, carefully . . . it's her voice."

Mark cocked his ears. It took a moment, but yes, then he heard it, too. It was coming from the opening of a vent above them, a small ventilator that Dean knew was part of the fresh-air system and wasn't up and running yet. It would completely change the air in the apartments every ten minutes, even better than on airplanes. They were in the small, tight room off the center elevator shaft that the fire stairs led to, the room on each floor where, for now, the construction elevator arrived, and where, in the future, service people would access the plumbing, heating, wiring, all the building's guts. "I hear her," Mark said.

"She's reciting something . . ."

Mark listened again. "Reading something."

"Thank God," Mark said, "that means she's all right."

"But how the hell do we get in there to help her?"

Chapter Twenty

Audrey finished the letter, very moved. Her father had told her that if he should die before Melba, without being able to talk to Audrey about these things, please know that he loved her, that he had the greatest hopes for her and her future, but that he feared she would not take her life in the direction that her Aunt Melba would want. *I have the distinct feeling, dear Audrey, that once you know the secrets (and I believe you* should *know the secrets, that is why I give the combination to my safe to you before anyone else), once you see the truth you will want to wash your hands. "Firm moral fiber" is how someone once described me in a puff piece. I said no, that is my daughter you are describing. My path in life was set long before I had any control over it, but yours could be different, dearest daughter. Perhaps I hope it shall be. To make up for some of my own sins.*

He was referring to what she'd already seen in the safe, the Kaneohe Project, the Makena Villas debacle, the illegal Chinese money flowing through Victoria Towers and probably countless more schemes like them. Audrey almost wished she'd known none of it.

"He left you this," Ben said, holding out the red-velvet pouch. "It was the only thing in the little safe."

Audrey took it from him. Her hands were trembling because she knew this was very important. To her father, and thus to her. Whatever it was, he went through great lengths to protect it from her brothers and Aunt. Audrey untied the bag's strings, broke the plastic seal of the chop, and slid the contents into her palm.

It was a beautiful light green jade pendant, the shade of an apple, the finest jade in the world, consistent in color, pure. The carving of a peach was of museum quality, set on a base of twenty-four-carat gold. It took Audrey's breath away.

"Wow," Ben admired. "Pretty cool."

"It was my mother's. I saw it when I was a little girl. I remember reaching up for it, trying to eat it, I guess. There is a portrait at Aunt's house of Mother wearing it. I'm told the artist had no trouble capturing my mother's beauty, but great difficulty getting the beauty of the stone on canvas. It's the most exquisite piece of jewelry I've ever seen."

"And worth a fucking fortune."

Audrey couldn't care less. "Its meaning far outweighs its value." She opened the clasp on the hefty gold chain and lifted it around her neck. She had trouble closing it, however, and Ben came around. The feel of his fingers on her neck and back made her shudder. But he clasped it and moved away.

She stood and studied her reflection in the gilded mirror hanging above the fireplace. She was startled—for a moment it seemed she was actually looking at her mother!

"Why a stupid peach?" Ben asked.

"It isn't stupid at all. The peach is a beautiful fruit. It stands for happiness and fertility." She thought warmly of the baby she was carrying inside her.

He got it, too. "Fertility? How fitting," he glibly added. "Fuckhead's baby."

"Why do you hate Mark so? What's that got to do with revenge?"

"If you had only wanted me," he explained, "I might have given it up. Or killed old Dragon Lady instead."

"Jesus, Ben. One minute you don't have any interest in me, and the next you sound like I jilted you for Mark."

Ben grabbed the pendant and looked at it again. "You like jade?"

"Very much," she said, giving in to the change in conversation. "The most interesting thing about jade is that it changes colors depending on how you are feeling."

"Huh?"

"If you are well and happy, it's light in color."

"What if you're sick?" he asked.

"Then it is dark." She pressed it into his hand and then looked at it. "Very dark."

"Fuck off." He laughed, handing it back to her. "What else does the peach mean in Chinese culture?"

She glared at him, nearly spitting out the words. "Long life."

"I would say," he responded with a glimmer of delight, "that ancient legend is not all it's made out to be."

"She's stopped," Dean said as soon as he heard the silence. "She's stopped talking."

Mark was helping him back into his wheelchair. "Wait, I hear him this time." They heard Audrey and Ben talking. "And her again."

Dean made an assessment. "Sounds like they're in the library. We're hearing them either through the fresh-air intake to the fireplace flue or the recirculation vent."

"You have your cell phone with you?" Mark asked.

"No. Flew out of the apartment without thinking. You?"

"It's in there with her. Nutcase didn't give me time to gather my things."

Dean's eyes flashed. "Maybe Audrey used it."

"Battery was dying on my last call."

Dean's ears perked. "They're talking too softly, I can't make out what they're saying."

Mark nodded. "We need to get the cops."

"We're going in there."

Mark fought him. "How?"

"However you got out."

Mark thought for a moment. Then he said, "We're helpless out here. This man is dangerous—look what he did to me—but Audrey obviously is keeping him at bay, giving us time to get help."

"It's two against one," Dean reminded him.

"He's got weapons," Mark argued, pointing to his head. "Might have a gun."

"We can't abandon Audrey," Dean pleaded, thinking the conversation was backward, that Mark should be saying what he was.

"I'm going to get help," Mark said with finality.

Dean was incredulous. "What?"

"You're in a fucking wheelchair! What good are you?"

"You bastard."

Mark said, "It's not personal, but I've got a point."

Dean was seething. "I'm *here,* am I not? How do you think I got here?"

"I'd stay here and send you, but I think you'd agree that I can move faster. I'll be back with the cops."

"No!" Dean pleaded. "I need you! Audrey needs you—"

But Mark was gone.

"Coward," Dean muttered, loud enough, he hoped, that Mark could still hear him. "God-damned coward."

* * *

The elderly Chinese couple and their mainland friends listened to Bobbi finish describing how two people who claimed to be them visited Victoria Towers that morning and left in mock outrage.

"Impersonators?" Patricia gasped, incredulous.

"But for what reason?" Curtis added. "Why would someone go to such lengths to preview an apartment?"

"Why would they say they were us? And to see Audrey, to risk the fact that she might have seen a photo of her father with us or even remembered us herself." The woman shook her head. "Didn't they think, even if they got away with it, that we would find out one day?"

Bobbi said, "Maybe it wouldn't matter—one day. Their reason had to be more immediate."

Jesse Walker interjected, "You said they came and left in a limousine? It was probably rented. You might call the companies and track it down."

Tim Hillard asked a question. "Have any of you seen the news report that's been running all afternoon and evening, the bodies they found at the airport?" The blank faces told him no one had. "An elderly Chinese couple were found dead, execution-style."

"My God," Bobbi gasped.

Tim continued. "The only reason I connect it is the confirmed reports of a black limo in the area about the time they think the people were iced."

"Oh dear." Bobbi went pale. "Someone shot the

Yees?" She looked at the startled faces in front of her. "I don't mean you, I mean the Yees. The other Yees. I mean *them,* whoever they were."

Tim rose. "I'm going to call a couple of people I know. I think the police will want to speak to you about this, Bobbi."

She nodded in agreement.

"Tim's well connected," Jesse offered. "He was a newsman in Seattle for years. He'll get answers fast."

There was a long, uneasy silence. Loretta Ables started singing again, a soft ballad, but none of the Yee party were listening. They were lost in thought. Finally Curtis Yee said, "I have a feeling I know what this is about."

Curtis rubbed his chin, and then asked Bobbi, "Did you or Audrey show them Hiram's vault?"

"Of course."

"Did they go inside it?"

"No," Bobbi assured him. "It's locked. Why?"

He looked very unsure. "I spoke to Hiram from Paris the day before he died. He told me he'd helped out a friend in trouble by moving some of his records from the colony to his safe in Honolulu."

Bobbi nodded. "Yes. Several locked boxes arrived a couple of weeks before Hiram died."

"Why's that important?" Jesse asked.

"The reputation of the man he was helping is what is of importance here," Mr. Yee said.

"Who?" his wife inquired, her eyes beading as if to prepare herself.

He wasn't happy to say the name. "Tung."

"Portuguese Tung?" she gasped. It looked like her suspicions were realized.

"Holy shit!" Bobbi gasped, breathless. "Excuse my language, but he threatened Audrey when she was in Hong Kong for the funeral."

"I don't doubt it," Yee said.

"But who is he exactly?" Bobbi asked.

"One of the most notorious organized crime figures in Southeast Asia," Jesse offered. "Tung is his real name, they call him Portuguese Tung in the colony—"

Curtis Yee interrupted. "Or more commonly Pearl River Tung because he controls crime across the Pearl River delta from Hong Kong."

Bobbi looked at Curtis again. "That's what came in the locked boxes that were put in the safe? Hiram has this guy's 'records' in his safe in the building?"

Old Mr. Yee nodded. "And we can safely assume these are most incriminating."

His wife put the pieces together. "I see what you're driving at. Tung trusted incriminating documents to Hiram, knowing he could count on him. They were pals from the old days. But Hiram dies. Tung is worried. He needs to get the documents back. He sends two people to impersonate us to do just that."

Jesse agreed. "Easy access, no questions asked, no suspicions on your part."

"But they didn't get into the vault," Bobbi reiterated. "And why would someone blow them away?"

No one had an easy answer.

Tim hurried back in. "Come on, everyone, we're moving the party to the police station."

"What did the cops say?" Bobbi asked as they got up.

"I didn't talk to the cops," Tim explained, "just to a reporter I know. He told me that he heard two things: the two bodies match descriptions of killers-for-hire being sought in Manila, Kuala Lumpur, and Bangkok."

"My goodness," Patricia Yee said, looking scared now for the first time.

Bobbi was incredulous. "Those people we thought were you," she said with a nod toward the Yees, "were actually hired assassins?"

"And probably have other talents as well," Tim continued, "because the initial tests on the bodies showed evidence of high-tech explosives."

Bobbi gasped. "What? That's what killed them?"

"No," Tim assured them, "they were shot to death. The explosive residue was all over their clothing."

"I see," Patricia Yee said, grasping her husband's hand.

Jesse said, "They were sent to destroy the information in Hiram Goh's safe."

"My God in heaven," Bobbi said as it dawned on her, "the woman, the other Mrs. Yee, she carried this big heavy bag she said she got in India . . ."

"Bingo," Jesse exclaimed.

"She wouldn't let go of it," Bobbi remembered, "lugged it all over the apartment."

"Did she have time enough to plant a bomb?" Jesse asked.

Bobbi gasped, "Sure. When Audrey fell on the girder, the woman was in the bathroom for about twenty minutes."

They were all chilled into silence.

Then they hurried for the doors.

Audrey could not be pulled from the image in the mirror. The jade peach pendant had mesmerized her. Audrey's father had obviously kept it after her mother died. Many times she'd asked him what ever happened to it, and he would shrug and say he didn't know. He'd secretly held on to it through the years, saved it for his beloved Audrey. He knew she alone would appreciate it. She was almost moved to tears.

Ben called for her to come to the safe again. When she did, she found him standing with a pile of papers in his hand. "He left you some great reading as well," he announced.

"What do you mean?"

"I mean this stuff. Here's a list of hits from 1994."

"Hits? Songs?"

He laughed at her naivety. "Hits, like murders. And here's all the companies Tung secretly has control of."

She froze. "Tung?"

"Portuguese Tung."

"We've met."

"Your daddy was obviously involved with some pretty shady types."

"That doesn't make Dad a criminal."

Ben laughed. "That's what they said about Sinatra." He leafed through the pages. "There's enough here to indict him for life. Amazing. I could get a lot of money for this."

"How did you—?"

He held up a hammer that he'd used to pry open the locks on the boxes. "This thing has come in handy tonight."

But Audrey wasn't hearing him any longer. She was staring at something she'd never seen before. It was a rectangular woven sea-grass box that was sitting under the computer table just outside the safe, against the wall. She walked closer and stared at it. Where had it come from? She knew everything in the apartment from the forks in the kitchen drawer to the stored toilet paper. "Did you put this here?"

Ben poked his head out from the safe. A bunch

of Tung files fell out of his arms. He kicked them in front of him. "What?"

"This box?"

He saw it. "Nope."

Audrey walked to it, stooped down to examine it. It was about the size and shape of a toaster. She reached out to pick it up. Only it surprised her. Thinking it weighed almost nothing, she was startled to find she could barely lift it. She brought it up and set it on the table with both hands, next to the computer keyboard. Then she lifted off the sea-grass cover. Inside was a hard metal box that looked like ones she'd seen in war movies where they stored the telephone out in the trenches. It had been soldered shut. "What in the world *is* this?" she said, intrigued.

Suddenly they both heard the sound of an alarm. It was a HAL warning, not a fire alarm but a pre-smoke signal. Audrey thought it probably was the kitchen, where there was the most chance of smoke or fire.

"What is *that*?" Ben asked about the sound.

Audrey set the strange box down. "I don't know. Maybe I left the oven on."

"Let's go check." Then he brightened. "And we'll have that surprise dessert."

Audrey could figure out the box later. She needed to play his game. "Yes," Audrey replied, thinking, Yes, oh yes, just come to the kitchen with me.

* * *

Melba Goh sat impatiently erect in front of a desk in an old cinder-block precinct building not far from Victoria Towers. Graced by palms and verdant plantings at the entrance, the building was nevertheless completely out of place. It looked more like a pumping station on the tundra than a public building in Honolulu. Melba thought it smelled like a toilet inside, dank and unclean. It was all she could do to sit still.

She had talked first to a young and handsome officer, Ralph Randazzo. When he told her the police couldn't start until Audrey had been missing for twenty-four hours, she demanded to speak to his superior. Melba and her ancient driver, who had accompanied her into the station, sat in silence, he tapping his feet, she rapping her fan in rhythm against the edge of the desk.

When Lieutenant Aucoin entered, a tall, energetic-looking man with marine-cropped hair, he greeted her with respect, saying it was an honor to meet one of the community's most influential members.

She stood and allowed the compliment, but got right down to business. "You are most gracious, but I have not come here for niceties. My niece is missing. She has been stalked by a man who has sent her threatening notes and she is now in grave danger. Detective Wong is already on this case. We must locate him."

"Whoa," the no-nonsense cop said, "back up, and tell me how you came to believe this."

Melba sat back down and repeated most everything she'd said to Sergeant Randazzo. As she spoke, another cop, snarky-looking and grossly overweight, came in and began noisily shoving papers into a filing cabinet that looked bursting already. As Melba continued her story, the portly cop stopped what he was doing and started listening to her. ". . . it isn't like Audrey to disappear, so I fear something grave has happened to her," Melba finished. "Detective Wong knows most of this already, but he is not on duty tonight."

"What has Wong found out?"

Melba shrugged. "Nothing that I know of."

The lieutenant said, "Where do your niece and her boyfriend work?"

"Mark Carson has a menial job at the Bank of Hawaii," Melba said with an obvious lack of respect. Then her voice turned proud. "Audrey is the head sales agent at Victoria Towers."

"Any problems at work," the lieutenant asked, "that might have led her to believe someone was out to harm her?"

"Not that I know."

"So this is speculation based on what?"

"Excuse me, Lieutenant," a voice interjected. It was the fat cop at the file cabinet. His name tag said Alan Holcomb. "I heard you say Victoria Towers."

"Yes? So?" The lieutenant sounded impatient.

"Well, Jimmy Stewart called in earlier, reporting a woman in danger up there tonight."

Melba Goh gasped. "Audrey!"

The lieutenant said, "Impossible."

Officer Holcomb nodded. "Told him that, but he insisted."

"He's a screwball," the lieutenant said.

"Who?" Melba demanded. "Who reported this?"

The lieutenant explained. "Guy in a wheelchair, Dean Carlucci's his name. I'm from Maui, he grew up there as well. Was a famous skier till he was in a bad car crash—"

"I know him, of course," Melba insisted. "My brother hired him to design the security system for the Towers."

"Yeah, well," the Lieutenant added, "that's not all he does. He watches the Towers, and all the other buildings around here, sees everything, always reporting some crackpot sighting or another."

Melba slammed her fan down on the desk. "You had best begin to listen! This man saw Audrey and said she was in danger. Did you not even investigate? Not even send a car to look? Shame on you, Lieutenant!"

The lieutenant looked up at Officer Holcomb, then at Sergeant Randazzo. And then he said, "She really missing?"

"She was supposed to go to Lanai, but she

never made the plane, never showed up. She's vanished."

"Or she's up in that building," Randazzo said.

The lieutenant punched one of the phone buttons. "I'll send someone to check."

Dean heard the alarm stop. She had shut it off. He figured they must be in the kitchen, for he could no longer hear their voices. He had given up trying to find an opening where Ben had dragged Mark through. There was the fire door leading to the bodyguard's room, but that was locked as securely as the front doors. He was stymied. The only possibility was that there must be some kind of space leading to the apartment that only a construction dick would know about. There had to be another way to go about getting in there.

Thinking of Audrey shutting down the smoke alarm at the computer panel gave him an idea. He wheeled over to a long metal box positioned on the wall of the center elevator shaft and opened it. Inside was a mass of wires and cables, all relating to the computer for Residence Twenty-three. Next to them was a small LCD screen like in a palmtop computer and a minuscule keyboard.

He had created and installed the computer software for the building. Maybe, he hoped, he could uninstall the security program for Residence Twenty-three. Maybe he could destroy HAL, and thereby save Audrey.

But he couldn't see. Then he remembered that

as he left the take-out place earlier in the evening, he'd reached out and grabbed both a mint, a toothpick, and a pack of matches. Sure enough, they were all still in his pocket. He lit a match and held it up so it illuminated the keyboard. And in the dim light, he went to work.

Audrey had just pressed the code to turn off the smoke warning. "Dumb me," she muttered, "I left the gas on under the roasting pan."

"It started smoking," Ben added, pushing buttons on the Gaggeneau range panel to shut them off. "Why'd you have those burners on anyway?"

"I was going to degrease the pan," she said in a fast save, "for gravy. But I forgot to go back to it."

"You could have burned the place down."

"Better way to die," she said.

He smiled sardonically.

She had to get him to the dishwasher, had to get him to bend down so he wouldn't see what she was going to do. "Go get the platter on the table," she said.

"Then we'll have dessert," he added.

"Fine," she said, donning mitt pot holders.

"Why are you shaking?"

"I'm not," she said.

"You are." He looked suspicious. "What's wrong?"

"I'm upset," she said, acting. "I'm on the verge of tears because I can't figure you out. I don't know whether I should believe you when you say you want to hurt me or when you tell me you're my friend."

"Could be both."

"Please, Ben!" She held her hands to her ears for effect.

"Audrey, I'm sorry. Just teasing."

"Don't harm me, Ben. I'll do anything you want."

He stared at her for a moment, then leaned forward and slowly kissed her on the cheek. She wanted to vomit, but she smiled instead. He bought it. He said, "I'll get that platter for you," and, with a wink, went into the dining room.

She gripped the tall brass handles sticking up from the sides of the copper pan. It was heavy to begin with, but even more so with the fat. Yet she knew she could do it. The trick was protecting herself. So she set it down for a moment and donned the apron that hung on the back side of the pantry door. Then she grasped the pan again.

Ben brought the serving dish in, admonishing her about not eating enough. "The lamb was perfect; you really missed out."

"I'm okay. Slide the leftovers onto the cutting board there and put the platter in the dishwasher."

He opened the door and pulled out the bottom rack. Then he bent down to put in the platter—

That's when she struck. She thrust the pan toward his face, and then let go of the bottom handle, so all the boiling grease would splash outward. He let out an intense cry of pain, and threw his hands up.

And then she ran. She didn't take time to assess his condition, to see where she'd hit him. She ran through the apartment with speed she didn't even know she possessed. When she passed the table just outside the safe, she glanced at the strange metal box again, but she couldn't even wonder about it then. Quickly, she found herself in the guest bedroom. From somewhere behind her came the cry of a wounded animal.

She went directly to the closet, yanked it open and fell to her knees at the panel that looked like it had been chiseled away from the wallboard. Sinking her fingernails into the slit in the wall, it popped forward when she applied pressure, and she tossed it aside. And found herself looking into a black hole. She heard more cries of pain coming from the kitchen. He sounded enraged, like an animal caught in a trap. But unlike an animal with steel teeth on its leg, he might be able to move. She had to work fast.

Chapter Twenty-one

Audrey crawled on all fours, a distance of only about four feet, until she rapped her head on what felt like cement, but rattled. She knew right away it was steel. Steel? A fire wall or door of some sort! Then she recalled that each floor had a space along the service corridor near the central elevator shaft for workmen's storage and tools and such. Perhaps that was where she was. She frantically groped for a handle or lock to open it with, then recalled the lock would be on the outside. This was accessible from the service hall, not the apartment. Ben had just known how to get into it from the interior of the closet. There had to be a handle—

And sure enough, there was, but under it was a padlock. A big, locked padlock. Ben had the key. He either had anticipated using this or someone had put the steel door on backward, facing the wrong way. In any case, she was locked in. She felt the flat and cold steel wall separating her from freedom. She pounded on it violently, shouting,

"Mark! Mark, can you hear me? Please, Mark, answer me!"

Audrey sucked in her breath and pounded again, and then slumped, exhausted. There had to be some other way—

Her thoughts died as she heard the rapping on the pipe, a steady soft clang that told her someone was answering her. Mark! He could hear her. He was out there somewhere beyond this steel plate. "Mark," she cried, banging on the steel again for all she was worth, "I'm here, I'm here! Help me!"

But she heard nothing in response.

She started groping to her right, to feel what was there. More steel, and what felt like insulation. She turned to her left and moved her hand up and down the wall of the small space. She had to hurry.

Then she screamed, as Ben's hands clasped around her legs, and he began violently dragging her back into the apartment.

At Honolulu Police headquarters, Bobbi and the Yees finished telling Detective Wong what they suspected. He had finally been called when they explained this was about Audrey Goh, and he had rushed to the station. He was reluctant to believe that the murders at the airport tied to his investigation of someone sending Melba's niece threatening notes. Until he put a call into Detective Jules Gordon of the Homicide Division and learned that his colleague had been trying to reach Audrey because her business card had been found in the pocket of the dead man. Then he learned of the traces of plastic explosives on the murder victims.

The man still seemed reluctant, but he did pick up the phone. "Give me Aucoin," he said, and waited, tapping his foot. He brightened suddenly, "Donald, Matthew Wong here. I'm going to ask your opinion on something, the building's in your jurisdiction—"

"What building?"

"Victoria Towers."

"Jesus," Aucoin muttered, it seemed all of Honolulu was talking about that place tonight. "Funny you should mention it."

Wong said, "Got some folks here who believe the airport incident—"

"The murders?"

"Yeah. Folks here think the deceased were hired to plant a bomb in Victoria Towers and then were silenced so they couldn't talk about it."

Aucoin laughed into the phone. "It gets crazier."

Wong grinned as well. "That's what I said."

"Gimme the phone," Bobbi ordered.

The man did no such thing. "I heard a rumor"—he looked up at Tim Hillard—"of forensics finding some residual explosives, and that they were known killers."

He was silent for a moment. The man on the other end was talking. Bobbi could stand no more. She suddenly punched the detective's speaker phone button and shouted, "There's a bomb up in Victoria Towers! This is no joke. You've got to do something about it—"

Bobbi stopped because she heard a voice from the other end of the line that sounded distinctly like Melba Goh's. "Bobbi?" the shrill voice intoned.

It *was* Melba! Bobbi shouted, "Melba?"

Lieutenant Aucoin started to tell them that Miss Goh was in his office and that he'd just sent a man to investigate a report that Audrey Goh was up in the building right then.

Bobbi was panic-stricken. "My God, my God," she cried, "of course. *That's* where Audrey and Mark are. They just stayed there."

"And there's a bomb up there," Patricia Yee whispered in fear.

Bobbi turned to Detective Wong and said, "I want *you* to tell me you're going to get Audrey out of that building before the whole thing blows sky-high!"

Audrey screamed and kicked in an effort to get free of Ben's grip, but she could not. He grunted and groaned as he dragged her back into the closet, over the trail of Mark's blood, to the bedroom. She tried to grab hold of the piece of drywall she had ripped down, wanting to use it as a weapon, but he was pulling her too quickly.

His wounds were visible in the light of the bedroom. She saw a grotesque red blotch on his right cheek and chin, and all over his shoulder and arm, where he'd pulled the shirt off to expose his burned flesh. She knew he had to be in great pain, and his face was contorted. He was also raving. "How could you do this to me? You little fucking bitch, I didn't hurt you. I never touched you!"

"Get away from me!" she shouted, trying to wrestle her foot free, but to no avail.

"Talking nice to me was all your clever little game to get me." He was kicking her now, in the legs and buttocks, fired with rage.

"No, Ben—"

"You let me kiss you, and then you betrayed me."

"I was frightened, I—"

"I trusted you, I wanted a beautiful evening with you, I gave you that pendant, and you—"

"Look! The jade's dark 'cause it's near you, you sick bastard," she screamed. She managed to shake her foot loose and kicked him directly in the crotch. He doubled over in pain with only a whooshing sound of the air being sucked out of him.

She didn't look back. She hightailed it—where to go?—down the hall and looked into rooms, trying to figure out which was the safest. She found the bodyguard's room and checked the emergency fire door leading to the stairwell. It was electronically locked, and she didn't have a clue how to open it, for it never had been necessary to know, only to speak of its attributes to prospective clients like the Yees.

But the room did have the major security computer station, and she took a seat there and switched on the monitor. She called up a map of the apartment. The whole floor plan appeared, with a red mark for Ben and a purple mark for her, made possible by infrared sensors in the ceilings. He was still in the guest bedroom, but the red mark moved slightly to the right, then the left, then to the door of the bedroom, staggering from side to side, but progressing.

She pushed two keys, and one of the most touted of features in selling the apartment to prospective tenants went into action: a steel panel suddenly cut Ben off at the end of the corridor, completely blocking his way.

Dean had felt Audrey's rattling of the storage-closet firewall all the way on the floor above. He could hear her pounding on it, an echo that sounded like someone thumping on an oil drum. He looked away from the computer panel and wondered for a moment how to answer her. Then he wheeled his chair to a pipe that rose from the floor below, and twisted himself quickly so that the footrest knocked against it. It was faint in comparison to her sounds, but he did it again and again, harder and harder, hoping she would hear that someone was responding. Yet nothing had happened, and he feared Ben had found her. He had to find another way.

Dean was almost out of matches. Reprogramming his system was a difficult undertaking even in the best of light, requiring a lot of time and deep concentration. This wasn't working. Uninstalling the program was impossible, but perhaps he could break into the code for locking the doors and open the apartment's entry doors. He knew where the codes were located, and knew how to access them. Trouble was, nothing was labeled anything so easy as Entry Doors or Fire Door. It was all in digital code. Which he didn't have stored in his head. The codes were lost in a sea of remembered numbers. He knew he could not accomplish such a task without the three-hundred-page book he'd printed for the men who would one day monitor the building's system.

He played around with the keyboard for a few more moments, and then, frustrated and angry, he started to rethink. How else could he get into the apartment? That was the only question. By shutting HAL down. But he could not do that by the computer. So how about manually, the way he'd overridden the construction elevator to work? Sure! Murder HAL by brute force!

But to do so, he'd have to go to the twenty-fourth floor, where the important wires connecting to Residence Twenty-three had nearly burned up that morning. Getting to the next floor by stairs was impossible when alone in a wheelchair. To get to twenty-four, he had to go back down the stairs to twenty-two, to take the construction elevator back up—that was, if Mark had sent it back up when he ran off with his tail between his legs. He'd done this before in his two years as a handicapped person, once for the challenge of it, once quite by accident, an incident in which he nearly killed himself a second time. Wheelchairs could descend stairs if you knew precisely how to do it, and had something substantial to hang on to. He was now about to try for the third time.

He gripped the railing with both hands at the top of the steps, then brought his right hand to the wheel and moved it forward enough that he dropped to the first step. He hit with a thud, his whole body shaking. He held tight to the railing as he steadied himself. Piece of cake. Down another, thud. Down one more, thud. Yeah, he would be the Evel Knievel of wheelchairs when this was over. Down yet another. He'd get there.

Audrey watched the diagram as the red mark moved back from the way he'd come, toward one of two halls that connected to the rest of the bedrooms and the living areas. Audrey hit the keys, and again he was stopped in his tracks, forcing him to turn around. He stood there, facing the other way, she could tell, until he made a dash for the living room. She was ready for him. She cut him off just as he reached it, and could tell by the lack of movement of the red mark that he'd run right into it.

As she waited for him to regain his strength, she typed into the computer: HELP! BEING HELD CAPTIVE BY A MADMAN WHO WANTS TO ILL ME! She scanned it, went back and changed ILL to KILL and wrote in her name, the building name, but before she could go any farther, HAL's screen blinked and suddenly replied: PLEASE IDENTIFY RECIPE YOU ARE TRYING TO LOCATE. She knew HAL was going on the fritz again, and cursed. When she checked on Ben, there was no red mark where she'd last seen it. In fact, the doors, which had been indicated by strong black lines across the corridors, were gone. HAL had freed him. Damn!

Her eyes scanned the entire floor plan until she saw him, moving from room to room at the far end, trying to determine where she was hiding. He poked his head into the library, then the music room, the conservatory, the office, and then he walked into the safe. The red mark stopped just inside the vault door. She took her chances and prayed that HAL would obey her. "Don't fail me now," she whispered as a few strokes told HAL to close the safe door and lock it. Which it did.

Ben was trapped behind two feet of solid steel. She smiled, thinking he could spend his time reading while he waited for the police to get him out. Then she realized that she was no further ahead, for how would *she* get out of there? She ran to the front doors. "Mark?" she shouted. "If you're there, if you can hear me, pound on the door!" She waited. "Please, Mark!" Nothing. Then she put her head against the door and closed her eyes. She was about to succumb to despair when her fingers felt the jade peach around her neck. And she knew she couldn't give up.

With renewed energy she kicked and banged on the door. "Mark! Mark! Help me!"

Mark Carson, wearing nothing but his undershorts, was standing in the middle of Pacific Street at that very moment, bending over to speak into the window of a patrol car. Melba's big black Lincoln approached from the right. Almost at the same moment, from the left came Bobbi's bright yellow Beetle. "It's Mark!" Bobbi shouted. The Yees, in the rear seat, were rapt with attention. Bobbi gunned the car, it lunged forward, and she slammed on the brakes right next to Mark's butt. Tim and Jesse drove up in their rented Pontiac. Lieutenant Aucoin and Officer Holcomb stopped immediately behind them.

Mark turned from the police cruiser and was astonished to see Bobbi's Bug. And Melba's big boat. What the hell? There was Melba, running toward him. And Bobbi getting out of her car. And who were all these other people? It looked like half the police force on the island had arrived.

"Thank God you are safe," Melba cried to Mark, her hopes up. "Where is Audrey?"

"That's what I'm telling them," Mark said. "She's still up in the building."

Melba sucked in her breath. Several more police vehicles converged on the spot. Wong and Gordon got out of one of the unmarked cars. The situation seemed chaotic, no one knowing quite who was in charge.

Bobbi was at Mark's side now. "Mark! There's a bomb up there."

"A what?"

Melba asked, "What happened to you?"

"Hit me over the head, tried to kill me." He saw the cops were listening now, all of them.

"Who hit you over the head?" Bobbi asked.

"Ben," Mark answered.

"Who's Ben?" Aucoin asked.

"Ben Benedict," he said, "he's the head electrician on the project. He wants to kill Audrey."

"Huh?" Bobbi thought she heard wrong. "Ben is Audrey's good buddy."

Mark moaned, "Not anymore." He tried to play the hero. "He mashed my head something awful, but I fought back. I wasn't about to let him harm Audrey, I'd let him kill me first! I woke up tied to a girder in the dark." He shivered, turning white. "There's really a bomb up there?"

"How'd you get down?" the lieutenant asked.

"Construction elevator. He got it working."

Bobbi said, "But all the power's off after six."

"Somebody tell me what this bomb thing is about!" Mark pleaded.

The lieutenant turned to the sergeant and ordered him to call for backup, get a chopper in the sky fast. Gordon told Mark that they had reason to believe that the people who were found dead at the airport that day had planted a bomb on the twenty-third floor of Victoria Towers.

Mark turned white. "The airport?" he gasped, remembering following it on TV earlier. "They were here?"

"Where the hell's the bomb squad?" Wong muttered. This was a bigger order now that they knew there were people in the building.

Bobbi pressed Mark. "How'd you get free?"

"Dean."

Bobbi gasped. "Dean? Dean Carlucci?"

"Yeah."

Bobbi felt her head spinning. "How many damn people were up there?"

"Carlucci is Jimmy Stewart," the lieutenant offered. Then he seemed puzzled. "But he's handicapped."

"I helped him as much as I could," Mark boasted, "and then we decided someone should get help and he ordered me down. I could run, you see."

Bobbi gasped, "You mean he's still there, too?"

"He sure is," Mark said, looking up at the blinking airplane lights on the edifice a couple of blocks away.

"Audrey!" Aunt shouted. "What about Audrey?"

Mark shrugged. "When I left, and I left reluctantly, believe me, she was still in there with him. But she was okay."

"How long ago was that?" Aucoin asked him.

"Fifteen minutes, twenty maybe. Took me a while to get down."

"A lot can happen in that time." Wong said, looking up at the tower. Then the bomb-squad van rounded the corner, and he waved to them. "Come on, let's get over there, fast!"

It seemed to take forever for him to get down the stairs, but finally Dean rolled onto the construction elevator and pulled the level for it to rise without even closing the gate. When he reached twenty-four, he rolled off and moved his wheelchair over to the exact spot where he'd located the smoking wires that afternoon. But he could not reach the control box from the chair, just as he'd been unable to do when Ben was there. Having no one to help him this time, he raised his arms and managed with brute force to lift himself by his hands. He remembered the hands of that stranger who pulled him from the burning car, incredible force and power you could never imagine a human to muster. Holding himself up there by his hands, he sucked in his breath, and then let one go. He swung on one hand only, one hand supporting all two hundred pounds of him. And with the other, as he swung in midair, he grasped a handful of HAL wires and ripped them out with a vengeance, as if he were ripping out Ben's eyes.

* * *

Back in the guardroom, Audrey saw the screen pop up with a warning: SYSTEM FAILURE. And then it went blank, and so did the lights. The room, the entire apartment, was plunged into darkness. She could hear the music stop, the air vents quit blowing, the ovens beep a final time, and the steam jet in the master bedroom let out a final whoosh. Everything was dead. She heard a series of clicks in the electronics in the walls and doors that told her HAL was deceased. It became eerie and silent. She realized the door to the bodyguard's room, which she'd locked when she entered, was now open.

And if it was open, she hoped, the front door would be, too.

She got up from her chair and made her way into the corridor. She knew where a big Mexican church candle was sitting in a gilded holder, and found it, wrapping her hands around it. Then she found matches in the living room and lit it. And pointed it toward the front door. She gasped, "Oh, God!" when she saw that the front doors, the entry doors which had locked them in at six that evening, had snapped open. Freedom awaited her.

Just before she moved toward the door, she heard something. Then it dawned on her: if all the doors had unlocked, even the time-set entry doors, the safe must have as well! With no computer to control anything, nothing worked. Ben was on the loose. And he was looking for her. "Audrey!" she heard him call.

She heard him coming. She put the candle down on the floor and reached out for the only heavy object the dim light let her see: the mysterious steel box. She grabbed it in both hands and held it over her head. When Ben rounded the corner, she brought it down on his head. He slumped to the ground. She tossed the box to the floor, where it landed with a thud. And then—she swore—she saw something she had not seen before. A little red light seemed to glow from the box, from the crack where the lid had been soldered to the body.

But this was no time to speculate on what it was. She grabbed the candle and dashed out through the front doors. The candle immediately blew out as she hurried through the small service corridor leading toward the staircase at the center of the building. She threw it to the ground. She ran to the end of the corridor to see where the construction elevator was. She first looked down, but it wasn't there. Then she held securely to the elevator gate, where a window frame would be when the construction elevator was removed, and leaned out from the edge of the building. It was above her, on twenty-four!

But where was Mark? Had he taken it up there? Or was he indeed, as Ben had said, beneath her? She faced a dilemma: which way to go? Down was certainly the better choice, for it was the direction of freedom, toward help, away from Ben.

The elevator might be faster, but it was simply not possible. Besides, she had to find Mark.

She ran down the metal stairs to the twenty-second floor, her heels clattering loudly. If she couldn't find Mark, she would just hightail it down all twenty-two floors to the ground, to get help. "Mark?" she whispered in the stairwell. She stepped onto the vast floor. "Mark?"

The level was not only dark and forbidding, but filled with stacks of plastic five-gallon paint cans, coils of wiring, piles of plywood, boxes and crates of things. He was probably unconscious. He could be hidden by any of those objects. She resisted the urge to run; she couldn't leave him. But where would she begin looking? "Mark! Mark, where are you?"

"Audrey!" It was Ben's voice. She could hear it reverberating from inside the stairwell. "Audrey, I'm going to find you . . ."

She cringed, ducking behind a pile of boxes containing toilet tanks. As she did so, her left foot slid suddenly, coming out from under her weight on something slippery. She ran her finger over her shoe and brought it to her nose. Blood. She gasped. This was where Ben had taken Mark. And then she reached down and felt the congealing puddle with her fingertips. Was he still alive?

But then, scaring her half to death, there was a shudder and she heard ropes and pulleys moving. The bottom of the construction elevator came into view. It was chugging downward, down toward her. Dear God, let it be Mark! she prayed as she looked up at it, watching it take forever to get to her. Sure, Mark had broken free, and he was coming to help her.

But Ben was coming closer. "Audrey!" he shouted, and it sounded like he was breathing down her neck.

The elevator was closer as well. Audrey prayed she'd get on it before he got her.

"Audrey, where—?" His voice stopped when he realized the elevator was running. He dashed over toward it.

He was standing just inches from where she was crouched, but he did not notice her because he was intent on the elevator. Mark, he thought suddenly, just as Audrey had. The fucker had gotten free—he turned and sure enough, Mark was not where he'd tied him.

When the construction elevator finally lumbered into view, Audrey could not make out Mark's silhouette. She couldn't make out anyone at all, for from her vantage point she could not see Dean in his wheelchair. She sprang from her hiding place, risking all, shouting, "Stop! Stop! I'm here, help me!"

There was a clanging of gears, and the floor of the elevator came to a stop about a foot beneath the twenty-second level. "Audrey?" the voice called out.

She blinked. It was a voice she knew, but it wasn't Mark's, and she was startled. "Audrey, behind you!" But she didn't have time to guess at his identity, for Ben grabbed her from behind and pulled her away from the open elevator gate. She attempted to put a knee in his crotch for the second time that night, but she couldn't maneuver herself into position. Her head struck a box of toilet tanks, knocking one to the cement floor, and she heard it crack into pieces. The box broke on contact, however, and she found her hand lying on a piece of jagged porcelain. She wrapped her fingers around it and jabbed it backward, hitting Ben as hard as she could.

He was dazed momentarily.

Which was just enough time for her to rush onto the elevator. The door closed as Ben's hands rattled the chain link, and she descended from his sight. And only then was she able to look up and see that the operator of the elevator—that voice she knew but couldn't place—was none other than Dean Carlucci.

Chapter Twenty-two

"It's all right," Dean said to a startled and frightened Audrey as the elevator descended. "It's all right now."

"You?" She was flabbergasted.

"Me."

"How—?"

"It's a long story."

They both heard Ben shouting from above them. But they were safe now. The construction elevator was slow, but even if Ben ran down the stairs, he couldn't do twenty-two flights faster than the elevator could. The horror was over.

"What happened to Mark?" she asked.

"He ran." Dean practically spit it out.

"Ran?"

"Said he was going to get help. I wanted *him* to help me get you out."

"He left you up there? In a wheelchair?" She was incredulous.

"He was scared, eh?" Dean wanted to call him a fucking yellow-bellied coward, but he had too much respect for her to do so. "Maybe he wasn't thinking clearly. He'd been hit on the head."

She blinked. And realized he was making excuses. "My God," she said as she realized something: it fit. Perfectly. Running off would be consistent with his manifesto up in the apartment a couple of hours ago. But she was now more curious about something else. "How did *you* get here?"

"Just crossed the street," he said facetiously.

"Seriously, why?"

"I . . ." He had had nightmares of her confronting him about the telescope, accusing him, being outraged, and hating him. He'd dreaded this moment. He didn't want to tell her, but the police certainly would be coming, and they knew about his little hobby, and thus so would she. Better to hear it from him directly. "I saw you through my telescope."

She was amazed. "Telescope?"

"I'm in a building a block from here." He pointed that way. They were passing the eighteenth floor. "Twenty-fifth floor. I check the Towers now and then to make sure everything's all right."

"You've been watching me?" It was an accusation, understandable because the cryptic notes had made her feel stalked.

"Well, yes. But I'll bet not like little Benny up there has been."

"My God!"

He could see she was very upset. He reached up and took her hand and clasped it tightly. "Audrey, I have long wanted to know you better, and yes, I've often watched you because you're the most beautiful girl in the world. But I never meant harm, only meant to protect."

She realized something. "And you did."

He nodded. "I saw it and tried the cops, but they wouldn't believe me. I missed the security truck on the street, so I rammed the fence and got up here myself. Mark was tied to a girder on twenty-two, but he was conscious by the time I got to him."

It occurred to her now. "You did something to HAL to open the doors."

"Murdered the bastard."

"I love it." They were passing the fifteenth floor. "It saved my life, I think."

"God Almighty, what was that nut trying to do?"

"Get revenge."

"Revenge?"

She looked down. She could see the flashing lights of police vehicles on the street. "Look!"

Dean saw it, too. He could make out police cars, a small yellow automobile, a big black one, a van or truck. A second later, a searchlight hit him in the eyes. He waved with both hands through the chain-link wall of the construction elevator. "Well, at least he came through."

"Yes!" Audrey shouted with glee.

The elevator suddenly creaked to a halt. Stopped dead.

Dean pulled on the levers. Audrey looked over the side, up, down, back to him. "What happened?"

"I don't know," Dean said. But he did. The dusty LCD panel had changed from MANUAL OVERRIDE to COMPUTER CONTROL. "The cops must have gotten into the control trailer and reprogrammed us. But why would they—"

The elevator shook and started moving again. But it was going the wrong way. It was going up instead of down. "What the hell?" he muttered.

"Why are they taking us up?" she cried.

She and Dean stared at one another, knowing the answer to that question wasn't one they wanted to hear. The reason the elevator was ascending again was because Ben was controlling it, not the police.

Less than half a mile away, on a deserted stretch of beach, a burly man dressed in an Aloha shirt and khaki shorts found a piece of sand he liked. It afforded him a perfect view of the night over the ocean, the low-hanging clouds that seemed to cling to the water like foam to beer, the twinkling lights of ships out on the sea, the sight of lovers walking hand in hand along the shore. It also afforded him a perfect view of Victoria Towers.

Which, he knew, in a little while would be no more.

* * *

Once the elevator had descended past his reach, Ben ran back to the apartment, into the guest bedroom, and dug into the backpack he'd worn when he arrived. He found his emergency computer programmer—something that Dean himself had created—and quickly accessed the elevator control. They thought they were pretty smart, getting away from him. And Carlucci, of all people, how the hell had he gotten there? What was he doing on the elevator? And where had the boyfriend gone?

He quickly stopped the elevator and reversed its direction. They were on their way back up. He'd teach them to try to fuck with him. His rage grew more intense as he felt the stinging burns on his face and chest. Then he slipped the programmer into the back pocket of the tux pants and started up the stairwell, taking two steps at a time, from twenty-two to twenty-three to twenty-four and on and on.

The best meeting place, he figured, would be the farthest from the ground.

On the ground, there was chaos. Everyone was talking at once, trying to figure out how to get into the securely locked building. The construction fence had been rammed by Dean's van, but the building itself was shut tight. The roaming security men, whom Dean had been unable to flag down earlier in the night, had arrived and were insisting they were in charge, so the lieutenant said, "If that's true, open the goddamned trailer and get the computer to unlock the doors!"

"I can get into the trailer," one of the security gorillas said, "but no way do I know that computer." No one was sure how to get into the building without the help of Craig, the master foreman—who'd been called—or Dean. And he was busy upstairs.

Nearby, Melba was thrusting her fan in the face of every policeman she saw, demanding they rescue her niece, while Bobbi dug through the trunk of her car to find Mark a sweatshirt and a pair of sweats. They were a little tight, but certainly more modest than his Calvin Klein briefs.

Detective Wong took Bobbi aside and instructed her to describe the apartment to the bomb squad. Three men would go up in antiexplosive gear. They needed to know where they would most likely find it. She explained what corner of the building the vault was nearest.

"Corner?" Wong reacted.

"Near it, on the southwest side."

He looked sick. "It could collapse. If it blows out the support columns, it might not hold the weight above."

"My God."

The area was swarming with people. Countless police cars arrived with backup officers and the SWAT team, which followed the bomb squad into the construction compound with high-tech gear on their backs. Fire trucks stood ready. Paramedics from an ambulance rushed to Mark, ordering him to their stretcher, which he refused. "Not till I know my Audrey is all right."

Bobbi rolled her eyes. She believed it was all an act. "Come on, Mark. You'd have stayed up there till she was in your arms if you really loved her."

"But, Bobbi," he said, whining, "I wouldn't have been any help." He made his voice reek of sincerity. "I'm like you. I'm deathly afraid of heights."

"We didn't stop on twenty-two," Audrey noticed.

"Where's he taking us?" Dean mused, looking toward the black sky.

"The cops are down there." Audrey's voice was growing impatient. "Why don't they stop the elevator."

"Probably don't know how."

They traveled in silence. Only the sound of the motor, the pulleys, the gentle shaking of the chain-link fence that wrapped around the elevator permeated the silent night. They passed twenty-five, twenty-six, twenty-seven.

"My God," Audrey said. "He's taking us to the top."

"Get some light up there!"

"Won't reach, sir." The cop shining one of the spotlights showed the lieutenant that the beam wouldn't carry twenty-some stories with any degree of sharpness.

Another cop ran up. "Sir, the master foreman for the project is on his way. And we are trying to reach the head of security, he has the codes as well. Also a Mr. Carlucci."

"He's up there, you asshole," Aucoin snapped. "Bust the doors in if you have to. Two lives are at stake."

A tanned, fit, gray-bearded and white-haired doctor carrying a black bag seemed to appear out of nowhere. He faced Mark. "I'm Dr. Appleton, and I want to have a look at your injury."

"I'm fine, fine," Mark said, staring up at the building. "All I care about is Audrey."

"I'm sure you do," the physician said, "but you're not going to be any good to her if you have a massive head injury."

"Dammit!" Mark reacted, "I don't need anybody—" And then he started to go sideways. Bobbi reached out quickly to steady him, and the doctor indicated to the paramedics to put him on the gurney. "I guess I'm a little dizzy," Mark finally admitted.

"That's not all you are," Bobbi muttered under her breath as the paramedics took him into the trailer.

"We should have a chopper up there in moments," the lieutenant explained to Melba and Bobbi.

They all looked up again. "The elevator is still rising," Melba Goh said.

"It's going all the way to the top," Bobbi added. She turned to the Yees, who had been standing in amazed silence. "That's the apartment Hiram wanted you to buy. Top floor."

"Yes, but why?" the policeman said. "Why are they going back up there?"

They passed twenty-nine. Now they were sure of Ben's intention. "He's taking us to the top."

"What are we going to do?"

Dean wheeled himself to the gate, so Ben would be facing him when the elevator stopped. "Outwit him. Again."

The elevator stopped.

But Ben was nowhere to be seen. Dean surveyed the top floor of the building, which was relatively easy, for it was half the size of the lower floors. "No one's here," Audrey said over Dean's shoulder.

"Don't bet on it." Dean was cautious. He didn't want to exit the elevator until he needed to. He looked around again. The airplane lights were bright, and they illuminated the floor much better than down on twenty-two, which was all dark shadows and nooks. The floor was almost empty of construction paraphernalia because the bulk of the cement floor had just been poured that afternoon. But Ben could be hiding out of sight behind the central elevator shaft.

Audrey tried to get the elevator moving by pulling on the levers, but it didn't work, as Dean knew it wouldn't. "What are we going to do?" she asked.

"Sit here," he whispered, "till he makes a move. The more time we can buy, the better."

She nodded. "It's just a matter of time until the cops get up here." It gave her hope.

But then hope died. For the airplane lights disappeared in a flash. So did each floor's work lights. In fact, every light in the building and surrounding it, in the construction trailer and even on the billboards at the end of the street, went dead, and Victoria Towers faded deep into the night.

Dean knew Ben must have used the programmer to douse the lights. Which gave him an advantage. For Ben knew precisely where they were, and they didn't have a clue where he was lurking.

Audrey and Dean waited in the construction elevator until they heard the sound of a helicopter somewhere in the distance. "A chopper!" Dean exclaimed.

"Yes! Way to go!" Audrey was encouraged.

"They might be able to get us down from here by helicopter," Dean assured her.

"I remember what they used to do on *M*A*S*H* reruns."

"We're going to be okay now—"

But he didn't finish. Ben's powerful hands gripped the front right footrest on the wheelchair, yanked him forward, off the elevator, and onto the plywood over part of the wet floor, and spun him around and around. Dean cried out, hung on, but it didn't stop. He saw the building spinning, the sky spinning, and he was dizzy. Several times he'd somersaulted over and over on a fall when skiing, and this gave him the same sensation of a slow-motion free fall, and the same worry of whether or not he'd end up alive.

Audrey held her breath as she heard—and could almost make out—Dean spinning in circles in the chair. Suddenly, with a great shove, the chair went sailing, not off the edge of the floor into midair as had been intended, but into the not-yet cement that had been poured that day. Because of the humidity of the islands, the flooring material consisted of a mixture of concrete and other compounds designed to provide minimum shrinkage caused by any changes in temperature. One floor had been poured each afternoon, giving it the night to dry and set, but thirty had been laid just that afternoon, and it wasn't hard enough yet to support the wheelchair. The wheels dug grooves into it and sank into the ten inches of half-set concrete.

Dean fell forward out of the chair and down into the cement on all fours, sweating and shaking from vertigo.

"Audreeeeeeeeeeey," Ben's voice then sang in a soft, melodious, and creepy tone. "It's time to get off the elevator. Penthouse floor, all out. Watch your step, please."

But before Ben could get near her, a brilliant light hit the building, slashing through the open sides to give Audrey a glimpse of Dean slumped down in front of his quicksand-bound wheelchair, then of Ben standing nearby, caught off guard, the beam highlighting the rippled muscles of his chest as well as the terrible burns along his side and face.

The light disappeared as the helicopter turned for another pass at the building. That's when Ben leaped into the elevator and grabbed her. They grappled for a moment. She was feisty and furious in her desire to see him die. He put an arm around her waist and another over her mouth. He pushed forward, forcing her off the elevator, but as soon as they were on the hard plywood which had been set over the drying cement, she bit his hand. When he jumped in startled pain, she took the opportunity not to run but to try to shove him over the edge.

But he grabbed hold of a post in the nick of time.

The chopper returned, the halogen projector lamp illuminating all three of them. Dean could not move out of the cement to help her. Ben was clinging to the post, the wind knocked out of him momentarily.

"Run!" Dean shouted to Audrey, trying to get her to take advantage of the moment. "Go down the stairs, run!"

"I can't leave you," she called back.

"Sure you can, go!"

"No!"

Ben was catching his breath, watching them arguing. The light showed Dean that Ben's face was contorted in anger. Then the chopper's lights were gone again. But a voice boomed like God's, talking from behind the clouds: *"The building is surrounded. You cannot escape. Toss your weapon over the side."* Audrey thought it was a joke. Dean shook his head. "Some help Mark got us."

"Don't you come near me!" Audrey said to Ben. She was aware of his silhouette in the darkness, facing her, only feet from her again. "Don't do it, Ben."

Dean watched. "Audrey, careful, don't back up—"

"Ben, stay away from me!"

"—stay away from the cement."

Ben whispered her name. "Audrey, Audrey, I don't want to hurt you. It was all a joke, okay?"

"No!"

"I just wanted to scare you, play with you—"

"Stay away from me," she warned.

"Audrey," he continued, reaching out toward her, "don't fight me, it's fate, remember?"

"Get the hell away from me!"

Dean shouted, "Audrey, watch out!"

Ben lunged and grabbed her again, this time around her legs, toppling her to the floor. Then he righted himself and started pulling her slowly toward the edge of the plywood. She kicked and squirmed. "No!" she screamed, trying to grab on to something. "No, please, Ben, no."

Dean knew he had to do something. Being helpless wasn't acceptable. He really had been helpless once in his life, when a stranger risked his own life to pull him from a burning automobile. No, he couldn't cop out. So he did the only thing he could think of doing, with the only attribute he had left. He grabbed the cold steel of one side of the wheelchair with his hand and, mustering all his will, counting on his arm strength, pulled it up from the wet cement and lifted it over his head. With all his might he threw it, sending it flying. It smashed into Ben's back. It then careened off the edge of the floor, into the sky, but unfortunately didn't take its intended target with it. Ben had been knocked down, but not driven off the edge of the building.

And now he was in a rage.

In the glow of the searchlights that engulfed the building, the spectators watched as an object sailed off the thirtieth floor and became airborne, the chrome glinting in the lights, sparkling. "Heavenly days," one of the cops said in astonishment, "what the hell is that?"

Bobbi cringed. She knew what it was immediately, even before it was clear to the others. "Dean," was all she could manage.

Yes, it was a wheelchair, but thankfully a wheelchair without a person in it. The spectators below scattered. The chrome missile plummeted toward earth, twisting over and over, until it landed on the roof of one of the police cars. The chair exploded into a hundred pieces, leaving the top of the car smashed into the seats.

"Dean!" Bobbi called out, her stomach turning. She'd never liked him much, but it was obvious she was a terrible judge of character. Dean was the good guy here. Ben had been her buddy, and now he was an attempted murderer. At least she had been right about Mark. She turned to the lieutenant. "Damn it, why can't you get men up there?"

"Going in now," she said to her, taking his mouth away from his walkie-talkie. "The team just broke into the building. They're on their way upstairs now."

"I only hope," Melba Goh said in a cold voice that betrayed the fear she felt for her niece, "it isn't too late."

On the beach, the bodyguard dialed the international number again, and said, "I'm in place, boss," when the voice answered.

"Almost time?"

"Go boom very soon."

"I want you on a plane outta there as soon as you see it happen."

"Want me to come back?"

"Get lost, disappear. Fly to Kansas or someplace and hole up."

The bodyguard stretched on the sand. "Why, boss?"

"You seen CNN? They're reporting someone saw a limo near the catering truck."

"No shit."

"It's shit, all right, you big fuck. They're looking for the driver."

"Fat chance."

"I'm worried."

"Listen, boss, I'll call you a minute before the fireworks. That way you can hear it, too."

"Okay."

"Man, that place is going to just go to the moon on a—" The man on the beach glanced up at Victoria Towers and he could not continue speaking because he was watching fireworks of another kind. Helicopters and searchlights lit up the night sky. The building seemed to be under attack. He'd heard the noises but hadn't paid attention, thought it was some fire or such nearby. He was speechless.

"What is it? What is happening? Are you there?"

He tried to say something, but words wouldn't come. All he could think was; What in the world is going on?

Chapter Twenty-three

Ben looked at Audrey and Dean with inflamed eyes. He had risen to his knees where the chair had knocked him down. Powerful helicopter lights cut through the floor again and again, making a strobelike effect. Hatred bubbled inside him, and he was no longer confused about what he was going to do to her. He wanted only one thing now: to kill them both.

Dean was still mired in the cement. Heaving the wheelchair had saved Audrey perhaps, but it had done nothing to rid them of the madman. What could he do next, so useless in his handicapped state? "Audrey—" Dean started to warn her, but she saw Ben moving toward her on all fours, and she stood up. Which surprised Dean. "Stay down," he called to her, "there's less chance of falling off!"

But Dean did not see the trowel behind her back. She walked to the wall of the central elevator shaft and leaned against it, giving herself both protection and leverage. "Come and get me, you monster," she challenged. She was trying to get Ben to turn his back on Dean, so Dean could do something.

But what? There had been only one wheelchair; there was nothing else in reach to throw at him. And Ben wasn't falling for it; he was intent on taking Dean out first and having his final moment with Audrey.

Dean thought fast. There might not be any object to throw, but his hands were touching fairly damp cement. As Ben lunged, to grab him by his useless legs and dump him off the side, Dean scooped up a handful of cement and tossed it into Ben's face. He cried out as it hit his eyes and fell to his knees again, trying to wipe the gritty compound off his burned skin. Audrey came up from behind and struck him with the flat metal trowel as hard as she could. And he slumped, motionless, into the mucky floor.

"Good girl," Dean complimented her.

"Jesus," Audrey said, out of breath, allowing herself to collapse to a kneeling position where she stood. "We did it."

"He could be faking—"

There was a booming voice from one of the two choppers circling about. *"Bomb squad is in the building. Give up now. Come to the edge of the floor and hold your hands in the air. We have guns trained on you."*

"Wave to them, acknowledge them!" Dean

shouted to her, afraid they'd shoot him, thinking he was Ben.

Audrey jumped up, rushed to the edge, and began to flail her arms full-length, like a flagman on an airport tarmac. "Here, here," she shouted, "it's okay, it's okay!" She continued to wave until the loudspeaker crackled again. Suddenly it occurred to her what they had said. *Bomb squad.* She had to have heard wrong.

"Acknowledging. We see you. Men are on the stairs. Evacuate the building, Audrey. We believe there is a bomb in the building. Get out, both of you, as fast as you can."

The chopper was so close that the spinning blades caused her shredded skirt to flutter. She waved again and then, feeling delighted, exhilarated, she threw them a big kiss and kicked one leg up behind her. It was then she realized she'd lost her shoes somewhere. She looked down at her beautiful dress. The front was virtually ripped to shreds, and every inch was covered with dirt, dust, or concrete. But all she could think about was the startling words the loudspeaker had said: *we believe there is a bomb in the building.* She turned to Dean.

But he was dead. The blood drained from her at the unexpected sight. At least he looked dead. He lay flat on his back in the cement, his arms out at his sides, his face smeared with blood that was draining from a huge gash on his forehead. And Ben was gone.

She froze again in fright. She'd thought this was all over, she'd believed they'd won, that there was no more danger. And now it was starting all over again.

She knew what had happened. The minute she'd turned to focus on the helicopters, Ben had whacked Dean with the trowel. It was lying there with blood on it. Ben had been faking, been slumped over to wait till the right moment to surprise them. She couldn't hear what was happening behind her through the roar of the helicopter blades.

She rushed to Dean, feeling for a pulse. Ben was still nowhere to be seen. Meaning he was either in the stairwell, or he wasn't on that floor at all. She shivered with a renewed shock of danger, trembling so that she could not even press her fingers to Dean's wrist tightly enough. She looked around. Nothing. Then she looked at Dean's chest. It rose, it fell. He was breathing. Thank God! But where was Ben? And was it true about a bomb? How would she get Dean out if he was unconscious?

There was no place to hide. The floor was a flat sea of wet cement and plywood walkways. He had to be behind the elevator shaft or in the stairwell. The stairwell! She could hear voices already, the cops on their way up, but what floor were they on?

She looked at the prone body at her feet. No

matter what, she had to get help for Dean. She could alert the policemen on the stairs.

Swiftly she crept to the stairwell, expecting Ben to come from around the elevator shaft. But he didn't. She made it into the dark stairwell and held on to the metal railing for a moment, catching her breath, then started down. Directly between floors, however, she found herself suddenly in the strong embrace of a man's arms.

At first she thought it was a cop, maybe one of the SWAT team. But when he started kissing her, she realized it was Ben.

One of the searchlights made the stairwell glow for a moment, and she saw his hungry, burned face with wild eyes and leering grin. He was kissing her, licking her, trying to nuzzle his lips down to her breasts, as his hands pawed at her, ripped her dress even more, trying to lift her skirt. She tried to get her knee up to get him in the crotch again, but he was protecting himself, standing sideways, preventing her from injuring him. "Audrey," he whispered passionately, "don't fight me, give in to it . . ."

"I hate you," she growled, seething. "I hate you, and I want to see you dead, you miserable prick."

He grabbed her head with his hands, pulled his own head back and looked into her eyes, and then spit into her face. "For my father," he snarled, "and my mother, and my dog."

She was so startled she let out a moan, closing her eyes, heaving inside.

And then he kissed her again, licking the saliva from her cheeks and nose.

With all her might, she ducked down, slipping out of his clutches, and as he turned, she slid between his legs and ran down to the next floor, shouting, "Help! Up here! I'm up here!"

She could hear voices somewhere below her, but there was no telling where. She continued down, but he was right behind her, and he jumped her at the door to the twenty-ninth floor. They grappled, rolling on the hard cement floor, smashing into boxes and a line of window-glass pieces. "They're coming, you can't get away," she cried to him.

"Fuck yourself," he growled.

She managed to pull away from him slightly, and her attention was drawn to moving pulleys to her left, at the edge of the building. He saw it, too. The construction elevator was moving! The cops must have gotten it started downstairs, it was moving down. If only she could get on it—

She ran for the elevator gate, but he tackled her by the legs, and was on top of her as it slowly passed the floor. "No!" she cried, seeing the top of it moving out of sight. He laughed as he groped her, reaching with his right hand under her skirt, trying to force his fingers into her underpants. "Noooo!" she screamed, and violently rolled with him, until they were near the edge of the building. She felt the gold chain around her neck break away, the jade pendant flying.

"Do that, go ahead," he taunted, "and we'll be in heaven together tonight . . . go ahead, I don't care, I'll go with you!"

"I hate you!" she screamed.

"We're going to blow up together anyhow, baby," he said, trying to kiss her again.

"No, we're not, *Corky*! No fucking way!"

"They said there's a bomb—"

"They're crazy!" But then she paled. She remembered the metal box she had used to thwart him. "My God, that . . . that box!"

"It's a bomb, and we're going to die here." She saw that he was trying to unzip his pants—God, was he going to try to fuck her right in the midst of this madness? She brought her knee to his hand with such force that the zipper actually cut into the skin of his arm. With a deep shudder, he went limp, and she seized the moment and pushed him, rolling him the two feet to the edge, and over.

He was gone.

She had to think fast. She was fine, she could get out, but Dean might be dying. How could she help him? By getting paramedics up to him, a doctor, someone who could really help. Would they have time? Would the box explode? Instead of going up to wait with him, she started down the staircase, seeking help, running to twenty-eight, twenty-seven.

On her way to twenty-six, she heard one of the cops call out, "Twenty-three!"

"I'm on twenty-six!" She shouted as loudly as she could. "We need a doctor!" They were running up, she was running down, they would meet on twenty-four or -five. "I'm coming, I'm coming!" But as she passed the door on twenty-six, a mighty arm reached out to grab her legs, and she went flying.

She tumbled headfirst through the doorframe onto the level cement floor, which was as open and uncluttered as the top floor had been. Ben was on his knees back by the doorway. "You forgot about the elevator," he said. "I landed right in the center of it. That disappoints you, doesn't it?" His voice was a venomous taunt.

"Greatly," she whispered.

"Revenge," he said, drawing himself up to a standing position.

She did the same.

"Going to join your father now," he said, and began to rush toward her like a sprinter.

It happened in slow motion in her mind. She had to outsmart him. *Think!* He was coming at her, only two feet away. He was going to grab her and push her off the edge of the building, twenty-six stories in the air.

Just as he was about to make contact, she balled her body up at his feet. He could not stop and instead he flipped right over her.

Three cops in SWAT gear entered the level, with guns drawn. But there was no one to aim them on.

Ben was gone. Vanished into the black hole behind Audrey, the huge refuse chute which had an opening on every floor, a hole she hadn't even realized was there. She and the cops heard the voice, Ben's cry in the darkness, as he descended floor after floor, down, down, faster and faster, and then it was gone.

As was he. Dead at the bottom of the chute, dead with all the rest of the trash.

"Bomb squad is in the apartment," the leader said.

Audrey was out of breath. "I saw it," she gasped hurriedly. "I threw it at him—a metal box, it had light coming from it."

"We've got to get you out of here."

"No!" Audrey whispered, "Dean Carlucci, he's badly hurt, top floor." She slumped down to her knees.

A walkie-talkie crackled. "Device confirmed. Twenty-third-floor apartment. Attempting to open and disarm. This is gonna be a tough one, guys. Sophisticated timer. I'm gonna do this one alone. Everyone out of the building, now. If I can't stop this, we're gonna have Oklahoma City all over again. Over."

"Evacuating the area," Aucoin's voice crackled from the speaker.

The leader of the SWAT team grabbed Audrey's arm. "Come on."

She wrenched it away. "Not without Dean."

The man thought for a second. "Can we get to the roof from where he is?"

She nodded. "He's right underneath it."

The man pressed the walkie-talkie to his lips. "Get the chopper over the roof. We're taking them out by air. Over."

Chapter Twenty-four

The captain of the Honolulu Police Bomb Squad had gotten his training disarming mines in the jungle underbrush near the Cambodian border in Vietnam. He had seen hundreds of explosive devices, but in all his years, he'd never seen anything as sophisticated and difficult as what he was facing now. And as powerful. Positioned correctly, this one could blow the World Trade Center clear into the Hudson River. He ordered his two backup teammates out of the building. If this sucker was going to blow, better it take only one life.

But his best backup man wouldn't leave. They'd worked together for twelve years, and he wasn't about to take an order to hightail it out now. He had the can with him, the heavily insulated drum in which a bomb could be moved, which would severely lessen the impact should it explode. If it couldn't be disarmed in the next few minutes, they'd put it in there. He could tell by the digital timer that it was due to go off at one in the morning. It was, by his watch, exactly twelve fifty-four.

* * *

On the top floor, Audrey bent down and held Dean's head as he started to regain consciousness. He couldn't speak, and she told him not to. She took the shirt one of the SWAT team had taken off and handed her and wiped the blood from his face. "Just hold on," she said. "We're getting out of here in a minute."

The helicopter had already positioned itself over the roof. It had hoped to land there, but the huge antenna already erected from the center of the building prohibited a safe set-down. There was a helipad already constructed to the side of the building, over part of the parking garage, from which the rich and powerful could access Honolulu International Airport. It did no good now, however.

They pulled Dean from the cement and put him on a makeshift stretcher that two of the men fashioned from a piece of plywood. They pulled their belts from their pant loops and secured him to it. Then they carried him up the stairs to the roof.

The blast of white light from the chopper made them look surreal, ghostly. Audrey held her hair and her skirt down as the whirling blades kicked up the tropical night air. Dean was hooked up to the line leading to the helicopter. Then she watched him rise effortlessly, swinging back and forth. In a minute he was safely inside the chopper, and the line was coming back down. For her.

* * *

The bomb expert felt perspiration running down his nose. His wife always warned him to powder it, but he never could fathom doing that. Once a drop of sweat fell to the tip of a wire he was attempting to remove, just enough liquid to conduct electricity from the wire to the sensitive metallic contact point, setting off the device. He'd lost his right little finger. But he still didn't powder his nose.

The sweat was for good reason. He'd never in his years of doing this dangerous job seen quite the likes of what he was attempting to disarm here. The thin blue wire he thought led to the timer turned out to do nothing when he clipped it. In fact, just as he cut it, it tripped another timer. He heard it, felt it, but he couldn't see it. A backup? What was going on? "Shit," he muttered. Then in a measured tone, he said, "Manny, time to can this." He wasn't going to go any further. They had less than a minute left.

Audrey was secured with a harness. "Just hold on tight and let your feet dangle, don't move them," the man instructed.

"I've had practice doing this," she joked, remembering her earlier rescue that day. Never, she promised herself if she lived through this, never again selling a high-rise. Low buildings, four or five floors tops, or better yet, houses, one-story houses, they sounded immensely appealing. Then she felt the building sway. She knew she must be moving. But the chopper had not yet begun reeling her in. It wasn't so much that her feet had left the roof: it was more that the roof had left her feet.

There was a great distant roar. Seventeen floors below, steel began to twist. Audrey's feet lifted into the air because the roof of the building moved with the force of the tremendous explosion. The top part of the tower, from floor twenty-three on up, was swaying like a ginger blossom in the path of a hurricane, and beginning, with a stomach-wrenching creaking of metal, to collapse.

They began reeling her in. As she dangled, she stared openmouthed in horror as she watched the cops on the roof flatten themselves to it, hanging on for dear life as the building quaked, rocking back and forth. A whoosh of air, filled with smoke and debris and dust, like the storm clouds that so often appeared from nowhere over Waikiki, blew from the twenty-third floor and rose all around the framework of the building. It appeared to be dense fog when light from the chopper caught it.

The bomb had exploded.

Melba, Bobbi, Mark, everyone on the ground, had been ordered to pull back when the lieutenant got word that the bomb had been located. They knew that anyone on the ground was in grave danger. Not knowing the capability or strength of the device, they weren't sure how much damage it might do. They evacuated the immediate area.

Two blocks away, windows shattered within

seconds of the blast, and glass fell like rain up to a mile away, for several minutes afterward. The rumble reverberated up and down the side streets. Some people thought it was an earthquake, or Diamond Head erupting. Everything shook and rattled.

One wall of Residence Twenty-three blew out into the air—furniture, steel, toilets, plaster chunks, plumbing fixtures, appliances suddenly became missiles. A second later, a great cloud of dust rose from the guts of the building and continued skyward.

Bobbi reached into her Bug to put her sunglasses on, for her eyes were suddenly filled with dust. Melba could not breathe, the debris caught in her throat. Mark was too shocked to speak. The Yees, their arms around one another, stood in awe and disbelief at the sheer power of the explosion.

On the beach not far away, a man raised a cellular phone into the air, hoping Portuguese Tung had heard it. He stared in proud wonder at the sheer beauty of it. Man, he thought, I'll get a bonus for this one. "Boss," he said, bringing the phone back to his ear, "it's fucking magnificent."

The voice oozed with relief and pleasure. "Sounded good. Sounded real good."

Audrey was being reeled up, up and away from the smoke and the sound of wrenching, crunching steel. She peered down. Was the whole top of the building twisting? Or was it because she was spinning in the wind as they pulled her up to the chopper?

"Oh, my God!" Bobbi squealed as she dug her fingers into Melba Goh's tunic.

Melba covered her mouth with her broken fan and held her breath. The building was doing a macabre dance of death in the glare of the police floodlights. The entire upper part of the structure, from the floor where the blast had occurred on to the top, was slowly turning. They could hear the sound, like fingernails scraping over a chalkboard, a creaking, wrenching cry of death as the steel girders twisted and bent. They heard pops and crackles as ductwork metal twisted and broke, as glass exploded, as pipes burst. Water shot out from the side of three upper floors. And then the whole top of the structure, from the roof down to twenty-three, leaned at an angle—

But did not fall.

"Audrey," Melba cried softly, "dearest Audrey."

Bobbi consoled her. "She's going to be fine; nothing's going to hurt her."

"You're cutting off my circulation," Melba snapped.

Bobbi removed her hand. "She's all right, I know it."

"I am glad my brother did not live to see this day," Melba said.

Bobbi answered, "If your brother had lived, none of this would have happened."

Detective Wong hurried to them, walkie-talkie in hand. "She's on the chopper," he said. "They got Audrey off the building in time."

Audrey felt her heart thundering in her chest as hands yanked her the final precarious inches into the helicopter. Landing on the hard, metal floor, she felt, for the first time, safe.

"You guys okay down on the roof?" she heard one of the pilots say into the mike.

There was a crackle. "If this thing doesn't do a swan dive, we are. Jesus." Audrey recognized the voice as the leader who was still on the roof. "Not sure we can get down by stairs," the man added. "Not sure there are stairs anymore."

"We're dropping the ropes right now," the chopper pilot said.

In a few minutes, all of the policemen on the roof had been hauled upward as well. Then the chopper swerved—Audrey's stomach took a dip—and they flew toward the water, on their way, she guessed, to a hospital downtown or on one of the military bases nearby. She looked at Dean and slowly brought her hand up to touch his shoulder. His eyes fluttered open for a moment.

"Hi," she said.

A slight smile appeared on his lips. "I'd rather be skiing," he said, and he was out again.

The man who had reeled them up took over.

He was a paramedic, and he began to take Dean's blood pressure, wrap his head with gauze. Audrey gave him room, turned, and looked down. They were over the beach. Below them she saw another commotion, the flashing lights of several police cars, spotlights directed on someone on the sand. For a moment she wondered what that was all about. Then she put it out of her mind. It certainly paled by comparison.

"Put your hands in the air," the cop ordered loudly and firmly. "Drop the phone."

"Come on, man, what the fuck is this?" the burly guy standing in the midst of the lights said.

"Drop the phone to the sand and raise those arms," another cop ordered again.

"Aw, man!" the guy moaned, and did as he was told.

The police approached him, patted him down to find a revolver in the band of his baggy shorts. They turned him around and put cuffs on him. They started reading him his rights, but he stopped them, swore he had nothing to hide. He demanded to know what this was about. Finally, as a cop on either side of him took his arms to guide him to the waiting cars, another police officer explained. "Want to ask you a few questions."

"Like what?"

"Like what were you doing this afternoon?"

"Driving around."

"At the airport?"

"What? Hell, no. I went up to Turtle Bay."

"In a limo?"

"Limo? I don't ride in no limo. I ain't rich."

"Maybe you drive one?"

"You crazy?"

"Then why was there a chauffeur's uniform in your room?"

"Costume party. Man, you got the wrong guy."

"We don't think so," the cop said, as they shoved him into the waiting squad car.

Audrey sat drinking coffee in a waiting room at Queens Hospital in the Punch Bowl, eager for word on Dean's condition. They'd landed on the roof.

Audrey looked out the little window. She could make out the glow of fire in the distant sky. She knew it was Victoria Towers. Then a nurse poked her head in and asked if she wanted to watch it on the television with them. She joined several of the staff members in a lounge to watch the building where she'd been trapped with a madman half an hour ago, a twisted, wrenching mass of broken steel, going up in flames.

She, like Melba, was glad her father had not lived to view this moment.

Chapter Twenty-five

Audrey was told that her family and friends were on their way, but she could not see them until the doctor examined her. After he pronounced her fit, if a little shaken, she showered and put on the only clothes available, a navy blouse and pants that someone had found in an unlocked locker. Then Detective Wong and Lieutenant Aucoin talked with her. They explained that Mark had been found, but that the two men who had been trying to disarm the bomb had died in the explosion.

She asked her most perplexing question. "Who put the bomb in the apartment?"

"The Yees," the detective said.

She couldn't believe it. "The Yees?"

"Who weren't the Yees at all." They explained who the couple had been, and what they were trying to do.

"You're kidding!" Audrey exclaimed. "The couple they found murdered at the airport? That's who we showed the apartment to?"

When they mentioned the name of the triad and "Pearl River Tung," it all fell into place.

"Interesting thing," the lieutenant said, "was that by picking up and throwing that box, you moved it away from the wall of the safe, and that's just where the bomb squad worked on it, so it hardly damaged it. And probably prevented the whole building from collapsing."

She blinked. "So they can still get Tung?"

The lieutenant nodded.

She smiled.

A call came through that told Detective Wong that the bodyguard had been picked up. He left to question him, but as he departed, Aunt Melba, Bobbi, and Mark rushed in. They took turns hugging Audrey. Bobbi's was the warmest, a genuine heartfelt embrace. Mark seemed filled with emotion and tried to embrace her tightly, but she wouldn't allow it. Her body remained rigid and closed.

When Audrey embraced Melba, she felt overwhelming sadness. The hug was as cold as the woman's demeanor, as phony as the rouge on her cheeks. Audrey felt a handshake might have been more intimate.

They sat and tried to calm down. They had a million questions. Wong told Melba he wished they could have learned all this sooner, but thank God they had made it in time.

"You wouldn't have without us," Melba snorted.

The lieutenant said, "Audrey, normally I'd ask

you to come to the station to file charges, make a statement, but under the circumstances—"

"He's dead," she said about Ben. "What point is there filing charges?"

"Necessary formality."

So she told her story in as much detail as she could recall. A police stenographer got it all on tape, and often the lieutenant had to admonish Bobbi and Melba for asking too many of their own questions. "You'll have all the time in the world with Audrey to ask her these things later," he explained.

Mark's comments were welcomed, however, because they filled in the blanks Audrey didn't know. What Ben had done to him, what happened after he left Dean in the service area outside the apartment. But Audrey had a question of her own. "How could you have just left him there?"

"What do you mean?" Mark answered.

"In a wheelchair."

"Christ," Mark said, "I learned later that he'd busted into the gates, gotten in the construction trailer, up a ramp to get into the elevator, gotten all the way up to twenty-three, then down to untie me. I mean, how handicapped do you think this guy really is?"

"He risked his life!" Audrey said. "Almost a stranger. I mean, I hardly knew him before this."

The lieutenant could sense an argument brewing, and he headed it off. "He's certainly a hero tonight, I'll give him that."

"Surprised the heck outta me." Bobbi laughed.

Audrey looked at her and nodded. "I told you he was a good guy."

Mark felt threatened. "You know he's a Peeping Tom? That he's been watching you through a telescope?"

"Thank God!" Audrey exclaimed.

Mark bristled. "Listen," he said, "someone had to get the cops. We decided I could run, that I had the advantage."

"Dean said you left him there," Audrey challenged. "He said he begged you not to leave."

"He just wants to be the hero."

"You didn't get the cops," Bobbi interjected. "Melba and I did." Bobbi was loving it. Mark was finally showing his true colors. "The police were two blocks from the building. We would have been there in less than a minute."

Mark folded his hands on his chest, and said, "Some gratitude."

Audrey gave him a look of pity.

Audrey didn't understand one important piece. "Why were you looking for me, Aunt?"

"You were to dine with me," Melba offered.

"You hunted me all over town because I didn't show up for egg drop soup?"

Bobbi called Melba on it. "Didn't you want to get back some papers that you'd given Audrey to sign?"

"Ah," Audrey said, "that's more like it." Then she sucked in a deep breath. "Were you fearing, dear Aunt, that I'd really read the document and figure out the truth? Unlike all the schemes I put my name to in the past, that I might actually object?"

Melba shook her head in her straight-backed chair. "I do not know what you mean, Audrey."

"I'll tell you what I mean!" she shouted. "I understood everything when I read the files on the Kaneohe Project tonight."

Mark shook his head. "Audrey, don't—"

"Don't what?" Audrey tossed back. "How about Makena Villas, Auntie dearest? Remember that one? Remember the builder, Bob Benedict, who was driven to suicide because of what you and Father did to his family?"

"This is an outrage," Melba said.

"What's outrageous," Audrey shot back, "is that you set up Ben's father, which destroyed him, his mother, and ultimately Ben's mind. He lived only to get even with the monsters who'd ruined his life. I almost don't blame him."

"Shit," Mark muttered, disgusted. "I can't believe you're defending the asshole who just tried to rape and kill you!"

"And you certainly made it convenient for him, running with your tail between your legs," Audrey barked back.

"Go, girlfriend," Bobbi said, urging her on.

"Audrey, I demand you stop this at once." It was Aunt's turn. She even stood for it.

But Audrey was undaunted. "No. I'm not stopping anything except living the way I had until tonight, trying to please everyone but myself, hoping people would fit my fantasy of what I wanted a husband and father to be, turning a blind eye to the scheming and cheating of the family business. No, never again."

She walked over to Mark. "I'm a changed person, Mark. I'm not crazed with fear because of what I've been through, I'm not in shock. I'm—"

"Audrey," the Lieutenant interrupted, "perhaps you have been under too much strain and—"

She cut him off the way he had her. "Shut up," she said. "I answered your questions, and if you don't want to sit around and listen to this, leave. But you're not going to tell me what I feel, and you're not going to stop me."

Bobbi kicked her shoes off, pulled her feet up under her on the chair. "I like this," she giggled. "Go girl, go."

Audrey continued talking to Mark. "I was looking at all the wrong qualities for a future husband, just skimming the surface. It's like looking at that beautiful building without realizing that, while secure and expensive and luxurious in its own right, it's a front to bleed Communist Hong Kong of money."

"Audrey!" Aunt gasped.

But Audrey was undaunted. "Bobbi was right all along. I should have been digging deeper than the tan and triceps, into the heart, into dreams and hopes. I should have been opening doors to feelings for love and responsibility, to feelings for children, because that's where you find bravery and integrity, that's where the heart makes the commitment and insures lasting love."

"What is this hearts and flowers shit?" Mark responded.

"It's about you, you moron. I'm saying that you're just like her"—she gestured to Aunt—"in her greed and disregard for the law." She let out a howl. "It's amazing you never liked him, Aunt. He's the best nephew-in-law you could have hoped for."

Mark stood up. "I almost got killed tonight because of your crazy plan to lock us in there, and this is the thanks I get?"

"Oh, go home, Mark," Audrey said.

"What?" He was dumbstruck.

"Get out of here, you coward. And don't even bother coming back when you grow up, because I sure as hell can't wait that long."

Mark started to open his mouth to say something, but no words came. He turned on his heels, and slammed out the door. Audrey wasn't through. She faced Melba, who was about to follow Mark out the door. "Where do you think you're going?"

"Audrey, you are in no condition to speak rationally. I will see you at home tomorrow. We will discuss matters then."

"I'm not coming 'home.' "

"Audrey."

"I don't *have* a home, Aunt, only a cell in your prison."

"This is disrespectful," Aunt said, shaking with anger and embarrassment.

"What's disrespectful," Audrey snapped back, "is the files I read. My own blood!" She gave Melba a look that said shame on you.

Officer Holcomb rushed in. "Excuse me, folks, but somebody found this on the ground where everyone had been standing under the building. Belong to one of you?" He opened his fist to display the jade peach pendant Ben had ripped from Audrey's neck.

Aunt gasped. Her eyes seemed to double in size. "Where did you—? That is—" She was utterly speechless.

"Mine," Audrey answered, taking it from the man. "Father saved it for me after Mother died. The key he left me opened her safe. It must have blown out of the building in the explosion. It's fate that it found me again. It is the only thing I will ever cherish from this family."

Aunt stood upright, appearing even taller than she actually was. It only added dimension to her already imperious aura. She looked down on Audrey and whispered, "May the gods of our ancestors forgive you."

That made Audrey even more angry. "I'm starting my own life tonight, Aunt, and you'd better not oppose me or I swear, I'll have you thrown in jail. And I have the proof to do it. You should wish the imposters' plan had worked. The safe didn't blow up."

Melba Goh studied Audrey for a moment. "You bring great shame on our family," she said sadly.

"No," Audrey corrected her, "you do."

Melba could say no more. She snorted, turned, and left the room without another word.

Detective Wong said, "Is there anything more we can do for you tonight?"

"No, thanks," Audrey replied.

"I'll have to ask you to come down to headquarters in the morning. We believe we have the bodyguard in custody. We need you both to make a positive ID."

Bobbi jumped at the chance. "I can't wait."

Audrey nodded. "It will be our pleasure."

Sergeant Randazzo entered with an ashen look on his face. "Sir?" he said to the lieutenant.

"Yes?"

"Sir, this is very strange. We went into the Dumpster at the bottom of the refuse chute, sir, to retrieve the body. But there wasn't any."

Audrey felt prickles on the back of her neck.

Bobbi's mouth dropped open.

"What do you mean there was no body?" the lieutenant demanded. "How could that be?"

The cop shrugged. "Dunno, sir. We went through every inch of that Dumpster, nothing. We even checked inside the chute, up the first five floors where it bends to slow the refuse down, but nothing."

The lieutenant looked at Audrey.

"He went down the chute. He screamed. I heard him hit bottom."

Aucoin was becoming agitated. "How about higher?"

"Every floor, shined lights between, nobody in there, I mean he wasn't hanging on or anything."

Audrey burst in with, "But I heard him, I heard him screaming as he went down."

"Ain't in there, folks," the cop said with puzzlement on his face.

"Die in the blast?" Wong asked.

"That," the cop said with a nod, "or he caught hold on the opening on one of the floors and escaped in the panic downstairs."

"My God," Bobbi said in a low, frightened voice. She turned to look at Audrey.

But Audrey wasn't aware of her, of any of them any longer. She was lost in a world in which only she and one other person existed, she and that guy who worked as an electrician at Victoria Towers, that guy with the beat-up old green lunch pail full of Cinnabons, that cute guy with the smile named Ben . . .

Audrey closed her eyes, felt ice-cold and then hotter than she ever had in her life, and as all the blood drained from her head, she slumped to the floor at Bobbi's feet.

Chapter Twenty-six

Dean opened his eyes to palm trees swaying in a fierce wind outside the window. At first he thought he was in his bedroom, but where had the trees come from? His apartment was well above them. Victoria Towers was nowhere to be seen. So he looked around and realized, oh yeah, he was in the hospital. Damn, but his head ached.

Someone in white had told him he had regained consciousness at four in the morning. What time was it now? He had no idea, but it looked like late afternoon. Was that possible? Had he been sleeping or was he out again? It was dark because it was raining; he could see the spatters on the window glass. That storm they'd predicted, the one that had devastated the Philippines last week, had arrived. But it didn't look like something to fear.

He could feel that his head was bandaged, and there was a bag hanging there with saline, probably, being pumped into his arm. The last time he'd done this he remembered how he still felt his legs, how he was sure he'd walk again, how he refused to believe them when they told him of the spinal damage and the fact that he was paralyzed from the waist down. Until he actually tried to move them.

This was easier, and he was under no such illusion, unless, of course, Ben had actually killed him and all this was just a heavenly dream. Then Audrey walked in. And he knew he was not dreaming.

"Hi." She warmly took his hand.

"Hi."

"You look like hell." She leaned against the side of the bed.

"I must have an honest face. 'Cause I feel like hell."

"Headache?"

"Like the worst hangover ever."

"You wish that was the cause."

He laughed. "How are you?"

"I'm okay, actually."

"Honest?"

"Yes. I was here last night—early this morning—but you were sleeping."

"Or out cold?"

"No," she explained, "they told me you regained consciousness, and I came down to see you, but you'd fallen asleep before I could get in the door. I sat here a while, just watching you."

It hit a nerve. "Tables turn, eh?" But he felt uncomfortable with the reference to his Peeping

Tomism, so he changed the subject. "That today's paper?"

"Read all about us," she said, unfolding it from under her arm.

He was thoroughly unprepared to see the headlines, FAMED HONOLULU BUILDING IN RUINS, and the photograph of the twisted, burning mass of steel that had once been their beloved Victoria Towers. He looked at Audrey. "Only thing I can say is fire that feng shui master you've got on retainer."

She laughed for the first time since Ben had appeared in the dining room.

"What the hell happened?" he asked incredulously.

"I could explain it all, but I've done it too many times, for the police, for the reporters. Just read, and I'll rest a while."

As he did, Audrey walked over to the window and peered out at the parking lot, which was being drenched by the downpour. Everyone held an umbrella. The mountains were covered with fog, and everything green looked like it was already getting greener with liquid nourishment. Hawaii was luscious, she thought, the most beautiful place on earth. But she wasn't sure she wanted to stay there any longer.

Dean peppered his reading with gasps and words like, "Bomb!" or "Imposters?" He read the accompanying article, AIRPORT MURDERS TIED TO BOMBING, and saw the photo of the man charged in those killings, the "bodyguard," a man the report said was identified both by Audrey Goh and Roberta Kicherer. "Chinese Mafia!" he exclaimed. Then his voice was truly sympathetic when he said, "Two members of the Honolulu Police Bomb Squad died in the explosion."

When he finished, Audrey was already thinking about where she might want to start a new life. She knew it had to be a big city. She was a big-city girl, after all. San Francisco might do, or Seattle. No, too many Chinese. Too many reminders of Hong Kong, and Aunt's spies would be everywhere. She needed to find someplace not on the West Coast of the mainland. Maybe Philadelphia, or Washington, D.C.

"Audrey?"

"Yes?"

"I didn't know any of this." Dean was truly blown away.

"You slept through it."

"You're amazing," he said.

"And you're my hero."

He turned away. "I did what anyone would have done."

"Anyone except Mark." She took a breath. "I'm a new woman today. They put me here in the hospital for the night because I fainted, but they let me go down to headquarters with Bobbi this morning to identify the bodyguard. I came back to see you."

"To say good-bye, huh?" He sounded sad at that prospect.

"Good-bye?"

"I figured you'd leave the islands after this."

"Well, not till I take you home first."

He brightened. "Will they let me go?"

"Saw the doc in the hall; he said yes."

"Great!"

"But you have to take it easy. I thought I might help."

He blinked. Was he hearing correctly? "Help what?"

"You take it easy."

"Oh," Then he brightened. "Oh!"

"Dean, listen," she said, "I am going to leave, start over somewhere else. You've lived other places. What's good?"

"Oh, Toronto is a great town," he said with enthusiasm, "but it's damned cold."

"I can buy a fur coat." She giggled.

"Florida sucks."

"So I hear." She opened the big bag she had been carrying. "No bombs, I promise. Bobbi went out and got you some things to wear this morning. Hope they fit."

"That was kind of her."

"I think she has a new respect for you." She set the khaki shorts, Aloha shirt, boxers, and white socks on the bed.

"Mmm. Good taste," Dean commented. "Nautica, nice."

"Maybe you'll give me a tour of Utah someday," she said, just to feel him out.

"Sure," he responded eagerly. "And I'll take you to Deer Valley, oh, you'll love it. Park City is still a little sleepy village despite Robert Redford's band of Hollywood types who descend once a year. You ski?"

"Always wanted to. But it's something a girl from Honolulu doesn't get a lot of chances to do."

"This boy from Hawaii did. I could teach you—" He stopped. He was pressing too hard, looking for too much here. He'd loved her from afar, and now he was assuming they had some kind of relationship, some kind of bond. Well, hadn't they developed one last night? Yes, but still, it was only as someone who'd helped someone else. He hadn't fallen in love with the man who rescued him from the burning car, after all. Why was he assuming she now had feelings for him?

"Stop trying to figure all this out!" she berated him gently. "I can hear your mind going a mile a minute."

He stopped thinking and smiled.

"Here, let's get you dressed."

As she held the bright green Aloha shirt covered with palm trees and parrots out to him, she said, "And when we get to your place, you've got to let me look at the world through that telescope of yours."

"Audrey, I'm truly sorry about that. It was an invasion of your privacy."

"Forget it. In fact, it may come in handy."

"Handy? Why?"

"Because," she said, drifting to the window, looking out through the rain, "Ben may still be out there somewhere, waiting for that chance to do it again."

Epilogue

New York City, Sixteen Months Later

The Mercedes M340 pulled up to the curb outside the elegant building on Fifth Avenue, just across from the Metropolitan Museum of Art. "Oh, look," Audrey exclaimed, "the signs are up. Nice, huh?"

Indeed, two small but tasteful signs advertising the fact that the renovated residences were now for sale flanked the entry doors, gold-leaf letters shining in the early-morning sun. Pretty classy. But advertising was hardly necessary, for the address belonged to one of the premier buildings in Manhattan, and Audrey had already sold three apartments sight unseen. Today the building opened to the public (by appointment only) for the first time, and Audrey was dressed in a great new soft green Prada suit she'd bought just for the occasion. It complemented the peach pendant perfectly. She looked like a million bucks, which certainly fit her job of selling million-dollar apartments.

The toddler in the car seat in the back gurgled something.

"Yes, Harry, Mommy is going to work," she said, almost singing. "Daddy worked here for a long time, now it's my turn to make us some money." She got out the passenger side, ran around the car, waving good morning to the doorman they'd just hired, and kissed her son through the open back window. "Be a bad boy," she ordered, "Make Daddy's day!"

A dog, a big Irish setter, nudged her face from behind the baby out the window, and Audrey kissed it, too. "Yes, yes," she said to the slobbering animal as the baby giggled, "I'm going to miss you, too, jealous old Melba darling."

Then she put her head in through the driver's window and kissed Dean on the lips. "Six o'clock?"

He nodded. "Six o'clock."

She giggled. "But there's no time lock here, so it's okay to be a little late."

He grinned. "I love you," he said.

"Love you, too," she responded. "Oh, did I tell you? I heard from Pat Yee? They may be coming to look."

Dean rolled his eyes. "Just be sure it's really them."

She laughed. "And her purse goes through a metal detector."

"Okay," Dean jokingly said to the passengers, as if he were a pilot or bus driver, "buckle up. Hold on to Melba, Hiram, Daddy's gonna put his thumbs to the floor and we're gonna beat the traffic across the park!" And he was gone.

Audrey watched them disappear into a sea of yellow vans, the new New York checkers. As she approached the elegant limestone-and-brick building, she studied the signs in detail, and felt proud when she read the glowing words at the bottom: GOH/CARLUCCI PROPERTIES. The doorman greeted her with a nod. "Howdy, Mrs. C.," he said, "big day, huh?"

"Hope so, Trevor."

He opened the door for her, and she entered.

Inside the vastly expanded and beautifully appointed lobby, workmen sat on the marble floor taking a breakfast break. They'd been working all night in an effort to get everything finished by the scheduled ten o'clock opening. "We on time, boys?" she asked.

Lots of voices said, "Right on, Audrey!"

Another said, "Nice outfit, lady."

Another just whistled.

Audrey laughed, and straightened her skirt with one hand while she pushed the elevator button with the hand that held her briefcase. While she waited, she showed them a little leg. Catcalls.

From all but one.

One worker, wearing coveralls, sat just to the side of the entry door, where she had not looked.

He always tended to sit out of the sight lines because he was self-conscious about the scar on his face. He balanced a beat-up lunch box on his knees, held his coffee in his right hand while he fed himself a Cinnabon with his left. But his eyes were not on his food. His eyes were on Audrey.

Even after the elevator doors closed behind her.